BERKLEY TITLES BY ALEXANDRA BURT

REMEMBER MIA
THE GOOD DAUGHTER

THE
Good
Daughter

ALEXANDRA BURT

BERKLEY
NEW YORK

BERKLEY
An imprint of Penguin Random House LLC
375 Hudson Street, New York, New York 10014

Copyright © 2017 by Alexandra Burt
Excerpt from *Remember Mia* copyright © 2015 by Alexandra Burt

Library of Congress Cataloging-in-Publication Data

Names: Burt, Alexandra, author.
Title: The good daughter / Alexandra Burt.
Description: First Edition. | New York : Berkley, 2017.
Identifiers: LCCN 2016030296 (print) | LCCN 2016037167 (ebook) |
ISBN 9780451488114 (paperback) | ISBN 9780451488121 (ebook)
Subjects: LCSH: Mothers and daughters—Fiction. | BISAC: FICTION / Suspense. |
FICTION / Contemporary Women. | GSAFD: Suspense fiction
Classification: LCC PS3602.U7694 G66 2017 (print) | LCC PS3602.U7694 (ebook) |
DDC 813/.6—dc23
LC record available at https://lccn.loc.gov/2016030296

First Edition: February 2017

Printed in the United States of America
1 3 5 7 9 10 8 6 4 2

Cover art: *Tree branches* © vertyr/Adobe Stock; *Water background* © Dutourdumonde
Cover design by Natalie Slocum
Book design by Kristin del Rosario
Interior art: *Tree branches* © Ihnatovich Maryia/Shutterstock

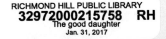

To those who live under beds,
and pass through walls.

To old and battered houses
with creaking wooden floors.

ACKNOWLEDGMENTS

I would like to express my gratitude to the many people who saw me through this book; to all those who gave their time willingly and generously, provided support, offered comments, and allowed me to quote their remarks.

Thanks to my editor, Michelle Vega, and the Berkley Publishing Group, and everyone who assisted in the editing, proofreading, and design. As always, thanks to my agent, Laura Longrigg.

I thank my husband, my daughter, and the rest of my family, who supported and encouraged me in spite of all the time it took me away from them.

Thanks to those whose names I have failed to mention. You too are deeply appreciated.

All the great stories have witches in them.

—UNKNOWN

Prologue

THEY stopped once for the night, in Albuquerque. The name of the city intrigued the girl, so she looked it up in the encyclopedia she carried with her. It was her most prized possession.

Albuhkirkee . . . She silently repeated the word until it lost all meaning. The girl caught herself drifting off into some paranoid daydream, not knowing what time it was or where they were going. They had never driven this far for so long, never had to pump gas so many times.

Weary with the burden of her heavy eyelids, she was drunk with sleep by the time her mother stopped at a hotel. *Rodeside Inn,* the sign read. All she'd remember later were the weeds that grew through the cracks of the concrete parking lot.

The next morning, her mother bought donuts at a drive-through and they got back on the road. The girl went to sleep, but when she woke up and looked out the window, the scenery hadn't changed at all. After days on the road, she felt as if she was leaking electricity. The hours stretched, and she wished her mother hadn't thrown her bag in the trunk of the Lincoln—she longed for her *American Girl* magazine and the jelly bean–flavored ChapStick.

She opened a bag of Red Vines, sucked on them, and then gently rubbed them over her lips until they turned crimson.

Running her fingers across the cracked spine of her encyclopedia—the first pages were missing and she'd never know what words came before *accordion; a box-shaped bellows-driven musical instrument, colloquially referred to as a squeezebox*—she concentrated on the sound of the pages rustling like old parchment as she flipped through the tattered book.

Her mother called her Pet. The girl didn't like the name, especially when her mother introduced her. *This is Pet,* she'd say with a smile. *She's very shy.* Then her mother moved on quickly, as if she had told too much already.

Pet, the encyclopedia said, *a domestic or tamed animal kept for companionship. Treated with care and affection.*

The girl opened the encyclopedia to a random page. She remembered when it was new, how the pages and the spine had not yielded as readily, and she wondered if the pages would eventually shed. She attempted to focus on a word but the movement of the car made her nauseous. Eventually she just left the book cracked open in her lap.

"My feet are cold. Can I get a pair of socks from the trunk?" she asked somewhere after the New Mexico/Texas border.

"Not now," her mother said and checked her watch.

The girl fell asleep again and later awoke to the slamming of the car door. She rubbed her eyes and her surroundings came into focus: redbrick walls, a large sign that read *Midpoint Café,* her mother standing by a pay phone only a few feet away, rummaging through her purse for change. It was noon and the girl felt ravenous as she stared at a display poster of fries and milkshakes in the café window.

"I'm hungry," she called out to her mother.

"It has to be quick, we have to be somewhere," the mother said, and the girl slid on her sandals in a hurry.

In the gloom of the dingy café, their knees touched under the narrow table. The mother opened up a newspaper left behind in the booth and scanned the headlines.

The girl had so many questions: *Why are we rushing?*; *Who did you call?*; *Where are we going?*; *Why did we drive all the way from California to Texas?*—she had the whole conversation planned out, knew exactly what to ask: short, direct questions that left no room for vague and elusive answers. The place was loud and crowded and the diners competed with one another to be heard, creating an overall atmosphere of raucousness. In the background, a baby cried and a waitress dropped a plate.

They ordered lunch—French fries and a strawberry shake for the girl, coffee and a Reuben sandwich, no sauerkraut, for the mother—and while they waited for their order to arrive, the mother excused herself. "I have to make another call, I'll be right back."

She ate and watched the diners and minutes later, her mother returned. She had seemingly perked up, now appeared bubbly, almost as if in a state of anticipation, and her eyes moved quickly. "Let's play a game," she said and opened the paper. "Tell me a number between one and twenty-two."

The girl loved numbers. *Numerology; belief in divine, mystical or other special relationship between a number and a coinciding event.* The number 7 was her favorite one. 7 meant she was a seeker, a thinker, always trying to understand underlying hidden truths.

"Seven," the girl said and silently recited random facts: *seven ancient wonders of the world, seven days of the week, seven colors of the rainbow.*

They ate silently, the girl devouring the fries, then taking her time with the milkshake, studying the people around her while her mother skimmed page seven of the newspaper. She wondered how naming a number of a page was a game to begin with, but her mother seldom answered questions posed to her, and so she didn't ask.

The mother paid the check and the waitress counted out the change.

Just as the girl attempted to decipher the headline the mother had been studying, she called out to her. "Hurry up, Pet."

The girl did as she was told.

Later, the mother rolled down the window and the girl watched her check her face in the rearview mirror. When a siren sounded, the mother licked her lips, fluffed her hair, and pulled into a dirt patch where three wooden posts formed an entrance with a cow skull nailed to its very top. An officer appeared next to the car.

"Your headlight's out," he said and scanned the car's interior.

The police officer was lean with closely cropped hair and skin the color of nutmeg. The mother got out of the car, pulled her red scarf tighter around her head. Her hair fluttered in the wind, her clothes clung to her body, and her arms were tightly wrapped around her.

The girl noticed a boy in the back of the police cruiser. "What did he do?" she called out to the officer.

"He didn't do anything. That's my son, Roberto," he said, "he's just riding along."

The next time the girl turned around, her mother and the officer were standing in the shade of a large oak tree. Her mother's voice trailed toward the car like pearls rubbing gently against each other. The officer leaned back and laughed at something her mother said.

Later, the mother drove to a motel, where the girl fell into a deep sleep. The next morning, after free coffee from the dingy lounge and day-old donuts, they emerged from the Aurora Police Precinct with paperwork in their hands. When the girl read the paperwork, it stated Memphis Waller and her daughter Dahlia Waller had been robbed by the side of the road, including the mother's wallet and identification.

Dahlia; flower, symbolic meaning of a commitment and a bond that lasts forever.

The girl did not ask questions. She was glad to finally have a proper name and no one, not even her mother, would refer to her as Pet ever again.

Later, she would remember that the sky was overcast and turning darker by the minute.

Part One

What is this madness blazing in your hearts?

—ACHILLES

One

DAHLIA

I⊤ all started with the crickets.

My mother sweeps them off the porch but to no avail: they seem to multiply exponentially—*They're taking over,* she says melodramatically—and she sprays lemon-scented Raid in every nook and crevice until the fragrance of artificial citrus descends upon her Texas bungalow and becomes part of our lives like the unsightly boxes in her room she hasn't managed to unpack in decades.

April and May bring more rain, which in turn brings more crickets. By June, the porch is covered in shadowy forms climbing up the wooden posts, reaching the horizontal rail just to fall off the precipice and pool under the porch. Come July, my mother is convinced that a rogue crowd of crickets will work their way up the brick walls and discover small pockmarks and cracks along the exterior. *Eventually they will invade the house,* she says.

I explain that last year there were the frogs, and the year before there were the crane flies, and before that—I can't remember, but I make something up—there were the potato bugs. "Next year it'll be something else. Just relax," I say, but she won't have any of it.

"I just can't stand those crickets," she says, getting more irate with every swipe of the broom.

"Let me go for my run. I'll think of something when I get back," I say, feeling myself getting impatient.

Over the past months, I have become a master in avoiding fights with her, yet the better I've become, the more she insists on the drama. The world always revolves around her, she sees no point of view other than her own, no explanations occur to her but the ones that make sense to her and her alone.

I step off the porch and stretch my calves, yet my mother is determined to discuss the crickets.

"I hate the sound they make," she says and follows me into the street.

"*What* sound?" I ask. If I wait any longer it'll be too hot for a run.

"It's like an old hardwood floor when the flooring nails rub together and they squeak," she says and holds her hand behind her ear as if she is attempting to direct sound waves into it. "You don't understand, Dahlia . . ." She pauses as if something important just occurred to her. "They crunch when you step on them. At least no one can come in undetected," she adds as if her logic has a special shape that fits a special key which in turn fits a special lock.

"I'll call an exterminator," I say and jog off before she can say anything else.

I regret having come back to Aurora.

Months ago I stood in front of her door and I realized the house hadn't changed at all—the same crooked solar lights from fifteen years ago were stuck in the cracked soil like elfin streetlights. The same drab curtains covered the windows; the paint was still chipped; the door chime hadn't been fixed. I knocked and my mother opened the door and as we embraced, I felt a hesitation, but I was used to that. She still looked impeccable—wore a dress, had done her makeup, didn't have a gray hair to be seen—yet she seemed grim and dark, and rarely was she without a cigarette between her manicured nails. And now she obsessed about crickets.

Leaving my mother's subdivision behind, I make my way down a rural road toward the woods. It's July and the sun that was orange an hour ago is about to turn into a yellow inferno. Another hour and everything will cook.

About two miles into the run, I realize I haven't stretched nearly enough. I feel a slight stinging behind my left knee, an old injury that has been flaring up lately. When I reach the top of the hill leading into the woods, I stop. Hands on my hips, I attempt to catch my breath. The heat bites into me and the sun eats my skin and eyes. I ignore the pesky insects swarming around me, barely wipe away the salty beads trickling down my neck. I scan an unfamiliar tree line to my right—haven't I paid close enough attention, or have the columns of rain that have swept North Texas for the past few months somehow changed the vegetation?—and I long for shade to stretch my leg.

Squeezing between the trees, I step into the woods and the temperature drops twenty degrees. The scorching sun loses its grip and the air turns dank and muggy. The beauty of the woods takes me by surprise; it's not just a collection of trees but there are paths leading toward what looks like ancient tree cities; some are still standing, and others have turned into mere skeletons. The springy ground is an array of leaves and chunks of rotted wood, the dark wet earth soothes my feet after the unforgiving asphalt.

I follow deer tracks, and brambles claw themselves to the mesh fabric of my Reeboks. With my palms I lean against a gnarly Texas oak, stretching my calves. The bark is sharp, leaving painful imprints on my hands. The burn in my leg ceases and as I bend over and pull brambles off my shoes, I catch a glimpse of a crescent indentation in the ground, like a burrowed tip of a boot in the soil. Next to it, a speck of red, a shade somewhere between scarlet and crimson. I can't make sense of it, as if my mind is trying to fit a square block into a round hole.

I step closer and my brain catches up; the colorful speck is a fingernail, a half-moon rimmed with dirt, resting among the tree scraps. A pale hand with nails a shade a teenager would wear, one with a silly name like *Cajun Shrimp*. The hand is motionless, just lies there, bare and helpless, a peculiar intruder disturbing the methodical layers of the forest's skin.

I scan the ground. There's a pale silver bauble—a coin maybe, larger than a dime but smaller than a nickel. The sun hits it just right and throws a sparkle my way. There's a luster to it, radiant and sparkling, illuminated as if it wants to be observed. I believe the hand and the sunlit glint among the browns and greens of the woods to be a figment of my oxygen-deprived runner's brain.

I bow down to get a closer look. Eyes peek from within the ground. They are surrounded by a spongy layer of pine needles.

Still the square block doesn't fit into the round hole. Broken and cloudy, the eyes stare beyond the cathedral high pillars. The lids seem to quiver ever so slightly.

And then the hand moves.

Run.

My body obeys. Ten steps and I lose my footing and stumble, hit the ground, left shoulder first. I roll down a hill and sharp branches nip at my skin. I tumble farther and farther, a steady and painful descent that I'm unable to stop. I come to a halt and I feel a sharp pain hit me right between my eyes. Then my world goes dark.

When I come to, everything is quiet but for the thumping sound of my heart. I swallow water. I'm drowning. My head throbs but I manage to push my body off the ground. I'm in a creek, facedown. The vision of the hand has carved itself into my brain. *I must be mistaken,* I tell myself.

I catch my breath and return to the very spot. I kneel down and a burning sensation moves up my arm, to my face, then to my neck. There is an anticipation, a nervous kind of energy tingling through me, as if electrical sparks are traveling all the way to my toes. A scent hits my nostrils, an olfactory hint of something . . . unpleasant . . . out of place within the otherwise fresh forest. The scent is sickly sweet, a mere hint one moment, then a good stench. Something is dripping onto my lap— warm moisture spreads onto my bare thighs—and I realize my nose is bleeding profusely. My shaking hands are covered in blood.

A buried body, I think, as if I have finally solved a riddle I've been pondering for a while. My mind tumbles, spills into itself. My sense of smell is heightened and the soil and decomposing leaves make the atmosphere thick. I feel a sense of paranoia, I imagine someone watching me, no, I don't imagine, I *know* there's someone watching me.

I scan the trees around me. I know what I am; prey. A small sob works its way up and out of my throat.

There's no visual clue, just knowledge and intuition, and my eyes find a narrow path with knotted roots. *Run,* I repeat to myself, and again my body obeys.

I reach the road and wave down a truck filled with men in overalls. There's a large ladder covered in paint splatters extending beyond the truck bed. I scream and point at the tree line and they rush in that direction.

One man stays behind and says words in Spanish I don't understand.

I FEEL AS IF I HAVE TRAVELED THROUGH A TIME MACHINE: I REMEMber the clinic well —Metroplex, a three-story building, aged and tacky, from the industrial carpet to the disassembled pay phones left deserted on linen fabric–covered walls.

I recall the emergency room—every strep throat, every fever that wouldn't go away, every sprained ankle, every cut that required stitches resulted in arguments with nurses and administration. My mother refused to sign paperwork, wouldn't give them any information but our names.

There's this rage inside of me that I feel toward my mother and I wish my memory was a sieve, yet it maintains a detailed account of her transgressions, all fresh, all defined, neat and organized. They sit in waiting and many have come back to me lately, so many memories have returned, yet not a single one of them pleasant. Lately, all it takes is an image, a smell, a faint recall, and the dam of restraint breaks. It sloshes over everything, unforgiving in its clarity.

They say—I've done the research—humans are hardwired to retain negative memories as a matter of survival.

Survival; the act of surviving, especially under adverse or unusual circumstances.

EL PASO, TEXAS, 1987

I roll down the car window to allow the night to seep in. I hear trucks idle. I listen to the drone of the engines; observe them maneuver in and out of the parking lot. They hiss and scream; sometimes their engines fall silent. Men emerge and climb from the cabs.

It's their house on wheels, *my mother tells me.*

My house is the backseat of my mother's car. From there I watch the constant movements of trucks and men. I arrange my pillows and blankets just right. I have learned how to tuck myself in. I am to remain underneath, hidden.

It's just a game, *my mother says.* So no one knows you are here.

I listen to their radio until it jitters, and then there is nothing left but silence. Underneath the many layers, I hear my mother talk to the truckers.

One man said, I saw a black dog, so I pulled over.

I'm afraid of the black dog. I watch the road sometimes, expect him to stand in the middle, drooling, baring his fangs.

I spread out my crayons over the seat. When I run out of paper, I flip through my drawings until I find one that's blank on the back.

We wash up in a sink in a nearby building. The floor is cold and my bare feet leave dirty wet trails all over the white tiles. I wiggle and struggle to get away from the cold that makes my skin turn into tiny bumps.

Is the black dog coming for me? *I ask my mother.*

She just laughs.

The dog's not real—it's when you drive too long and you see things. It's time to pull over and sleep. That's all.

I know the feeling of seeing things. I will keep an eye out for the black dog anyway. To make sure.

Mom leaves and when she returns, she smells of food. She hands me a donut, and I eat in the car. I get powdered sugar all over everything but Mom doesn't seem to mind.

Those days don't feel real. It's almost as if I travel while I sleep. When I wake up, I'm in a different place but still in the car.

I love the car. All my toys are in the car.

Two

DAHLIA

THE ER waiting room is quiet but for the hypnotic tick of an old plastic clock hanging on the wall. A whiff of latex and disinfectant hangs in the air.

Bobby's uniform is tidy, his blue button-down shirt and navy-colored slacks pressed immaculately. His hair is short, his face freshly shaven. A lifetime ago Bobby and I went to high school together, but he stuck around and I left Aurora days after graduation. We haven't spoken since I've been back in town.

"I can't believe this," I say and struggle to line up the events. My clothes are wet; so is my hair.

Bobby smiles at me. "You've been back in town for what . . . a few months, and I see you're still the same old troublemaker."

For a split second I'm a teenager again, remembering how we'd roam through town, wandering around in abandoned buildings, acquiring cuts and bruises and sprained ankles along the way. "Seems that way, doesn't it?" I finally say.

"I waved at you the other day, at the gas station. I was going to follow you and pull you over."

I feel some sort of way about his words. That's how we met a long time ago; his father pulled my mother over by the side of the road.

Bobby sat in the backseat of his father's cruiser, I was in the backseat of my mother's car, and we stared at each other.

I ignored Bobby at the gas station because of the way I'd left fifteen years ago. That and the fact that my life is nothing to be proud of. I have been dreading having to make small talk with him, catch up, swap stories about our lives.

"How long has it been?" Bobby asks. "Just about fifteen years?" he says as if he's kept track of time.

I do the math. I arrived in Aurora just shy of thirteen. I did one year in middle school, then went to high school. In high school, I saved every dollar I made; I bagged groceries, worked at the car wash, even put away my allowance. There wasn't any money for college, and I didn't have any motivation or big dreams short of getting out of town—but Bobby was going through something then. His mother had cancer, had been well for years, but then it returned. There seemed to be something else; he was preoccupied with things I knew nothing about, things he was reluctant to share. I left Aurora at eighteen. Fifteen years exactly.

The last time we spoke was the night I left.

"If you think about it, why not go to Colorado, or California? If we're going to leave, might as well go far," I had said but he had remained quiet. We had talked about leaving Aurora for years, leaving Texas altogether; we had imagined it many times.

"You want to hear what I think?" he finally asked.

I sensed sarcasm. He started talking about having a different perspective and maybe I should be thankful for what I have instead of griping about what I don't. That night, he made his way through a six-pack in no time, and by the time he was on the last beer, he didn't make a whole lot of sense. He went on and on about choices some people have that others don't. Had we not talked about leaving Aurora since tenth grade, had we not imagined what life could be like *somewhere else?*—but suddenly there was no more *I vent and you listen.* He was judgmental and mean and not what I needed that night. We parted ways then; he was drunk and I was angry.

At home, I saw my mother hadn't lifted a finger to fill out the paperwork I needed to apply for financial aid. I threw my clothes and a few books in a duffel bag, waited for the sun to come up. When I heard my mother rummage around in the kitchen, I went downstairs.

"You still haven't filled out the forms." It came out sharply, just as I intended. All my life there had been missing paperwork and incomplete forms. "Are we still doing this? We still don't have the right paperwork?" I asked. There were the missing papers when I was a kid—what I now know to be shot records and residency documentation—and school was the mother of all wounds. She would never let me leave, wanted to attach an eternal tether to me, to make sure I'd never be more than she was.

We argued. I told her I'd leave. She said she'd pay for a community college close by. I told her I wanted to go out of state. We argued some more. Eventually she turned silent and ignored me.

I left that night. I drove down the highway, leaving Aurora behind me. I had about five hundred dollars, a fifteen-year-old car, and my high school diploma—a pretty meek start for a life on my own. There were regrets about that night: I had fought with my mother, and I had never said good-bye to Bobby.

I felt panic rise up. The streets felt alien to me, yet I drove on until I reached Amarillo. The city was depressing, with nothing but dust and yellow grass, far away from everywhere and close to nowhere. I found work the very next day and a place to stay. *Help Wanted* signs at motels were plenty along the two major highways running through town, and my mother had taught me well: the right motel and the right owner, and you can offer free work for a week in exchange for a room. One week's worth of work for the room each month, cash for the next three weeks of work. I knew that many employers didn't mind turning a blind eye to the fact that I insisted on getting paid under the table.

I got a second job at a nearby motel, and after a year of saving every penny, I felt confident I was in a good place. One day, on my way to my second job, a tapping and slapping sound under the hood made me pull over. The car, by then sixteen years old, was no longer fixable. The next day I went to apply for a car loan, for a used older model Subaru—though it was still better than what I had—but I needed my social security number.

"I'm sorry we can't process the application," the car salesman said. "Do you have your card on you?"

"I think I lost it," I lied.

He scrambled through the papers. "You might want to go to the social security administration office downtown."

"How about I pay you cash for the car?" I hated to use every penny I had saved up, but I needed transportation. I haggled some, paid for the car. I never went to the local social security office. It was just like it had always been, the old and familiar hurdle that was *paperwork*.

I worked more jobs to save more money and eventually moved out of the motel. I knew better than to try to rent an apartment, but I waited for a sublet to come available—there'd be no credit checks, no paperwork, and no contracts to fill out. I lived in a three-bedroom apartment with two other women: a flight attendant and a pharmacy student from Ecuador.

I thought about starting my own residential cleaning business, but I knew the business license would never happen. Again, there'd be *paperwork*. There were better jobs I qualified for over the years— cruise ships taking off from Galveston—but I needed a passport. I kept my head down, never forming lasting friendships or getting seriously involved with anyone. Fifteen years passed, and I saw myself going nowhere but down a lonely, dead-end road of minimum wage jobs and double shifts.

I thought about returning to Aurora, but those moments passed. I thought about my childhood, and those thoughts lingered. My early years remained sketchy at best; I couldn't name my favorite childhood food, stuffed animal, board game, friend, place, or person. Glimpses emerged, yet none of them could be verified; there was no attic stuffed with trunks and boxes holding dolls and toys and old bicycles. When my mother and I did move, we started completely from scratch; no phone calls to left-behind friends, no letters, no Christmas cards. Everything was final, never to be revisited.

I imagined myself twenty years from now and I panicked. I needed a social security number, a birth certificate, and proper documentation so I could emerge from the shadows of my bleak existence.

With those thoughts, I got on the same highway that had led me to Amarillo and I went back to Aurora. The trunk was filled with hardly more than I had left with fifteen years before. On the highway, I folded the visor down, and in the mirror I saw my reddened face. I was going to appear back in my mother's life the same way I had left; one minute there, then gone, then back again.

I had questions. The kind of questions that, once raised, demanded answers.

SITTING IN THE ER, I WANT TO APOLOGIZE TO BOBBY FOR IGNOR-ing him all these months.

"You okay?" His words pull me out of my lulled state.

I attempt to speak, but my voice fades into unintelligible croaks.

I hear a gurgling sound from the water dispenser and he holds my hand steady as he places a cup of cold water in it.

"Drink this." He raises his hand and brushes my wet hair out of my face.

Water spills over my hands. I remember the creek. There's that odor, the one I smelled in the woods. Sweet and pungent—roadkill is what comes to mind, a recollection of hiking and coming across a deer cadaver, weeks old, dissolving in the heat. All blood leaves my face and I grip the paper cup so tight that I nearly crush it.

"Maybe you should spend the night in the hospital? You look hor-rible. You don't seem well at all."

"I'm fine. Really, I am. How's your dad?" I ask to change the sub-ject. I wish I looked more put together, hair done, makeup, a shower.

"You know, he's old." Bobby pauses for a moment, and a shadow falls over his face. "He's not the man he used to be."

A nurse behind the counter turns up the volume of the TV mounted to the wall. Bobby and I both look up, glad to be distracted.

There's mention of a breaking news about the girl from the woods coming up and immediately a vision of the tree line appears out of nowhere and my mind pops like an overheated lightbulb. The hand of a dead woman with red fingernails. There's no sense in fighting the image of her fingers prodding through soil layers, a hand stealing a glimpse of the underworld.

"You're shaking." Bobby waves his hand in front of me as if to fan me some air. "You look like you're about to pass out."

"Is she alive?" I haven't dared ask but I must know.

"Yes, barely. She's in a coma."

I'm back in the woods, bent over her body. Someone dug a hole and shoveled dirt on top of her. Buried her alive. How long ago? A day? Hours? Minutes, even? The possibility that someone watched me discover her—stood behind a nearby tree, his boots covered in soil, his heart beating in his chest, sweat on his brow, watching me— is mind-boggling. I manage to wipe the thought away like a determined hand removing fog from a bathroom mirror.

"You're right, I look awful," I say. My reflection in the glass doors that lead into the emergency room speaks for itself.

"How are you supposed to look after falling into a creek and busting your nose?"

"I need to call my mother," I say. It's been hours since I took off running; she must be frantic by now.

"They sent an officer over. She was a bit . . . well, a bit feisty about the police coming to the house. Took a lot of convincing to get her to open the door. What's that all about?"

I ignore his question. I imagine the doorbell ringing, a suspicious *Who are you looking for?* through the closed door, an insistent *Are you Memphis Waller?*, her silence on the other side, the officer attempting to convince her to open up. Did *This is about your daughter* prompt her to let her guard down? Did the entire conversation happen through a bolted door, or did she reluctantly allow the officer inside, just to regret her lack of vigilance?

"Do you know who the woman is?" I ask.

"She's still unconscious. We can't interview her," Bobby says. "We haven't IDed her yet either." Bobby hesitates ever so slightly and leans forward in the chair. "Did you see anyone?" Every muscle in his face communicates tension.

"I was running the trails. My leg started hurting and I needed to stretch. I went into the woods. It was just one of those things, I guess. I just happened to be there."

"So you don't remember anyone? Other joggers? Trucks? Hikers? Even just cars passing by? Anything?" His voice sounds breathless, but then he seems to compose himself. "What are the odds, huh?" He checks his wristwatch. "You'll have to give an official statement once you feel better. So . . . someone will check you out before you leave. I'll come back and give you a ride home. They'll let me know when you're ready to go, okay?"

I nod. My head pounds and I have lead in my veins, my limbs heavy and saturated with exhaustion. I watch Bobby push the square stainless steel elevator button and the large doors swallow him as if he is a ghost of times past.

After the doctor looks me over and concludes that I'm *just a bit beat up and bruised*, a nurse helps me take off my wet clothes and change into a pair of gray scrubs. In the waiting room, with my wet clothes in a plastic bag on my lap, I sit and wait for Bobby.

The TV is still tuned to the local news. First, the reporter focuses on the closing of the road, detours, and forensics being done out in the woods. Then, with one hand tight around the microphone, a piece of paper in the other: "According to an anonymous hospital source, the woman was in the woods for a very short time before she was discovered." *An anonymous source?* It sounds clandestine, but someone probably knows a nurse who's overheard a comment or read a file. In small towns like Aurora it's really as simple as that.

The reporter smiles and promises to keep the viewers updated. KDPN has told me nothing more than I already know.

I feel an odd sense of kinship with the woman I found in the woods and figure there is no public plea for her identity because law enforcement expects her to wake up and tell them her name at any moment.

Suddenly the screen switches to a black-and-white sketch of a woman. I catch a few words here and there—*similar case . . . mystery woman . . . almost thirty years ago . . . sketch artist . . . cold case.* The woman was reported missing by a man who had no photo of her, hence the sketch. It is an image drawn with pencil on paper, facial features created by a forensic artist to identify unknown victims or suspects at large. Old-fashioned wanted posters far from present-day digital images created by computer programs. The reporting then turns to high school football scores.

A nurse appears and informs me Officer de la Vega is waiting for me at the ER entrance. When I stand up, the world around me spins, then stills.

Instead of departing through the two large sliding glass doors, I take the stairway. Holding on to the railing, I walk up two stories. I have one more place to go before I leave the hospital.

THE THIRD FLOOR LIES ABANDONED BUT FOR A SECURITY GUARD whose silhouette I see strolling down the hallway. He then disappears around the corner. A board on the first door on the right says *Jane Doe,* scribbled with a dry erase marker. *My Jane,* I say quietly to myself, as if the fact that I found her gives me the right to claim her.

I enter the room. I shut the door behind me, and as I part the curtain, the plastic gliders gently purr in their tracks.

I approach Jane in a very pragmatic way, partly to calm my nerves, partly not to miss anything. First, I take in the visuals; her weight, height, and skin color: five seven, one hundred and forty pounds, plus or minus five pounds, pale complexion with a gray undertone. Her hair is ashy blond, medium brown maybe, slicked back, hard to tell.

The monitor above her bed is busy; Jane's heartbeat is rushing along in one neon green jagged line, unsteady like the jittery crayon stroke of a child. There are two other lines, one red and one yellow. Measuring blood pressure and oxygen saturation, I assume, but I can't be sure. But it seems that's what those machines ought to track. A body needs circulation, oxygen, a heartbeat.

There are three tubes in all. One in her left arm, one leading from under the blanket to a urine collection bag. The third is a breathing tube. With a rhythmic hissing sound that raises and lowers as the machine cycles, a ventilator blows air into her lungs. Jane's chest is rising and falling in a steady wave. The side rails of the bed are pulled up as if there is a conceivable chance she might spontaneously get up and make an attempt to get away.

I'm taken aback by the measures required to keep her alive. I feel the desperate energy her body radiates in its lulled state of unconsciousness, compensatory for some unknown act of violence inflicted upon her. I spot Jane's likeness in the reflection of the large window, her ethereal body an apparition, and beyond that lies the town of Aurora, a faraway carpet of glitter, like an otherworldly background of sorts.

I step closer and I allow my hand to hover over Jane's hands. They are now scrubbed clean, but some dirt remains under her nails. They are jagged, as if she tried to claw her way out of the grave someone had put her in. I lower my hand and feel her skin; it's warm to the touch, alive, prickly almost.

An odd scent fills the air. I tilt my head back and sniff at it like a dog. *Is that cinnamon?* My mind slips like feet losing ground on a slick floor, then the pressure behind my eyes becomes unbearable. I can't quite interpret what message is coming from her, but I *know* she's trying to communicate with me. That's it—how else can I explain the tremor in my hand that slowly works itself up to my shoulder? It then rushes through my body and a metallic taste develops in my mouth. I plunge into what feels like madness in the making; images of trees, branches clawing at me. Someone has turned a switch, making reality hard to identify; it's blending with visions of Jane in the woods, digging a hole with her own bare hands. I can smell dank creek water, feel it seep into my nostrils. Is that what my Jane went through or am I reliving falling into the creek and losing consciousness? Suddenly we are one and I am inside Jane's body, *I* am the one in the woods, not her.

I'm not sure when I fall, but I hit the floor, knees first, then my body folds in on itself. Cold linoleum seeping through the thin scrubs snaps me back into reality. There's a voice coming from above, almost as if I'm at the bottom of a well and someone is talking down to me. A pinpoint-sized speck of light seems to appear out of nowhere. The speck turns into a beam, then the beam turns into something brighter than the sun, so bright that it sears my eyes, hot and sharp like a blade.

"Are you okay?"

I know the voice. *Dahlia. Dahlia. Dahlia.* Over and over. I want to answer but I can't. The pungent cinnamon scent is trapped in my nostrils, bitter and sharp. There's pressure under my arms and then around my waist. I'm nothing but dead weight, yet Bobby manages to place my body onto something rather soft and comfortable.

All that is left of what's happened is a pounding headache and aching joints. I'm beyond hungry. Famished.

"What happened? No one is allowed in here. Did you pass out?"

I find my voice: "I think she just tried to communicate with me."

Bobby cocks his head to the left; his eyes go soft. "Look at her," he says. "Does she look like someone trying to communicate?"

I have taken a long hard look at her. I know it sounds nuts.

"You smell that?" I ask.

"Smell what?"

"Cinnamon," I say.

"I don't smell anything. Let's go," Bobby says.

How can he *not* smell that? It's all over the room, pungent, sharp, biting its way up my nostrils.

"Wait. You really don't smell that?" I ask and resist when he tries to push toward the door. "Just breathe in."

"I don't smell any cinnamon, Dahlia. But we're about to be in a shitload of trouble if they find us in here. I'm taking you home. Now."

The scent remains with me as we depart through the sliding glass doors and even when I fasten the seat belt in Bobby's police cruiser. I stare straight ahead, my head against the headrest. Something feels different, as if a part of me went AWOL in Jane's room. What that missing part has been replaced with I can't tell.

The police radio squelches and splats until Bobby turns the volume down, the communication now white background noise.

"It'll be okay. Just try to relax," he says and rests his hand on top of mine, which are shaking in my lap.

His hands are familiar, sinewy, with short fingers and large palms. I roll down the window, close my eyes, and allow my hair to blow in the breeze. The silence between us is natural, soothing. We used to be that way, comfort for each other. I feel myself calm down, almost as if hardly any time has passed between us at all.

FIFTEEN MINUTES LATER MY MOTHER'S HOUSE APPEARS ON LIN-den Street, a road ironically lined with Mulberry trees. The scent remains, yet watered down, the pungent part now in need of detection, no longer presenting itself without any effort. The sweetness, now replaced by an earthy, nutty scent, reminding me of something pure and uncontaminated, not the syrupy and artificial kind drifting through the mall when you pass the Cinnabon counter in the food court.

"She's in a coma?" I ask Bobby one more time as I reach for the car door. "You know that for a fact?"

Bobby nods. "It's all over the news."

I try to tell myself I just went through a lot—finding Jane, hitting my head, falling in a creek, seeing her comatose and hooked up to machines—and that I have the right to feel out of sorts and that it's really no surprise that I'm beside myself.

I nod and as we shuffle along the driveway, I see the front door is ajar, my mother kneeling on the porch. She sees us, stands, and goes inside, slamming the door shut.

"It'll be okay," Bobby says. I'm not sure if he's talking about me or my mother. "Get some rest and call me when you wake up, okay?"

I trust Bobby. Trust him with my life. And so I just come out and say it again. "She tried to tell me something." Just like that. I don't know of any other way to communicate what just happened to me in that room.

He doesn't acknowledge the comment, but doesn't tear at it either.

"Don't come inside," I say. "She's in a mood." There is no such thing as rest in my mother's house, there is no resting from my mother's moods. She is unpredictable at best.

Bobby looks at me as if he is going to argue, but then his shoulders drop. My eyes follow his cruiser lights as he drives off. He taps the horn three times and I smile. It's something he used to do a lifetime ago.

I catch another whiff of the cinnamon scent. I turn my head, expecting to see its origin, but I know better. What if this is it? This is how it starts. Soon there will be crickets in my world too. Have I been a sitting duck, a sure victim of my mother's faulty and mentally deranged DNA?

At the threshold I sidestep a cricket that looks like a miniature black raven on its back. But there are others I can't avoid, and as the tip of my shoe crushes the carcasses to dust, I hear my mother's voice.

"Where've you been?" She appears calm but her voice is higher pitched than usual. She wears makeup and a dress; her hair is a couple of shades lighter than it was this morning. She is barefoot as if somehow she forgot to complete the illusion of having it together.

"You've heard what happened?" I ask.

She turns the kitchen faucet on full blast. The microwave stops running, then beeps. The scents of burnt popcorn and cigarette smoke sting my nostrils. The cigarette between her fingers is short enough to burn her. She leans forward and crushes it out in an already overflowing ashtray.

"Have you heard what happened?" I repeat, my voice louder than I want it to be.

"You had some sort of an accident. They wouldn't tell me anything else," she says.

"I found a body in the woods. A woman. She's alive but in a coma." I shudder at the mental image of my Jane covered in forest debris.

My mother shifts in place as if she is trying to find a way to perfectly position herself, like she is expecting a blow. "You should've stayed home and taken care of those crickets. You never listen to me."

I stand next to her, pass the dish soap, and watch her swirl her hands around in the water.

"I was running but my leg hurt and I went into the woods and—"

"Where did you find her?"

"Let me tell you the story from the beginning." My mind is still attempting to make sense of everything and recalling the moment. Allowing me to relive what happened might help me do just that, might help me separate truth from imagination. But as always, my mother won't have any of it.

"What woman and where?" She scoops up dirty silverware and immerses the pile into the sudsy water.

"Will you just be patient," I say and then lower my voice. "If you'll allow me to tell the story without—"

She stomps her foot on the linoleum, and it strikes me how silly the gesture is. I watch the sudsy water turn into a pink lather. It takes me a few seconds to realize what has happened.

"Mom," I say gently, "you cut yourself." I grab her by the forearms and allow the water to rinse off the blood. There's a large gash in the tip of her middle finger; a line of blood continuously forms.

"I don't understand," she says, and I realize she's begun to sob.

I hug her but she remains stiff, her arms rigid beside her body. She has never been one for physical affection, almost as if hugs suffocate her. I rub her shoulders like she's a little kid in need of comfort after waking from a bad dream. *There, there. You'll be okay.*

I speak in short sentences; maybe brevity is what she needs. "I found a woman. She's okay. I'm fine. Everything's okay," I say as I wrap a clean kitchen towel around her fingers.

"The police came to my house." She pulls away from me, dropping the bloody towel on the floor. "I don't like police in my house. You know that."

"I'm not sure you understand. A woman almost died. I found her while I was running and they took her to the hospital. If I hadn't—"

"You've been here long enough," she says and starts banging random dishes in the sink, mascara running down her cheeks. "You came for a visit and you're still here."

"Mom." *She doesn't mean to be cruel—she's just in a mood,* I tell myself. *She needs me.* I don't know what's going on with her but I can't even think straight and all I want is to go to bed and sleep. "Please don't get upset."

"Can't you just . . . lay low?"

The tinge of affection I just felt for her passes. I recall the time I didn't lay low, years ago, right after I started school in Aurora. It was the end of summer, the question of enrollment no longer up in the air. I wondered how she had managed to enroll me in school, how she had all of a sudden produced the paperwork. "But remember," she said, "stay away from the neighbors. I don't want anyone in my house." The girl—I no longer remember her name but I do recall she had freckles and her two front teeth overlapped—had chestnut trees in her backyard. One day, I suggested we climb the tree. When I reached for the spiky sheath that surrounded the nut, it cut into the palm of my hand and I jerked. I fell off the tree and I couldn't move my arm. I went home without telling anyone my arm hurt. The next day a teacher sent me to the school nurse. They called my mother—I still wasn't caving, still telling no one what had happened, still pretending my swollen arm was nothing but some sort of virus that had gotten ahold of me overnight—and an hour later my secretive behavior prompted them to question my mother regarding my injury. When I finally came clean, her eyes were cold and unmoving.

Laying low is still important to her. "What did you want me to do?" I ask with a sneer. "She'd be dead if it wasn't for me."

Even though she hardly looks at me, I can tell her eyes are icy. Her head cocks sideways as if she is considering an appropriate response. Her responses are usually quick, without the slightest delay in their delivery, yet this one is deliberate.

"I don't need any trouble with the police," she says.

"That's what this is about? The police? What did you want me to do? Just leave her in the woods because my mother doesn't want to be bothered? You can't be serious."

"I'm very serious, Dahlia. Very serious."

"I have to go to bed. I'm exhausted. Can we talk later?"

"I've said all I had to say."

I lie in bed, staring at the ceiling. I don't want to think anymore—just for a few hours, I want to not think. I envy Jane in her coma. I wonder if she's left her body behind. Has she returned to the woods, reliving what's happened to her? And did she hear me when I spoke to her? Can one slip out of one's body and back into the past, removed from time and space?

My mind has been playing tricks on me lately—all those childhood memories that have resurfaced, at the most inopportune moments, memories I didn't know existed. I haven't even begun to ask my mother the questions that demand answers.

Aurora; a phenomenon. A collision of air molecules, trapped particles.

I'm exhausted, yet sleep won't come. I didn't think coming back to Aurora was going to be so unsettling. There is no other explanation. It must be this town.

Three

QUINN

THE old, detached garage had been in desperate need of a paint job for years. The layers were peeling off and the bleached birch wood had been painted numerous times; multiple coats had merged into a shade that was hard to identify.

Killing time in the swinging chair on the front porch, Quinn listened to the metal poles screeching with every painful descent. First, the garage was there. Then it was gone. There, gone. She wished everything was that easy, that she could make things disappear. She went over the list in her mind; PE on Tuesdays and Thursdays— she was too heavy and sweated profusely—even though she liked watching the boys play football and loved the sound of the rumbling buzzer; church on Sundays came in a close second. She could do without the itchy tights and the leather shoes pinching her feet, the dress stretching tightly over her body, the scent of Play-Doh and gossip and old hymnals with gold-rimmed pages. But most of all, she wanted to make a woman disappear—the woman she was waiting for on the porch.

She hadn't met her yet; in fact, she had just found out about her the previous morning. Her father had waited for her to come down for breakfast—she couldn't remember the last time they'd had breakfast together—and he hadn't even given her a chance to eat.

"I met a very nice lady," he had said and set the coffee cup down. "And I hope you'll grow to love her as much as I have."

Just like that. There'd be another woman in the house. All those days and nights of business in some town were nothing more than a lie. He'd been out looking for a wife.

Quinn thought about all their plans, traveling for the summer—he had even promised he'd take her to Galveston this fall, had told her all about the hotel, the Galvez. He had described in detail how only rich and famous people and American presidents had frequented it in the past, Roosevelt and Eisenhower, even famous actors, like Jimmy Stewart and Frank Sinatra, and Howard Hughes. Suites were named after them and Quinn had been looking forward to the trip.

"What about Galveston?" Quinn had asked. "The hotel? The spa? Are we still going?"

"Don't you worry," Mr. Murray said and patted her arm, "we'll go soon, I promise. Really soon."

"The two of us?" Quinn asked.

"Sure. Maybe we all go?"

He had all but *promised* it would be just the two of them, and there'd be spas and a theater and restaurants where they'd serve fish with the head attached and he'd teach her how to use one of those fish knives with a spatula blade to separate the fish's skeleton from the body. In a moment of clarity she admitted to herself that she'd have to give up on Galveston—it was never going to happen.

Quinn continued swinging with brisk speed, hypnotized, running her fingers through her hair. It was poufy and frizzy and regardless of how diligently she used the flat iron, it returned to its untamed state once she stepped into the humidity of a Texas summer day.

Quinn's mind started to rush and her hands began to fidget as she recited ingredients from a cookbook. The old ladies at church, smelling of talcum powder, were always impressed.

"What's your daddy's favorite dish?" they'd ask, and Quinn tried not to stare at their hands covered in dark spots with veins like blue rivers running through them.

"Chicken-fried steak," Quinn said and elaborated on the cut of meat—cube steak—and how she had to pound it fiercely with a meat mallet and then dip it in seasoned flour, pan-fry it, and serve it with a cream gravy made from pan drippings.

As Quinn continued to swing, she yearned for that night's dinner, could almost smell rosemary and chives on her fingertips and the scent of the pot roast with mashed potatoes and okra cooked to perfection wafting through the house. She loved the comforting clinks the fork made against the fine china as she scraped off every last morsel of food.

Quinn forced herself to abandon this culinary vision—after all, she was waiting on the porch for her father and her new mother to show. He hadn't given her a time or date, just said he'd pick her up—and so Quinn had been waiting out on the porch for the second day in a row, waiting for a car to kick up a cloud of dust on the winding road up to the house.

Quinn stared at the cracked floorboards. She mistook the fissures for spilled paint but then looked closer and recognized an orderly army of ants marching along it, carrying food back and forth. Soon there'd be hundreds, even thousands more, carrying away everything in the house, and even though they were small and insignificant, moving mountains seemed only a matter of time. She hated insects, bugs, beetles—pests, all of them. She didn't even like butterflies.

Kneeling down, she was painfully aware of her stomach pushing against her lungs, forcing her to make a wheezing sound. Out of nowhere, almost like a hummingbird flapping its wings, she felt anxiety flaring up inside her.

Hours passed, and her anxiety became a peculiar state of being. Sitting there with nothing to stare at but the wall with chipped paint, she began to drift into an unpleasant daydream, a memory of the last time she'd been on this porch waiting for someone to show.

For her twelfth birthday she had handed out invitations in school, and she had sat in this very swing when her classmates showed up, gift bags in tow. Quinn knew they didn't come for her friendship's sake but out of sheer curiosity.

At the birthday party, the kids ran through the house, opening and slamming doors, entering rooms no one had any business going in. "What's in there?" they'd ask and rip the door open so it hit the wall behind it with a thud.

"A study. You're not allowed in there," Quinn said but they entered nevertheless, giggling and intruding, leaving the door wide open. She heard distant, hazy chatter. She couldn't make out the words, but laughter rang loud and clear and didn't seem to stop.

Due to the commotion her father had appeared at the top of the stairs. Everybody stared at him, the last button of his dress shirt undone, gaping open, exposing his belly. And they snickered when they saw him, mocked him, his waddle gait, how he used his body weight to swing his leg up, like a pendulum.

After everybody left, cake crumbs and smears of icing were all that remained of the once-triple-layered Victoria sponge cake that had taken her all morning to make. No one had admired the light perfection of the cake itself and the richness of the frosting, none of the kids had said anything, but they had scraped the icing off and made a mess on their plates.

NOW THIS WOMAN, HER NEW MOTHER, WAS GOING TO LIVE with them. For a split second, she felt the need to run to one of the trees up front and climb up so she could see farther down the road. To everybody's amazement, despite her size, Quinn was proficient in climbing trees. She was strong and not afraid of falling and even though she scraped her legs and skinned her knees in the process, it was all worth it; to peek into a nest—she would *never* disturb it; after all, momma bird was taking care of the baby birds—and to be able to catch a glimpse of her familiar surroundings that seemed so different from a higher viewpoint.

Her new mother didn't appear until nightfall. She wore one of the prettiest green silk dresses Quinn had ever seen—the color of beans dropped in ice water just at the right time to stop them from cooking—and her hair smelled of oranges and bergamot pear and when the light hit it just right, the colors and highlights reminded her of autumn leaves, amber hues melded together like a crown on a princess. And in the middle of her face sat her eyes, deep green and dark as a lake. Quinn couldn't help but imagine how pretty she'd be if she'd been given half of her new mother's beauty.

Quinn was adept at hiding her feelings, yet her heart had a life of its own. It picked up a beat or two, stumbled even, causing her to draw in a deep breath. She didn't know what to say to her and so she just stood watching her father busily wiping his shiny face with a handkerchief. He seemed happy, his eyes were wide in anticipation, and he stood close to the woman, who was so small that three of her would fit into his body. Quinn could tell by just looking at her that she'd never love him. She was too exquisite a woman to love a man like her father.

"Call me Sigrid," the woman said and she grabbed Quinn's hand, hanging limp by her side. Her smile was small, then fleeting. "I've heard a lot about you," she added but it sounded as if she had just told a lie.

Quinn felt the woman's eyes wander from her round face down her plump body and back up. The woman's cheeks had a rosy hue, but the rest of her skin was quite pale, as if the warmth had recoiled the moment she realized Quinn was not what she'd expected.

"Call you Secret?" Quinn asked, stretching the first syllable.

"S-I-G-R-I-D," the woman replied, spelling out her name.

"Where are you from?" Quinn asked, since she detected an accent.

"Austria," the woman said.

Quinn didn't know what to expect of living with a mother or a woman functioning as a motherly figure, because she had never had one. There was a certain kind of pain and longing for her very own mother—a woman she had never met and who wasn't spoken about unless Quinn brought her up herself—yet the pain was vague at best, elusive, as if Quinn was unable to assign any true meaning to some-one she had lost but who had never been there to begin with.

Sigrid turned out to not be very domestic. It took her hours to get ready in the morning, and she never seemed to have time to prepare breakfast or lunch. She drove into town, to the local beauty salon, frequently, however, and always returned in high spirits with arms full of bags and packages. The laundry piled up, and after a few months, it was decided that Mrs. Holmes would return to resume the responsibilities of maintaining the house.

In due time, Sigrid made it a habit to stay in her room. Mrs. Holmes brought her tea on a silver tray with dainty fine china Quinn's father had ordered from Austria as a gift to Sigrid, and she ate all her meals from the plates with gaudy peacock-looking birds and orange and blue flowers. The set came with cups and saucers, sugar bowl and creamer, a soup tureen, and serving plates, dessert bowls, bread plates, a cake stand, and a gravy boat.

"Where did you get those peacock dishes from?" Quinn asked, fascinated by how every dish had its very own bowl or container.

"It's not a peacock, child," Sigrid said as she gently caressed the shiny smooth surface of the dainty plate. "It's a pheasant bird of paradise. The pattern is called Eden."

"Eden like Adam and Eve Eden?" Quinn asked, tempted to reach for the plate, wanting to feel its smoothness and weight, since Mrs. Holmes had been instructed to serve Quinn's food on simple Pyrex plates with a thick red border.

"Adam and Eve? Not so much. More like a perpetual place of bliss, you know, like your father and I."

Quinn knew it was all a lie—there was no paradise, no Eden, not even close. There was, however, Cadillac Man.

Less than one year after her father had married Sigrid, a man in a midnight blue Cadillac had pulled into the driveway. Quinn had dug her shoes into the porch and halted the swing with a violent screech. The man was tall and wore a gray suit and shoes shinier than a newly minted quarter. He retrieved a suitcase from the trunk, nodded at her on his way to the front door, then knocked. Mrs. Holmes wasn't expected for another two hours, but Sigrid must have been standing behind the door, because it opened just seconds later.

"Go play, child," Sigrid called out, and Quinn wondered what kind of games Sigrid thought teenagers played these days. She remained on the front porch for a while, then snuck into the kitchen. She ate the leftover cobbler, wondering what kind of cake and ice cream Mrs. Holmes would serve after dinner. She wasn't supposed to eat before dinner nor roam or sneak about or spy on Sigrid, but Quinn was curious and if she was careful not to step on the wrong floorboard, if the slats remained silent on her behalf, she might be able to peek into Sigrid's room.

Quinn tiptoed as softly as her body size allowed, avoiding the raised edges of the boards. She turned the knob silently, and after releasing it, she pushed the door inward, allowing for a gap. She waited.

The first thing she became aware of was Sigrid's perfume lingering in the air. She took in the rich scent, a fruity and floral aroma like the sweet peas growing behind the house. The curtains were drawn, but an inch-wide gap let in a beam of light. After her eyes adjusted, she made out the man's jacket draped over the back of a chair. The breakfast tray sat abandoned on the nightstand; the jelly-stained knife rested next to the shredded remnants of a biscuit.

Cadillac Man was kneeling on the bed, next to Sigrid. She must have fainted—her body flat on her back with one leg hanging off the side of the mattress—but there was no shaking of Sigrid's shoulder, no fanning of air, no smelling salt wafting toward her nose. She watched him undo the top button of Sigrid's blouse with one hand while pushing her skirt up with the other.

Quinn straightened up as if she'd been awakened by a bang of cymbals, her heart pounding and blood rushing like a fierce river through her ears. Cadillac Man's hand made Sigrid's body glide effortlessly with a swaying motion, peeling off her skirt. It rustled to the floor. His pointy shoes hit the wooden planks. Sigrid sat up, propping herself up by her elbows, watching him. Sigrid's body had the shape of a violin and as Quinn stood watching, she imagined her own ample body struggling to execute such deliberate moves.

Cadillac Man opened Sigrid's blouse slowly, twisting each button.

He ran his fingertip from her throat toward her breastbone, barely dragged it across her neck, but it had left behind a reddish streak on Sigrid's pale skin. The blouse fell open and he studied her body. He held her left breast, gently at first, then, as if he thought otherwise, his hand clutched and covered it, making it entirely disappear. He lifted his hand, barely grazing her nipples, and meandered down her stomach, then back up, and paused again at her breastbone. He shoved Sigrid back onto the bed—for a moment Quinn wondered why Sigrid didn't struggle against him when it seemed so violent, making her entire body bounce on the mattress. Cadillac Man crudely removed Sigrid's underwear, the fabric cutting into her thighs. He got off the bed and on his knees. He kissed her just above her pubic bone, and a finger disappeared inside Sigrid.

Sigrid in turn moved into his hand until he stopped suddenly, removing his finger. While she propped herself up on her elbows again, Cadillac Man got up and unzipped his pants. He grabbed Sigrid by the back of her head, wrapping her hair round his fingers, and then pulled her head back so she had to strain to look at him. Their bodies were statue-like but something seemed to unleash, like horses when the starting gates open. Quinn watched as they moved with the constant sound of flesh on flesh, only interrupted by the man flipping Sigrid onto her stomach. They switched places over and over and then Cadillac Man's round backside heaved one last time and there was nothing but the sound of heavy breathing.

Quinn was captivated as if she were a hare spellbound by the talons of an eagle. An unfamiliar scent lingered in the room, a scent she couldn't quite place. Something much more powerful than red velvet cake with cream cheese frosting, something that reached deeper than the stomach, surged through her, sank its teeth into her, leaving her with a terrible feeling of throbbing and longing.

Leaving the way she had entered, silently, unbeknownst, Quinn went back to the swing on the porch. For a while, she kept momentum, but then allowed the swing to come to a stop. Still shaking, her body two steps ahead of itself, she couldn't erase the image of Cadillac Man's shiny shoes, their tips pointing upward as if to aim toward heaven. Like her father, he too was no match for Sigrid—he was a man who just showed up and stayed for an hour or two just to move on.

Quinn lost her appetite. It wasn't that her hunger had ceased, but a knowledge had emerged that food was no longer what she was after. The thought of meat roasting in the oven and the sound of swirling and rattling ice cubes in a glass of iced tea nauseated her, no longer made sense as a means of comfort. She pushed it all aside just to feel a sadness she had never felt before. How easily people throw each other away. She knew, in due time, she'd look just like her father and people would make fun of her too. The thought of him made her eyes sting—not the way people ridiculed him, nothing like that—but how he had easily cast his daughter aside for a beautiful woman who had never loved him in return.

There she was—Quinn Murray, who had stopped growing at five feet five inches, who had the kind of face people forgot even before they'd stopped looking at it, a girl who had gained thirty pounds since her fifteenth birthday, all of them around the hips.

Satisfying her hunger suddenly seemed no longer suitable. She felt that yearning leave her and she was fully awake, had only one mission. She longed to be like Sigrid, with violin hips and men adoring her, never to be discarded for anyone. Yet there was also a seed of fear inside of her, and she was unsure of its origin, like a dream she was unable to interpret.

She wanted to be powerful, like Sigrid, as if this world was an instrument to be played. She wanted to be powerful, yet there was also this vulnerability that seemed too familiar to shake. And it terrified her.

Four

DAHLIA

IN the Barrington Hotel parking lot, I take one last look in the rear-view mirror; the bruises around my nose are still noticeable but the swelling has completely subsided. I run my tongue over my chipped front tooth. The flaw is barely visible but the tip of my tongue is tender from persistently running over the sharp edge. I'm part of a crew of women who clean the guest rooms. We have been hired on probation and get paid under the table. We go unnoticed—we are actually told to never make eye contact nor speak to the guests—yet we are held to the same standards as the room attendants in their black uniforms with white aprons. They are a step up from us; they help unpack, assist with anything the guest might need, they don't scrub toilets or change sheets. I get out of the car, fluff my bangs, and check my likeness in the window; my baby blue housekeeper's uniform is starched, pressed, and fits me impeccably, just as management demands. There are no allowances for stains, wrinkles, and snug skirts or fabric pulling against buttons. At the Barrington, even my crew of undocumented help isn't allowed to slack off.

Every single time my sore tongue touches the tooth's jagged edge, I'm reminded how long it's been since I found Jane in the woods. Seven days—*an entire week*—and not a word about her identity; she remains in a coma and her name is still a mystery. Watching the local news, I'm taken aback by the absence of appeals to the public and the overall lack of urgency. I am able to abandon the image of Jane in her hospital bed, attached to monitors, but I can't forget what happened to me in her room.

Since the day I saw Jane last, I have had another episode. I have decided on the word *episode* until I figure out a more appropriate word.

It happened earlier this morning, in the shower: the calcified show-erhead's water pressure was mediocre at best, yet I felt my hands tin-gling, starting at the tips. The prickling traveled up my arm, past my neck, into my eyes and nose. I didn't only *feel* the water pounding on my body but I smelled the minerals, tasted them like miniature Pop Rocks exploding on my tongue. Every single drop thumped against the wall of the shower stall—individually and all at once—as if the world was magnified while simultaneously zooming in on me, allowing itself to be interpreted. I dropped on the shower floor before my knees could buckle on me. It was over as quickly as it had started. I was left with an anticipatory feeling, a nervous kind of energy that tingled through me like electrical sparks as if I was positioning myself on the blocks to prepare for a race. I remained on the shower floor for a long while, only getting up when I realized I was going to be late for work.

Housekeepers are forbidden to enter through the front door but I'm late. If I hurry and my supervisor, Mr. Pratt, doesn't catch me between the door and the lockers, I can clock in without a lecture.

The revolving mechanism makes a gentle *sswwsshh* and Pratt lies in wait behind a marble column, motioning me to approach him, curling his index finger as if he has caught a kid with muddy shoes trampling through the house.

I follow him to his office. He does not offer me a seat and the lecture is short. "We have to let you go," he says, and within the same breath, he assures me of the Barrington's empathy for what I have been going through after finding Jane in the woods. "But you've been con-sistently late and you are unable to complete your assigned duties. We only pick the best for our full-time positions, you were informed about that policy. I will escort you to clear out your belongings."

Later, as Pratt watches me from the door of the locker room, I dump the few accumulated belongings—a change of clothes and a brush, and granola bars—in my purse. I hesitate when I see the stuffed giraffe at the bottom of the locker that I failed to take to lost and found days ago. One of its eyes dangles on a thread, and I attempt to stuff it back in its socket.

"Your last check will be mailed to you. I was hoping to offer you a full-time position, but we do probationary part-time for a reason. Sorry it didn't work out."

I always knew it wasn't going to work out. A full-time position includes paperwork, forms I don't have. For as long as I can remember, less than eight hundred a month—the cut-off for tax-exempt wages— has always been the magic number.

I leave the Barrington through the back door. When I reach my car, I steady myself, lean against it. As I drop the giraffe in the near- est garbage can, a memory hits me: my mother waking me in the middle of the night, thrusting a stuffed animal into my arms: a lav- ender bunny. Another one of her cloak-and-dagger operations, leaving everything behind—*grab the papers, anything with our name on it*—and off we went to a town unknown, unaccustomed rooms and a bed unfamiliar to me. There aren't too many memories but this one is clear as day. I wonder what happened to the lavender bunny.

Above me, moths' wings make contact with the streetlight.

I bend backward, looking up; the moths swirl around like snow- flakes. Hundreds of them spin aimlessly in the harsh whiteness of the LED light.

Snow. A blizzard. That too is a memory I can't place.

Five

AELLA

THEY appeared at Aella's door by nightfall. There had been signs; first the dog had raised his head, then his ears had perked up, and he had let out a deep bark, shallow and low. Atlas was a crossbreed, half wolf, half dog, and she trusted him with her life.

Aella opened the door and stepped outside. Atlas followed her, stood motionless to her left, let out a bark. It was a mere warning on his part, giving her a sign: *Watch me. I'll tell you if there's trouble.*

A man with an unkempt beard and teeth too perfect to be his own stepped forward and Aella knew he had rapped on her door. There were more; she heard their mumbled voices in the dark from where they were standing, to the right where the road had led them to her trailer in the woods.

Aella's eyes got used to the dark and she realized they were all men, with beards and grimy clothes, who had parked their cars by the road, car doors propped open. The men had gathered around, smoking, talking, and stretching their backs.

Atlas continued to keep his distance from them, remaining next to her, his nose darting out occasionally, only to retreat immediately. Bad news, yes, but dangerous, no. Atlas was a skillful judge of people and therefore Aella was not afraid.

"It's a bit late for a visit," she said and watched a couple of cats scurry off into the dark.

"We are just passing through and were wondering if it'd be okay to camp out back."

Out back was a field with cedar stubs caught between shrubs and trees releasing pollen in explosive puffs of orange-red smoke whenever cold winds blew from the north. Like gnarly little fishhooks, the pollen invaded nostrils and sinuses. It wasn't a place to camp out, but it was all the same to Aella. It wouldn't be the first time they had passed through—not the same men, but their kind. "Who's passing through?" Aella asked, shushing Atlas as he let out a low growl.

"It's twelve of us. Just for one night."

"I can count," Aella said, even though the night was pitch-black and she could barely make out the men's silhouettes. "But who are you?"

The man paused for a second, then stroked his beard downward. In the light coming from the trailer Aella saw strong hands, uncut and clean, maybe a man working with gloves? His arms and face were sunburned and the knees of his jeans worn.

"We are travelers," the man finally said.

"I see." *Tinkers,* Aella thought. Irish travelers passing through, looking for employment. "I guess one night is okay with me."

The man mumbled something Aella couldn't make out, and another man from the group called out to him. They conversed in a language with soft vowels and words Aella hadn't heard before.

"You are here why?" Atlas had settled down, yet he kept his distance.

"Roofing jobs, after the fall storms."

"But why are you coming here? To my house? You can park anywhere and spend a few days. Who told you about me?"

"Well"—he scratched his beard again—"we've heard from travelers that they sometimes pass through here and that you allow them to camp on your property."

He spoke the truth. Tinkers passed through all the time. Mainly bad seeds, the ones that trick the old folks, scam everybody out of some money, and before locals know they've been had, they've long since left town.

Aella didn't care about their dealings but she didn't want people in town to know they stayed on her land, didn't want to be connected to them. Aurora had never got used to her, and people gossiped. Women like her didn't want to be the talk of the town. Too many people came snooping, and then there were the teenage dares, and it would all get out of hand so easily.

The local men were reluctant, shook their heads at the sight of her; some spit in the dirt as they passed by. The women worried. *How can you live out there, all by yourself? Aren't you afraid?* they'd ask, and Aella just grinned. *I'm the baddest thing out here,* she'd say, and they'd stare at her and then break out in a nervous giggle. Yet the people of Aurora flocked to her: meek boys who wanted the pretty girls, men who couldn't keep beautiful women in their beds, lacking money and prowess. They asked for potions and salves and bottles containing strange things. Reconciling with a lover was what men were usually after—nothing a black cat bone and lodestones couldn't fix—but the women looked to cure ailments. Ringing in the ears was a big one— no doctor can help with that; no ear drops or pills can cure the dead talking about you because you've done them wrong while they walked this earth. Some women wanted to keep their men, bind them so they'd never leave, not thinking about the future when they'd long for them to go, and then they'd return and the unbinding would cost thrice. Mothers came for their children: a cleft palate, a head tremor making other kids scatter in disgust, the inability to read or write, infants who stared straight past their mothers, struggling to make eye contact. Mothers were the most desperate of them all.

Aella held the man's gaze and cocked her head, as if to say, *What's it worth to you?* The man shoved a hand at her, causing Atlas to growl again. This time Aella didn't correct him. The man took a step back, then extended out his arm again, his hand facing upward. In his palm was a substantial wad of dollar bills held together by a rubber band. Aella reached for the money.

"Wait," the man said. "There's something else. One of us needs to stay here for a few weeks. We'll get her on our way back."

Her. Aella scanned the group of men, and a woman of petite stature emerged from the backseat of one of the cars and walked toward them, dragging her feet. Atlas approached her and sniffed the air. When the woman stepped next to the man and the moonlight illuminated her, Aella saw an expanding stomach that seemed overly large, almost freakish. Her elfin frame had nowhere to put a baby but to push it outward, and then there was her age; she seemed young, too young to be pregnant, and her eyes were vacant as she protectively placed a hand over her stomach.

"She doesn't feel well. We thought a bit of rest would do her good."

Aella grabbed the wad of dollar bills and counted the money. The amount was more than generous, more than double what they usually paid to camp out on the land behind her trailer. It was hard to admit, but she looked forward to having company, especially during a time of year when storms kept her indoors for days on end.

"You can spend the night in the field. She can stay with me." Aella pointed at the pregnant woman and then back at her trailer. Aella beheld the belly underneath the filthy shirt poking out from an unzipped jacket one of the men must have given her. There was something in her eyes—not so much what was there but what was lacking—that made Aella consider her longer than she would have any other woman. Atlas continuously sniffed the air, tracking invisible scents, veering left to right. He approached her and put his nose on her hand. He slinked back and hid behind Aella.

It was a sign. "What's wrong with her?" Aella asked.

"Nothin'." The man scratched his head, then shrugged.

Inside, after the men had carried their tents and belongings past the trailer, Aella took a good look at the woman. She wasn't a woman after all; she was merely a girl, barely grown. If it wasn't for the obvious signs of pregnancy, the belly and the engorged breasts, she would have assumed she was barely sixteen years old.

The girl lowered herself into a chair, her feet clearing the floor by several inches as they swung back and forth. Her face had an unhealthy look to it and her eyes were open as she stared at nothing on the wall. Her pale skin was a peculiar backdrop for her black hair and bushy eyebrows. "What's your name?" Aella asked.

The girl sat, still and quiet, scooting farther back into the chair. "Tain," she finally said, and it seemed as if the word had fallen from her mouth by accident.

"You can stay with me until they come back."

Her brown eyes then lost their emptiness, became rounder, glossier. Her face buckled, her breathing stopped momentarily, and tears streamed down her face.

"What's the matter? Why are you crying? You're safe with me, if that's what you're worried about."

"There are storms coming soon," the girl said. "I'm afraid."

"It'll be all right," Aella said. "It's not so unforeseeable, you know. If you pay attention to certain things you'll be able to tell exactly when the storm is coming."

"Like what?" Tain seemed fascinated by the fact that Aella could predict the weather.

"Watch the bees," Aella told her. "Horses shake their heads a lot, and there are lots of cobwebs in the grass. Most of all, the clouds are pink in the evenings."

"I've always been afraid of thunder and lightning."

"Nothing to be afraid of. It's like this here in the summer, but usually storms are severe on the coast, never this far inland. No need to worry. Just a little bit of rain and thunder." The words didn't seem to calm the girl, who wrapped herself in the jacket and continued to stare straight ahead, burying her hands in the oversized pockets. She looked cold. "Let me make you a cup of tea."

Tain's face remained blank. Aella thought about the chamomile she had collected in the nearby fields and how she'd brew the blossoms for a long time so they'd be strong enough to calm her, and maybe she'd add valerian root.

When Aella finished brewing the tea, she extended the cup. Tain's tiny hands reached for it and they touched Aella's ever so slightly. Tain's hands were cold—icy as if the girl was merely a ghost or was about to turn into one. Aella had felt that sort of thing before, people who didn't have a lot of time left, as if they were already part of another world—and she watched Tain cup her hands around the hot tea and then something gave way, as if a floorboard had shifted. Tain's form shimmered and fluttered, and Aella held on to the table. She wasn't worried; everything around her had been gleaming for a while—the woods and the trees, the cars passing her, even Atlas and the red cardinals outside—and it was always like that in her head when a storm was gathering strength. The girl was right to be afraid of it. It would be a big one.

Later, as Tain slept on the couch, her stomach tucked off to the side to allow her to breathe easier, Aella regarded her; her face was softly flushed with sleep, and her dark eyes shone through her thin and heavy lids.

The girl seemed ethereal, as if painted into this life with a fine brush; with every stroke the colors faded so quickly that she was dissolving in front of Aella's very eyes. Aella knew it was a sure sign that the girl wasn't going to be on this earth for a long time, or maybe the baby's life would be cut short—Aella wasn't sure.

She tried to make sense of this girl, wondered how easily people who didn't know any better could fall victim to her. Tain was like a gentle uprising of heavy clouds in the distance on a windless day—but then there was a distant *boom*, announcing what those brooding clouds had promised all along—a powerful storm.

Aella watched Atlas. It was true that the dog cared for no one but his master, yet he always allowed for courting by strangers, especially women. He remained at a fair distance from Tain at all times, didn't make any attempt to approach her.

That too was a sign.

Six

QUINN

QUINN placed one foot in front of the other, skipping the third step from the top, the one that screeched like an angry old woman. She paused at the bottom of the stairs. Out of the corner of her eye she caught a movement beyond the hallway, inside the darkened kitchen. It was formless and indistinct, like a shadow, barely shifting, and she knew it was her imagination. She calmed when she reminded herself that Sigrid was sleeping upstairs and that it was nothing more than the fear of being found out that made her see shadows and other spooky obscure shapes. Without as much as a creak of the wooden floorboards, Quinn made her way through the kitchen and out the back door.

Outside, the darkness disturbed her, as if there were feathered beasts baring incisors lurking beyond the shadows, yet Quinn vowed to embrace the feeling, for she was no longer a child, easy to impress. As she marched down the dirt road toward the fields, near the woods, a faint wind brushed against her, making her skirt cling to her thighs. Her gait was nimbler than it used to be, than it had ever been, really; her body was now as agile as a dancer's. Quinn could no longer conceive of inventing recipes and chatting with old ladies in town, she was no longer preoccupied with harvesting vegetables in the backyard and the planning of future meals.

Taking a lover was what she called it. It was an expression Quinn had pondered and concluded was something that would make her powerful beyond comparison. To *take* him implied power, yet her lover was merely a boy, hardly a couple of years older than herself, and far removed from Cadillac Man. But to Quinn he meant everything.

After she had watched her stepmother and Cadillac Man in her father's bedroom—along with the many times since that encounter, in secret, through the same crack in the door—Quinn had begun to wonder about it all. It seemed to be a matter of men succumbing to a certain kind of beauty; not the cheap kind that came from loose behavior and tight blouses, no, but the power of women who were what she liked to call *mysterious*. The less a man knew about a woman, the more he seemed to be enamored of her. Cadillac Man, after all, knew nothing of Sigrid's true self—her indigestion and frequent belching after large meals, or the way her eyes were red and puffy when she woke and how ill-tempered she was before noon—but he got to enjoy her company after she had bathed and dressed and curled her hair. Quinn had read about geishas and how they were considered artists and could seduce a man with just a hint of their necks, but only if they chose to, as if all the power was within them, a power so intricate Quinn had problems understanding it herself. Supposedly you could tell a prostitute from a geisha by her clothes; prostitutes tie their kimonos in the front while geishas have help tying them in the back.

She thought of geishas when she watched men stare at Sigrid, their eyes eating her up, with her restrained makeup and tasteful appearance, always crossing her legs and appearing helpless somehow so random men would offer to lift groceries into the car, carry packages, and pump gas. Some men were even in the company of other women, yet they couldn't refrain from staring, their eyes wondering what it would be like if she belonged to them. Maybe they thought possessing her somehow would automatically elevate them to some higher standard.

Wiles, Sigrid called it; *the wiles of a woman.*

Quinn's father had had a coronary during a city hall meeting the previous year. Seconds after he had pulled a starched handkerchief from his pocket, beads formed on his brow and the room watched his large frame drop and hit the floor with a *thud*.

"He was gone before he knew what was happening," the doctor told Sigrid later and went into detail about how it took six grown men to lift him up onto an ornate desk, where the doctor performed CPR with a high degree of difficulty due to the circumference of his body.

"Don't worry, child," Sigrid said to Quinn after the doctor had told them the news. "You'll stay with me. He wouldn't want it any other way," Sigrid added and uncrossed her legs.

"He was a sick man and he was sick for a long time. The town will remember him. He was a good man," the doctor said while taking in Sigrid's face underneath her new hat, a veiled half-moon-shaped affair with matching gloves.

Oddly, in the days after his death, Quinn imagined he was still alive, and it seemed quite plausible because her father had never been home when he was living, never spent a lot of time with her, so he might as well still be around, just not present in the house. She preferred to retain the memory of him this way, absent yet still alive somewhere. As with her mother's passing, the word still was a strange concept, implying a movement from one state to the other, yet she couldn't imagine what or where that place was. And so Quinn thought of her father often, with great sadness but also with great reverie, knowing that his body no longer held him back. Diabetes had caused ulcers on his legs, and he should have retired years ago, should have taken better care of himself, seen doctors—it was not as if one can cure diabetes with magic water—but he had seemed to be content going on as long as he had. Quinn prayed for him often and kept his watch in her jewelry box. When she did cry she thought mainly of the trip to Galveston they'd never taken. How she'd love to have that memory of him, on chairs by the pool, dining at fine restaurants, strolling along the harbor with Spoil Island in the distance. She would have held his hand. She wished she had this memory, but maybe one day she'd get to go after all. As time passed, imagining this lost opportunity became more and more painful, and eventually Quinn tried not to think about it anymore.

That night, as Quinn made her way to meet her lover, she knew her trim body was powerful; she now ate only two small meals a day, but mostly she was thin because she had decided for it to be so. Her new body was a mere mouthpiece of her never-ending dominance over her hunger. She had stood in front of a mirror that morning and admired the part where her thigh curved into her hips, the dimples above her buttocks, and her defined collarbone. Not a single part of her hidden below a layer of flesh. Feeling the power of her new body, she strode through the bright night with a crescent moon overhead and imagined the pressure of her lover's hands all over her, even though he hadn't dared touch her quite yet.

QUINN CALLED HIM BENITO, AND THEY HAD MET FOR THE FIRST TIME when he and his uncle had delivered bales of hay to her house to fertilize the rosebushes. Sigrid, after the death of her husband, had insisted on growing roses, and even though the bushes looked measly and were speckled with what seemed like large black pepper flakes, she wouldn't give up on them.

"Hay is good for the soil, it makes it fertile. You'll see," Sigrid said and had Benito and his uncle drop the hay next to the forlorn flower bed. The uncle inspected the soil, rubbed a clump of dirt between his fingers and promised to return the next day and till the flower bed and fold in the hay.

Benito wouldn't look at Quinn that day, but when he returned the next, they struck up a conversation even though the uncle gave them sideways glances. From then on, Quinn waited on the porch until she heard the rumbling engine of the old truck become more powerful with every passing second that it approached the house, imagining the pipes spewing twin plumes of black smoke. Once the uncle was tending to the flower beds, Benito was the one who was sent back and forth for a forgotten tool or to empty a bucket of rocks they had dug up from the soil. Quinn sat on the front steps and watched Benito jump in the bed of the pickup, the muscles of his long skinny arms quivering under his brown skin when he lifted wood, bags of mulch, and gardening tools.

"What school do you go to?" Quinn asked.

"I'm not in school," he said. "I'm from Palestine. I went to school there," Benito said and reached for the hand tiller, pushing it to the very edge of the truck bed. He jumped out and landed on his feet like gymnasts Quinn had seen in school. Then, seemingly without strife, he lifted the heavy tiller and placed it gently on the ground. His hair had a sheen like deep dark mahogany wood and it swished gently in the wind, swaying with each word he spoke.

"Palestine. Where's that?" Quinn asked, merely trying to be polite. She crossed her legs like she had seen Sigrid do. She feared she didn't look half as sophisticated as her.

"About thirty miles from here, a small town."

"Do you always work with your uncle?"

"I do a lot of work for lots of people," he said and wiped his forehead with the back of his hand. "I'm saving up to start my own business."

Soon Benito's uncle had enough of Benito taking his time collecting tools or dumping buckets and he began interrupting their conversations by tossing random items to and fro in the truck bed and then walking off, mumbling something under his breath. After a week of protest, the uncle called from the backyard every few minutes, making it impossible for them to have a conversation at all.

"*Ven aquí*," the uncle shouted at first, then he'd yell, "*Me estas escuchando?*" and by the end of the third week, when the soil was tilled, the hay folded, the rosebushes planted, and all that was left was to attach a trellis to the back porch, Benito no longer accompanied his uncle.

"Where is Benito? Please, tell me," Quinn begged and watched the uncle holding a nail below the head with the fingers of one hand.

The uncle simply replied, "*No hablo inglés*," and Quinn watched him tap the nail gently to set it in place, then he grasped the hammer firmly at the end and hit the nail straight on. A few smacks and it was done. "*Todo ha terminado*," he added and turned his back to her.

Days later, after school, Benito waited for Quinn by the hardware store she passed every day on her way home. They drove out of town and parked in secluded places, knowing people would talk about the daughter of the late town treasurer and the Mexican farm help, but that too was power to Quinn, the fact that she did as she pleased. They sat in Benito's truck and he told her about his hometown, where he had lived before he came to Texas. A mesa in Mexico, *Mesa de Sagrado*, an elevated piece of land with a flat top, and on one of its steep sides, his family owned a small farm where they raised goats and chickens. He spoke of his grandmother, who still operated the farm with her cousins, and how she lived for the one day a year when the gates of heaven opened and the spirits of the deceased reunited with their families.

"There's a day for that?" Quinn asked, wondering if this was real or something the superstitious people who had their futures read at the yearly carnival believed in.

"*Día de los Muertos*," Benito said, and crossed himself.

"What's that mean?" Quinn asked and tried to pronounce it the best way she could. "Dee-oz dayla merde," she said and they both laughed and scooted closer to each other.

"It's the Day of the Dead and the only night of the year my *abuela* sleeps in her bed."

"Where does she sleep if not in her bed?"

"On the floor."

"But she's an old woman. Why would she do that?" Quinn thought of Sigrid and her large bed covered in the finest linens.

"When my grandfather died, she promised to never again sleep in their bed unless it was with him. That one night she believes he joins her and she cooks and sets out a plate of food for him, and washes his clothes and lays them out on the bed."

Quinn tried not to think about Benito's story too much, for it made her remember her father, and Sigrid hardly even visited the cemetery to leave flowers on his grave.

"Does her husband ever show up?" Quinn asked, but the image in her head was not one of old *abuela* waiting for her dead husband to join her, but rather of her father in the blue suit, his head resting on a satin pillow in the cherrywood coffin, propped up at Mitchell's Funeral Home in town. His face had appeared waxen and bloated, he had looked nothing like himself.

"It's just something you do. The dead don't show—I mean not really, but in spirit—it's a matter of honoring them," Benito said.

Later, careful as to avoid curious eyes watch Quinn get out of Benito's truck, they agreed on another day and time when they'd meet again. The following Sunday, after they walked the fields by the forest, Benito showed her how to pick grass with the widest and coarsest blade. He put it between his thumbs, pulled it taut, and pursed his lips and blew into it. Depending on how he cupped his hands, the sound changed. He said that the grass in his hometown grew higher than any grass he'd ever seen in Texas. Soon they began meeting after dark and with every passing day, with each stride she made toward him, she felt more in command of her own life. She felt like a girl walking toward her destiny, and geisha stories seemed silly and thoughtless and she imagined leaving Aurora with Benito to start a life someplace where no one knew them.

THAT NIGHT, WITH THOUGHTS OF A FUTURE TOGETHER, QUINN forged ahead, mesmerized by the moon above. It offered a brilliance and silvery light that she had never seen before and even as she stumbled over dips in the ground, she continued to stare into the night sky. Some stars were rather dull, merely flickering into existence every now and then, but some were powerful enough to illuminate the night. She walked on, down the rural road, and at some point she cut across a field and ended up on the dirt path leading into the woods. When she entered, low-hanging branches tickled her cheek ever so slightly, making her jump.

The woods seemed different that night, the surroundings suddenly unfamiliar. The trunks were slanted and the paths had all but vanished, the trees were higher than in the daylight and they were spreading toward something way beyond their reach, up into the night sky, almost touching the moon. There was talk about these woods. Always had been. The trees *whispered*, locals said; on certain nights you could make out voices and it was best to walk in the other direction and not turn around. Quinn knew that the cottonwood trees were abundant and the leaves were flattened sideways, conducive to a particular type of movement in the wind, and that was all there was to it, even though she had to admit when the wind picked up and rustled the leaves, the noise level seemed unnatural, even to her. When she finally reached their secret place, an oval clearing within the darkest part of the forest, she sat on a fallen tree and waited for her lover.

"Mi corazón." She felt the words more than heard them.

They embraced and his wet hair tickled her cheek. His wrinkled shirt smelled of soap and some faint odor of food that was unfamiliar to her. Everybody in his family called him Benito. He was nineteen with a strong body from the hard labor of setting up fences and removing trees, stints at farms where they'd brand cattle and build barns. He had a broad face with a hooked nose and his skin was soft with barely a hair on his entire face.

They spread a blanket on the forest floor and they became lovers. Quinn was a virgin but Benito wasn't and he was gentle and whispered words in Spanish Quinn didn't understand yet that sounded like a melody to her. Even though his hands were coarse and calloused, they felt soft as he took hold of her face, forcing their eyes to meet. A beautiful stillness descended upon them as they lay on the forest floor and even though he was not inside her yet, they were one. Their bodies were trembling and Quinn felt something take hold within her, some entity clinging to her as if she'd done this a million times. His mouth captured hers and he kissed her slowly as he moved with her. Her chest rose as she drew in a breath and held it while his body shifted. She felt a tinge of pain and cried out. Benito stopped moving. Finally Quinn let out the breath she'd held in and then she slowly drew in another. Everything she'd ever believed this to be was a mistake, this was not crude and vulgar, there wasn't any power *over* Benito, not like Sigrid and Cadillac Man, but the power was within her, and pouring out of her into him. It was like the lunar eclipse she had watched with her father years ago, an event so momentous that every time she thought of it, she felt as if she was reliving it. That's how this moment would feel to her for all eternity.

Benito reached out and touched her, running his fingers over her flushed cheeks. He drew her into a hug, then covered her face with kisses. El Dorado was real, a golden city, he told her, the land of a king who was covered with gilded dust so thick he seemed to be made of solid gold. Quinn wasn't sure if it was a legend or if a scrap of truth rested beneath his words but she didn't care. She thought of Benito as a prince who would soon become a man and then rule some sort of kingdom. And she'd be his queen.

"I have to go," Benito said. "I have to work with my uncle early in the morning."

"Come see me after school on Monday? At the hardware store?"

"Yes, *mi corazón*, I'll try but it's a big job. A deck. It will take all weekend and maybe all of Monday. I'll wait for you Tuesday, maybe Wednesday," he said and held out his hand to help her up. "Let me drive you home."

"I'll leave in a bit. I want to see the sun come up."

He bent down to kiss her and Quinn watched him disappear between the cottonwood trees. She heard a faint sound of a car door opening, then slamming shut, followed by the revving engine. Quinn imagined Benito skillfully maneuvering across the potholed dirt road.

She propped her arms behind her head and stared at the night sky. The wind had died down and as she lay under the stars, she still felt

Benito's soft breath and his heartbeat. She was nothing like Sigrid, and whatever wiles were, they didn't apply to boys like Benito. She was too much in her heart and not at all in her head, so whatever advice Sigrid had given her was no longer relevant, maybe never had had any significance at all. Forever she wanted to remember the moment she became Benito's lover. Quinn closed her eyes and drifted off into an inky darkness.

She awoke to a gunshot sounding in the distance. Quinn opened her eyes, but only for a second, and when all remained silent she drifted back to sleep, thinking she could have been mistaken.

The last image she'd remember later was the moon looming overhead with a sharp point, almost like a hunter's horn.

Seven

DAHLIA

AFTER leaving the Barrington for the last time, I rack my mind, wondering what the next step down from hotel housekeeper is going to be. On my mother's street, I find her house sitting quietly without a sign of life. The glaring and lonely porch light illuminates the impeccably clean front porch. I can't make out a single cricket in the harsh light of the bare bulb.

When I cross the threshold, beneath my feet something crackles as if I am stepping on a cracker or a piece of popcorn. I take another step and again I hear a crunching sound. Another step, another crunch. I swipe the light switch upward. Arranged two inches apart like cookie dough on a sheet pan is a carpet of cricket carcasses.

"Mom?" I call out, but there's no answer.

The back door gapes open, leaving a hole big enough to swallow a body. After I check the house and search for a note haphazardly left atop newspapers and magazines, I step out into the backyard. The fence gate is wide open.

My mother's neighborhood sits in rows of identical houses, all bungalows, no basements, small upper windows above narrow porches and square bays. The only differences are the conditions of the lawns and an occasional hanging basket, but mostly the houses are uniform.

I call out her name every so often and I tell myself that she went for a walk and forgot to shut the back door. And the gate. And forgot to leave a note.

When I arrive at the nearby park, less than half a mile from the house, I find the parking lot deserted. The entrance sign states that entering after dark is prohibited but around here no one really cares. The walkways are concrete and the silver maples, planted many years ago, now reach all the way up to the streetlights. No faint trickle of a nearby creek, not in the summer, not in Texas.

I stride down the walkway, past park benches and a small pond. I catch a whiff of garbage cans from the dog park to my right and I smile, for once certain this is not a figment of my imagination or my nose betraying me. About half a mile later, I hear a whining sound coming from the playground. Then I hear a whimper; this time it seems almost childlike.

"Mom?" I walk toward the general location of the whine, stop, and wait for it to resume.

"Mom?" This time louder, more urgent. I hear hissing that sounds like a snake, but then a cat scurries past me and disappears into the bushes.

I return home and dial the Aurora precinct number. I ask for Officer Roberto de la Vega and leave a voice mail. I tell him, "My mother has walked off into the darkness." I realize how melodramatic that sounds. "Call me back," I add. "I don't know if I should wait at home or look for her. Or where to look. I don't know if I should worry, even. The back door is open and she's gone." I'm trying not to sound too alarmed, it's not an emergency, but it *is* the middle of the night. "She didn't leave a note or anything."

I am exhausted and I prop my legs up on the coffee table and fall asleep.

I awake to harsh lights shining through the kitchen window. Parting the curtain, I see a police cruiser parked in the street with its nose poking into the driveway. A face stares at me through the window and Bobby points toward the front door. After I open the door, Bobby fumbles with the radio attached to his shoulder.

"Hey, troublemaker," he says and smiles. Then, more seriously, "I got your message. A couple of patrol cars are out looking for her. Do you have any idea where she could be?"

"She goes out without telling me, but never in the middle of the night. I told her to always leave a note so I know where she is. I checked the park earlier. That's where she goes often."

"Was she upset or acting strange at all?" Bobby asks.

My body blocks the view into the house and the crickets on the floor. I step outside and pull the door shut behind me. No one needs to know about the crickets just yet.

"Not that I know of," I say. "I got home and the back door was wide open. I wouldn't have known she was gone if it hadn't been for that door. I thought she was upstairs, in bed. She's usually asleep by the time I get home."

"Well, sit tight, we'll find her. Call me if she shows up?"

"Sure," I say.

I follow Bobby down the driveway to his cruiser and watch it crawl down the road. He never really speeds up, and then he stops and puts it in reverse. He rolls down the passenger's seat window and leans forward.

"Just got word. They found her."

"Where?"

"Down county road 2410, toward Elroy."

"2410 and Elroy? That's miles from here."

Bobby doesn't answer. He fumbles with the mobile computer and, without looking at me, he says, "They're taking her in."

"Taking her in for what? Did she rob a gas station or something?" I say, trying to sound lighthearted.

"She's okay, but she has a few scratches. And she refused to tell the officers her name. They asked her repeatedly but she wouldn't tell them. Told them she was out for a walk."

FM 2410 is nothing but a deserted country road and I don't know of any houses out there at all. There's an occasional mailbox, and driveways leading to properties, most of them just plots of deserted land. Walking down 2410 is a peculiar thing to do. Not telling the police her name is a new one, even for my mother. And then there are the neatly arranged crickets in the house. A voice in my head is whispering, telling me that none of this is remotely in the realm of *normal*, reminding me that lately she has been talking without punctuation or taking a breath, but all I can think is that I'm glad she's okay.

"They're taking her to Metroplex," Bobby finally confirms. "They will call you."

He goes on, but I stop listening. I don't mean to tune him out but I can't erase the picture of my mother walking down a dark country road. I imagine her defiant, ignoring the officers, stomping off: *I don't need to tell you my name, walking down the street isn't illegal.*

I spend the rest of the day sweeping the crickets out of the house, and I do the long-neglected laundry. As I finish folding the towels, a Dr. Wagner calls me from the hospital. He's calm but curt. Emotionless. After scribbling down his number and asking him to repeat it back to me three times, I ask him about my mother.

"Your mother is a bit confused," he says, and I wonder if that's a word a doctor ought to use regarding the mental state of a patient. "I have her on a mild sedative and we'll keep her for a few days. She has asked to stay and seems content for the moment."

"When can I see her?"

"No visitors for the time being."

"But she's okay, isn't she?"

"She's requested a few days of peace. That's what she called it. No reason to be alarmed." I hear him take in a deep breath. "Something seems to have happened?"

A few days of peace seems like something she would say. In the back of my mind I hear my mother's voice during our last conversation, sharp as a knife, the day after I found Jane.

"Why did you bring the cops to my house?"

"I told you last night, I found a woman in the woods."

"You lied when you were a child," my mother said. *"You'd tell stories, get people in trouble."*

"You mean when I broke my arm?" There were many incidents but the one with the broken arm was big.

"There were others," she said and kept wiping the sink that was already clean.

"Give me an example. I don't remember any of them."

"Reliving your glory days? I'm not repeating any of your stories if that's what you're trying to get me to do."

"Why don't you tell me something else then?" I asked her, feeling myself getting upset. That sharpness in her voice, the cold eyes. *"Tell me why we moved so much, why I never went to school. I don't even recall going to school until we moved to Texas."*

"No one remembers their childhood. It's not unusual."

"Why didn't I go to school like everybody else?"

"I homeschooled you."

"You were never home."

"I worked, more than one job at a time. You're going to blame me for not being home?"

"If you worked so much, why did we live in squalor?"

"You want me to hand you a résumé? What's with all the questions?"

Her spotted, blue-veined hands held the dirty rag, shaking ever so slightly, hardly noticeable, but I knew there was a storm brewing underneath her cool and calm demeanor.

"Who is my father?" The question hung between us like a heavy gray rain cloud about to unleash its fury. *"I don't remember him at all."*

"He ran off when you were a baby, I told you that. He was—"

"I remember Bobby's father taking us to the police station. I remember when they filled out the paperwork and you told them my name was Dahlia."

There was a long moment of silence. It stretched beyond the kitchen, beyond the house, beyond both of us, her need to keep secrets a gaping divide no bridge would ever overcome.

"Dahlia was not my name," I add. *"You called me Pet before that."*

Finally she broke her silence. *"I don't know what you're talking about. He stopped us because we had a broken headlight. You know that."*

I KNOW BETTER. I KNEW BETTER THEN AND I KNOW BETTER NOW.
There was no broken headlight. There are, however, questions that I
must ask before she drifts off deeper into this murky world of hers,
infested with crickets and her fear of police. Our love for each other
is fierce, we are all we've ever had to hold on to, and it was enough
when I was younger, it was even enough when we just talked on the
phone the past fifteen years, but it's not enough now.

LATER THAT NIGHT, I WAKE UP. WHEN I OPEN MY EYES, I CAN FEEL
something is wrong. *Off* somehow. It's dark outside—not even six
judging by the lack of light—but something is glowing up ahead of
me, almost like a pinprick-sized dot of light at the end of a tunnel. I
blink and blink again. Is it possible to observe light and it remain
obscure at the same time? It takes me a while until I realize that it's
not an actual glow but more a feeling of being lit up from the inside
out that is reflected off my eyelids. It remains within me, never leaves
my body. My hand tingles, then twitches. My skin feels snug and hot
and I remain completely still, hoping it will just go away. My hand
twitches again, stronger this time, no longer just a feeling but a visible spasm now. As quickly as the feeling materialized, it vanishes.

I don't hear the AC humming and that's all the explanation I need.
Nothing wrong here, just the heat. The air is thick and heavy, making it hard to draw a breath. Stagnant and idle, capable of melting
candles. Texas heat has a fierceness to it, everyone knows that. It makes
people lose their minds, my mother always says.

I lie in the dark, unable to shut off my thoughts. Like a bundle of
yarn, my mind loops around itself, repeating things to me, no matter
how hard I try not to think at all. It's been ten days since I found Jane
and still there's no update. I have no job, no money. My mother is in the
hospital after wandering down a country road in the middle of the night.
I want to call her, talk to her, and convince myself she is okay, but then

there are these fears I have. That I'll call and she'll be confused and dismissive. That I'll never get to the truth if her mental decline continues—I am halfway there myself, it feels like at times, with my headaches and smells and twitching limbs. I am as afraid for her sanity as I am afraid I'll lose my own before I ever get any of the answers I need.

When the sun comes up, I check the news on my phone, call the hospital for a report on my Jane (I call every day even though they are not allowed to give me any information, but they have taken to *No change* now instead of *Only relatives may inquire*). Just as I hang up, I get a call. It's Dr. Wagner.

"Your mother is well," he says and after a short pause he adds, "Relatively speaking. She agreed with me that it would be best if she stayed with us for a few more days. Her exact words were *Going for a walk is not a crime.*" Dr. Wagner goes on and on about how she doesn't think there's anything wrong with her, although he believes there's a personality disorder or two but "without proper counseling and an official diagnosis I'm unable to categorize her just yet."

He calls her actions *a behavioral pattern of impairment in personal and social situations.* I don't care about what he's saying—his medical gibberish is redundant; after thirty years I know my mother is teetering on the edge of crazy. She hasn't quite fallen in, yet she's staring into the abyss. That's what I know during this moment of clarity: the crickets, her secretive nature, the suspicion she feels toward just about everybody aren't normal. When we go shopping and the cashier asks for ID, she holds up her wallet, and when the cashier reaches for it, she gets irritated; *Don't touch it, I don't like germs. See with your eyes, not your hands.*

"Has anything stressful happened in your mother's life lately?" he asks. "Any specific event you can tell me about may be important and could help me gain a better insight into what triggered this."

I can't help wondering if the police showing up at her house is what did her in. I tell him about the woman in the woods, how I was in the hospital and the police came to the house and how she's an overall suspicious person. He listens intently, does not interrupt me. I drift into talking about myself, the strange odors coming out of nowhere, passing out or whatever those episodes are, the forgetfulness, at the same time remembering things I'm not sure about. I want to talk about everything, I even use the appropriate terms, *cognitive problems* and *dizziness*, just so he doesn't think I'm like her, because I'm nothing like my mother.

"All in all I'm still pretty shaken up about this woman in the woods," I concede. "Please forgive me if I'm not making much sense. I don't really understand what's going on with my mother. Is there anything you can prescribe for her? Someone she should see?"

"Your mother's diagnosis isn't just a matter of a blood test or therapy. It's hard to pinpoint any diagnosis at this point. I need to know more about her, but she seems tightlipped, which makes it difficult for me. There should be some extensive counseling and I have offered to set up an appointment with a colleague of mine, but"—I can hear him switching the phone to the other ear—"she just flat out declined."

I punch down the urge to ask him the question that is rising like mutant dough over the rim of a bowl: the possibility of heredity.

"I prescribed her anxiety medication that should mellow her out some for now. Your mother isn't bothered too much about anything but her purse. She is quite upset about it. She told me she lost it where the police picked her up. I assume she had her wallet and credit cards in there. She didn't elaborate, but if you could make an attempt to locate her purse that would make life a lot easier. Not just on her."

"I'll see what I can do."

"We are testing her for Alzheimer's but I don't think that is the case. We just want to make sure. She is scheduled for release in forty-eight hours. I really want to talk to you in person so I can get a better picture of what set her off. Do you think you can pick her up Wednesday afternoon? We can talk then?"

"Sure," I say. "Anything else I can do?"

"Keep all stress away from her when she comes home, make sure she takes her medication, and just basically do what you can to keep her even-keeled."

After I hang up the phone, I check under the sink for cleaning supplies. I rummage past the balled-up plastic bags and dirty sink towels, deformed and dried up. Empty spray bottles tumble out. There is Borax and some foam promising to do the work for you. Not a single sponge or glove. There is a jar. It seems to be an empty jelly or pickle jar, with the label pulled off partially but not quite; lots of white residue and glue sticks to the glass.

I lift it out of the dark below the sink and into the light, hold it up. It is a jar full of crickets, their antennas and legs tangled beyond recognition. There are about twenty of them, if not more. I shudder, wondering what that's all about. Do people freeze and eventually cook them? I don't know and I don't plan on dwelling on it.

Later, at the market, I'm greeted by the scent of rotisserie chicken and a smile from a seventy-something age-spotted man with orthopedic shoes and a heavy limp. He offers me a cart and I decline, making my way straight to the cleaning supply section and grabbing one bottle of multipurpose cleaner, a box of wet mopping cloths, and yellow latex gloves. The lines are long; children are fussing and leaning out of carts, reaching for candy planted enticingly nearby. I don't care to interact with anyone and use the self-checkout at the far end of the store.

The image of the crickets in the jar remains with me, even though I no longer ponder the logical reason as to its existence. I am realizing that most of my mother's peculiarities cannot be explained by a sane mind. As I make my way back to the entrance, I pass a bank, a customer service counter, and a Western Union. On the wall that separates the restrooms, I see a poster dotted with pictures of children of all ages, declaring that *Every Second Counts*. I step closer. Individual pages behind document protectors are thumbtacked to a large blue board. I do the math; altogether there are eighty-four pages. Every page has a picture of a child, a name, gender, age, height, weight, eye, and hair color. *This child was last seen on*, then a date, sometimes a description of the circumstances—*disappeared walking home from school* or *didn't return from a friend's house*—and some have an additional age-progressed picture. I scan the missing dates and realize they reach as far back as ten years. Just a few of the pictures have a red *Located* banner across them.

I wonder where they are. Have they willingly abandoned their families or are some held captive? I cannot conceive of the fact that so many people, children at that, just float around somewhere, on the fringes of society, forgotten, abandoned, and written off. Those who are no longer alive ended up . . . where? In basements, ditches, hidden graves? Washed up on shores, floating on ocean surfaces in plastic bags? Hidden somewhere in basements just to be recovered decades later, in shallow graves in backyards? Or buried in some woods, underneath branches, shed leaves, bark, acorn caps, and other vegetative debris in various stages of decomposition.

The images of missing children overlap and tilt my mind; suddenly I sense a zigzag pattern, like a contorted screen between my eyes and the physical world. I see flashing lights and my skin starts prickling. It begins in my fingertips and travels slowly up my arm and my shoulder blades, all the way up to my temples. As they start pulsating, I feel as if I am on my back in a field of prickly grass or some golden yellow crop that suddenly turns black right in front of my eyes. It grows all around me, tingling and pinching my skin. I want to scratch my entire body but my hands won't cooperate and then billions of spores fly off the black crop and I can no longer breathe. The world around me is shrouded in hot and aromatic pungency and trying to escape this odor is like trying not to smell food cooking on a stove. I desperately bury my face into the crook of my elbow to make it stop, to escape this almost resinous compound. The scent reminds me of a place I can't be sure of, for I don't recall the location itself, but I stand barefoot on rough wood, a porch maybe, peeling away squeaky corn husks and handfuls of silk.

By the time I get home, the feeling has dissipated. The Texas summer sky is a doodle of colors, hesitant brushstrokes at best. The sun is about to set and the entire picture will soon turn into a canopy of luminous stars; minute specks of light will shine within the blackness.

I have never hulled the husk of an ear of corn in my life. Not that I know of. Just like the snow blizzard, maybe this is all just my brain misfiring?

Eight

MEMPHIS

DAYS ago, when, through the peephole, Memphis laid eyes on the distorted bodies of two police officers standing in front of her door, the first crack had appeared. *This is it,* she had thought, *now it all comes to an end.*

That night, on a whim, when she had left the house and had tried to find the farm again—merely wanting to know if it was still standing, still out there at the end of a dirt road with its barn and shed—she had lost her purse. Just like that; it was in her hand one moment, gone the next. At first she hadn't noticed, but once she did, she didn't dwell on it. She was preoccupied with the scent of the night and the memories that rushed toward her.

Not a single car passed her as she made her way down the road. It was cool, at least in relation to the three-digit daytime temperatures, and her legs moved all on their own as if they were on a mission. Before she knew it, she was on the outskirts of Aurora, on FM 2410, and it seemed as if those three miles took her less than an hour to walk.

Thirty years had passed since she had left the farm, maybe more; she wasn't so sure anymore. The departure had been hasty and unorganized and she had left everything she owned behind. After their time on the road, she'd lived right here in town, yet she had never been back, never so much as looked at it from afar, not until the police had come to her door.

She had been unprepared for the police, hadn't even heard them approach. Too many cars passed by the house, too many doors slammed, too many children went to school or walked home, rapping twigs against fences, screaming and running and laughing. Over the years she had let her guard down, especially since Dahlia had left town. There had been over fifteen years or so without Dahlia, years she had lived alone, working menial jobs, and during those years she had become less vigilant.

She loved cleaning houses the most—the people were usually at work and money was left on some foyer table for her to collect—she enjoyed the solitude and she'd imagine those houses were her home and she'd walk in and for a split second she'd picture Dahlia as a child, running through the hallways, playing in backyards, so far removed from what reality had been.

The care of the elderly was also something she didn't mind, mostly Alzheimer's patients, still capable of living with their families, not so far gone that they needed 24/7 supervision. She'd play the radio as she cooked for them, did the laundry—sometimes she'd sit and read books she found somewhere on a nearby shelf, and then she'd imagine that one day she'd be one of them and Dahlia would care for her the way she cared for these strangers. She watched their old wrinkled faces, eyelids drooping over their eyes, staring off into space. At times she was jealous. Not having any worries, any consideration for people watching them, not fearing the doorbell, not dreading the ringing of the phone. Compared to what she had been through, their existence was bliss.

So yes, her guard had been down and when the police showed up, when she saw the uniforms, every muscle in her body went tight, preparing for her escape. Her brain shouted at her, *Run run run,* her mind a merry-go-round of fears, and with every turn another thought developed, one more disturbing than the last.

"Are you Memphis Waller?" the female officer had asked.

Memphis stood in silence. Frozen. Then she nodded.

"This is about your daughter."

Memphis still couldn't move, stood in the doorway to keep the officers from entering.

"Your daughter," the officer then said, "is at Metroplex. Don't worry, she is fine. She's just being looked over right now. If you want to, we'll give you a ride to the hospital?"

It wasn't easy to shut off the adrenaline and so she just stood there blocking the door; she couldn't move an inch.

"Are you all right? May we come in?" the second officer, also a woman, asked and leaned in slightly.

She would have asked them in if she had had any power over her body, but she was reduced to a pillar of salt. The officers all but pushed her aside and entered the house, looked around, nosy and prying, intruded into the dining room, even up the stairs, as if it was any of their business. After they'd left, she sat with her heart beating out of her chest. It wouldn't stop thrashing and at times her own reflection in a window prompted her to call out, *Who's there?*, and she'd stand still and so did the shadow, and then she'd move and so did the shadow, and she realized she couldn't trust her own eyes. She had looked out of the window and seen shapes moving across the yard; then a branch swiped against a window, making her jump.

She took to creating acoustic clues then, arranging dead crickets in a carpet of even rows and columns to alert her if someone came in, no longer trusting that the shadows mocking her were born of her imagination, so their dry and rigid bodies would crunch beneath someone's feet and there'd be no mistaking the actual weight of a real person, for shadows and ghosts are weightless and luminous.

When she couldn't stand it another minute, it got worse. There was another knock at the door—yet a glance out the window revealed nothing but a porch bathed in the harsh light of a bare bulb—and she ran out the back door then, leaving it wide open.

She had to lay the ghosts to rest, silence them somehow. She had to see the farm one more time. Yet again, it was the little things she didn't take into consideration. If Dahlia had thought her to be in bed, Memphis would have made it out to the farm and back home by the time the sun came up, before Dahlia woke. She could even have waited until after Dahlia was asleep and taken the car, but she didn't, just ran out, and that was another blunder in her thinking. The only reason she'd agreed to stay at the hospital was to calm herself, get her story straight. She could have fought the hospital stay—no one was able to keep her against her will, that wasn't even legal—but she needed time to think. Time to put her ducks in a row.

That night, after Memphis realized she had lost her purse, it took her some time to find the dirt road behind the trees and shrubs. Over the years, property lines had been redrawn, new roads had appeared, and if it hadn't been for the old wooden bench she would have never found the place. The fact that it was still there meant there was money in the bank to pay property taxes, even though she had never checked up on how much exactly was left, but Bertram county had only a couple of schools and taxes were low and the money must have been enough or the farm would have been sold by now, or even torn down.

That night, she didn't plan on setting foot onto the property at all; she just wanted to look at it from afar. It was still so vivid in her mind—the winding dirt road, the meadow, the shed, and the barn—and decades later reality matched her memory. The farm was still intact—the barn slightly warped, the meadow in full bloom—but as she stood peeking through the trees, crickets started chirping all around her, and one did jump at her, pecked at her leg, or maybe it was something else, she couldn't be sure. And she stood by the road, determined not to set foot on the property, as if history was going to catch up with her, as if merely walking the grounds was going to infect her with some contagion.

Her muscles were tired, her limbs heavy from the long walk. She licked at her cracked lips, feeling the thickness of her saliva. She looked past the shed, and there it was. The cypress. She couldn't make out anything underneath, but the old cypress stood there, firmly anchored; had gained a few more feet in height, even. She beheld the tree from afar but still she felt mocked by it, as if it said, *I've guarded the secrets, but they are still here. Don't you get any ideas. You haven't escaped.*

In a way, she had it coming, Memphis knew that. And she decided to stop fighting.

Nine

DAHLIA

I T'S almost as if there's a hole in the ground somewhere, swallowing lives, like the hole in the woods was supposed to swallow Jane. At home, I throw the bag of cleaning supplies on the couch and power up my laptop.

The numbers are staggering; thousands of people go missing every day, adults and children alike. Other crimes take priority and missing persons' cases are mostly solved by sheer accident or coincidence; there are tens of thousands of unidentified remains waiting in coroners' offices all over the country; more than a hundred thousand cases are open at one time.

The computer freezes. As I wait for it to recover, I imagine a map with tiny dots for every buried body, missing, undiscovered. And there's my Jane, found, safe, yet no one seems to know her. It seems impossible that no one but me seems to care who she is. But maybe nothing is as it seems, maybe the police have a clue, maybe found DNA even, but how would I even know? Bobby should know, or at least he should be able to find out. I dial his cell and he answers after two rings.

"I'm on patrol. Something happen?"

"No, nothing happened." I don't know how to ask the questions that bounce around all day long in my head.

"I'm in your neighborhood. I can come by."

Fifteen minutes later we are in the very house and on the very couch where we used to sit together as teenagers.

"I can't believe no one knows who she is. Someone must miss her. Is there anything you can tell me? The hospital won't talk to me."

"They expect her to wake up from the coma and tell them who she is. Who did this to her."

"How do they know she'll wake up and be okay?"

"They don't know. They've done tests but they won't know for sure until she wakes up. But we know she's not matching up to anyone reported missing."

"Why don't they make her picture public? Someone might recognize her."

"She's got a tube in her mouth, her face is swollen—I'm not sure that would do any good. I've seen people after car accidents, or fights, and they are so swollen not even their own family recognize them."

"You've seen her lately?"

Bobby pauses, ever so slightly, then takes a sharp breath in. "No, not really. Detectives are working on the case and I don't really know any more than you do."

"Are there others?"

"Other what?"

"Missing women. In Aurora." There is a hint of a shadow descending over his face. His cheeks become stiff, no longer a friend sitting here, catching up, but a door just closed, like the gates of a fortress. "What if there were other victims, in the past? How can you explain the way he buried her? What if he was right there, watching me? What if I interrupted something and he knows who I am?"

"Dahlia—"

"There must be others. What he did to her, that's not something that someone does once. There's someone out there, maybe, I don't know. Really, I don't. But it's not impossible. You can't say it's impossible."

"You're going overboard. I—"

"Bobby, what if there are more missing women? And no one does anything about it."

"You need to stop worrying. There's no reason to believe that he was watching you. How do you—"

"Are there others?"

"Dahlia—"

"Missing women. Cases like this. As a cop you should know if there've been any cases in the past ten years or so."

His expression goes blank. I know the face, have seen it before. We used to get into a lot of trouble, back in high school. We smoked behind the gym, broke some equipment in the chemistry lab, but Bobby—the most honest person I know—changes when he lies. His face turns indecipherable with no signs of life. *Your facial expressions give it away. Learn to have a poker face,* he used to say to me.

"She'll wake up. It's only a matter of time."

"So there are others?"

"Just allow it to play out for now. I think she'll wake up and then we'll know what happened. In the meantime, try not to worry. You saved her life. Isn't that enough?"

His radio goes off, the voice of a female dispatcher squawking, just a couple of words at most, clipped, short. Bobby gets up and walks off to the side, pushing radio buttons, talking into his shoulder mic. "Let's talk some other time," he says and ends our conversation.

After he leaves, I go back to skimming through the articles. When I run across something with additional information, I hit the print button—I can't stand reading on a computer screen—and finally I pull up the FBI site, which lists the missing by state.

I'm just about to compare online photos of missing girls with any resemblance to my Jane when I remember my mother and her lost purse. Lately, forgotten tasks enter my mind in completely unrelated moments, like an air-filled float popping to the surface of the ocean. The purse had completely slipped my mind, yet here it is, urging me to go find it. It's too late to go out and search for it now; it's about to get dark.

The composite woman pops back into my head, and the report on TV I watched that day in the hospital. I do a search for her and come across an article.

I see a red blinking light coming from the printer on the kitchen counter. I reload the tray and wait for the last few pages to print. I grab the stack and sit on the couch in the dining room and I start reading.

Last week, a jogger found a young woman on the brink of death in the woods of Aurora, Texas. The very discovery has stirred up a cold case of another alleged missing person that began with a man appearing at the Aurora police station over thirty years ago. The headline in the 1985 *Aurora Daily Herald* reads as follows:

MAN BOOKED FOR RESISTING ARREST AFTER REPORTING DISAPPEARANCE OF A WOMAN

Aurora, December 12, 1985
A man by the name of Delbert Humphrey appeared at the Aurora police station claiming his girlfriend, a woman known to him only as "Tee," had gone missing after he looked for the woman at the Creel Hollow Farm in Aurora. Two deputies questioned Humphrey extensively but even the police chief, Griffin Haynes, was unable to make sense of his story. Questioned further, Humphrey admitted he was not licensed to drive a vehicle and he was also unable to produce a photograph of the missing woman. He did, however, offer a pencil drawing of her. When the police doubted his story, he insisted on a sketch artist. A composite was rendered of the mystery woman.

The deputies asked permission to search his vehicle. During the search, they recovered what looked like drugs, commonly referred to as rock cocaine or crack. The rocklike substance, however, had a strong fragrant odor. Upon questioning, Humphrey referred to it as "High John the Conqueror Root" and "Balm of Gilead." Humphrey explained that the missing woman was part of a group of travelers working at local carnivals, reading palms and selling herb and plant resins, the very rocks deputies thought to be rock cocaine.

The deputies also recovered an old rudimentary brass scale and weights. Humphrey was booked for driving without a license, on suspicion of possession with intent to distribute an imitation controlled dangerous substance and possession of drug paraphernalia.

The young woman who was found by a local jogger in the woods, which locals refer to as the Whispering Woods, is on the mend, however. It's been over a week but police are confident that her identity will be revealed as soon as they are able to question her.

At the end of the article is a rudimentary pencil drawing of the woman who went missing in 1985. Her individual features are flat, barely dimensional. The composite, however, shows more depth and dimension. She seems to be a woman in her twenties, long hair parted in the middle, full lips.

When I emerge from the stack of papers, it's dark outside and the cold air coming in through the open sliding glass door makes me shiver. I sit on the floor and fan out the papers on the coffee table. There are Jane's articles, and the woman whose only likeness is a composite.

When I run out of room on the coffee table, I arrange the papers on the floor. I get lost in sorting them and realize no one cares about Jane as much as I do. They can't possibly know what I came to realize the day I snuck into her room; how I saw and felt that she wanted to communicate with me. And that she holds the key to her very own identity and she wanted to tell me. How else can I explain what happened at that moment, the whiff of cinnamon, my mind slipping, feeling as if I'm tumbling down a staircase, the tremor going through my body? How can I explain what I saw that night? The vision of the woods. It can't be nothing, I'm sure of that.

The printer behind me feeds more paper and I grab the last of that stack once the motor goes quiet. The mystery woman without a photograph was a rather big story—even papers of surrounding counties had picked it up. The articles revolved more around the man going to jail for the possession of an antique scale and some resin than the fact that he was there to report a missing person.

The papers on the floor get mixed up. Short of stapling them there's no way to keep them in order. I collect them into a stack, and with thumbtacks I pin them to the wall. I run out of room; I have covered the entire wall behind the couch with papers.

I tuck the composite underneath the mirror frame. The woman looks to be about twenty years old. Her eyelashes are long, her eyes slightly bulgy between prominent cheekbones. Her face is gaunt. Her picture floats to the ground but I am out of tacks and nothing would irritate me more than the wall not being complete. I stick it back under the mirror and this time it remains.

I step back and take in my wall. The pattern of the pages—aligned with perfect angles and grouped by person, sequenced by date and positioned in a star-shaped design in the center of the wall—seems to shift, appears to close in, yet the pages remain, as if all my senses are tuned in to this design I just created. A strong emotion overcomes me—I feel afraid of what's happening but all my senses kick in at the same time—I see the composite face, the wind outside plays with the leaves, a sprinkler hisses somewhere down the street, I smell the dank soil of my neighbor's lawn. *Fusion.* That's what it feels like. A fusion of all my senses. It must mean something. I just have to figure out what. There is a feeling of anticipation and my senses seem to battle with one another, not to dominate but to achieve equality. It is overwhelming, as if some *thing* makes itself known, telling me not to be afraid. The images of the two women jumble, like dice in a cup, just to emerge again, tumble out on a table that is my wall.

There is a hunch, a premonition of some sort.

A spark of the whitest light I have ever seen sears into my eyes like a camera flash. The ground shifts as if someone is picking me up. I am on my back, looking up at the ceiling fan blades as they *wop-wop* like helicopter blades. They slice the air, disturb the light, turn it into snow.

I'm in a blizzard yet again, the same blizzard I keep seeing over and over. I can't escape it—can't hide from it either.

Like a monster, it just won't go away.

ROSWELL, NEW MEXICO, 1988

Camelot Mobile Home Park. *I read the sign. I don't know what the word* Camelot *means. But I know what a mobile home park is. It's where I live now. Small paved walkways lead to similar houses just like ours. They are not really houses, I don't think they are— they shake and hum when it rains and strong winds come through the cracks in the wall. Mobile homes are what they're called.*

Outside my window I see a long driveway with occasional weeds peeking out from cracks in the concrete. Sometimes I can see Mom through the window as she walks from door to door. She collects the rent, she tells me. I watch children play through the window. They must be smarter than me, must be *because they get to go to school and I don't, and so I study more, study harder, force my mind to make connections, do my math even though I have to imagine things like balloons or pizzas to understand the concept of multiplication and subtraction. And one day, once I catch up with those children, then I'll get to go to school too.*

The coffee table is covered in books. Most of them have torn pages and crayon marks but I don't care. I love books. I read anything I can get my hands on.

I have many questions when Mom comes home for lunch: Do airplanes fall out of the sky and what's the meaning of "Lockerbie"? What are the rules of tennis? *Most of those questions I can't ask because she'd know that I changed the channel from the only one I'm allowed to watch. Mom only stays for a little while and when I tell her I have more to ask about she tells me she'll get me a book that will answer all my questions.*

"All of them?"

"Yes. *All the words in the world are in it," she says and hugs me. I hang on to her shirt, I don't want her to leave, and I need to know about that book.*

"*When?*" *I ask and don't really believe her. There's no such thing as an answer to all questions.*

"*Soon.*"

I want to cry. Soon *is like saying* never. *Like* soon *I'll be going to school.* Soon *we'll have friends over,* soon, *everything that never happens is* soon. *I cling to the thought of owning such a book, vow that the first words I'll look up are* Camelot, *then* Lockerbie, *then tennis game rules.*

I have a schedule. Reading Rainbow *after Mom leaves. I write down all the words I learn as I watch and then* The Jetsons *comes on. After* The Jetsons *I read until Mom comes to make lunch and checks my workbooks. I have so many questions:* Why can't I get on the bus with the other kids in Camelot? Why am I not allowed to play outside?

I did sneak out that one time. The girl's name who was playing outside I never asked as if I knew I wasn't going to see her again. We stole chalk from the bucket by the community board and we drew squares on the concrete, picked the biggest rock we could find—there were plenty in between the patchy grass and the crumbling road—and we played as the sun was beating down on us. When Mom pulled up in her car, I ran back to the trailer and locked the door behind me, pretending to be studying. As if I could trick her, make her believe that she had seen another girl looking just like me outside while I was inside practicing my upper- and lowercase letters. She was mad, but not that mad. But I can't do that again. Ever.

As I learn to read and draw, as I begin to prefer the news channel to The Berenstain Bears, *as my mind expands, the road leading to the trailers crumbles a bit more with each passing day. And then we leave.*

The stolen chalk, the stones, and the memory of the nameless girl are all I take with me from Camelot the night we pack up the powder blue car and drive farther west.

West, is what Mom says, We are going west, *as if it is going to be the end of all our troubles.*

Ten

QUINN

QUINN was awakened by the sound of slapping wings intensifying in the trees around her. Morning faded in like a scene on a stage accompanied by a screeching murder of crows. She gathered the colorful woven fringed rectangle of a blanket and tucked the wet, reddish stain into the innermost fold. She wasn't sure what to do with the blanket and even though Sigrid didn't care where she was and when she returned home, walking in through the back door with a sapphire blue-and-maroon-striped Mexican blanket might cause her to ask questions.

Quinn decided on the route through the woods instead of the dirt road, even though it would take longer, but there was no rush, Sigrid didn't rise before noon on any day of the week. In the soft morning light, the trees were no longer menacing with their long and dark shadows, and sun rays fell through the branches, warming her skin. She stopped in her tracks when a sound pierced the air like the whip on the back of an unruly horse. There was a voice, then two, maybe even three? They multiplied, projected toward her.

Quinn found herself standing in front of a man who fixed his eyes on her rumpled dress and tousled hair. His thick lips and his unkempt beard made her uneasy.

"Who we have here?" he asked and turned a bottle of beer upside down, his lips sucking every drop out of it.

Quinn clutched the blanket closer to her chest, suddenly remembering the way her body had left an imprint on the earth after she had gathered it up off the ground. If she had left one hour earlier or one hour later, they would have never met. Strange how life is. *I should have gone down the dirt road,* Quinn thought, shuddering as she became aware of more voices around her. She caught a glimpse of three other men in camouflage pants and shirts approaching them.

The woods suddenly seemed dark and musky, the canopy of live oaks shielding the sun from reaching the forest floor, merely lifeless sticks emerging from the ground. Quinn stood motionless. The man held up the empty beer bottle, inspected it, and then tossed it into the woods. The amber glass landed gently on a bed of pine needles and moss, hardly making a sound. Without a word, he unzipped his pants and released a powerful stream of urine merely inches from her feet. Quinn felt a warm droplet touch her left foot when he fanned the stream left to right.

As her fingers clawed themselves into the blanket, she thought of something to say. "What are you all up to?" She hated that her voice shook. She watched him unshoulder his shotgun and gently lower it to the ground. Quinn managed to get the words out with a smile but then realized the man hadn't zipped up his pants.

"Huntin' season," he said.

"What are you hunting this time of year?" Quinn asked, no longer able to force even a hint of a smile on her face. She was shaking. Her brain was only able to gather one characteristic per man: Beard, Bony Fingers, Pony Tail, and Pimples. Beard was staring at her when she faintly became aware of his hand moving rhythmically by his unzipped pants. She scanned Bony Fingers', Pony Tail's, and Pimple's eyes. Not one of them was going to stop Beard. There was no way they were going to stop, period. Not a single one of them.

Run.

Like a rabbit, Quinn turned on her heels and bolted down the path. She barely got ten feet away, didn't even have time to break into an all-out sprint, when she stumbled over roots and skeletal branches strewn about like bones. Her legs had springs and she recovered quickly. As if her mind had no mercy, everything was magnified, her surroundings in the light of day seemed like an alien landscape and the man pursuing her was a giant—but then her brain flooded and nothing mattered but the path in front of her.

Quinn quickened her pace but each of his steps was worth two of hers and just as she recognized the clearing to her right—beyond it the road, not too far—his hands grabbed her. One snatched her neck to the side, the other clamped tight around her right upper arm. Quinn felt panic rise up in her throat as the scent of beer and something foul like deer urine consumed the air around her. She yanked and wouldn't have minded if her arm had dislodged just so she could get away, but his hand didn't budge and so she went for him with her free arm, her nails searching for his face. His skin was slippery with sweat and she couldn't get a hold of him.

"Hey," he screamed, slapping her hand away, "stop that."

He crossed her arms in front of her and held her by her wrists, one of his hands big enough to latch on to both of hers, and with the other he slapped her, twice, left, right, then his fist, three, maybe four times. Quinn tasted blood, metallic, she could smell it even through his stink of animal and liquor and filth. She dropped to the ground but he pulled her back up, pushed her against a tree, the bark hard against her back.

Please, she wanted to say, *please let me go. Don't hurt me. Don't do this. Please. Please. Please. Please please please please please please please please please please please.* She searched his eyes, hoping for a hint of mercy, but they were amber like the eyes of a wolf. The only sound was the man's breathing and then he looked at her, his lips curled backward, exposing yellow-stained teeth.

The woods went quiet. Even the birds chirping their morning's sweet cantata became silent. And he waited for the others to catch up.

LATER, BY THE TIME QUINN REACHED HOME, THE WIND HAD DRIED her hair and her dress was merely damp where it hugged her body. She entered through the back door, into the kitchen, where the aroma of bacon and syrup hung heavy in the air. Her mouth felt swollen and dry and she doubted she'd ever be able to eat another morsel of food. She showered, changed, and went to bed, where she remained for three days. Sigrid never so much as checked on her; she barely looked at her as they passed each other in the hallway on the way to the bathroom.

"What's going on?" Sigrid asked on the fourth day, after dinner, during which Quinn merely rearranged her peas and flattened her mashed potatoes on top of a pork cutlet.

Quinn felt hot one moment, cold the next, her cheeks flushed and her skin clammy. "Nothing's wrong."

Sigrid took one look at her plate. "Are you going to eat that?"

"I'm not hungry," Quinn said and took a sip of water, hoping it would cool her swollen tongue. Her throat barely allowed the water to pass. She pushed the plate toward the center of the table.

"Your father didn't leave me a rich woman and wasting food is not something I condone."

"I understand." Quinn bit her lip. "Maybe I have the flu or something."

"In July?"

"It feels like the flu. I don't know."

"Eat."

"I can't. I don't—"

"Eat." This time sharper.

Quinn remained silent.

"Eat, child." Sigrid's voice was steady and low but carried the fury of a tornado.

"I can't eat. I feel sick."

Quinn didn't even recognize her own voice. She pulled the plate closer, picked up the fork and began eating. Her stomach lurched and gurgled, but she finished her plate. Later, after she threw up, she sank back into bed. When Sigrid came to check on her hours later, she was delirious and hallucinating. *Strawberry fields, you said,* Sigrid later told her. *I need to get to the strawberry fields.*

When Quinn awoke, she wouldn't have known where she was if it hadn't been for the constant stream of nurses and doctors. The diagnosis remained elusive to Quinn. *Pelvic infection,* the doctor said, *hydrosalpinx,* he told her. *The infection caused your fallopian tubes to be blocked and filled with fluid.*

Benito, Quinn thought. *I wonder if Benito knows what happened. What they did to me.*

"How long have I been here?" Quinn asked when her thoughts became clearer.

"Two days. You are on heavy antibiotics. We have to wait for the infection to completely clear up. You are young and healthy, but . . ." The doctor paused and lowered his eyes. "I'm sorry to tell you that your fertility will be affected."

Affected. Quinn wasn't sure what that meant, had never thought about anything remotely related to fertility, was detached from the whole diagnosis. Nevertheless she tried to make sense of it all, but not for one second did she consider telling the doctor what had happened.

After her fever ceased and the pain was dull and manageable, she tried to erase it all from her mind. She imagined that a fine paring knife cut out the part of her brain that held the memory of it, but regardless of how hard she tried, the images didn't disappear, and instead she felt a longing for the woods, the pure creek and its cold water running over her. She longed to immerse herself in it, even wondered how far down the bottom was.

After the doctor left the room, absolute clarity was bestowed upon her. She wondered if it was possible to live life as a ghost. She could not live one more second in this body as the person she used to be, and that's what she felt like anyway, a mere ghost of the girl Quinn. It was that or nothing at all.

Eleven

DAHLIA

WHEN this latest episode is over, I'm famished. I pop a TV dinner in the microwave. I've been living off microwaved and prepackaged food all my life. I haven't developed an aversion to it—its American ingenuity comforts me: the divided trays, the thin plastic covering, and the eventual sliding of the empty tray into the box. Even now I stick with the foods I ate in my childhood: meat loaf and mashed potatoes, chicken-fried steak and corn.

While I eat, I stare at the papers I thumbtacked to the wall the previous day: composite woman, *my* Jane. I refer to them as *my* missing people as if it is up to me to tape a red *Located* sign over their pictures.

After I eat, exhaustion takes over. I want nothing more than to close my eyes and stay on the couch for the rest of the day, but it's Wednesday and I have to pick up my mother at Dr. Wagner's office.

My hair is still wet from the shower when I pull into the parking lot of the clinic located next to the Metroplex compound famous for same-day lap band surgery.

Minutes later, a middle-aged woman in pink scrubs shows me into an office. I've barely had time to look around when Dr. Wagner enters the room. The first fragrance I notice is the minty scent of hand sanitizer as he furiously rubs his hands together. When he's satisfied, he extends his right hand toward me.

"Dahlia Waller. I've heard so much about you."

I manage a cheerful smile and shake his cold hand. He sits and inserts some sort of ID card in a slot of his laptop. With his posture straight and his coat as white as snow, he hits the keyboard, his every movement precise and purposeful.

"How's my mother doing?" I ask and the image of the finely arranged crickets pops into my head. I imagine her with her packed bag on her lap staring at mauve-colored plastic cups on the tray of her bedside table, her hair styled, her eyes staring straight ahead, impatiently looking toward the door.

"She's ready to go home."

"Good," I say and clear my throat.

"Did you ever find her purse?"

"Not yet, I don't know the exact location the police picked her up," I lie. My mother's purse had completely slipped my mind until last night. "I'll track it down after I drop her off at home."

Dr. Wagner takes a deep breath in. He seems annoyed by my inefficiency, and I feel the need for him to like me. I want him to know that I'm here for her, that I love my mother. Despite her craziness. Despite everything. And that I need her to be okay, but I also need her to answer my questions.

"She's upset about her purse, and I think if you keep her away from any anxiety-inducing thoughts, the better her mood will be. Anyway." A short pause and another key on the keyboard, then there's eye contact. "This is not how I usually go about this but . . . would you mind telling me about your mother?"

"Tell you what about her?" How can I possibly make him understand her ways? And most of all, do I even trust my recollections? Sometimes flickers of memories pop into my head so outrageous they might as well be out of books or a movie, or someone else's life altogether. I furrow my brow and I realize that words are just going to fail me. I don't know where to begin. "You'll have to be more specific."

"Well, whatever strikes you as significant?"

When I ask him how much time he has, he raises his hands as if to say, *Whatever it takes.*

I'm a mere curator, but he asked, so I'm going to try to answer. Telling him about my mother is a difficult undertaking. I try to think of an analogy, and the best I can come up with is catching a fish with my bare hands. Not impossible, yet it requires very specific skills.

"She's very private. Always has been." I say that as if it makes up for my inability to categorize her and tell him what he needs to hear . . . to what? Come up with an appropriate diagnosis? "Suspicious. A recluse, in a way. She has her routine, doesn't deviate much from it. Easily angered."

"How are her social interactions?"

"Nonexistent." She has no friends. No interactions with the world at large. A few men came and went, all for places to stay, jobs, never love. There is just me, no one else. The moment I grant myself this directness, the moment I accept that I'm somehow the key to her motivations, I'm accepting his invitation to revisit the past.

"What kind of a mother was she?"

"My childhood is nothing I dwell on," I say, and that's not a lie. If it wasn't for the walls I erected over the years beginning to crumble, if it wasn't for wanting to have my questions answered, I wouldn't revisit any of this. My past has been more or less a torrent of disconnected thoughts, but nevertheless, maybe it's about time to put everything in order and for someone to hear my stories. I need to make sure I don't make this about me—my Jane, my missing people—but like sap lazily making its way down the bark of a tree, I falter. "I'm . . . I'm . . . sorry," I stutter, "I've been going through a lot lately and I'm trying to think about this chronologically." If I don't, it gets mangled in my head and I'll repeat myself. I don't get the luxury of order often anymore, not since I found Jane, not just externally, but also internally, being organized, having things compartmentalized, and tidy.

Words pop into my head. *Razzle-dazzle. Flimflam. Double-dealing. Shell game.* Those are words from the book I used to have, but I don't want to get dramatic, carried away. To tell her story is in a way telling mine and I can only refer to her behavior through how I perceived it as a child. It's hard getting to her innermost core. She's a vault.

"First of all, I didn't know other kids didn't live like I did. I thought my world was nothing but a mirror of everybody else's life. So I didn't ask questions for a long time." Once I figured out that my life was anything but normal, I learned to deceive. *Don't volunteer our names, or where we lived before. My name is no one's business; neither is yours. Nothing we do is anybody's business, remember that.* I scoured my book, found words for what she asked me to do. *Strategy. Slyness. Cunning.* "In order to understand my mother," I say and look past him, scanning the wall, "you must understand that I have to talk about myself. I'm not a doctor, I have no insight into her that way, all I can tell you is what I've observed over the years.

"Chronologically speaking, my first memories are of wind and dirt. Just that, dirt and wind. Reddish dirt. I want to say we were homeless but that's not a memory in itself, just the dirt. The kind that kicks up under your feet as you run, leaving a cloud trailing behind you. And whirlwinds, dust devils, sand augers, whatever people call them. I guess it depends where you're from." *Whirlwind; a column of air moving rapidly around in a cylindrical or funnel shape.* The kind of whirlwind the Navajo refer to as *chiindii*: ghosts or spirits of dead people. If it spins clockwise, it is said to be a good spirit; if it spins counterclockwise, it is said to be a bad one. I don't remember who told me this or where I read it.

"I remember old ladies watching me in houses without other children, not a single toy, not as much as a swing in the backyard. I was about four, maybe five. All I had was a coloring book and crayons." I pause. I'm not used to not censoring myself. It's time for the truth. "Promotional crayons from chain restaurants they give to children to color in placemat menus while waiting to be served.

"I remember my mother arguing with a woman, and a yellow paper being passed back and forth, which I now believe was my shot record. I didn't know it then but I think she was some sort of school official.

If you ask my mother, she'll be elusive, so I can't be sure what that was all about. She said she homeschooled me, but she was never home."

Dr. Wagner scribbles on a sheet of paper and occasionally nods.

"We moved a lot. I know we lived in California for quite a while. I have memories of New Mexico and I know I was able to read by then, so I must have been about eight or nine. My mother brought books home, some from libraries. Others I got to keep, they were used, I could tell by the broken spines and ripped pages that they weren't from a store. I had this encyclopedia I carried everywhere. It was heavy, one of those A-through-Z editions." The mention of the book brings a smile to my face.

"She worked at a restaurant. I remember her bringing home food in take-out boxes. And I remember a gas station. We lived above a gas station for a long time. My mother worked the night shift there. By then the supply of crayons and coloring books had dried up. I had collected all my drawings and I remember making those scratch art pictures, you know, you cover the entire picture with black crayon and then you use an empty ballpoint pen or something sharp enough to scratch away the black, and the rainbow colors underneath come through. I never knew how the picture would turn out until I started scratching and revealed the colors."

He chuckles. Barely, but quietly he chuckles. Not in a funny way— I didn't tell any funny stories—but in a nostalgic kind of way. We all have those stories, they don't mean anything until we're older and we look at them in the present, evaluate them with a grown mind.

"So she changed jobs frequently. How about her relationships? Friends? Boyfriends?"

Men. Her *men*. I'm trying to line them up chronologically, but it's like attempting to merge a narrative without an apparent structure or plot. They get jumbled easily. I open my mouth to say something but then I think otherwise. I don't want to go back there. Having lived through it was atonement enough, no one should have to revisit this again. One drank, one made me uncomfortable just by looking at me. Suddenly I don't blame my mother for not wanting to go through therapy twice a week for however long. I can't stand to be here and it's been all of ten minutes. And it's not even about me.

"I really would like to just take my mother home. I have to be at work in a bit," I lie. "I'll be happy to bring her in for therapy if she's up for it."

He pinches his lips into a thin line. "I understand," he says and gets up and extends his hand. "I think it is very important for your mother to see somebody. Anything you can do to get her to agree would make a big difference."

"I'll try," I say and together we walk down a corridor to a nonde-script door. We enter the room and my mother sits by a window.

"Are you ready to go, Mrs. Waller?" Dr. Wagner's voice is too loud, a volume reserved for the deaf and the mentally disturbed.

Suddenly I become very protective of her and before he can say, "Your daughter is here to pick you up," I'm already by her side.

My mother sits in a faux leather chair the color of a robin's egg. Memphis Waller is no longer a Pollock painting, full of vibrancy and complex colors. She is a mere watercolor image, watered down so much she almost vanishes.

"What's going on with her?" I ask and my chin starts to quiver.

"Please don't be alarmed. She's just getting used to the meds. She'll perk up in a day or two. If not, we'll reduce the dosage. I wish there was an easier way but we have to wait until the meds reach a thera-peutic level. I'm so sorry."

I watch Dr. Wagner put his hand on her shoulder. He bends down and she looks up at him. "Your daughter is here. You're going home today." He keeps it short and to the point as if she's unable to com-prehend longer sentences.

I grab the already packed bag sitting on the bed, and a nurse with a wheelchair appears.

"I'll bring her down in the wheelchair. If you can just pull the car around?"

Later, in the car, I try to make small talk. *How was the food, are you happy to go home, do we have to go by a pharmacy,* that sort of thing. She's

THE GOOD DAUGHTER   89

short with me, nothing new there, *bad, sure, no*, her usual economic brevity. When we get to the house, she makes straight for her room. "I'm tired," she says as she walks past me. "What about . . ." She doesn't finish the sentence, looks around.

"I cleaned the house. I did the laundry." I'm afraid. Afraid that she'll ask about the crickets—*Please don't start with the crickets again,* I want to beg.

"My purse," she says as she stands in the doorway, her feet firmly planted on the threshold, as if she's afraid to step into her room. "Where's my purse?"

I panic, but just for a second. "Don't worry, just get some rest. I'll get it for you."

Her face goes soft; it's no longer rigid. She nods and takes a step forward, into the room. She pulls the door shut and the house goes quiet. I hear the mattress springs and then there's silence.

DECADES AGO, FM 2410 WAS A COUNTY ROAD CONNECTING A rural area to the town of Aurora. It still does just that, in a way, but the part it used to connect to isn't there any longer. There's hardly anything out there—an occasional warped trailer on a couple of acres of patchy grass, boarded-up houses with sagging porches, overturned Little Tikes toys, and empty doghouses in abandoned unfenced yards—and the farther I drive east, the fewer signs of habitation I find. The distance from the last traffic light on Aurora's main street to where, according to Bobby, my mother was picked up, is less than two miles to marker 78.

When I pull over at the marker, I stop on a bed of gravel and get out of the car. There's a lonely bench under a tree—maybe a remnant of an old bus route, but I can't be sure—and it's not one of those cast-iron benches with wooden slats as a seat, but a crude construction of gray and weathered wood nailed together a long time ago.

I scan the road and the surrounding area for a fleck of goldish brown leather amidst the greens and grays of grass and buckled concrete road.

A fragrance presents itself—I can't put my finger on it but some sort of shrub smells syrupy and oddly familiar—and I don't see anything remotely resembling her purse. There's still a lot of daylight left; it's barely late afternoon. The light is the kind of warm you only find at the end of a day, because afternoon light is that way, yellow and welcoming, just the opposite of morning blue light. It comes at you, building in strength because it had all day to get better, more vibrant, and it contains everything that's been building up for hours, like moisture and dust and atmosphere, so it's always warmer than the morning light and it's always just a little bit more golden.

I am captivated by the scenery around me, especially the old wooden bench, odd and warped, its placement as much as its sheer existence, and I can't imagine an old bus route leading through here.

I walk past the bench and there's a remnant of a path left leading through trees and bushes and shrubs, half overgrown, but still, it's a path. I follow it. It suddenly turns sharply to the right, as if it was meant to deceive, to take followers on a twisted journey, like a maze. I continue on, keep my eyes on the ground as not to stumble or twist my ankle, but then I look up and see a farmhouse.

I can see it clearly through the trees, and the overgrown trail leading toward it turns into a path and then an assertive dirt road, where shrubs become scarcer and none of the ground cover has dared to reach across the road. With each step I take, I feel the farm is the end of a journey I didn't know I was on. From a fair distance I behold the structure, consider it as if I were a photographer looking for the perfect shot. Farther to the right sits a dilapidated barn.

The farmhouse itself is a square two-story building with a porch. Time has taken its toll: the exterior has the worn color of unfinished wood, weathered by harsh elements and baked by decades of hot summer sun, cracked, warped, and twisted by the shrinking grain of the wood. It is an old relic at best, with a shingled roof and a sagging porch. I approach the house, the dirt beneath my feet solid, and I no longer worry about stumbling over roots. I reach the front steps and as my feet make contact with the porch, I freeze.

Unexpectedly there is movement. Not an animal scurrying by or a fleeting shadow even, but more a visible trembling of the space around me, as if the wind grants me a glimpse of itself mingling with its surroundings. Like a conduit, the farmhouse allows for the breeze not only to be heard, but *seen*; the way it rattles the screen door, the quivering of the worn shingles, brittle leaves caught in the nooks of the window.

I approach the window to the right, by the front door. I cup my hands and shield my eyes, the sinking sun behind me distorting the image inside: a kitchen sink, the faint outline of a table, chairs upturned. The lack of birds chirping makes it eerie and the top part of the window still has remnants of a curtain of indeterminable color. A pitcher sits on the ledge, cracked and old as if it could dissolve into dust at any moment. There's something in the other corner of the window sill, something that strikes me as familiar, yet I'm not sure what in my brain calls up its memory—and at first glance it is a container with dust and debris gathered at its bottom. Given the disrepair and state of the entire property, yes, that is the most likely guess—a glass that has collected dust and other debris.

I lean into the window and I focus on the content, really focus on it. My mind claws at the image—I have a strange sense of not being able to turn around and walk away, and so I panic. I force my body to step back, then forward again to peer through the window once more, like a child hoping the monster is gone. But it's still there.

I've seen a jar just like it before. Underneath my mother's sink. Filled to the brim with crickets.

Her nighttime excursion to this farm. Her lost purse. Nothing makes sense to me anymore. But it totals something. It's not nothing, *that* I know.

Before I can continue the thread in my mind, my body gets tingly and I walk backward until my back hits the railing. The tingling in my body turns into visual shapes, snowflakes, but stronger, impenetrable and dense and thick, making it hard for me to breathe. It looks like snow slowly descending from above, but then it turns into a blizzard. Thousands of little white ghosts fly around me and at the same time my skin turns icy and the ghosts find their way down my neck and underneath my clothes. My blood cools, I'm disoriented in a ghost blizzard, and the world around me is being erased.

I wait it out, that's what I do—wait for it to pass—and I step off the porch and make my way back to the car. I start the engine and take off. I almost drive right past a golden square by the side of the road, a few feet off the mile marker. I don't understand how I could have missed it earlier. I pull over, open the door, and grab the purse without even getting out of the car. It is dusty and there's a visible tire mark cutting across it.

I turn around. There is nothing but a line of trees, nothing else letting on that there is a farmhouse behind them, yet its presence is undeniable now that I have laid eyes on it. My heart beats faster than it should. The sun is about to go down, that's what makes this place scary, nothing else.

Does wind just arrive—isn't there usually a gradual buildup? There hardly was a breeze earlier, but there is one now. Things move and shake and tremble.

That's all this is, I tell myself. *The wind.*

Twelve

QUINN

QUINN sat by the window, staring. Cars driving up the long windy dirt road to the house created a cloud of superficial dust, shrouding the visitors in a cloak of lifeless powder. Not even the tires were capable of leaving an impression in the parched ground. The cracks reached deep into the barren soil, which had been baked hard by the sun. The flower bed behind the house hadn't been soaked by the rain in weeks and the soil had turned from brown into an ashen colorless shade unable to deflect light. Withered grasses emerged from the thirsting soil like burlap strings. The roses struggled to grow, for this environment was no more hospitable than a bed of river rocks.

Quinn barely managed to get out of bed and she hadn't been in town at all. She kept catching herself jerking out of some sort of tranced state and inspecting her nails. They had grown back then, no longer ripped, broken and bleeding from clawing at the mud to escape. Regardless how often and how harshly she scrubbed her body, she longed to immerse herself into the stream in the woods and wash off the memory of that day. She wondered if the stream had turned into a lazy creek when it had stopped raining weeks ago, and if that creek would soon turn into a mere trickle, moving listlessly over the boulders and stones it usually disregarded in its swift passage when it was bursting with the rain from up north. Even if she could go back, there was no sense wading into it; no amount of rocks in her pockets could drag her to the bottom of something that no longer existed. She envisioned her feet not reaching the ground, kicking into the vastness of the water, and every day she imagined drowning, for it was the only thing that mimicked what her body felt, the panic of her heart hammering against her ribs, and she knew she would welcome the oxygen deprivation and how it would erase all other thoughts.

When it became too hot on the porch, she'd move back to her room, lay on her bed, still longing for the feeling of her legs struggling to get her to the bottom of the stream. She wanted to sink to its lowest point, yet she knew she could step across its entire width by now and still have dry feet. She imagined the fragile plants on the banks of the river, lifeless and weak, vanishing as they turned into dust between her fingers. Like Benito. For he had all but disappeared.

There was talk in town; Quinn wasn't sure about the specifics, but there was talk. Of a Mexican boy and a white girl and a rape, but no one was sure if it was true. Quinn wasn't even sure who started the talk—for all she knew it was Sigrid wanting to get rid of Benito. No one knew who or when or where, it was just a random story of what happens to some girls. Benito's uncle came by for handiwork now and then but when Quinn asked about Benito, the uncle just shook his head, panic in his eyes. Quinn stared out of the window every day, sat on the porch, waiting for Benito to appear, take her in his arms. He never showed. By the time summer passed and fall showers trenched the soil, her head had cleared and all she could think about was getting away. High school was over with and the thought of going to college out of state appealed to her. But Sigrid had other plans.

"There's no money for college. Find a man to take care of you," Sigrid said one day, preparing dinner. "Find a husband."

"A husband?" Quinn asked and wrinkled her nose in disgust. "I'm nineteen."

"I know what you've been up to, so don't play me for a fool."

Quinn's throat closed up on her thinking about marriage. Her reflection in the windowpane was vague, like her sense of self, and she barely recognized the now thin and emaciated body that belonged to her.

"Sneaking out at night," Sigrid went on, "doing who knows what. I'm not stupid, you know. It was just a matter of time until something bad was going to happen." She was silent for a while. "Did that boy do that to you? The boy who worked on the rose beds?"

Something bad. Quinn knew what would happen to the men who had done this to her if she were able to identify them, but many hunters came to this part of the county during the early summer months, especially when the deer population got out of control. Every year open season started and the woods were overrun with local and out-of-state hunters looking to make a kill. She had never seen the men who raped her before and she knew just about everybody in town. At times, their faces merged into one grotesque face, combining their features, and she was no longer sure if she could pick them out of a lineup if she were asked to.

But it wasn't *that* simple. Nothing was ever simple anymore. Quinn pushed the thought of that day aside like a plate of pot roast she didn't ask for, was determined to keep the rape a secret, not out of misplaced shame, no, she had managed to cope with the shame—that part was straightforward enough—and all those weeks on the porch, staring into the distance, waiting for Benito's truck to show, she had come to accept the girl those hunters had turned her into. She just didn't want to deal with it, couldn't even imagine the police questioning her, having to describe what they had done, said, made her do. The horror of imagining the way people would look at her, what Benito would think of her, how this small town never let anyone live anything down. First they'd lower their eyes, then they'd turn and whisper. Forever she'd be *that* girl. *What did she do in those woods? What was she wearing? She should have stayed home.* Not one question as to why the men took those liberties, hurt her, raped her, beat her, humiliated her, as if her mere presence in the woods was justification for the crime they'd committed.

"Men take what they want, every woman knows that. And I know you've been messing around with that boy," Sigrid continued on.

"He had nothing to do with any of this. I haven't even seen him since," Quinn said.

"And you won't either."

"What does that mean?"

"He's gone, that's what that means."

"Gone?"

"If he tries to contact you, you have to tell me."

Quinn held back her tears. Sigrid would think she turned them on, was crying on cue, wanting sympathy, weeping crocodile tears. And faced with such judgment and callousness, she sat stoically, removed from herself.

"Change and wash your face. Put on a nice dress."

Quinn didn't think she'd have the strength to even get up and walk upstairs.

"And smile, for heaven's sake, will ya? Doesn't cost a thing."

"Where are we going?"

"Out," Sigrid said.

The corners of Quinn's lips fought for a split second, but then she managed a smile. She kept practicing that fake smile, knowing nobody would be able to tell a forgery from the genuine thing. Her cheeks hurt but Quinn knew that eventually it would all come natural to her.

In a dress, her hair in a ponytail, she accompanied Sigrid to a nearby estate sale at a white monstrous Greek revival of a house that belonged to the widow of a man who had made a fortune as a cattle farmer, then an even larger fortune in oil. There were lots of floral prints and an old dusty phone with a large dialing disk and curled cable dangling from the receiver on a console table. Above it, on the wall, there was a mirror framed with what looked like golden leaves from a willow; atop the frame, a cherubic face stared down at her. The mirror was tarnished and Quinn wasn't sure if it had been polished a few times too many or maybe that's just what happened with age, but her reflection looked nothing like her—she even thought she was looking at a painting of a woman, didn't recognize herself at all. The bony frame made her feel light and the hollowed face now showed her cheekbones, making her oddly beautiful. The console table itself was, though heavily ornate, nothing but a Chippendale look-alike with cabriole legs.

"Today is the preview but you can put in a sealed bid. It has to be at least half of the asking price. You'll get notified if the bid is accepted," a raspy voice greeted them, and Quinn turned around.

Sigrid visibly vibrated with anticipation. Their house was large and beautiful, yet nothing like this mansion with gazebos, a greenhouse, and a pond out back. There was a sunroom, a garden with topiaries, and something resembling a ballroom, even. She watched Sigrid lick the seal of the envelope for a bid on a piece of furniture. *Like a cat about to pounce on a mouse,* Quinn thought as they walked through the old dusty mansion. A man approached them, his right leg fluid but the left one moving jaggedly, as if he couldn't control it. He wasn't much over thirty and had a strong look about him with his dark hair and glasses, his clean-shaven face with a square jaw. If it wasn't for the cane and the limp, he'd have passed as attractive.

"Are you the executor?" Sigrid asked in her most classy voice, almost without an accent.

"It's my aunt's estate; I'm just settling it for her."

The conversation drifted off into the distance as Quinn turned the other way and ended up in a sitting room where floorboards creaked underneath. Quinn felt removed from the world, this house, the furnishings; even her feet felt as if they weren't touching the ground at all. Smiling at people was one thing but her insides were dead. She felt no need to do anything; just moved about waiting for the day to end, to go to bed, and then get back up. She was a ghost, waiting to go to the other side, wherever that was, to join the dead.

From across the hall she watched Sigrid and the young man in deep conversation. Sigrid was sparkly while the man smiled with ease and made fluid arm movements to accompany whatever story he was telling. He seemed out of place, as if he typically didn't wear a suit or usually didn't stand in mansions such as this one, looking to sell its contents. His flailing arms exaggerated his speech and finally he shook Sigrid's hand, then turned and shuffled toward her.

"Hello," he said. "My name is Nolan Creel. You mother just put in a bid on that console table over there."

Quinn smiled her fake smile, the one she'd been practicing. She squinted ever so slightly so it looked right, including the wrinkles around the eyes. She maintained the smile while he told her of his aunt's estate and his being the last Creel in the family. It was the first day of the sale, the very first hour, and there were only a few people to see the furniture and the mansion.

When Nolan held out his hand for Quinn to take, she complied, but instead of shaking it, he brought her hand to his lips and kissed it. Something stirred inside of her. Not a burning of love like she'd felt for Benito, nothing like that, but something stirred. She didn't know what the feeling was; it was a rather bizarre sensation once she allowed it to unfold, and it wasn't unpleasant at all. Nolan Creel adored her in some way, was enamored, even.

Nolan Creel and Quinn walked and talked and she listened to his raspy voice. He seemed kind and so were his eyes, and for a while she got lost in their conversation. At one point Quinn looked past him and met Sigrid's gaze from across the room, who in turn watched her like a hawk. Quinn's smile never left her face, lips perfectly curled over perfect teeth, and she was surprised how easy it was. She felt as if she'd stepped out of her body and constructed an imprint of herself, a second skin with a much more cheerful demeanor. At times reality drifted off completely and Quinn imagined this man to be her husband, children's feet running through these halls, filling the shells that were this house and her body with life. It was just a game she played in her mind, yet something took hold, an epiphany of sorts, of having no choice but to go on with life. It wasn't a matter of hope for the future, just the extension of the person she had created, seeing her through until the end.

"Where are you from again?" Quinn asked and took the arm he offered her, hooking her hand into the crook of his elbow.

"Aurora, Texas. A small town west from here. Creel Hollow Farm."

He told her of his estate in the country, and she wanted her life to have something more to offer her than those nightmares, and waiting on porches for lovers who don't show, and living in her childhood home where she was merely tolerated. It didn't sound glamorous at all, Creel Hollow Farm, but it seemed peaceful and safe. Nolan told her of his late father, who had been an artist, painting hundreds of paintings of the farm and the surrounding estate. Quinn listened and smiled when it was appropriate, especially when he mentioned that he wasn't married.

"Will you be delivering the table to our house if we win the bid?" Quinn asked.

"I wouldn't mind a bit," Nolan Creel said, and he struggled to keep himself steady as Quinn strode ahead of him over the creaking floorboards. Quinn slowed her steps, making him believe he could keep up with her.

QUINN CREEL. SHE REPEATED THE NAME OVER AND OVER AS she, suitcase in hand, stepped on the front porch of Creel Hollow Farm. Quinn Creel sounded like the name of a boat, one of those paint-chipped tourist skiffs tied in choppy rows at the Corpus Christi Harbor, where they'd just spent a week on their honeymoon. It was October 1970. Quinn was nineteen, Nolan thirty-one. The farm was run-down and she wanted to cry.

"You'll love it," he had said on the drive up. "There's a meadow by the side of the house, full of buttercups," Nolan had told her on the five-hour drive from Corpus Christi to Aurora. "Buttercups," he had recited as if he was being quizzed in some silly botany class in school, "*Ranunculus* in Latin, meaning *little frog*. The name *buttercup* comes from the belief that the plants give butter its yellow hue when the cows eat it." Nolan paused as if some revelation was to follow. "Not true. In fact, they are poisonous to cows and livestock in general. Did you know that?"

Quinn neither cared nor planned on retaining any of this useless information, but she smiled and looked at him adoringly as he kept going on and on, until they had reached the farm. She was appalled by the state of things; had imagined a stately property; not *this*.

"Some people call them *coyote's eyes*," Nolan said, then preceded to tell her about some legend in which a coyote tossed his eyes up in the air and an eagle snatched them up, leaving the coyote without eyes, and so he made himself new ones from the buttercups he found. "Buttercups are poisonous when they're fresh, but their taste is quite unpleasant anyway so they are usually left uneaten. Cattle only eat them when they are abundant and there's not much else growing, so it's pure desperation when they do and—"

"Nolan."

"What?"

"I didn't imagine it like this." Quinn heard her shaky voice, was taken aback by it.

Nolan paused for a long while. "Cold feet, babe?" He then laughed and kissed her hand with the shiny gold band. "A bit late for that, isn't it?"

Cold feet, Quinn thought and glanced around the farm, the weathered barn, and the grooves in the ground from the flash floods. *How muddy it must be after it rains,* she thought, and she felt as if she was floating. There was nothing to keep level around here, no familiar thing, no comfort—even the soil below and the sun in the sky above were unfamiliar. So were Nolan and this marriage she had entered into.

"It's, it's . . . ." Quinn didn't find the words to express her disappointment.

"I love you. And you love me. It's not really that complicated. We'll have children, raise them; they'll grow up the way my father grew up here, the way I did. This farm is solid and it keeps people grounded.

We can do some fixing up and make it look just like the way you want it." He paused, then said, "I can't imagine it any other way."

Quinn thought she was going to snap, just break apart. The pain in her lower back was unbearable and suddenly everything seemed like a really bad idea, something she had agreed to in a moment that had passed. Yet here she was, on the steps of Creel Hollow Farm, and she sat her suitcase on the front porch and stared at a wooden door. The knocker was rather large, shaped like a lion above the letter C, and the name Creel started to grow on her. Quinn Creel didn't sound so bad and some paint might do wonders, and there was a farm and a door knocker with an initial involved.

Nolan came from behind and scooped her into his arms. His cane leaned against the door frame. When Nolan moved slowly, his limp was barely noticeable. Quinn thought of it as him moving with care more than a disability, and it seemed as if he didn't dwell on his limp at all. He was a strong man and he'd keep her safe, she was sure.

"Mrs. Nolan Creel, how do you like your new home?" Nolan said and took Quinn's hand in his, leading her through the door.

"I like it," Quinn lied, and it struck her as odd that there weren't any farmhands rustling about or cows in the meadow. There was no smell—isn't there supposed to be a smell on farms?—and the barn sat silently by the side of the house.

Quinn entered the farmhouse, hitting the light switch by the front door. She tried to ignore the wallpaper with the vertical stripes that was competing with the occasional dots of mold and, once she looked closer, she saw how the wallpaper peeled at the seams and the house smelled slightly of mildew. Nolan made for the stairway as if he was about to take two steps at a time, not holding on to the railing, like a boy looking to claim his room upstairs, but then he thought otherwise and calmly ascended the stairs. Quinn crossed the foyer, the hardwood planks underneath her feet producing unnerving sounds: a creaking from her heel pressure, a clacking and groaning as she rolled her feet toward the tips, as if the wooden strips meant to get her attention, wanting to tell her some old story. She quickly entered the kitchen—the floor was tiled, and though it was chipped, it made no sound—and opened the grimy curtains with a swift flick of the wrist, exposing blind and warped windowpanes coated with a layer of dust. She pulled open the oven door and was startled by the screech it made. Oddly enough, the interior was immaculate. She walked around the kitchen and touched every surface, opened every drawer, and even gave the tap a try. Nolan appeared behind her, making her jump.

"There's a well behind the house," he said and dipped his finger into the water stream. "We'll never run out of water."

"I see," Quinn said, staring at the deep sink stained with rust. The house seemed strong and worthwhile but it was neglected in many ways, as if Nolan hadn't bothered to maintain but its very basic functions, like the roof and walls, water and electricity. It was a house, but it wasn't a home. She turned off the tap, wrapping her arms around herself. The house seemed to make her shiver, and the air had a chill to it even though it was barely fall. The window above the sink had six panes on the bottom and six on top. The panes seemed organized and structured and Quinn noticed that the frame had been painted multiple times and the paint was caked on, running in spots like tears, and so she made no attempt to open the window and let the warm air in. The view was beautiful, that she had to admit—the barn was to the left, a big tree to the right, and the winding dirt road snaked toward the main road straight ahead. A lacy curtain drooped off a crooked rod and when she pulled it to the side, she flinched. She wanted to cry—she was nineteen and not capable of doing any of the things that needed to be done on a farm and then there was the pain. Excruciating pain. In her stomach, and stretching and twisting and turning always made it worse.

"It's all ours. Just needs a bit of work," Nolan said and hugged Quinn from behind.

"Looks like it," Quinn replied, pressing her stomach against the sink. Pressure seemed to take away the pain at times, but now all she wanted was to go to sleep. The farm made her shift in place, as if it was difficult to find the right spot, the right room to be in, as if she didn't belong here at all. Like a fish out of water, she felt as if she were suffocating, not getting enough oxygen to sustain her. "What's in the other rooms upstairs?" she asked and unwrapped herself from Nolan's embrace.

"There's one bed in the second bedroom." Nolan stood in silence for a while. Then he said, "But we'll have to buy a crib."

Quinn smiled but didn't say anything and later, after they stocked up the fridge with the groceries they'd picked up at a store in town, they sat and ate supper, fried eggs and potatoes, and Nolan laughed and giggled, holding her hand across the narrow table. Tired from the long ride, they went upstairs to bed while it was still daylight. Quinn watched Nolan's chest rise and fall, then he moaned in his sleep. She pressed her body against his until there was no more space between them. Such closeness usually made her feel uncomfortable but Nolan was asleep and she felt safe even though she couldn't explain those emotions.

Quinn woke early and couldn't go back to sleep, the pain in her stomach getting worse. It was sometime between night and day, a liminal moment, and she felt her heart beating rapidly inside her chest. She got up and stood by the window, looking at the winding driveway, and the small shed to the right. She opened the window, gently as not to wake Nolan, and a flapping shutter in the distance made her heart skip a beat. She watched the night dwindle, the first sun rays of the day were about to appear and in the meadow to the right of the house the colors were melting from an ominous array of grays into pale yellows and smoky browns. There was no sign of buttercups, not a single yellow dot, and the grass seemed dead, as if nothing was going to grow there ever again. It seemed early in the year for a meadow to be dormant but Quinn didn't dwell on it. She smiled and resolved that soon she'd get to know everything about this place. Quinn Creel of Creel Hollow Farm. It was *something*—not perfect, but something. What else was there for her?

"Hey," she heard Nolan's voice, even more raspy after he woke in the mornings. "You okay?"

"I'm fine," Quinn said and she saw his eyes pause on her hand resting on her aching stomach. "I feel pregnant," she heard herself say. It was as if another woman had spoken those words. Quinn didn't understand what made her say that, a comment so unnecessary and uncalled for. No one had pushed her, no one had made her say it, yet she had spoken words that were so far from the truth. She'd just given Nolan, her husband of less than thirty days, the impression she might be with child. Was it because when they were together, all she did was imagine Nolan's sperm burrowing itself into her egg? She had imagined the egg dividing into cells, moving into her uterus, attaching itself—*implantation*, it was called. Such a crude word for a miracle. She'd left out the part of the fertilized egg traveling down the fallopian tubes because they were blocked and the doctor had told her in so many words that she may never have a baby of her own. *Difficulties, conception problems*—that's what they had told her. As if she could forget. She knew what the doctors had said, they had spoken of *scar tissue*, and she imagined those scars like welts on skin, and why not, why would her body not display what she felt on the inside—scarred she was—but just like she had reinvented herself, she also wanted to conjure a healthy body. *I feel pregnant*, she had said. She had gotten carried away, a small mistake on her part, nothing more.

Quinn felt bloated, full; something inside her was gnawing at her, had been gnawing for days. She felt it growing inside of her, the feeling at times so uncomfortable that she'd propped up a pillow and rested her stomach on it with her body facedown, pressed hard against it, and she'd allow the weight of her body to push against this feeling of fullness. She didn't know how she was supposed to feel, didn't know what to do, maybe she ought to call Sigrid and ask her. She knew she wasn't pregnant, just knew, couldn't explain it, but she knew with certainty. She felt as if a cannonball was lodged inside of her, and that was the best she could describe it.

Nolan rose and hugged her. He held her for a long time and then he let go of her and she heard the toilet flush shortly thereafter. Quinn was unable to move, she felt paralyzed, her legs no longer under her control. Her mind began to spark erratically. A voice in her head spoke. *Why?* it said. *Why did you just say that?* And she stood by the window and watched a golden-bronze hare emerge from the knee-high grass. First it moved slowly, and then it lolloped in an ungainly way. Suddenly the wind picked up and somewhere a shutter slammed and the hare went up on her hind legs, black eyes staring seemingly in every direction.

After breakfast Quinn stepped on the porch and watched Nolan retrieve the rest of their suitcases from the trunk of the car. His movements were unwavering despite his limp and Quinn wondered if anything could ever throw him off. She had noticed how his gray eyes never traveled down her body, but were always focused on her eyes, as if he saw something in them only he could fathom. Maybe his adoring nature led him to be captivated by her, always in thought, always observing her, but it was hard to read him in return. Nolan then made a gesture of recognition, raised his right hand, pointing behind her, past the house.

"We just missed them," he called out.

"Who?" Quinn asked.

"The buttercups. They were in full bloom a few weeks back. I guess we have to wait until next spring. Do you want to go for a walk in the woods?"

His words made her jerk. Lately, after all those moments, after she thought she had conquered the past, that day in the woods had become more and more consuming. It wasn't as if she didn't know she had no fault in this, *she was not to blame*, no one is to blame for being raped, but it was her *lot* of having to live in this body, day in and day out, knowing what had been done to it. That's why no baby was going to grow inside of her—her body wasn't worth it. Having a husband who knew nothing of what had been done to the body he held every night, the violation of it all, the knowledge she could never escape, for this was the only body she had been given and she'd have to take it to her grave one day, was unbearable at times.

And every day she encountered new moments that made her think just how tainted she really was. The way the man at the Corpus Christi gas station had pointed at the dead dog in the bed of his pickup truck, a head wound seeping crimson, and how his calloused hands had wiped tears off his cheeks, not the least embarrassed about his feelings. He'd told Nolan right there among the gas fumes that the dog had killed one of the chickens it was supposed to protect and he wasn't good anymore. He had to shoot it, *no ifs, ands, or buts about it*, a dog that had tasted blood wasn't good for anything anymore, but he'd loved that dog. *He was a good dog, best one I ever had*, but he couldn't stand for the fact that the dog had killed, *He clamped his teeth shut and shook that chicken, swinging it*, and *that* you can never erase from a mind. All the love in the world couldn't make up for one's actions.

There was the roadside diner in Conroe, and the two siblings, a boy and a girl, who argued over an ice-cream cone, and the boy declared, *Now that you licked it, I don't want it anymore*, and nothing the mother told him could change the boy's mind. And then the cone ended up on the linoleum floor of the diner and the mother apologized to the waitress, who scooped it up with a napkin. You love it, but it's tainted.

Her memories seemed to unwrap in layers lately. There were noises she couldn't place and she wondered if her ears would be able to distinguish the sounds with time or if her mind would continue to stack bricks of paranoia that seemed to mount in her head with every passing day. Every snap of a twig was a predator, every slamming door the dropping of a gun on the forest floor, a never-ending message to her body to brace herself for what was to come. But there was more. How she smelled semen and sweat and deer urine, a scent as strong as it was on that July morning. Most of it she swiped away like a bothersome swarm of gnats circling her, but *certain* moments remained like a sticky residue that just wouldn't come clean. How Pimples made her admire him, how Bony Fingers made her say she liked what he was doing to her, how Beard made her beg for him to penetrate her, over and over. *Beg.* She had to repeat the exact words and when she got them wrong, even just one word, he'd slap her. Hurt her. The thought of it all made her gag, her insides attempting to purge the words he had made her say.

Each one of those insights was a thing in itself, another finger digging into her wounds. If her attempt to not dwell on the past also meant that she didn't look to the future, what did it matter that she told him she might be pregnant, what did it matter if she handed out a little hope for Nolan and for herself?

"Maybe we should think about buying a crib," Quinn said then, smiling her most brilliant smile. And when Nolan took her hand and embraced her, she felt almost normal. Almost, but not quite.

Thirteen

DAHLIA

I slide my mother's purse over the kitchen counter. Her eyelids droop, seem to be made of lead. She nods, faintly, but it's a nod.

"Thank you," she says, and even those two little words are dangerously close to being slurred.

"How many of those pills have you been taking?"

She mumbles something like *Nonyopism*.

"How many?" I repeat and steady her as she gets up and sways.

"None of your business."

With her purse in hand, she makes her way toward the stairs, holding on to the kitchen counter before she stiffly grabs the handrail. She passes my wall of the missing, yet she neither beholds it nor says anything about it. Instead, she climbs the stairs as if her legs are cast in concrete.

She looks like an actress from the Golden Age, I think, and a definition pops into my head. I remember the cumbersome encyclopedia edition, can almost feel its weight on my lap, its dank scent, the onionskin pages, the gilded edges of those pages between my fingertips. Something in my head flaps its wings, opens its beak, and I hear a faint melody. And just like a cuckoo bird emerging from its enclosure, a definition reveals itself.

Tightrope walking; the art of walking along a thin wire or rope at a great height. A tightrope artist usually performs in front of an audience.

I watch her reach the upstairs landing. She's swaying slightly, losing her balance, figuratively and literally, yet she manages to hold on. She drags herself the length of the hallway with her head up, arms out and flexible, keeping her weight on the balls of her feet, her hand gliding along the railing. Her legs are slightly bent. That's my mother. Performing.

Later, in my room, after tossing and turning for most of the night, I get up and go downstairs. On the laptop I do a search for *Aurora, woods, found, Jane Doe, unidentified.* By now, several forums are speculating about my Jane. There is someone by the screen name of *MommyDearest* laying out the case for human trafficking in the Rio Grande Valley. I-35, according to her, is a major artery, yes, she's using the word *artery,* in the trafficking trade. *IamFiftyOne* begs to differ; aliens are involved. The pyramids are proof. *PsychStudent* is convinced that Jane is mentally ill and will remain unidentified, withering away in some psych ward. *NoLongerAVictim* is convinced Jane has escaped decades of a life in a closet eating paint chips, "nothing but paint chips her entire life," which have poisoned her brain, making her incapable of remembering her name.

I no longer know what to make of any of this; the farm, my mother, Jane Doe, Composite Woman. I worry I will never make sense of anything.

I wait until the sun comes up and I call Bobby. "Meet me," I say.

"Where?" he asks.

"Gas station, at ten," I say.

Later, for the first time since I returned to Aurora, I see him without his uniform. He wears jeans and boots and drives a pickup truck. He pulls into the parking lot of the gas station where we had waved at each other weeks ago, his hair still wet as if he's just climbed out of the shower. We embrace and there's a moment of awkwardness when we let go of each other and we stand close.

There it is, the way he cocks his head ever so slightly—I can tell he sees me in a romantic way. There wasn't a person in high school who believed we were just friends, but we were, always have been. *Friend zone* is the expression people use now—back then we didn't have words for it. And maybe we both didn't have an explanation either; we just never went there. There was some invisible wall around the both of us that was going to deliver the equivalent of a lightning strike if we had come any closer.

The hug was a simple gesture—an old friend wrapping his arms around me—but I felt *something*. Is it affection? Something small, maybe the fragile remains of what we used to be? The truth is that our bodies being so close to each other soothes me more than I'd have expected.

We remain casual for a few minutes—*how are you, how's life, this town has hardly changed, how long has it been*—that sort of thing. Then we get more personal. He had married—his eyes stoic as he tells the story—and divorced three years later. She was a Realtor wanting to move to Dallas, while Bobby never thought about leaving Aurora. "The marriage was a big mistake," he adds. He's done talking about her and I don't even ask her name.

I tell him about Amarillo, all the jobs I had, not being able to get ahead, and about my mother's secretive behavior, her reluctance to talk about the past. I used to be covert when we were kids, kept the secrets my mother told me to keep. I wish I hadn't. To explain to him now what those years were like for me is difficult. When I tell him how it felt being without power, without choices all these years, I see the boy I remember; the raised eyebrow as he's listening, the kind eyes. A suspended moment of childhood and the long-overdue truth all at once. We let our eyes roam as we sit in the bed of his truck, and we remain silent for a long time. It's not an awkward moment of silence at all. I can smell the pines, see the boughs sway in the wind, and know their rough dark bark and the stickiness of the dripped resin where woodpeckers have jabbed away at the trees. I hear, even from this parking lot across the street, squirrels running up and down the tree trunks, and I know how it feels to stumble over their snapped branches on the ground.

"So what's the plan? You staying in town?"

"For now. My mother isn't doing well and I might have to if I want to or not. I'm looking for a job."

"Anything going on with her? What did the doctor say?"

"Old age, you know how that goes."

Sitting here with him feels as if I have never left, as if I walked over a threshold and whatever prior life I lived has somehow taken on the form of a dream. This town has this power over me, had it when I arrived when I was twelve, as if it somehow makes me forget what came before once I pass the *Welcome to Aurora* sign.

There are new buildings, and roads that have been redone, trees that were mere saplings a decade ago are now mature—the town has changed visually, but I can still see the past, feel it. I am somehow tuned in to this town, know every square inch of it, know its secrets as well as what it allows all of us to see. This is my hometown and it has remained with me while I was gone, but being here with Bobby, it's like the air carries me still, and the wind is saturated with the voices of people I used to know.

I take a deep breath and catch a whiff of something pungent. *Not now,* I think and I panic for a second, expecting another episode, but then I see the cedar trees across the street, mixed in with the pines. From them comes this pungent and spicy scent, sharp and intense, not as sweet as the pine trees, more of an intrusion.

I have a million questions but this one is as good as any.

"Do you remember the day we met?" I ask.

"Of course. You came into town in that old beat-up car all the way from the West Coast and your headlight was out and my dad stopped you. I was in the back of the cruiser because it was just another one of those days, you know . . . my mother wasn't feeling well, and I went to work with him a lot during that time."

"What else do you remember?"

"You had wild hair and a huge heavy encyclopedia you carried everywhere and I thought you were the most beautiful girl I had ever seen."

I was not yet a teenager, barely becoming one. We arrived after a long drive from California, stopping on the way, sometimes for days at a time. Was it a trip, a move?—I don't remember. I had given up asking *Where are we going, what's next?* A kite comes to mind—not like a paper kite batted around by random whips of wind, no, but an untethered kite, floating out there, flying off into the darkness, held by some invisible hand. I didn't know where we were going to end up, every single time. Were we going to stay in the car for a few days, a small room above a gas station, a motel, a trailer, an apartment with stained carpets and dirty walls? It never got better, that I knew. Until we arrived in Aurora.

I'm glad Bobby remembers that weighty encyclopedia, and I recall many of the definitions from that old dusty book. Heavy and cumbersome as it was, it was my salvation. Whenever I couldn't make sense of the world, I looked up words and things came into focus. And as the years went by, memories were born out of the words that I longed to understand.

Aurora—it pops into my mind—*a natural electrical phenomenon characterized by reddish or greenish streamers of light in the sky.* Or *dawn.*

"*Aurora*," I say and put my hand on top of his, "means *dawn* in Latin."

"Not sure if it's fitting for this town but I believe it if you say so," Bobby says and steps off into a patch of green, aimlessly ripping some of the dirty yellow grasses. Then he tosses them aside carelessly. From the shadow on his face a form develops.

I know Bobby by the way I feel around him, and when his features get dark and gloomy, I want to ask him what is on his mind. About his mother and cancer. About the way it was after she died. I never did. It always seemed as if I'd hurt him more by asking him to say things out loud, and underneath his composure Bobby is paper-thin. *A bleeding heart really gets you nowhere,* he used to say.

"Did you ever think that, back then, your dad and my mother had . . . you know . . . a thing?" I say it casually, as if I'm not really implying anything. There's a long silence.

"I don't think so. Not back then, no. He loved my mother and was heartbroken when she passed away. But . . ." He then looks at me with his eyebrows raised, straight into my eyes. "I think they knew each other. I can't tell you how I know, it's nothing that I ever overheard or was told, nothing like that. Just a hunch. Some things you just know."

I have never considered that possibility. We had lived in California for a long time and when we came back to Aurora, my mother knew no one. Not that she knows anyone now, she's not the kind who makes a lot of friends, but she knew Sheriff de la Vega and I never believed the story about the broken headlight, even though she still insists on it being true, to this day.

"You believe they knew each other back then, like when?" I finally ask. "Must have been before we met or even before we were born. I was young, but I remember states and names. We'd never been to Aurora before."

"I don't know, Dahlia, but I know there was talk in my family, about my father leaving Texas as a teenager, going to Mexico. Nothing more was mentioned, and I never asked. Sometimes an aunt would slip and hint at something. Maybe something that happened a long time ago, before he became sheriff. He was from Nacogdoches, by the Louisiana border, but lived in Beaumont for a while." He pauses and thinks, sipping beer. "Where's your mother from?"

"She never told me a specific town, just East Texas. She'd always say she's from nowhere in particular and traveled all her life." *Remember, it's no one's business where we come from and where we're going.*

"So why did she come here if it's all the same to her? I can imagine better places, all things being equal. Just picking a city from a map."

"Maybe it was random. Beaumont, you said? Your father?"

"He lived in Beaumont, then he went to Mexico. I don't know exactly when or why. He didn't come back until years later, and then he married my mother not long after."

"Can you ask him about my mother?"

Bobby's face freezes. "Oh, hell, Dahlia, that ship's sailed a long time ago. Señor Ramón de la Vega can't remember much about any-thing."

"Go for a drive with me," I say and slide off the truck bed.

"Like where?" Bobby's always up for anything, like a dog who gets up when you get up, stirs when you stir, loyal by my side.

"There's something I want you to see. Down 2410. I'll tell you where to turn."

We drive with the windows rolled down and when we reach 2410, the sun has climbed to its highest point in the sky, egg yolk–like and round, unwavering. But for a few wispy clouds drifting by, the sky is a perfect azure.

When I tell Bobby to pull over by the bench and I point to the overgrown driveway, he looks at me, puzzled.

"Where?" he asks. "There's no road."

"There's a dirt road, trust me. I've been here. Just park by that line of trees."

He slows to a crawl and the branches swipe the truck's windows, whip at them, but then they clear and eventually barely hit the cabin.

To my right, there's movement. It's not as if a deer ran by or a person hid in the thicket; it's more like a shimmer of mist, diffused and ethereal. The trees and the surroundings take on the inaccuracy of a poorly rendered photograph, but as the shimmer dissipates, I'm no longer sure of what I've seen. Or if I've even seen anything. It's hot and I'm overtired. The sun rises. The sun sets. Nothing is ever as complicated as we make it out to be.

Bobby parks by the bench. We get out and I walk ahead. Bobby follows closely behind me, but when he sees the farmhouse, he stops.

"Is this private property?" he asks.

For a second I see the boy he used to be, adventurous, carefree, now a man who can't even enter an abandoned property without thinking misdemeanor trespassing, but maybe I'm judging him too harshly.

"Abandoned," I say and hope he won't ask any further questions. I'm not ready to lay it all out on the table just yet.

"I didn't even know this place was out here and I know just about every inch of Bertram County." He pauses, then gives me the benefit of the doubt. "How'd you find out about it?"

Back-then-Bobby would never dig that deep.

"It's where I found my mother's purse, out in the road, by the bench," I say.

"I see" is all Bobby says.

I was here before at sunset, but now for the first time in the brazen light of day. When I step onto the front porch, I see the rafters are rotting, and another decade or so and there'll be rats roaming freely in and out through holes in walls. I cup my hands and look through the window.

"What do you think this is?" I ask and point at it.

"I don't know, a jar with rotten pickles?"

"I'm serious, Bobby. Look closer?"

"Damn." Bobby's voice is soft, he's dragging the word out. "Looks like bugs, like a bunch of legs and bodies . . . spiders maybe? No wait, the bodies are . . ."

I remain silent as not to put words in his mouth.

"Crickets. It's a bunch of crickets in a jar. What the hell?"

"You ever heard of such a thing? Why would people put crickets in a jar?" I wait for Bobby to answer and then realize he's no longer standing next to me. Bobby is at the front door. He jangles the rusty doorknob, then twists it. When it doesn't budge, he gently leans his entire body into it. It screeches and whines but still doesn't move.

I lean against the porch and look toward the dirt road that leads to the house. I wonder who stood at this window, washing and drying dishes, looking out. There's the old barn to the right, a tree to the left, the path snaking toward the road. Something catches my eye— nothing extraordinary by any means, just something that doesn't seem to fit in the otherwise flat landscape. The tree—a cypress judging by the delicate, light green foliage—sits in front of a rudimentary fence that has partially collapsed. Its trunk is scaly and shredding and has a lot of rough ridges and fissures. In front of the tree the soil is raised;

two oval shapes with a slightly concave top emerge from the ground, much like a mesa.

"What's that?" I ask and point toward the mounds.

Bobby steps off the porch and we walk toward the cypress. We kneel down and gently put our hands atop one of the mounds. It's pressed and hard as if it has been there for decades.

"It doesn't seem natural," Bobby says and scans our surroundings. "It's not recent, that's for sure. It's completely overgrown, looks like it's been here for years. But I don't know what it is."

I put my hand atop the mound next to it as if the soil can talk.

"Look," Bobby says. His voice is strained. "There's more."

"More what?" I ask and wipe the dirt off my hand.

"There's another mound, over there." He points down the fence line. There's one more, bigger. Longer. More pronounced. "There are three of them."

When I get up I feel dizzy. "Break down the door for me. I want to go inside." I reach for his hand.

Bobby remains close just long enough for me to get a whiff of soap and detergent. He then turns and makes for the front door, this time putting all his weight into it. The door gives a few inches, and just as he is about to repeat the motion, I panic.

There is pressure behind my eyes and I see a psychedelic whirlwind distorting the building's angles and something pulls away the ground from up under me. Again I feel as if I'm receiving a message of sorts, a vision for sure—like I did in the hospital when I spoke to Jane, and all those other times, in the shower, in bed, more than I can remember at this point—and I surrender myself completely to it.

My body gives in to itself, like a marionette void of strings controlling its movements from above. My muscles turn rigid and stiff, performing repetitive jerking movements, and I hear my foot hit the porch post, rhythmically as if to communicate by Morse code. I see a white shadow out of the corner of my eye. It seems to be levitating a foot off the ground, translucent, shimmery. I fall to the ground, knees first, but I can hear sounds like soft bouncing branches in the wind, then the words become clearer, more sharply focused.

Dahlia. Dahlia. Dahlia.

I wake to the image of dusty boot tips and Bobby's voice repeatedly calling my name. He grabs me underneath my arms and props me with my back against the porch railing.

"Help me up," I hear myself say.

"You scared the shit out of me."

"I'm fine, just help me up."

I stand and take a few steps. When I look up, toward the door, I see the white shadow lingering. I blink and then it's gone. I can feel gravity—can one feel gravity?—and the earth's rotation, as if the entire planet is attempting to align itself.

I RECOVER, I BLAME THE HEAT. DEHYDRATION. BOBBY DROPS ME off at the gas station. I feel like a dog—my nose focuses on a scent but I'm not sure where the scent is taking me.

I cruise down the streets of Aurora, keeping an eye out for *Help Wanted* and *Now Hiring* signs in windows. I pull into the parking lot of the Aurora animal shelter. As I approach I realize the sign on the door is nothing more than a flyer stating their primary mission is finding forever homes, proudly advertising their ninety-five percent adoption rate. That doesn't change the fact that the building is filthy, smells of drool, and is, most of all, noisy. It's no longer the pound but Aurora's Forgotten Paws, a city-run adoption shelter. They are hiring and I take an application from the counter. Cleaning motel rooms or cages, it's all the same to me.

The room where they keep the small dogs is nothing but kennels stacked on top of one another, newspaper-lined, with tipped-over water bowls in the corner. Some kennels contain one dog, most of them two, some three. All of them seem to be some sort of Chihuahua mix with bulging eyes and large ears that perk upright. They curl up with their backs to me but the ones that acknowledge me raise hell. A tsunami of barks, shrill and high-pitched, makes we wonder how anyone sticks around long enough to make any kind of connection with any of them.

I walk down a concrete walkway framed by about ten large kennels on each side. Here, everything is made of concrete and the echo multiplies the noise. I am surprised none of the dogs are spinning in circles or chewing their mouths bloody on cage doors. It's a loud and sad place; ear-piercing sharp barks and deep bays merge into something that makes me anxious and my ears ring.

I put my hand flat on the chain-link cage door of a shepherd-like female who looks like she's given birth recently. She doesn't lift her head and remains still like a statue. One of her eyes is off in color, not like a Husky with one blue and one brown eye, but gray and clouded. *Tallulah*, the sign on the kennel door reads, *age five to seven, sixty pounds*. Her nipples are enlarged and the skin around her belly is loose. I wonder what happened to her litter. An animal control officer in a navy blue uniform appears next to me. Behind him, he drags a large black dog on a leash. After he shoves the dog into an empty kennel, the officer latches the gate and smiles at me.

"Here to adopt?"

"I was actually looking for a job."

"Did you complete the course?"

"There's a course?"

"Required by law. Humane Animal Control Course."

I don't say anything, ignore the tug in my chest. *Paperwork.*

"Well, let me know if you have any more questions."

The baying of two spaniel-looking medium-sized dogs across from where we are standing becomes unbearable and my eyes twitch. The officer walks down the hallway, leading the female I'd observed on a leash out of her kennel. Tallulah, the dog with the cloudy eye, is digging her paws into the ground, her belly only an inch or so from dragging along the concrete floor. The white portion of her eyes is showing at the corners.

My mind is moving faster than my thoughts can interpret. I'm stuck on fast forward and the volume is jammed right up. I know what's happening, she knows what's happening. "Wait," I say and catch up with the officer just as he loops the leash around the dog's neck to get a better grip. "Where are you taking her?" My breath is coming out in short spurts.

He pinches his lips. "We need to make room for more intakes, she's been here a while and is just not adoptable. Her time's up."

"I'll take her," I call out. "I'll take her with me right now." I don't know what just came over me. The dog, all sympathy aside, is probably blind in one eye and has numerous health issues. I don't have the money for a vet but she moves my heart with a strength that is unknown to me; her saggy stomach with teats full of milk, the fact that she has just given birth not too long ago, the absence of her litter, the cloudy eye. I hope she's got some grit left in her.

After I sign the papers and acknowledge the neuter contract, we leave the shelter. She keeps her body close to the ground, her tail tucked under, and refuses to jump into the car. I walk her around the parking lot, I try to get some momentum going but every time I get close to the car door, she shuts down and refuses to budge, lowering her head and digging her paws into the ground. We are at it for quite some time but finally she leaps in, but immediately attempts to make an escape, not realizing that I've tied the leash to the headrest. She freaks and jumps from the backseat to the passenger's seat—as far and as high as the leash allows—and it finally gets caught between her legs. She struggles like an animal in a trap, jerking her limbs.

I start the car and I hope that eventually she'll run out of steam and I drive and allow it to play out. After a mile or so she cowers down in the passenger seat, panting hard, her tongue reaching all the way to the cushion, dripping with saliva. Her scent is yeasty and fermented, but not at all unpleasant. Another mile and Tallulah stops drooling. The stiff fur on her back relaxes and when she stops shaking altogether, I rub her head and her scruff. Eventually sheer exhaustion makes her curl up in the seat, and her eyes close.

At home, Tallulah sniffs the entire perimeter of the kitchen, partly curious about her surroundings, partly suspicious, I assume. I settle down on the couch, and after a few more rounds around the house, Tallulah becomes bold and settles by my feet. She lies on her side, panting heavily. She keeps one eye on me, the other on the front door.

From above, I hear closet doors and drawers open and close in my mother's room. I'm suddenly exhausted. The image of the crickets in a jar returns to me. Maybe it's really a thing, something people do around here, and I just haven't heard of it, like dream catchers above beds or wind chimes on porches, some sort of custom I don't know about. I stretch out on the couch and fall asleep to the sound of my mother rummaging through her piled-up boxes above me.

I jerk awake when I hear a noise coming from the top floor. Judging by the lack of light coming through the blinds, it must be somewhere around three or four in the morning. Above us, a door slams shut as if caught by a rogue draft. Tallulah stops panting, as if tensing for what's to come. There's thumping and banging and an occasional pushing of boxes across the floor and I wonder if she's been at it all night. There's a clatter as if she's dropped a drawer of silverware, followed by a loud crash.

Tallulah begins to bark, sharp and short, one bark after the other.

Smoke drifts toward my nostrils—another episode, another blackout, whatever it is that comes over me. I wait for something else to happen but my body feels normal except for the pressure in my bladder. The smoke remains.

I feel panic rise up and my mouth goes dry. The house is on fire.

Fourteen

QUINN

THE buttercups began to blossom in the spring and didn't let up until August. Their abundance gave Quinn hope that she might get pregnant soon. The world around her was in bloom and every morning the grass was thick and wet with dew, stood almost three feet tall, the stems hairy and hollow, swelling with juices and full of life. Yet every month she bled worse than the one before. It was a debilitating pain accompanied by a throbbing and cramps that radiated from her belly button through her body to her lower back and down her thighs. The worst part was the inability to get out of bed for days at a time. It usually started off with her thighs aching, a harbinger of the fact that she didn't conceive and hope had died yet again. It wasn't just her body, but her mental capacity to cope was reduced; there were frequent plumbing problems that she handled just fine any other day. A busted pipe in the kitchen usually meant Nolan grabbing the tools and Quinn running for a bucket and a handful of towels, but during those weepy days she was in tears within seconds, convinced she'd drown in this farmhouse altogether. She'd sob and cry and lament and then the bleeding would start and ahead of her would be ten days of searing pains, headaches, and more tears. September came and by then the soil was parched and the meadow lay in shades of browns yet again. Quinn watched Nolan drag the tow-behind brush cutter over the grass, severing everything in its wake.

Things were not how they used to be between them. All Nolan knew was there was no pregnancy, not when they'd moved to Creel Hollow Farm and not after that, and it had become clear to him that there never would be one. Month after month he watched Quinn bleed profusely, soak two or more pads every hour, unable to stand, never mind the cooking and cleaning.

Nolan waited on her hand and foot for the first few years but eventually he left her to her own devices and began tinkering around the farm. He did random work like replacing rotten parts of the wood fence and an occasional barn rafter; he sold a few bales of hay and it was all fine and well because as far as Quinn knew the farm was paid for and they were living off the proceeds from his aunt's estate sale years ago. There was no mortgage, county taxes were low, water came from the well, vegetables were given to them from neighbors, and at times there were dozens of wooden crates of vegetables stacked in the corner of the kitchen. Washing and preparing them took half a day; peaches and strawberries were always in abundance. When the tenth year of their marriage passed, the only time they left the farm was on Sundays, to church and then lunch. Afterward, they'd go grocery shopping and spent the rest of the week hardly speaking to each other.

At night, Quinn pulled the covers up to her chin and rolled toward the darker side of the room. She hated the moon, hated how she was forced to watch it wane, then wax, then wane again, as if it was reminding her of her life passing. All night, every night, she tossed from side to side, Nolan sleeping next to her, her side of the bed becoming a chaotic tangle of covers. She'd wake up just as tired as when she went to sleep. More often than not she'd panic during those nighttime moments when her guard was down, when there was nothing to protect her from the shadows, and she closed her eyes and breathed slowly and rhythmically, counting, forcing her heartbeat to slow, willing her brain to stop firing frenzied messages, attempting to contain the dread that spread quicker than she could possibly breathe it away. The nights had become longer and longer over the years and dark thoughts tumbled through her mind, thoughts of chores she had already resolved, like the leaking pipe underneath the kitchen sink, but they reemerged to be examined over and over again. There were things she wasn't supposed to forget, like the sheets on the clothesline she'd left out overnight, but the more forgetful she became, the more her thoughts nagged at her. After an eternity of nighttime with chirping crickets and howling coyotes, the room began to flood with light, the birds sang, and Quinn threw back the covers and stumbled out of bed to face another day.

Other women her age were busy with children and chores, and the next house was miles away, too far to walk. Quinn was friendly with Seymour, an elderly man who lived in a cabin a mile from the farm, but he was peculiar and most days he was brooding over books, mumbling about something Quinn had difficulty understanding. He was a retired history teacher and preferred to be left alone. Quinn hadn't seen Sigrid in three years but they had spoken on the phone every so often.

"What am I going to do?" Quinn asked Sigrid in a weak moment. "Nolan won't go for this much longer. It's been ten years, Sigrid, *ten* years. I'm thirty, how much time do I have left? I don't know what to tell him. It's just a matter of time until he runs around with some girl from town and she'll end up pregnant and knowing him he won't go for having a bastard. He'll leave me, divorce me. I'll have nothing. *Nothing.* Where am I going to go? What am I going to do?" Quinn secretly hoped Sigrid would offer her to come back home and then that worry would be off her mind.

"Don't be silly," Sigrid said. "He's not going to leave you, not if you're smart. Now be the girl I raised and do what you need to do."

"What's that mean?"

"There must be some pregnant teenager looking to give away a baby somewhere out there," Sigrid said without missing a beat, as if that was the most logical conclusion in the world.

"What do you want me to do? Put an ad in the paper?" Quinn asked.

"You young girls have no imagination to get what you want."

It stung. Quinn thought of her father and how he had probably been just one of Sigrid's plans; marry a rich widower who won't last long.

"Have you been to a doctor?"

"More than one. They all say the same thing. Scar tissue from the infection. Nothing they can do. And to pray for a miracle." Quinn switched subjects, asking about the town, the house, and people she remembered by name, but she didn't dare ask about Benito. Quinn doubted Sigrid even remembered him. He was probably married by now with kids, living in Mexico on his family's ranch. Quinn's heart still ached but not as much as it used to. It was as if the dullness of her existence had also dulled the longing she used to feel for him.

After they hung up, Quinn pondered Sigrid's suggestion of finding a pregnant teenager and abandoned it just as quickly. Nothing in this town went unnoticed—*nothing*. A conversation she had overheard the other day after church popped into her head. Amanda Kingsley, a girl of about ten or so, known for flinching her fingers and being unable to speak in coherent sentences—at least that's how the story was told—went to see a woman who lived on the edge of town. Said the woman gave her herbs and smudged some sort of smoking aromatic plant all over the girl's body. Two grown men had to hold her down as she convulsed and twitched about. Then she fell into a long sleep—they said it was two weeks or longer—and when she awoke, she spoke coherently for the first time in her life. The girl's family didn't speak of the woman at all, not even behind closed doors or cupped hands, but the girl sat in church every Sunday, smiling, following the service. The people who gossiped about her were neither family nor kin, but random people flapping their gums, looking to tell a tale. Quinn thought it to be an outrageous story, but then there was a conversation overheard during lunch, or tidbits of conversations among groups after church, whispers at the grocery store. Talk about scorned wives' husbands returning to them, husbands whose wives had run off with other men coming back home, sick children becoming well overnight. People paid the woman any amount they could afford. If she helped you, you didn't tell, you didn't gossip, out of fear your good fortune would reverse. It seemed too impossible to be true but stranger things had happened and maybe the old woman was her best bet to have a child.

The same night Quinn made up her mind about seeing the woman, she had a dream: She stood in front of the woman's house and it was quiet but for the sound of crickets chirping. Quinn heard the faint *shoosh* of a snake sidewinding its way through the dirt when she spotted a slender branch underneath a tree. It was nothing but a common stick really, smooth and without leaves, and Quinn picked it up. When she turned around, the snake had disappeared but she decided to hold on to the stick. When she looked up, there was a pack of wolfdogs spread out by the side of the house and on top of wooden crates. Some were clearly visible; others only revealed themselves by the glow of their eyes in the dark. A majestic black wolf, the biggest one of the pack, perched on the front porch, lifted its head. Then, the rest of the pack raised their heads, their noses pointing upward in primal anticipation. Their nostrils flared, their cheeks flapped as they took in her scent. Their bodies, in one fluid motion, rose. Their eyes sparkled in the dark, leaving tracers in their wake. The pack descended on her as if an ancient code told them to encircle her from all sides. Quinn drew a line in the sand with the stick. The alpha circled her, followed by the pack. Then, as if the wolf thought otherwise, he changed directions and disappeared up a hill. The pack followed. Quinn started running after them and simultaneously jerked awake, screaming.

Nolan woke. "What's wrong?" he mumbled as Quinn turned away from him, facing the wall.

"Just a bad dream," Quinn said, knowing Nolan had already fallen back asleep. She felt the heaviness of her lids, her eyes sitting like dry river rocks in the cavities of her skull, and the stickiness of her parched tongue. She longed for a glass of water and she got up and stood in the kitchen, staring at the old pitcher on the windowsill, its white bisque porcelain with the hairline crackling like streets on a map, the slightly sandy surface, and how the finish had dulled over the years. The pitcher was old, like her body, cracked, beyond its prime.

Quinn went back to bed and Nolan scooted closer, grabbing her around the waist, pulling her toward him, until her shape fit perfectly into his. The embrace was nothing but an accidental gesture in the stupor of sleep. His hand on her body bothered her. Lately, the memories of the hunters seemed to disturb her more frequently, like a pebble in her shoe she just couldn't shake out. Her heart beat profusely and then Nolan's hand found her breast. Random the touch was, yet before she knew it, she was back in those woods, and she *felt* gnarly bark under her fingers as if she was touching its rough surface. There was a blend of pine, earth, and dew lingering in the air that made her body stiffen. Quinn attempted to move Nolan's hand, calloused and rough, but he wouldn't budge. The weight of his hand on her breast took her back to the oak tree where the hunters had—

Quinn managed to wipe it all away—the intrusion after all was in its infant stage, still ethereal enough to be pushed aside with a swift brush of her hand—but if she waited any longer, the woods would be inside her, roots taking over, tangling her legs, crushing her, and then there'd be no way out. The memories would choke her, do her in completely. Nolan stirred and rubbed up against her and she felt a slight breeze creep into the folds of her nightgown, making her shiver. As she remained frozen, Nolan suddenly stopped moving, as if he'd thought otherwise. He became motionless and then his breathing slowed, deepened.

Quinn hated Nolan then. He would not remember the moment, and if he did it would mean nothing to him, yet there she was, her heart beating out of her chest, her skin crawling, and it would take hours before she'd be able to forget. And then, just like that, it was too late. It had begun. Too long she had remained in the moment and her mind flipped, folded in on itself. There was no escape. The memory, more than a memory, a deep trench in her brain like a scar on her brain stem, evoked a vision of her facedown on a bed of acorns and leaves. Beard on top of her crushing her lungs, leaving her gasping for air. His weight lifted off her so quickly she could hardly think. Then she felt Bony Fingers dig into her. She caught a glimpse of blackened nails before he stifled her screams with his filthy hand. She could hear him panting, his breath the rhythm of an animal. He didn't speak, didn't tell her not to fight, didn't tell her not to make a sound. His fingers did all the work; he grabbed her throat as if it was the neck of a chicken, ready to be wrung. Bony Fingers would unhinge her head if any sound were to leave her lips.

What are you all up to?

Huntin' season.

And then they dragged her into the darkest part of the forest.

QUINN STOOD AT THE KITCHEN SINK, STILL TREMBLING. NOLAN ATE bacon and grits, then took a cup of coffee out to the barn and did whatever it was he did every day on a farm that didn't produce anything but bales of hay in the summer and pruney squash in the fall. She still shook when she set out to visit her neighbor, Seymour Vines, the retired history teacher turned avid wildlife watcher. Seymour lived on a small neighboring plot, in a cabin, a mile down the road.

Quinn had collected more stories about the woman—no one knew her name, everyone referred to her as *the woman*—and one was more outrageous than the other. Some said she made a magic salve from herbs that made it possible to communicate with the dead. A woman in town had been searching for a buried box filled with money after her husband's fatal fall off a roof. She had turned the entire property upside down and didn't find anything. Supposedly the woman had told her where to dig. Some people had observed her feed the mangy strays roaming the fields and watched them mate with wolves. Quinn knew there were no wolves in these parts of the country, and those stories were merely a legend: a male and a female wolf, living in a concealed thicket. Some folks from town said they had seen the woman feed them, always by hand, always one at a time. And no one knew more about animals and local lore than her neighbor Seymour.

"Is that even true?" Quinn asked him after she sat next to him on the wobbly bench outside his cabin. "Are there wolves around here?"

"Depends on who you believe," Seymour said and wiped the sweat off his forehead with a red-and-white-checkered bandana. He was about ninety years old and looked every year of it, but his mind was as sharp as that of a young man. "The buffalo wolf was extinct by 1926, the Texas gray wolf by 1942. The last two wild Mexican wolves in Texas were killed in the late sixties."

"So that's a no then?"

"The red wolves are supposed to be extinct too but I don't care what the books say," he said, "'cause there are two roaming around these parts"—he spoke fast, with long pauses in between, as if he was constantly testing the validity of his statements—"and I've seen them with my own eyes."

"I've heard that a long time ago, when there were only a few wolves left, they mated with dogs and those are the ones people talk about. Hybrids, they call them, or wolfdogs," Quinn said.

"I don't care what people say. I believe what I see with my own eyes and I know a wolf when I see one," Seymour said, his voice suddenly sharp. "Wolf eyes have a heavy black eye lining. And very large feet, not rounded like dogs. And they have a dark spot a few inches down from the base of the tail.

"It was early one morning, the sun was barely up. I was watching deer pass through the meadow by your house when I saw a wolf rolling in the grass. The male was a few feet away from the female and I watched him crush the head of a doe with one crunch, claws and jaws working together to hold down the meat while his jaws shred and broke bone. His teeth were large and more curved and thicker than a dog's, even a wolfdog. The female then ate the doe, ripping flesh and licking the blood. See, their tails don't curl in like a dog, they are always straight, and I've never seen a tail so straight on any dog. Ever." Seymour seemed to be lost in the recollection and Quinn wondered if it was a mere half truth lodged in his mind pretending to be a memory.

"Do they bark like dogs?" Quinn couldn't think of anything else to say. The story line about the old woman had faded and Quinn felt herself get impatient.

"Their bark sounds like a fast puffing sound, or a high-pitched yip that can almost sound like a coyote. They can scream when they're agitated but I've never heard that," he said and stared off into the distance.

"What about the woman though?" Quinn asked, but Seymour ignored her.

"A wolf's howl is one of the most haunting, beautiful sounds you'll ever hear." Seymour wiped his forehead again, then clutched the bandana in his fist.

"The woman, Seymour, what about the woman?" Quinn insisted.

"I don't pay any mind to old wives' tales. She's an old woman who grows herbs and lives alone and ignorant people call her a witch. Silly backward people live here, Quinn, you know that. I don't talk about her. It's none of my business."

"So you talk about magical wolves but you don't want to talk about her?"

"It's not a matter of believing," Seymour said, "it's just the way it is."

They sat in silence and Quinn thought about leaving and coming back to see him another day, bringing him muffins or a pie to get him talking some more. He knew everything going on around here and maybe he just wanted to play coy, wanted to be courted for his stories.

"I have to go," Quinn said and just as she was about to get up, she heard Seymour whisper something she couldn't quite make out. "What was that?"

"You've heard about the hunter?"

Quinn jerked, and then felt the panic rise. She yet had to discover all the words and places that harbored the memories of the woods and the consequences she lived with. Sometimes it was in Nolan's clenched jaw, in the cracking of his knuckles. Or in a word. *Hunter.*

"Back in 1834," Seymour continued, "there was a trapper, name was George Dent. He made his way up Devil's River. Dent's wife went into labor and there were complications and he went to get help. He found a Mexican shepherd who agreed to accompany him back to the camp and the shepherd brought his wife along to help with the birth." Seymour was quiet for a long time after that, as if he thought better than to tell the story.

"And?" Quinn said with an irritated tinge in her voice.

"They found Dent's wife dead from childbirth. The newborn was gone, and wolf tracks were all around."

"What does that have to do with the woman?"

"What woman?" Seymour looked up, confused.

"The woman who cured that kid, the one they call a witch?" Quinn said, hoping he'd tell her more.

Seymour spit out a mouthful of chewing tobacco, juices running down his chin. He wiped them away with the back of his hand. "I told you already, I don't talk about her. But I've heard stories, you know, years later, of a girl running with a wolf pack. Seminole scouts found small human footprints mingled with the wolf tracks. A search party tracked down the pack and captured the girl. She was so wild they locked her in a shed. At night the wolves came and attacked the men's horses. That was only a diversion, because the next day they realized the girl had escaped. For fifty years there were occasional sightings of the Wolf Girl of Devil's River."

"What are you saying?"

"I'm not saying anything. I'm just telling you what folks around here are saying."

"That's like, what . . ." Quinn paused. "That's like"—she did the math in her head—"over one hundred and fifty years ago."

"Well, folks around here have their legends," Seymour said and cocked his head.

"They say the Wolf Girl of Devil's River lives in the woods of Aurora?"

"They say they've seen her walk around in a white dress."

"So people say there's a Wolf Girl out here?"

"So the legend goes."

"But what about the woman who cured the girl in town? The woman who sells herbs?" *The woman who does spells and hexes and gets unfaithful wives to return home to their husbands and makes stray husbands fall in love with their wives again, the one who cures warts and ailments and burns foul-smelling herbs to get lost cows to come home, speaks words over twitching children. The one who helps women conceive.*

"Ghost," Seymour called out to a white dog with numerous markings of tan, approaching from behind the cabin. "Where have you been?" He stroked the dog's scruff and got up. "Always running off, that dog. No common sense."

THE CALL CAME ON A FRIDAY MORNING. QUINN HEARD THE PHONE ring, Nolan's responses short and to the point. He never handed Quinn the phone, but when he entered the kitchen, she knew something had happened.

"Sigrid is dead. She fell down the stairs and broke her neck."

"Who was on the phone?" Quinn asked and dried her hands with a kitchen towel, continued on when they were already dry.

"The housekeeper found her. She'd been dead for a few days."

That's it, Quinn thought. *Just like that. Now I have no one.*

"They want you to come and see about the house and the property."

"See about it? What does that mean?"

"I'm not sure. She said there's no will and the house is in your name. Your father must have put it in your name before he died."

Quinn got a whiff of a chemical odor, something like ether or chloroform, she couldn't be sure. Nolan's fingertips were white as if they had been dipped in paint.

"Can you drive me?" Quinn asked and took a step back, the odor so strong she felt nauseated. "I don't want to go alone."

"I'm working on something," he said, and Quinn watched him dip his hands in a sink full of cold water. "You can take the truck. The drive isn't that far."

Quinn didn't answer, but for a moment in time a thought flashed through her mind. It was a mere spark, neither logical nor feasible, really. Yet it grew, sloshed over everything.

She wouldn't mind at all if she never saw Nolan again.

THE NEXT MORNING QUINN GOT IN NOLAN'S TRUCK AND MADE her way to Beaumont, close to the Louisiana border. She took I-45 south and then cut across until she reached the town and the house where she grew up. She never entered the property—it had been Sigrid's house for so many years that even looking at it from the curb made it seem like it hadn't been home for a long time even before she'd left—and Quinn signed paperwork at the office of the executor of the will. Her father, always with "one eye in the future, the other on doing what's right," according to Horacio McCann, Esquire, had an ironclad will. The house had been promised to the Texas Historical Society of Beaumont, and a price had been set years before he passed. Sigrid had lived off her small pension but had never been entitled to the house. When Quinn left McCann's office, she was in possession of a cashier's check in an amount that was staggering.

Quinn took 146 South and within two hours, she reached Galveston. As a child she had imagined they'd have to drive all day, maybe even take a ferry, but now that she realized that it took a mere two hours from Beaumont, she felt anger well up inside of her. Galveston, the place her father had always promised he'd take her, was nothing but a stone's throw from her house, yet he had never bothered. She hated the fact that she felt resentment toward her father and so she thought of Nolan and the farm, where her anger felt more at home and appropriate. The fact that he was her only relation now made her feel untethered as if she was floating about without a binding thought in her mind. Suddenly being free someplace else—whatever that meant and wherever that was—seemed something she might consider. Maybe it was the check in her pocket, maybe it was the fact that there was nothing for her in Aurora, just like there was nothing in Beaumont for her either.

The Galvez was just as she had imagined it: a majestic brick building with a stately lobby of Corinthian columns, decorated ceilings, and marble floors. There were potted plants everywhere, area rugs, and wicker furniture, and the windows facing the coast allowed abundant light to flood in. She couldn't get enough of how it felt to sit in the oversized plush chairs, and every day she had her clothes laundered and returned pressed. On the grounds there were palm trees, a barbershop even, and boutique stores in the main lobby.

Yet in the company of the other guests she felt out of her element. The restaurant was extravagant and other guests stared at her because she was the only woman dining alone. In the evenings the dining room of the Galvez was crowded with men in suits and women who seemed to have been outfitted by professionals. She assumed the ladies in white coats with large suitcases scramming through the endless hallways of the hotel were the ones styling the women. The dress she wore and considered fancy was nothing but an average sheath that seemed way too casual—the other women wore elegant dresses and jewelry and lots of makeup, even in the mornings—and Quinn felt as if she set the cup on the saucer a bit too forcefully; couldn't help it when the knife scraped across the plate, making people flinch. Living on the farm for all these years—she did the math; eleven years in all—had made her rough around the edges. Her nails were chipped, her face freckled and burnt from the sun, and she always forgot to cross her legs.

And then there was the food. Quinn thought she knew about food preparation, had in fact cooked for her father since she was twelve, before Sigrid entered the picture, but now her attempts at cooking—shocking beans to retain color and allowing egg whites to adjust to room temperature before beating—were nothing more than a clumsy effort taken from country cookbooks with bland ingredients.

She came to realize that what had passed as a feast was merely a poor man's meal.

The tables stretched the length of the room and delicacies Quinn had never heard of or seen lined the walls; whole roasted pigs still turning on spits and Cornish hens arranged in zigzag patterns, their orifices stuffed with sprigs of rosemary; platters of fruits—one shaped like a star!—and nuts, cheeses, and breads, and all by the flickering lights of the overhead chandeliers.

There was a masterfully arranged glazed ham on a bed of greens with pineapple slices in a vortex pattern; grilled trout with lemon on a bed of wild fragrant rice. A table—its very own table!—of breads; French baguettes in flower shapes; dinner rolls that looked like seashells; and in between side dishes so plentiful that she couldn't possibly try them all. Quinn picked the trout and the rice, and when she returned to her table, a couple with two children had been seated. Quinn panicked, not wanting to hold a conversation with people such as them, rich and sophisticated—what was she going to talk about, after all, the farm and her husband riding around aimlessly on a tractor while he depleted the family's fortune?—and Quinn used *fortune* loosely. As if claiming the large round table had been an audacity of hers, she had relocated to a smaller square table by the window when a waiter appeared and asked her for her choice of wine.

"Madame? What wine would you like?" he said and bowed.

"White," Quinn said even though she preferred water with her meals.

The choices he named—Chardonnay, sauvignon blanc, dry Riesling—confused Quinn and she busied herself removing the baked lemon, fiddling with the fish that had its head still attached. She froze. Her father was supposed to teach her how to separate the bones from the flesh but he never did. Using the butter knife, she made a clumsy attempt to remove the head behind the gills. By the time she pulled the body away from the head, her plate was a mess of bones and eyes and silvery skin. She picked at the rice and felt the eyes of the waiter on her as he removed the plate and in a harsh and snappy manner pointed at the silverware. Quinn left the dining room without dessert and from then on ordered room service.

The next day she strolled across the boulevard to the beach and walked the shoreline. She wore shorts and a blouse and had tied a red scarf around her head to keep her hair from whipping her face. Large sunglasses hid her eyes.

Quinn must have walked for over an hour, had long left the fancy hotels behind, when she came upon a group of people. Vans parked by the side of the road, and they had set up tents and coolers. Some of the women held babies, and there was a handful of children, some of them naked, playing nearby, building sand castles. A cold fire in their midst—a sign they had been at the beach all night. Quinn rested on a nearby jetty and watched the group of people chatting and laughing. The women had hair that reached all the way down their backs and they wore sandals and flowing dresses; the men seemed scruffy and wore long beards. *Subculture* they were called, Quinn then remembered, had heard on TV, men and women opposed to war and government and society at large. Quinn jerked when from behind a man emerged from the water, dragging his surfboard with him. He wiped his long hair out of his face and it stuck to his skull and back. He dropped the board in the sand and sat on it, catching his breath.

"Strong winds," he said and smiled.

He leaned back on the board, his stomach concave, his body tanned and lean. He continued to make conversation even though Quinn just nodded and smiled. Eventually she engaged and he told her they traveled along the coast, and that they were on their way back to California. *Cali*, he called it.

Quinn told him about the farm and Nolan and he called over a woman who was balancing a baby on her hip. The man, Jason, and the woman, Amy, weren't married but lived in a commune in California. When Amy heard Quinn lived on a farm she perked up.

"What do you grow? Do you have animals?"

Quinn was embarrassed and named random produce. "No animals," she added. "Tell me about the commune," Quinn said, not really interested, just so she wouldn't have to talk about herself and the farm. She wanted to leave; the surf was making her cheeks prickle.

Amy told her about the dangers of chemicals in foods—"We grow all our vegetables and we don't eat meat at all"—and how they lived secluded on a farm with horse wagons and outhouses, and all the women gave birth at home.

Before she knew what was happening, Amy handed her the baby. Holly was her name and she was mellow and settled into Quinn's arms as if it was the most natural place to be. She smelled of sun and salt and something stirred inside of Quinn. She had thought she had wanted a baby before but this felt as if her wish had just been elevated and presented to her in a perfectly new light: *I want* . . . she thought. *I want* . . . and then an awareness manifested that she would settle. Settle for something lesser, less significant than her own child, but not in a sacrificial way, no, more like having what she wanted, just not in a way she had thought.

Quinn knew her womb was dead, it had died a long time ago that day in the woods, and nothing more would come forth from it but blood and cramps and the smell of defeat and death. But with this baby in her arms she wanted to tuck away that sense of defeat nicely, along with the memory of the creek, the moment Bony Fingers submerged her. His hands holding her shoulders and her lungs busting, straining, and then inhaling water. She felt as if holding this baby, someone else's baby after all, had allowed her to be born again with a new understanding of what needed to happen.

The scent of the ocean was intoxicating, how it churned and whipped the waves like a vortex, drawing her in. And she tucked the memory away in an orderly fashion, *away* in the past where it belonged, and the ocean roiled and thrashed and she began to shake, not from cold or wind or not having eaten breakfast, but from the center of her being, and the only calm was Holly, sweet Holly in her arms, the perfect weight to keep her from exploding, keep her grounded. Calming like a mother's cool hand on a fiery forehead, something she knew nothing about, having never met her own mother, but she *wanted* . . .

just wanted to *mother*. To *be* that, be it, *mothering*, holding, and keeping someone safe. Salvation and generosity all in one. She wanted *that*. Even if the child wasn't hers.

She held the baby for a while longer, maneuvered her from hip to hip, from one side of her chest to the other, and eventually the baby fell asleep, and as much as Quinn wanted to remain in this moment of her epiphany, she was in a hurry now to leave.

Everything had changed; she didn't want to keep driving east to get away from Texas and Nolan and the farm, start her life over by herself, even though with all the money she had now it *was* possible. She didn't fit with the women in the hotel, with their belted dresses and barrettes, purses and stockings, stiff and ladylike. And she wasn't Cali either, wasn't tall and slender, braless with sun-bleached hair and naked children building castles around her, growing vegetables and giving birth while other women cheered her on.

She was Quinn, the wife of Nolan Creel of Aurora, Texas. And there was no need to see any more doctors—they had told her as much, short of calling her *infertile*, she might as well be honest with herself, as if she were a stretch of land without any rain, and littered with rocks, unable to sustain life—but there must be a way. *Must.* The money from the house, her father's house, was in her pocket. A check for an amount so outrageous, she'd never even dreamed of so many zeroes.

The next morning she left the hotel and got back on the road to Aurora.

Anything was possible now. *Anything.*

Part Two

Everything is more beautiful because we are doomed.

—ACHILLES

Fifteen

DAHLIA

*T*HE *house is on fire.*

I feel the heat through my mother's door. My mind upturns—
I no longer remember if I should open the door or not open the door
but either way—I see gray smoke seeping through the gap underneath.
It bellows and moves upward, hugging the walls.

I yank open the door and simultaneously cover my nose and mouth
with the hem of my shirt. I feel my way along the wall to the window
and I open it. Smoke stings my eyes. Every breath I take, it gets worse.

In the middle of the room sit boxes with haphazardly open lids,
papers are strewn all across the floor. In the center of the boxes is a
blackened metal bucket from which smoke bellows in black clouds.
There are more boxes yet not much of them remains—some have
turned to dust. The scorched wooden floor is covered with ashes.

My mother stands in the darkest part of the smoke.

This is not a fire that came about within the past few minutes—
the amount of boxes smoldering, the scorching of the floor, even the
curtain on the far window is on fire—but it seems my mother struggled with the flames getting out of hand for a while.

Just when I think to call 911, I hear sirens in the distance. They
get louder by the second, yet my mother just stands there, her apathy
much more unnerving than the fire and the smoke. She is frozen,

watching the flames as if she's surrendering herself to the fire. She even takes a step toward the bucket, is about to take yet another, but I jerk her back by the only thing I can get a hold of, her cardigan. She breaks free from my grip; her cardigan left in my hand as if she's determined to be consumed by the flames. Thick smoke billows black across the room, filling my lungs.

We choke and cough; it is painful to breathe with my heart racing in my chest. The sirens become deafening and I scream her name as she bends down and picks up pieces of paper that are clearly on fire. She kicks the bucket. It tips over and the world turns into an inferno. The flames burn with kaleidoscopic colors—purples and blues and greens, shades of gold and yellow—and with each flare they lick across the floor as if there's something highly flammable present, not just a fluke, not a candle or faulty wiring: she used an accelerant to start this fire. To burn things.

Someone grabs me and pulls me backward. I can't make sense of anything until I open my eyes again at the bottom of the stairs and I'm staring into the eyes of a firefighter in full gear, a mask covering his face.

"My dog," I scream, "where is my dog?"

The mouth behind the mask moves but I can't make out any words. I wiggle and kick, attempting to get away so I can look for Tallulah. The man's grip is tight. He lifts up his hand and makes a robot-like gesture with it and it takes me a second to comprehend—thumbs-up—and I know Tallulah is safe.

He carries me outside, across the street, where he hands me to another man. People scream, voices give orders, but all those human sounds turn into white noise and my world is nothing but movement: men in yellow coats and helmets, bystanders in housecoats. A piece of vinyl siding slides off the second-story exterior like a dab of butter in a hot pan. Through the open window flames escape into the darkness, casting their yellow glow into the night. The wind carries off the smoke and ashes rain down. More sirens approach, wailing as they come down the street.

Air hisses into my nostrils. Another painful coughing fit shakes me, rattles deep down in my chest. Someone is pulling on my hands and I resist, jerk whatever I cling to toward myself, and clutch it in an embrace. I look down and realize that I still have my mother's knitted cardigan in my hand. My fingers have dug into it, stretched the fabric into a distorted shape beyond recognition. It is singed, yet I hold on to it.

MY MOTHER SITS ON THE BACK PORCH IN A LAWN CHAIR. I SIT ON the back stoop, not sure what to say to her, where to even start.

"Where'd you get the dog?" she asks, as if that's the most pressing problem at the moment.

"Her name's Tallulah. She's from the pound. They were about to put her down."

We both hear Tallulah yap and look up. She's standing in front of a tree, shaking her head. She turns sharp to the right just to stand in front of the fence, not moving, tapping it gently with her nose.

"The bitch's blind," my mother says.

I'm taken aback by her chuckle, her entire demeanor. She should be remorseful, should show some kind of emotion, yet she doesn't acknowledge the fire that could have burned down the entire house and possibly killed us. I had seen her medication bottles earlier in her bathroom—thirty days' supply was halfway gone and she'd only been home for a few days. With all those meds in her she should be passed out on the couch, yet she is slightly subdued at best. She must have a tornado living inside of her.

"No one told me she was blind." I now question Tallulah's eyesight even though she does make eye contact. But then there's her inability to jump into a car, the way she freaked out in the backseat—it's altogether possible that she is blind. "I'm not taking her back, if that's what you're getting at."

My mother tilts her head as if she just remembered something. "Where are we going to live?"

I want to know what she burned in that bucket, what was in those boxes, but none of those questions turn into words. "Why do you collect crickets in a jar?" It's out before I can rein it back in. I watch her closely.

Her eyelids twitch and she swallows hard. My mother laughs, deep, from the gut, almost diabolically. Then she just stares straight ahead.

A firefighter approaches. His gear spooks Tallulah and she takes off into the house, up the stairs. He kneels down; his face is sooty, his eyes are bloodshot. He tells me that it would be best to vacate the premises tonight.

"We have no place to go," I say and we both watch my mother get up and take a sheet down from the clothesline. As she folds it, she leaves soot marks all over it. She gives up, sits back down, waiting for someone to tell her what to do.

"I will allow you forty-eight hours to vacate. That should give you time to pack and make arrangements," he says, pity in his voice. "The ambulance will take your mother to the hospital. Between the smoke inhalation and her demeanor, she should be evaluated, but they'll sort that out at the hospital. Do not enter the upstairs bedroom. The floor is unstable and it's dangerous. I understand there are pets on the premises?"

"Yes, my dog."

"If you can't take the animal with you, please contact animal control. Surrender the animal until you find a place to stay."

After everyone has left, I find Tallulah hiding underneath my bed. She looks defeated, the way she is facing the wall, her tail tucked underneath her body. I grab some bacon from the fridge and sit on the floor, speaking gently to her.

I recall her behavior in the backyard earlier, and how her head doesn't always turn when I approach her as if she's waiting for acoustic clues. I realize my mother might be right. Maybe her cloudy eye means she is partially blind and her good eye is on the brink of darkness. This blind dog from the pound, cowering underneath my bed, drooling and shaking, may see shadows at best.

I wonder what shadows my mother sees. How it feels to live in her body. Maybe it's like having a nightmare and realizing you're awake and it just doesn't stop. I know one thing for sure: for years I've watched her eccentricity get worse, appearant even in random phone calls now and then, but these three months I've lived with her are no longer up for interpretation. I can only imagine what's the next step in her madness.

I pull a pillow on the floor and I just lie there, bacon beside me. My ears are ringing, my hands shaking.

All windows and doors are open. A pungent scent of smoke fills the air and from the backyard I hear the snapping of ashen bedsheets in the wind.

THERE'S SO MUCH GOING ON AROUND ME—HAVING TO PACK UP the house, finding rental properties that accept dogs, my mother's empty glare as they led her to the ambulance that would take her to the hospital. Out of all the things I could possibly obsess over, I focus on the jars of crickets. I can't let go of the black flattened bodies, the way their long antennae tangle and create a labyrinth of legs and spurs. I know I should be searching for employment opportunities online, but instead I check the Bertram County website for property information. I need the exact address of the property. There's no information given out over the phone, all inquiries have to be made in writing, so that afternoon I visit the courthouse.

The County Tax Assessor's Office is located in an annex building of the Aurora courthouse, a dank room with artificial plants and stained industrial carpet. In the background, I hear the faint melody of country music, interrupted by occasional static. At the window, I exchange polite tidbits about the weather, the fact that it's Friday, and Mrs. Winnipeg's leopard blouse. She is about sixty and tempted to take reduced social security payments in two years. I tell her I'm a photographer and that I'm working on a project photographing abandoned properties in the area and I'm here to check on the status of a property on FM 2410. "I'm not sure if you can help me, I don't know the exact address. And the property is vacant; actually, it looks like it's been abandoned for a while."

"All the information about deeds and properties is a matter of public record," she says and I'm engrossed by her red lipstick bleeding violently into the lines and wrinkles around her mouth. Her silver hair is fine and wispy and I can see her shiny scalp.

Mrs. Winnipeg puts on a pair of cat-eye glasses and grabs a form from the shelf next to her. "Tell me the approximate location of the property."

"It's on FM 2410, a couple of miles or so from the outskirts of Aurora, by mile marker 78. It's set back from the road by a quarter of a mile or so. There's a dirt road and an overgrown path, and a farmhouse on the property. And a barn. No close neighbors to my knowledge, not that I could see, at least. It's pretty deserted out there."

"And you need to know who the owner is?"

"I don't want to trespass," I lie. "I'd like to get permission to photograph the property." I watch her write FM 2410, the F and M so elaborate that the letters are almost impossible to decipher.

"Ranch or farm property?"

"There's a difference?" I ask. Livestock versus produce, I assume, but can't be sure.

"A ranch includes structures used for the practice of ranching, raising and grazing livestock such as cattle or sheep. A farm produces a harvest and results in a product used to sustain those who farm or in a commodity to sell. Sometimes a ranch engages in a limited amount of farming, raising crops for feeding the animals, such as hay and feed grains," she says, rattling off the well-rehearsed facts of farming. Mrs. Winnipeg is resolute and on a roll and I don't dare interject.

"Well," I say, "I don't remember seeing any cattle guards or troths, but I didn't see the entire property. There was some rusty farm equipment, so I assume it's a farm."

She checks off a box, moves her glasses up to the bridge of her nose. "Have a seat," she says and slides the glass door shut in my face.

I sit and wait on one of the shiny wooden chairs in a row of ten opposite the customer window. She returns after what seems like fifteen minutes, maybe longer. Her hands are empty.

"The property is not abandoned and we should be able to figure out who the owner is. The bad news is that the Official Public Records index does not include entries prior to 1976. I had to contact the Bertram County Archives. They will fax over a copy. It'll just take a minute."

"Thank you."

"Five dollars. Cash or credit card?"

"Cash," I say and push a five-dollar bill over the counter.

"Anything else?" she asks as she hands me a receipt.

"Yes, unrelated. Completely unrelated." I take a deep breath in. "Is there such a thing as collecting dead crickets in jars? Is it something people do around here? Like a regional custom, something like that?"

She stares at me for a moment. "Crickets in a jar? You mean like trapping fireflies?"

"No, more like for collection. Or storage. I'm not sure."

Her red fingernails scratch her shiny scalp. "It's not anything that people do around here, and I'd know." She pauses for a second. "But my late husband collected and preserved insects. He pinned them in, you know, in a curio box. House was full of them." Her voice trails off and her eyes become glossy for a moment as she's remembering bugs and beetles pinned behind glass. Then her eyes turn back to steel. "There's a certain protocol you have to follow. You put them in a jar, then add alcohol or some sort of chemical, I don't quite remember. Then they go in another jar so they don't fall apart when you pin them. That's about the gist of it. Other than that, no, I don't know why someone would collect bugs in a jar."

The fax machine rings and hums, and a tray spits out two pieces of paper. She inspects them and then slides them toward me. "So here's the deal. This here is the last known owner but"—she pauses, wets her finger, then flips to the second copy—"it was decreed to someone else after. It might just be a glitch in record keeping and, you know, things happen. We don't have the current address or name of the new owner on file. So I can't help you with permission for your photographs. If you want, I can request for some research to be done. It might take a while."

"No, that's all right."

"The owner is alive and up to date on property taxes but I can't tell you the name or their address. I don't have access to that information. I wouldn't worry about a permission. But don't quote me on that."

Later, in the car, I scan the fuzzy copies. Most of the words are typed, some are filled in by hand. *Deed Record.* I skim the typed portion, pick up on words like *grantor, State of Texas, lot 5, block 17, 48 acres, AURORA, Bertram County, Texas. Date: October 12, 1949.* There's a box in the corner with the word *MICROFILM* and a number that's hard to decipher. It reads as follows:

WARRANTY DEED
Mable and Rupert Creel, Creel Hollow Farm

TO
Nolan Creel

The second copy looks identical but the *MICROFILM* box has a decipherable number and completely different information. The date below the signatures reads *April 4, 1982.*

WARRANTY DEED
Nolan Creel

TO
Quinn Creel

I sit in the car and I read the deed over and over as if I'm going to find something of value if I just look long and hard enough. I come up empty. There's no obvious connection and maybe it was all a co-incidence, maybe my mother just walked out of town and ended up there for no reason at all, and I'm not sure what I even expected. I feel silly. What sounded like a Sherlock Holmes kind of move, a connecting of the dots—my mother's night excursion down 2410, losing her purse, the Mason jars with dead crickets—is now full of flaws.

There's so much going on in my head, but it's not like this is some sort of buried memory, nothing like that. Maybe I'm attempting to connect dots that are bound to end up in a jumbled mess: no meaning to be extracted here. My mother has always been random in her actions and maybe all this is random too.

I fall asleep with those thoughts and when I wake up, Tallulah is curled up next to me in my bed. Her body exudes warmth and her paws gently twitch. She relaxes and her nose rests so close to my arm that her breath produces moisture on my skin. I dare not move as to not interrupt her sleep. She hasn't eaten since the fire, must have come out from underneath the bed some time during the night.

The sun isn't up yet and I have to finish packing but I give Tallulah this moment of peace. As she lays there, I have time to examine her. I don't know anything about her past, but her thick calloused elbows make me believe that she's spent years on concrete floors. She's probably never seen any of her litter beyond eight weeks. Her pads are cracked as if she's walked across state lines. I wonder if an owner gave her up because she was blind or too used up or had too many litters. And I wonder what I'd feel for my mother if she had a heart condition or broke her hip. I would care for her, I know that with certainty, but this odd behavior, this madness is something completely different. What if I can't help? I stroke Tallulah between the eyes and she wakes and begins to walk in tight seemingly random circles and then stops, does a quick cursory spin before she curls up next to me again.

Tallulah, deep inside, is a wild dog with an ingrained instinct to pat down tall grass and underbrush to make a comfortable bed for herself. There's a reason for everything. There's never nothing behind something. Maybe there's a reason why my mother set fire to that bucket. Or rather—*what* was she burning in that bucket?

I get up slowly and enter my mother's room. It smells dank and smoky and I can see through a hole in the floor straight into the living room downstairs. The bucket sits in the corner of the room, filled with a mixture of water, soot, and paper pulp.

Several of the boxes were completely engulfed in flames and there is nothing left but a distorted pile of charred remains. I flip over one of the boxes that is still intact. Most of the papers are soaked and stick to one another. I gently peel them away from each other, so they don't fall apart.

There's the lease to the house, a life insurance letter—I can make out red lettering and the State Farm Insurance logo, but it seems older, the font and graphics seem vintage in an outdated kind of way—it's not a policy, part of the address is intact, but all I can decipher is the word *Aurora*, and an incomplete zip code and a partial name. *No____.* *____ll. Change in Bene____.* This could mean benefits or beneficiary, but then there's not a single complete line. There are also photographs. I flip through them, and as they separate, murky drops of water mixed with soot run off, as if they are hemorrhaging some vile, black blood containing a long-kept and dark secret.

There's a picture of me; I'm about thirteen, I can tell by the length of my hair. It is the nineties, summertime I assume, judging by the shorts and the tank top. I was skinny and lanky, didn't wear a bra yet, but one of those sports bras was flattening my barely developing chest. I flip the photograph and see numbers on the back. 199_, I can't make out the last number. It could be a zero, or an eight, maybe a nine. Then a name. *Pet.*

I know, *know*, that Dahlia isn't the name my mother has called me all my life. I have memories of her calling me Pet, and now there's a photograph with the name on the back. She went from Mom to Memphis Waller. I went from Pet to Dahlia.

Dahlia came about in Aurora. Somewhere between West Texas, en route to Vegas, then California, and back to Texas, something changed. We no longer ran; we settled down in Aurora. I went to school for the first time in my life. I ate lunch with other children, made friends. The woman who had dragged me over multiple state lines, from motels to furnished rooms, from living in cars to ramshackle trailers, settled down. Suddenly my mother felt safe enough to stay in one place. And she was Memphis from then on out. Not that I was aware of any other name—she was Mom, Mother, not a name—there were no IDs, no documents. And if there had been, would I have understood? Would it have meant anything at all?

A wet piece of paper flops around in my hand and I support it with my palm. The paper is without tension, its fibers no longer maintaining its original shape. The bottom portion of the document is partially burnt. There is, if one were to look for it, something resembling a seal.

I remember the paperwork from the tax assessor's office, the microfiche number, the seal. This one looks identical, yet it's difficult to make out the faint letters. Something catches my eye. *Creel Hollow Farm.* I tilt it toward the light, then stand by the window to get the best possible view of it.

WARRANTY DEED
Quinn Creel, Hollow Creel Farm

TO
Memphis Waller

Like a flash of lightning is followed by a rumble of thunder, parts of my body go numb. Something inside of me shifts, as if my bones move but my body doesn't, almost like I'm stepping out of myself. I feel a tug around my neck as if someone is jerking on an invisible leash. Nausea washes over me and my vision turns blurry.

Nothing makes sense but I know one thing for sure: my mother's world, the part that is unknown to me, the part she keeps secret, expands with every passing day.

I connect the dots: an older couple puts a property into their son's name, and that son is Nolan Creel. At some point, Nolan Creel puts the same property in the name of a Quinn Creel. That make sense, that's how farms are handed down through generations, gifted while the previous generation is still alive as to avoid taxes, especially when there are large estates involved. But then it gets curious; at some point my mother was given the property. From a Quinn Creel it goes to Memphis Waller. My mother never claims the farm. Allows it to sit there, somehow manages to pay property taxes. But she sneaks off at night to visit the farm in the dark. To see what? If it's still there? If the key still fits?

How do I ask her the questions I need answers to? She very seldom allows herself to get caught up in a conversation, is always on point, careful not to divulge too much. Not to give it away, whatever *it* may be.

How do I make her understand how important this is to me? She lives in her head and emotions are alien to her, she barely understands her own feelings let alone anyone else's. It isn't that she doesn't care— I keep telling myself she loves me, that I'm sure of it—it's just that she wasn't born with the faculties to understand how to relate to people. Maybe someone more skilled is better prepared to open the vault that is my mother.

CHARLENE, BLOND AND THICK AND CHEERFUL, HER ACRYLIC TIPS clacking on the keyboard, collects my money and as I sit and wait in Dr. Wagner's office, I roll a can of Diet Coke from the vending machine in the lobby over my eyebrows.

"Dahlia, what brings you in?" Dr. Wagner enters and, like the first time I met him, his hands are covered in glistening gel that smells overwhelmingly minty.

"I don't think that's my name," I say and my voice surprises me. Cold. Without emotion.

"What was that?"

"My mother started a fire, almost burned down the house. First she doubled up on her meds and before I knew it, the house was on fire. I found a deed . . ." I stumble over my words. I take in a big gulp of air but that makes it even worse. "Do you remember that I looked for her purse?" I pause and breathe but still the words get jumbled up in my mind. I'm not sure if it's my faulty brain or my mouth relaying words out of order. It takes all the concentration I have to sound coherent.

"Slow down, Dahlia. I don't follow. What happened?"

I start from the beginning. *Purse. 2410. Farm. Crickets. Fire. Deed.* When I'm done, he just stares at me.

"Let me see if I've got this right," he says and leans back in his chair. "The farm where your mother lost her purse, according to this deed, belongs to a"—Dr. Wagner flips the pages—"Quinn Creel. And after your mother set fire to the house and ended up in the hospital for smoke inhalation, you find among the things she attempted to burn a document that says that a Quinn Creel deeded a farm to your mother. And Memphis Waller, your mother, is the rightful owner of that farm. Something she never told you. But she also rents a house where you both live."

"Yes. But there's more." I'd be lying if I said I wasn't enjoying this. Some part of me is reveling in this mess of names and deeds and court documents.

"There's more?" he asks and stares at my hands pulling a photograph out of my purse.

"Here," I say, "that's me, I was about thirteen or so. Flip it over."

"Pet. 1-9-9 something. I don't understand?"

"My mother called me Pet for as long as I can remember. Some people thought my name was actually Pat, like Pat short for Patricia. And for all I know that's true. Then suddenly she tells me my name is Dahlia and hers is Memphis. Last name Waller. Out of the blue. When we came back to Texas after living in California and all those other places. She changed her name and probably mine too, and I don't know my real name. And Pet is not a name."

"Are you aware that you're slurring your speech?"

"I sound just fine to me."

"Why are you rolling that can over your forehead?"

"I've been having headaches. But I'm okay," I say. "I have weird moments, smells and memories, and sometimes I pass out." I smile to make it sound plausible, insignificant, even.

"Why is your front tooth chipped? When did that happen?"

"The day in the woods, when I feel into the creek. And I hit my head."

"You hit your head." He looks worried, his brows raise higher than usual, he's leaning forward as if not to miss anything I'm doing or saying. "You didn't tell me you hit your head that day."

"I found . . ." I pause. I am *not* going to call her Jane again, especially not *my* Jane. "The woman in the woods. I fell in a creek, hit a rock or something. And I chipped my tooth."

"I am ordering an EEG and an MRI immediately. Dahlia, you might be having seizures. They can range from anything like an odor without origin, seeing colors or auras, to full-blown grand mal seizures. Let me see if they can fit you in right now. And I'll call over to the hospital and check in on your mother."

"I think you are overreacting a bit. I'm fine."

You don't understand, I want to say, *I've been given a gift and I am onto my mother and her decades of secrets and variations of stories I know* not *to be true, she's a con and I'm onto her and therefore she tried to get rid of evidence. She is* not *who she claims to be. And neither am I. I don't even know who I am.* I want to tell him all of this but I remain quiet.

Something is hatching inside of me. Secrets. Why did she always demand that we be secretive about who we were, where we were going? Who were we running from? What is the secret she looks for at night on dark country roads? What are the secrets she attempted to reduce to ashes?

Then I go a step further. Do I have a secret too? One unwillingly imposed onto me? I don't have to ask another question: I felt it when I walked across the dirt road on that farm. It is in my mother's breath, in her bones. In *my* bones.

Something isn't right.

THE EEG TECHNICIAN MEASURES MY HEAD AND FITS ME WITH AN
elastic cap with electrodes. She studies the monitor. "During the first
part of this test I will be asking you to open or close your eyes. At
some point light will flash. The second part will just record the brainwaves while you relax. If you fall asleep, don't worry. The machine is
recording your brainwaves even if you're not awake."

I follow her instructions, open and close my eyes when she prompts
me to. A light flashes. I see greens, magentas, and yellows. I have the
sensation of being a rocket that's about to soar into the sky, but then
the flashes seize and it's all over—instead of taking off, I turn into a
dud. There are more commands, more flashes.

"You're all set. Imaging is right next door."

The imaging nurse—a radiographer by the name of Brenda—
pushes me into a large cylinder. She places some sort of helmet around
my head—a *head coil* she calls it—and sticks a call button in my hand.

"You can talk to me through the headphone system," Brenda says.
"I'll be able to see and hear you throughout the entire study. Press the
call button anytime to get my attention. Please remain completely
still or the images are useless."

I close my eyes. I can't move my head and the cradle-like helmet keeps
me completely stationary. After an initial period of silence there's a loud
tapping noise. It increases in volume and then turns into a bleeping sound.

"The machine has been calibrated and we are about to start. A
brain scan takes about twenty minutes."

About ten minutes into it, I open my eyes. Even though the chute
is stationary, it closes in on me, its walls a mere two inches away from
me. With each breath I become tenser and the stagnant air is crushing
me like bricks—I can feel the pressure in every bone of my body—I
struggle to prevent the fear from escalating into an all-out panic. It
rises like a bathtub filled to the brim and it's about to overflow. My
finger atop the call button jerks, I'm tempted to push it, abort it all,
but I can't bear starting again, all over, I'm almost done.

I try to remember the first memory I've ever had. I mentally move backward on the timeline that is my life, want to recall the very first image that my eyes sent to my brain to write on the slate that is my memory. It must be stored somewhere. My first memory. I struggle but there it is.

Warm skin. Itchy legs. Grass. Amber. Mustard. Saffron. Like paint splotches over a canvas, random and haphazard, flowers strewn across a meadow.

Gold like butter.

Buttercups.

Sixteen

QUINN

QUINN had called ahead and told the branch manager she wanted to cash a check. She even mentioned the amount, and after a pause he advised her it would take a couple of days for the money to arrive. "It's a rather large sum and it's going to take some time," he said in a nasal voice, coughing as he attempted to shield the receiver.

Days later, Quinn entered the Texas Commerce Bank and made her way to the counter and slid the cashier's check toward the teller. She instructed him to pay out half in cash; with the other half she wanted to open an account. After the paperwork was filled out, she watched the clerk count out the money. He creased the bills lengthwise down the middle so they remained almost flat on the shiny counter. She followed the movement of his hands, smooth as a cunning gambler he organized the piles; stacks of hundred-dollar bills, stacks of fifties, stacks of twenties.

"Please sign here," the clerk in the white dress shirt said and pointed at the dotted line on the withdrawal form. "I can get you the manager if you're interested in investing the rest. Savings bonds maybe?"

"Some other time. For now I'd like to keep it in an account." Quinn draped the red scarf she had purchased at the Galvez Hotel around her neck. It was last remnant of a life she had thought possible, even if only for a short moment. "Can you put it in an envelope, please?"

The man tapped the stack of bills on the counter, leveling the edges, then tucked them into a large white envelope with the Texas Commerce Bank logo. "Anything else I can do for you?"

Quinn looked at him, wondering how her life would have turned out if she had married a man like him—dress shirt, slacks, shiny shoes, and not whiff of formaldehyde—so unlike Nolan, mucking about on his family farm with nothing to show for it.

No. No no no no no. This was *not* one of those moments. This was a moment of joy; she had the money for the old woman, and since there would be a baby, Nolan would end his drab existence and start the life they were supposed to live, someplace else where young families belong. A life with a job besides the mediocre tasks he performed on the ranch—maybe he'd finally sell the farm and with the money they could afford a nice house in a subdivision in Dallas. She had left brochures around the house, of Ponderosa Forest and its houses with wall-to-wall carpeting, not those pesky screeching wooden floors scraped and dulled by decades of wear, pinching the bottoms of your feet when you walked on them barefoot. The new house would be drawn out on a piece of paper—they called it a *master plan*—there'd be architectural characteristics, *stable, established, and upscale*, just like the brochure said. There'd be a manicured lawn and a sprinkler sitting in the center keeping the grass green and lush during the summer. Quinn imagined making new friends, meeting neighbors, and maybe inviting them to dinner. Quinn had mentioned selling the farm before, on one of those days when Nolan was in a good mood—there hadn't been too many good days lately—and she had waited for weeks to mention the subdivision to him, the master plan with a powder room and the carport, and he had just looked at her and had shaken his head in disbelief, as if he couldn't believe she'd come up with such a crazy idea.

"What for?" Nolan had said, inspecting his hands for splinters from the wood he had just carried into the house. "Why would I sell the farm? It's been in my family for over two hundred years—and why would I move someplace where houses are so close you have no privacy whatsoever?" he said and threw the firewood on the floor where the logs scattered like they were about to play an angry game of pick-up-sticks. The baby would change him, she just knew it, would make him less agitated and less easily maddened, would turn him back into a kinder and softer person, the way he used to be, years ago.

This happened often now, Nolan losing his cool. Once in a fit of rage he had taken a bat to the clay pots on the back porch, smashed them to pieces right in front of her. Quinn could no longer remember what that was all about. Long past were the times when they'd sit on the front porch with their feet propped up, the nights when they'd go out to dinner and a movie. When they'd come home they'd sit in the truck and Nolan would put his arm around her and they'd kiss until their bodies were covered in a layer of sweat. No more picking paint colors and perfect spots for a swing and a sandbox as they listened to a dog bay in the distance.

By now it was difficult to pinpoint a specific moment of happiness, that's how long it had been, but eventually she uncovered the trail of a fleeting moment: the day Nolan gave her a yellow dress. Back then, Nolan still tried to make her happy. Still loved her.

"Open your eyes," Nolan had said and had looked at her with a grin from cheek to cheek.

A square box with a silk ribbon tied around it sat atop the bed. Quinn gently slid the silky strip off and lifted the top of the box. Tissue paper crinkled and then settled down. She unfolded it—left, right, top, bottom—and there lay the dress, neatly pressed and folded. Gripping it by the shoulders, she lifted it out of its cardboard home and held it up. The dress, a floral print on cream pale yellow background, was nothing like the musky and flimsy dresses from the secondhand stores she owned.

"It's beautiful," she said. Nolan *still* loved her then, he *still* cared for her, baby or no baby.

And there was a summer, it must have been the second summer on the farm, the year the frog population was out of control because the rain had continued far into the spring. Almost all the way through

May it had rained and the frogs were singing and croaking and grunting as Nolan put his arms around Quinn every night and that's how they'd fall asleep, holding each other, and everything was all right with the world. Nolan didn't even rule out getting a dog or two for the children they were going to have, and as soon as fall came around, he'd start building a playhouse in the backyard, one with a door and window shutters and a small bench in front of it. And if it was a boy, he'd build a tree house in that cypress tree by the fence because Quinn could watch him from the kitchen window. But nothing had turned out the way it was supposed to, nothing was as Quinn expected it to be, nothing was as Sigrid had told her it was going to be. There was more to life than being taken care of.

After she'd returned from Galveston, she had never told Nolan about the trip nor the baby, Holly, she had held at that beach, or how she had nestled into her arms. For that one moment she had completely forgotten about the darkest part of the forest where the hunters had done unspeakable things to her. It was as if by holding a baby the great forgetting had come over her, as if in the company of such innocence nothing evil could take hold, not even remotely materialize. A little baby was an antidote, so elfin and sweet, without sin. Quinn could only imagine how it must feel to have one of her own, but no, *no*, she had given up on having her own, but she could settle, could settle for less, for holding one that belonged to her. One that was all hers but not of her.

AFTER QUINN LEFT THE BANK, SHE TUCKED THE ENVELOPE UNDER the seat of the Ford truck. She felt giddy with excitement, her entire body seemed to hum, knowing she was going to see the old woman. There was no turning back—not after church last Sunday. Quinn had watched Nolan at the grocery store, how he'd stared at that girl who worked the register at the Market Basket, with her belly all swollen and her ankles unrecognizable. The way he had beheld her, the *want* written all over his face, his desperation coming off him like stink. It cut her—every single time Nolan stared at that cashier, it cut her.

And Quinn felt gawked at by the people around her, felt pinned down under a microscope. When she felt well, her stomach was flat as a board, and they stared, pity in their eyes. Quinn knew what they were thinking, that she was barren. Desolate. Sterile. And then she'd bleed and her belly would swell, and they'd smile at her, and then she'd skip a Sunday because she could hardly stand upright, and the Sunday after that, her stomach descended again, they'd lower their eyes, and pity it was all over again.

When Quinn reached the road leading into the woods, she expected to see a cottage tucked away, a line of trees around the house, vines trailing across porch rafters. She thought there'd be an herb garden with the scent of rosemary, pungent and pine-like, and sweet peas growing on homemade trellises made from willow branches. She had expected strange things hanging off trees, willow puppets and bottles filled with liquids and herbs, all the stuff locals talked about. Quinn was prepared, had money, and wasn't going to be turned away. She'd wait for her, even if it took hours.

Quinn stopped the car in front of a run-down trailer, warped and old, leaning into the wind in the middle of a clearing in a forest with mostly pines, juniper trees, and stunted shrubs by a tree line. She pondered if she should grab the envelope with the money but then decided to leave it tucked underneath the front seat. She hadn't told Nolan about coming here but Seymour, the old neighbor, probably suspected it, maybe even knew. The more questions she'd asked him that day, the more he'd paused before he'd answered, as if he knew what she was up to and didn't approve.

Quinn's heart beat in her chest like a feral animal as she approached the trailer. The garden to the right was nothing but chaotic shades of green dotted with pink and red and white, like a painting attempting to capture a mood rather than specific images. Hollyhocks were covered in an abundance of bees, and butterflies buzzed about, and most of the plants Quinn had never seen but some she recognized: spider flower and Rocky Mountain bee plant. St. John's wort, a staple of European doctors for depression and anxiety—Sigrid had sworn by it—and an abundance of a plant with long oval leaves. The bell-shaped flowers were purple with green tinges.

Quinn felt heat spread throughout her body. *How do I ask for something that hurts when I even mention it?* But this woman had done miracles and she could do one for her too. Holding the baby on the beach that day had been the antidote to all those demons chasing her—even the memory of the little body in her arms was almost as powerful as the moment itself had been, and if it had taught her nothing else, it taught her that there was hope. Nothing was ever lost; living her life with the constant memory of men violating her body, beating and humiliating her was not all she had left, it wasn't the end of things. If she thought it were, she might as well just give up.

"Who are you looking for?" The voice reached Quinn from below a willow bursting with leaves as if it was a giant drooping umbrella.

She was middle-aged, white, with freckled skin so pale that she appeared luminous. Her hair was long and colorless, like the redheads who don't turn gray but ashen as they age. Slipping her hand inside her jacket, the woman took out a pipe and a small satchel of tobacco. As if loading a gun, she pinched a batch of tobacco in the round opening, packing it evenly with her thumb, without so much as even looking down.

"What's your name?" was all Quinn could manage to get out. It sounded casual on the verge of being rude.

"My name?" Clamping the pipe between her teeth, the woman struck a wooden match on the deck, giving it time to burn back on the wood. Then hovering the match over the packed tobacco, she pulled the flame inward. "You've got some nerve walking on my property asking me my name."

"I'm Quinn. I meant no disrespect."

"Quinn. That's unusual." She was lost in thought as if she pondered the name. "Are you as wise as your name suggests?"

"I don't know about that," Quinn said as grand puffs of smoke curled around the woman's head and she detected an unfamiliar aroma swelling around her. "What do you want me to call you?"

"Aella."

"Is that Italian?"

"Could be."

To Quinn's right, a taut clothesline reached from the willow to the roof of the trailer. A rabbit hung on a hook off the line, head down, its legs covered in tiny nicks where the coat was cut to skin the hare. Blood, slow as molasses, dripped from its neck. Underneath, a litter of spattered kittens slurped the crimson blood out of a bowl.

"What do you want?"

Quinn had never thought about not being able to state her wish out loud. There was something about this woman, Aella, ashen hair and freckles like the Milky Way, strewn about haphazardly yet in perfect order that seemed to silence Quinn. There was no way she could just come out and tell her what she wanted.

"A reading," Quinn finally managed to get out. "I've heard you give readings. About the future. How much?"

"It doesn't cost anything. But you can give whatever you see fit. How much do you have?"

"I'll pay you ten dollars."

"Come closer." They sat at a small table underneath the willow. On a piece of white silky fabric, Aella cut a deck of cards twice, then laid out three. They were larger than regular playing cards, colorful, not at all like the card decks Quinn had seen. There was a queen on a throne in the middle, upside down. To the left a man with swords sticking out of his torso, his face distorted. Before Quinn could look at the third card, Aella had collected them and had reshuffled the entire deck. "Tell me why you're really here, Q."

"I can't," Quinn said before she even knew those words had come out of her mouth. "I just can't. Maybe we should just do the reading?"

"Sounds like it's a matter of life or death. You want somebody dead? Is that what this is?"

"No, no, I don't."

"So then what?" Aella paused, taking another hit from her pipe. "Where do you live?"

"Out on 2410, with my husband. Creel Hollow Farm."

"Oh," Aella said and cocked her head. "He knows you're here?"

"No."

"You have children?"

"Not yet," Quinn tried to keep her voice steady but failed. "No," she added, "no children."

"He running around on you?"

"No, he's a good man."

"A good man," Aella chuckled. "All those Creels have their heads in the clouds. If it wasn't for that farm going from one to the other, they'd be living under a bridge."

"We might sell the farm and move to one of those new houses, with carpet and a garage."

"A Creel not living on a farm, I don't know. What's he into, your husband?"

"I don't know what you mean."

"His granddaddy ran a rabbit-breeding operation during the Depression. He didn't have the heart to kill them or eat them, so that venture didn't turn out well. Nolan's daddy went off to work in the Ford factory up in Dallas for a while. Then he planted an orchard and took up painting. He painted fruit, mainly. A banana here and there, grapes, but mainly apples. His wife put a match to the barn one day, burning all the paintings. There were hundreds of them. Set fire to herself in the process. At least that's the story I've heard."

Quinn knew nothing about the Creel family history, but there was an area in the barn, covered in tarps. She had never bothered to look underneath.

"Set fire to herself?" Quinn said, crinkling her forehead. "Never heard that story."

"Those Creel men, they always come out on top, it seems like."

"Nolan went to college."

"Did he now?"

"Yes, he's a lawyer."

"Be that as it may, he should have an office downtown then. The Creel name goes a long way in this town. But you never answered my question."

Quinn cocked her head. "What was the question?"

"What's he doing now? He's not breeding rabbits. He's not painting apples. What's he doing?"

"Running the farm," Quinn lied.

"Your time's up."

"You never told me what you saw in the cards," Quinn insisted.

"You didn't come for a reading is what the reading told me. And that you lie a lot."

"About what?"

"About what's in your heart. About why you came here."

"He's not doing much of anything. He spends a lot of time in the shed. He won't tell me what he's doing in there," Quinn said, her hands folded in her lap.

Aella laughed, musically, as if she was repeating a melody. "From rabbits to fruit, to some shed. You could just go and look, you know?" She yawned, exposing tiny yellow teeth. And like an arsonist coming back to smell the ashes she said, "You seem very nervous, like you're hiding something. Are you going to tell me what you want from me?"

"Yes," Quinn said but didn't go on.

"I have rosemary for blood pressure, Aloe Vera for digestion, echinacea for infections. Any herb you can imagine. Tell me what ails you."

Quinn remained silent.

"Q., you have to talk to me. I've heard it all before—trust me when I tell you I've heard it all before. And some."

"I need your help," Quinn said after a slight pause. "I want to have a baby."

There was a long silence during which Aella smoked while Quinn watched her. There, she had made her declaration, had said it out loud. No going back now.

Finally Aella spoke. "You go to church?"

"Every Sunday."

"Why don't you ask your god for a baby? Why come to me?"

"He hasn't been listening."

"So your god is all out of answers then?"

"Yes. Yes he is."

"It's gonna cost you."

"I have money. I have lots of money."

"That's not what I'm talking about." Aella chuckled. "It's gonna cost you in other ways."

"I understand."

"Do you?"

"Just tell me what I need to do. I'll do anything for a baby." Despite her pounding heart Quinn smiled at Aella.

"First of all I need you to understand what you're asking for."

"I know what I'm asking for. I want a baby."

"Here we go already. That's vague. Very vague. You need to go home and think about this."

"I know what I want. I don't care how, all I want is a baby."

"I know what you want but you don't know what it takes. Let me see your hands."

Quinn extended both hands, palms up, toward Aella, who took them in hers, her thumbs rubbing gently over the ridges and lines. Aella leaned forward, some of her hair suddenly static like the spikes of a dandelion. A flow of words emerged from Aella's mouth, words unknown to Quinn, sharp and high-pitched as if accompanied by clanging cymbals. Then Aella wiped Quinn's palms with her own.

"How much money do you have?"

Quinn mentioned an amount that would just about deplete the stash in the envelope.

"Do you know the moon phases?"

"I do," Quinn said, remembering that Nolan had told her about being superstitious when it came to setting fences; how they must be cut during the dry, waning moon to stay straighter, while wooden shingles will lie flat if cut during the dark of the moon.

"Come back on the first night of the full moon. And write down what I'm about to tell you. I need you to bring a few things."

Quinn scrambled through her purse, pulling out an old gas station receipt, and started writing. The first three things seemed easy enough. When Aella named the fourth, Quinn paused the pen.

"I told you there was a price to pay. And if that troubles you"— Aella pointed at the paper—"I can't help you. Because that's only the beginning. Like I said, come back with the money and the items on the list. First day of a new moon. Or don't come at all." Quinn watched Aella empty the pipe by thumping it against the willow tree. "Asking for a life to be given isn't for the faint of heart. A life isn't free. You make a pact and that's that."

Quinn's fingers moved across the paper, wondering if a lifetime of penance but no deliverance was the worst life she could imagine. The thought of Nolan, the blueprint of the house she wanted to live in— she could almost feel the fluffy carpet beneath her feet, could smell the fresh paint—her longing, and she decided it was all worth it.

"Okay," Quinn said finally. "If that's what it takes. I'll do it."

Seventeen

AELLA

ALL the Bujny women were born during thunderstorms. There was pressure in the air and a rumbling in the sky as they were pushed from their mothers' wombs. The Bujnys were crazy, Aella had heard it all her life, but she doubted one could just blame it on the women. *They knew how to pick 'em,* her grandmother used to say, *them* as in husbands, and therefore crazy came from both sides of the family.

Aella's father had killed a man. *In cold blood,* they said. It started out as nothing, really, an argument, a harsh word here, an even harsher response, just a comment the man made while in a drunken stupor and her daddy didn't let it go. He wasn't good at letting go. The judge said he knew what he was doing as opposed to it being some sort of crime of passion, but Aella wasn't so sure about that. She believed that taking any life demanded passion of some sort, maybe not the raving mad kind of passion in the moment, but her daddy had a kind of passion that can fester and turn into something else altogether, like hot air and cool air meeting and before you know it, there was something dangerous brewing.

"But never mind that story about my daddy," Aella said when people asked. "That was a long time ago and no one cares about that anymore."

Her great-grandmother came from Poland and settled in the

mountains of Appalachia. Aella asked her often what made her pick those mountains and she said that when you leave the soil and the trees and the mountains of your homeland, you try to find a place to live that reminds you of where you came from. The Germans went to the Midwest, while the Russians went to the Northeast. Neither one of them could quit the snow and the howling winds and long nights and dark days. They would have withered away in Florida or Texas or Louisiana—too much humidity and heat to bear for someone who's got the tundra and the German forests in their bones. Her grandmother told her of Poland and that it used to be covered in forests, almost ninety percent of it.

Ever since Aella could remember, her mother used to sit by the fire and sing strange songs—Polish, she assumed, but she'd never known her to speak her native language—and she'd measure a leather strip by multiplying the length of her forearm. She'd knot the string and tie objects inside the knots, sometimes feathers, or bones, willow branches, rocks. And she'd sing, her voice growing louder with every knot, and then she'd end up with a long rope and she'd hang it by the fireplace. Sometimes those strings disappeared overnight; sometimes she'd undo one knot per day and then throw it in a nearby creek.

Neither her mother nor her grandmother ever worked a day in their lives the way people think one ought to work, backbreaking labor and such, but they made do. They stared at the bottom of teacups and made salves from plants she wasn't allowed to touch. Townspeople gave them food, produce, money, or anything they asked for. Those songs and feathers and bones were part of her childhood like other children read Bible stories and people pray the rosary.

All the women in Aella's family had gifts. Her grandmother was a healer of wounds, making warts and scars disappear in the time it takes an ice cube to melt in the sun.

Her mother was a seer. She knew everything about someone by looking at them; the mailman couldn't hide his love for another man even though everyone envied his wife and thought him devoted to her. The butcher's daughter hid her pregnancy but Aella's mother knew that her cousin was the father. When the dentist told her he wanted to move to Florida, she told him not to travel in the month of August. He didn't listen and died in an accident.

The most God-fearing people trusted her with her opinion and called upon her in their hours of need. Aella accompanied her as she burned incense beside dead bodies and then opened windows to allow the smoke to escape while draping all mirrors so the ghosts of the dead wouldn't linger. "The dead sometimes remain and nothing good has ever come from sticking around and some don't know when to leave, even after they're dead," Aella's mother said. "And without the proper actions, and I'm not talking about a horseshoe hanging upright above the front door, nothing will nudge the spirits along."

Eventually Aella settled in Aurora. It was never meant to be home, just a place to stay for a while.

One day a woman came along, Q. she called her, for she had an uncommon name that Aella could never recall. She was good with names and faces, never forgot anyone who had come to her for help. Yet Q.'s name eluded her as if there was a part of her she couldn't grasp, some sort of fracture. Life had broken her, fragmented her in body and mind. There was more than one of her, she made Aella fidget, made her nervous.

She read Q.'s palms then and she understood. The lines in both hands were identical and Aella had never seen such a thing in all her years of people shoving their hands toward her. The left hand showed what a person was born with but the right one told what kind of a person they had become and Q. was all fate.

Nothing lost, nothing gained; it was all set in stone.

Eighteen

DAHLIA

THE day after the fire Bobby and I return to the farmhouse. This time we drive through the line of trees and we park by the front porch, as if we've returned home after a day's work. We approach the cypress tree; it's the mounds we are interested in.

The tree hasn't tolerated the drought well and has shed its needles. It sits naked and barren. Behind it, the warped wooden fence has seen better days; the planks nailed loosely to a frame that is just as frail as everything else on the property. I imagine one good kick, maybe just someone leaning against it, and it will probably topple over. What holds it together are dry ivy shoots that made their way through the cracks and gaps in the wood, wrapping themselves around its worn planks like knotted snakes. We stand and consider the mounds, their perfect oval shapes, how deep the cracks in the soil are underneath the grass growing over them.

I tell Bobby the farm is in my mother's name and his eyes widen. He stews on it for a while.

"This is your mother's farm? Why didn't you tell me that last time you dragged me here?"

"I didn't know then."

"What's going on with her anyway? What's the doctor saying?"

"Physically, she's fine. It's just a matter of adjusting her medication.

They don't want her catatonic nor climbing up the walls. At least she can't start fires while she's in the hospital." I sound callous and I feel a tinge of guilt, but then I relax. "She'll be home in a day or two according to her doctor."

"Have you asked her about this farm?"

"First chance I get, I'll bring it up, trust me," I say.

Bobby scans the surroundings, shaking his head.

"These mounds, Dahlia. They don't look natural judging by everything else being pretty much flat," Bobby says. "It's not recent, that's for sure. I don't know what it is."

I reach for his hand. He holds it as if I'm breakable and even though my hand disappears into his, I know that he's at ease with the small and fragile things of this world. For a moment I feel like I belong here, always have, as if there's some long-forgotten connection to him and this place that I've denied all these years. Maybe it's just the land. This farm is a threshold, a forgotten place in time that has some sort of a hold on me. It's not that I remember it—there's no recollection of anything, not the structures, not the property—yet is feels as if the farm remembers me, as if the air is buzzing and I can't escape it regardless of how hard I try. If even for a second I manage to shake off its pull, it finds me again around the next corner, just to remind me it's been here all along.

"I need you to do something for me," I say and lean into him. I feel like Eve offering Adam the red apple, seductively stroking its red skin.

"Do something for you?" he repeats and for a split second I think he's going to kiss me.

I want it as much as he does, yet what I don't want are complications. I wouldn't think twice if I planned to leave town in a week or so, if I had a life waiting for me somewhere else—then I'd want to know how it feels to kiss the guy I was friends with, the subtle familiarity paired with the excitement of a spontaneous . . . what? Fling? I know there's a certain power I have over Bobby, a power I've always had, something everybody around us picked up on. I can't deny that I want to feel his lips on mine.

"Break down the door for me," I say. "I want to go inside."

He ponders it, I can tell. I handed him the apple; he wonders what it tastes like. He too wants to know about this place.

"Come tomorrow I have to be out of the house, remember?" Even I hear the sarcasm in my voice. "I can't play this game anymore, Bobby. I can't live in another motel. If this is my mother's farm, we might as well live here. At least for now."

We are caught up in this moment, this hint of the past and the present, and so Bobby says nothing, doesn't even take a second to think about it, but turns and makes for the front door, grabs the knob, and pushes the door with this shoulder. Just like before, nothing happens. He puts all his weight into it. The door shifts—there's now a visible gap between it and the frame—but the hinges hold tight as if they refuse to give way.

"I don't want to destroy the whole frame. I have tools in the car. Wait here," Bobby says and disappears down the porch steps.

I step closer to the door and run my fingers across the frame. There's a lighter patch where something is missing, like an old knocker. The wood has hairline cracks allowing the post to seep through from the inside outward.

A weariness overcomes me. Entering the farmhouse seems bold and heartless and evokes a kind of unpleasantness that stops me in my tracks. I feel as if I am intruding somehow, disturbing something that didn't ask to be disturbed. I find myself shivering in the summer heat. I no longer feel giddy with anticipation—the fact that we are about to enter suddenly doesn't feel right at all.

"Maybe we shouldn't do this?" I say when Bobby returns from the car with a tire iron in his right hand. My head is buzzing like a beehive and the colors around me are off, covering the world like a lace veil of pastel psychedelic cutwork.

"Okay, Dahlia, what is it going to be?" Bobby sounds almost impatient, as if he's talking about us and not the door he's about to break down. "Let's just do this. Step back," he says.

Bobby inserts the tire iron between the frame and the lock and wiggles it about. Then he hands it to me and gives the door one more shove. It screeches on its hinges, gives in, and flings wide open. It hits the wall on the inside.

I step over the threshold. *Step* isn't the right word; it seems like it's more a crossing over, as if I'm progressing from one state of being to another, immediately feeling the energy of the house, its abandoned walls and its shrieking floors. The air is hot and stale, and there is something unsettling about it, as if there's a familiarity that takes me back to a place I no longer remember.

The stagnant air smells of dust and wood, but more than the individual scents that cumulate into a thickness and heaviness, it contains an entire lifetime of scents that have gathered in this small foyer, the place where people come and go, take off and pull on shoes, prepare to step outside or inside, from one place to another. There's a woolen rug in the middle of the foyer and when I step on it, I can hear a slight crunching sound beneath my feet.

Bobby's phone rings and I hear his voice in the background, talking, pausing, talking.

"Dahlia," he suddenly calls out to me from the porch, his voice urgent and serious.

I don't answer—I'm almost annoyed by the disruption.

"Work. I have to leave."

I suck in the aroma of the wood and the walls to enhance the images but it doesn't help much. I struggle—maybe it's the fact that I'm cueing into someone else's life—but then I get an image of an upstairs room. I know better, *know* I've never been here before—and maybe the house reminds me of passing through for a borrowed moment in time and the scent of dry cardboard turning to dust, something I seem to remember from the moves during my childhood.

He's asking me to let the house go and move on but I can't. It's less than a memory but more than a dream.

AT HOME, I STARE AT THE PAPERS ON THE WALL—MY JANE, THE composite—and as if I'm seeing them for the first time, I recognize a familiarity in the image tucked under the wall mirror. The composite. I stand still and stare at the face. It's a juxtaposition of individual facial parts—lips, nose, cheeks, chin, forehead—and as I stare at myself in the mirror, my face and the composite merge into one. The same dark hair, full lips, large teeth, thick eyebrows. I look *like* her. No one can deny the similarities. Or do I just see myself in her?

This has to stop. I recognize the madness in all this, this preoccupation with Jane and this nameless woman who is no one, really. Am I replacing my Jane with a composite that I believe to look like me? My entire life is a spiral, nothing leads up or down, just in circles—coming here was a mistake, maybe having left in the first place was too. I'm exactly where I was fifteen years ago, as if I'm incapable of choosing a wiser way.

I take down the papers off the wall, bundle them up, tempted to rip them in half. Just when I'm about to tear a newspaper article to shreds, I pause. I don't know why, but my eyes skim over it. There, those words. They catch my eye. That name. I see the letters and then they blur. My hands steady, and I read it again. *Creel.*

MAN BOOKED FOR RESISTING ARREST AFTER REPORTING DISAPPEARANCE OF A WOMAN

Aurora, December 12, 1985
A man by the name of Delbert Humphrey appeared at the Aurora police station claiming his girlfriend, a woman known to him only as "Tee," had gone missing after he looked for the woman at the Creel Hollow Farm in Aurora. Two deputies questioned Humphrey extensively but even the police chief, Griffin Haynes, was unable to make sense of his story. Questioned further, Humphrey admitted he was not licensed to drive a vehicle and he was also unable to produce a photograph of the missing woman. He did, however, offer a pencil drawing of her. When the police doubted his story, he insisted on a sketch artist. A composite was rendered of the mystery woman . . .

Creel Hollow Farm. My mind flips. It's like I've stepped onto a staircase but every time I start to climb, I end up in the same place: Creel Hollow Farm. There's no further mention of any residents being questioned. No mention of anything but a farm that is in my mother's name.

I can't make sense of it. I stuff the composite and printouts in a nearby box. I take one more look around—there's no need to spend another night here. Followed by Tallulah, I grab the box from the counter.

On the ride to the farm, I look over at her, curled up on the passenger's seat. Something stirs inside of me. She was abandoned and dumped, minutes from stretching out on a cold concrete floor with a needle in her vein to stop her breathing. Maybe it's not just her, but also Jane and the forgotten woman without a photograph: they are special to me because they are lost. Do I collect the forgotten to make them relevant somehow? Because in a twisted way being lost feels familiar to me?

I snap out of my thoughts and reach for my phone. I need police files, about my Jane and the composite. Just as I dial Bobby's number, I see that I have eight missed calls. All of them from the same number.

"I'M GLAD YOU COULD MAKE IT ON SUCH SHORT NOTICE," DR. Wagner says between mouse clicks, the privacy screen making it impossible for me to make out anything, especially with that angle. Dr. Wagner's features are tense; he's making less eye contact than usual. "I'm not going to sugarcoat this, Dahlia. The MRI showed some suspicious activity. The EEG confirmed you had a mild seizure during the test."

"I don't remember any seizure," I say and fight the urge to turn the screen toward me and study the test results myself.

"The easiest way to explain this is that damage to nerves in a specific area can cause the brain to incorrectly function, creating odors that are not there. A phantom odor, hence the name phantosmia. It is connected to seizure activity. You told me you fell in the woods and hit your head. The smells you experience, the passing out, the"—he pauses slightly as if he's unsure—"the visions, Dahlia. We need to talk about your visions."

"What about them?"

"They could be related to your injury." He leans forward in his chair, pushing files and pens and paperwork out of the way. "Phantosmia is a condition that results in olfactory hallucinations, a sensory perception of something that has no basis in reality. The perception of a scent in the complete absence of any odor. And sometimes visions."

"All because I hit my head?"

"Possibly. I'm only going to talk to you about this in general terms. I need you to make an appointment with the neurologist before you leave here. You have to promise me to follow up on this? I was worried when you didn't return my calls."

"I was busy. I'm still confused though—"

"For one, please always return my calls. Second, I'm writing you a prescription for anti-seizure medication. Go to the nearest water fountain after you leave the pharmacy and take the meds immediately. The neurologist will be able to answer your questions in depth. Third, let me explain the basics, okay? One of the most common and well-documented causes for phantosmia are seizures. During seizures patients usually recollect having phantosmia just prior to blacking out."

I just look at him, puzzled.

"Your olfactory bulb produces odors and those odors cause your brain to seize. While some of them feel like a simple shadow or movement out of the corner of your eye, it is much more serious than you might feel during those moments. There will be a progression as to the severity of the seizures. They are going to get worse, culminating in a temporal lobe seizure."

The scents. The snow. The ghostly woman at the farm. It *felt* real. Like sitting here feels real. I can feel the chair beneath my body, my feet on the ground, the car keys in my hand. "Because I fell?" is all I can think of asking.

"That's the thing. We are not sure. It seems that way."

"Okay?" There seem to be consequences beyond what he's saying. There is more. I can tell.

"We can't really confirm the injury from the fall, not at this point. What I'm trying to say is we *know* you fell, you hit your head, and you chipped your tooth, but how that's related to the scents and the visions you told me about, we can't be sure about that." A slight pause. "The second leading cause of phantosmia are neurological disorders such as schizophrenia, with well-documented cases of hallucinations, most commonly visual and auditory."

Schizophrenia.

I watch Dr. Wagner, transfixed; his mouth is moving, but I can't hear him. My ears ring, tune out everything else. A realization hits me. Not like a brick, but more like ten thousand bricks all at once. I want to laugh out loud, from the gut, the kind of outburst that makes you throw back your head and just bellow out *I'm not hearing voices.* Not like that, not like voices telling me what to do. I don't care what he says. This is happening for a reason, and mental illness isn't it. I seem to understand what he's saying now—no, not *seem to*, I understand him just right. His words no longer reach me but there's a logic and a torrent of implications. *It's because of my mother.* I turn it any which way I can. Finally. The words escape my mouth in the form of a croaking sound.

"You say this because of my mother."

"In no way does your mother—"

"If you didn't know my mother, would you still tell me what you just told me? From falling in the woods, from seeing and smelling things to schizophrenia, that's a leap. I think you're assuming there's a possibility that I am schizophrenic *because of my mother.*"

"I did not say that, Dahlia. I'm not making a diagnosis as to your mental state in relation to your mother's behavior. But the fact that you regard this as a 'gift' gives me cause for concern."

"There's much more you need to know. I haven't told you everything yet. I found this article about a man who reported a woman missing, decades ago. There's no picture of her, but they drew up a composite, well, maybe not a drawing but like they combined facial features—anyway, I had her picture on a wall, not just hers, Jane's too, and this composite woman, and get this: *I look just like her.* I should've brought the papers but I'm moving and they are in a box, you know the fire I told you about? I've had lots of memories lately, lots. About growing up, moving, taking off in the middle of the night, but the more everything comes back to me, the more I believe that . . ." That *what?*

I'm just making this worse. Dr. Wagner's eyes are wide and borderline empathetic. *Look at the crazy woman rambling on,* they seem to say. Did I just mention visions and that I favor a woman who disappeared decades ago? I take a deep breath in and gather myself. I even feel my spine straighten, as if better posture is going to make him believe me.

"Look, I'll be happy to see a neurologist, but for now I need to stew on this for a while."

"I understand." He checks his watch, then takes off his glasses and starts polishing them with a cloth. "Get those meds and take them immediately. Make an appointment on your way out, okay?"

"I will," I lie.

I go by the pharmacy and I get the meds but I don't make an appointment. Not just yet.

As I make my way across the parking lot, I feel more determined than ever. There's something there, I just know it, and I'm not giving up. Any other day I would have dwelled on what he told me, but today I'm not. Funny how quickly I can overwrite *schizophrenia* and just push it aside. I'm not one of those people who stand on a street corner yelling about Jesus or demons chasing me. I am not a maniac running around with no consideration for tomorrow. I've been living on my own since I was eighteen. I *don't* believe there's a serial killer on the loose, I *don't* believe there's some secret society enslaving women, I just happen to believe that certain people around me are less than forthcoming with the truth. Like my mother. And there's *nothing* crazy about that.

Nineteen

MEMPHIS

MEMPHIS had time to collect herself during the last stay in the hospital. She'd made mistakes. First she had lost the purse, and then there was the fire. All those papers, random photographs and documents, she couldn't keep them in order, didn't know which to burn, which to keep. The yellow flames were obedient in the beginning, barely singeing the papers' edges, but then she became impatient and doused them in nail polish remover and it splashed across the floor and the orange flames went out of control. The curtain caught fire, black smoke started to choke her, and she helplessly watched the flames leap around her. She became oddly tranquil then, pondered locking the door, letting it all go up in flames, including herself. But then Dahlia pulled her out of the smoke and managed to open a window. Fire trucks came and Memphis never was able to check on those papers, which ones had been consumed, which ones had survived.

And now Dahlia is taking her to the farm. Memphis stares straight ahead with all the indifference she can muster. If it wasn't for the pills keeping her even-keeled and mellow, Memphis wasn't sure what she'd do. Her body recognizes every turn, every inch of every road, every pothole. Mile marker 78 will come up in no time. Dahlia must have done some digging, found out about the farm. That was Dahlia's way, a constant inquiring and digging to get answers.

If it hadn't been for the crickets, those godforsaken crickets—last year's toad plague hadn't stirred up anything, even though the roads had been dotted with their flattened bodies like large pieces of gum— she wouldn't have panicked, wouldn't have lost her purse and her cool, she would have gone back home without Dahlia noticing, but no, that night the crickets chirped, like fireworks they started exploding all around her. As she stared at the cypress tree, the chirping ripped at her eardrums and it all came back and panic started festering and by then it was too late. She had already begun to fall apart. The moment she had arranged the dead crickets on her living room floor to hear intruders step on their parched and barren bodies, she knew there was no turning back.

In the daylight Memphis realizes that the area looks the same but is also different; it's all there, all of it, yet the roads have changed, there are white lines now, not the gravel and pothole road it used to be. *I'm in a time machine,* Memphis thinks, yet it's nothing like one would expect, no tunnels, not like she's squeezing through something too small for her body. Just a simple blink of the eyes and *poof.*

Memphis hears a voice reaching her from afar. Dahlia has been nagging lately, asking questions, going on and on about things she knows nothing about. Kids are cruel that way, greedy and selfish, only remembering what they want to.

Memphis isn't worried about Dahlia at all. The girl is strong, strong as an ox. She had raised her that way, to be tough and robust and sturdy, fending for herself. Resilient is what Dahlia is. Memphis wonders how much she had to do with who Dahlia is today, the girl who had left Aurora without so much as looking back, making a life for herself. But then she'd returned, out of the blue, after years of snubbing her nose at the town. That might be a remnant of those years they had traveled—the kindest word for dragging her across the country, really—and how they'd always left one place or another be- hind, and maybe one can only run for so long, leave so many times. Isn't Memphis herself proof of that, how there must be an end to all that running? Dahlia's return has caused the messy part, as if their separation was merely temporary: this child has called on fate to stomp its foot, determined to resolve itself.

Mistakes she'd made, at every turn it seemed like. They had left the farm behind so long ago, had left the town of Aurora, left Bertram County, and eventually she had put state lines between the farm and her—first New Mexico, then Nevada. Eventually they had ended up all the way in California. Only when their lives became unsustainable had she decided that they'd go back to where it all began.

Memphis has been on the run for so long, in hiding, cloaked, out of sight—all those words Dahlia would use if she still were the young girl lugging the old encyclopedia around, reciting definitions day in and day out—that this farm literally feels like coming home. The irony isn't lost on Memphis. It was done now; no more looking over her shoulder, no more flinching when the doorbell rings, no more arranging crickets so the crunching announces a visitor. None of that.

When the dirt road appears on the right, just a few yards farther down and behind the old wooden bench, Memphis can hardly make out the specific spot, even though she must had driven down that road hundreds of times. But the road is narrow now, overgrown, and all but invisible from the street. As the farmhouse appears at the end of the driveway, Memphis feels as if she's burning from the inside out and she scrambles to get her head in a better place. Any moment she'll crack and the voices she hears will stoke the fire she's been keeping at bay for all these years. She can only rein in those thoughts for so long, but her hands give it away, they are trembling and that's something new altogether. With each tremor there is a creak of the bones, and she fights to hang on.

Dahlia stops the car and kills the engine. She turns to check up on the dog and Memphis can't help but think that Dahlia is to blame. Not in a fault-assigning way, but by default—a flash of clarity combined with a dissipation of confusion—Dahlia is a reminder of deeds done, crimes committed, a constant token of all her wrongdoings. This very moment, on this farm, has been in the making, as if every breeze, every drop of rain, every falling leaf, over the past thirty years has led them here to this place today.

They get out of the car and the dirt underneath Memphis' feet seems more forgiving than it used to be, more cushioned, as if the years without any living soul setting foot on the property have softened the soil, made it more pliable somehow. She expects a dust devil to appear, the way they used to; unexpectedly there'd be a brown blur of dust, swirling about. Some say the dead appear that way to the living, transparent in a bronze haze. Memphis wants to chuckle but it's not a laughing matter. Boldly she turns.

There's the shed.

Suddenly she is not Memphis any longer, but the woman she used to be a lifetime ago, the way she was so eager to please, and *that* woman allows Dahlia to drag her toward the shed. "Come on," Dahlia says and takes her mother's hand, pulling her from the car, "let's have a look around."

Don't go in there, Memphis wants to say to Dahlia, *don't go in that shed. It's haunted.* But the words won't drop from her lips.

And she sighs, unbeknownst to Dahlia, a sigh that signals the end of a deliberate effort on her part to remain vigilant—an effort she had been holding on to like pruney hands to a lifesaver at sea—and her true deterioration begins.

Memphis feels a layer of herself crack, hairline thin for now, but soon she won't be able to contain all that has been cooped up inside of her for all these years. Suddenly she sees the way the world is, some sort of divine epiphany has been bestowed upon her—the farm isn't just a decrepit old house but a state of being. And it will do her in.

Twenty

DAHLIA

'VE feared this moment but here we are. I want to pull over, take her hand in mine, and gently ease into the subject, but then I don't. My mother knows she owns the farm, and that's not the part that's hard for me to talk about. She doesn't want others in her business—not even me, her own daughter—but here we are, like it or not, and I need to know how the transfer of an estate of this magnitude came about and if it relates to the life we lived.

"You packed up the entire house?" my mother asks, hands folded in her lap.

"Most of it is in storage. Some of it is at the new place."

"Where is the new place?" she asks.

Why did she leave this farm behind? Why the secrecy? As much as she wants to believe that her vagabond ways were a notion of freedom, it was the opposite. Yes, we were able to pack up and leave, stuff our belongings in a trunk and the backseat of whatever car she owned at the time, and just move on, but there was one thing we never had: options. We were *free* by all accounts, *free* as in *untethered*, but we weren't free to choose where to live, where to work. We had to live where no credit checks or references from prior landlords were required. My mother worked jobs that required no skill and probably no W-2s, or any kind of résumé. We were free within the limited means of the lifestyle her poor choices imposed on us. Yes, owning the farm poses a question. The transferred deed is another thing altogether. I imagine legal ramifications, but I won't know until I ask.

How do I start? *No need to freak out, but . . . I know that you know where we're going. Why is this place in your name? Who is Quinn Creel and how did you get her to give you an entire farm?* I've rehearsed this in my mind, more than once, have weighed the pros and cons of honesty versus sugarcoating, and I decided to just allow it to play out.

"So, here's the thing," I say as I look straight ahead, giving the road more attention than it actually needs. I feel anger at the fact that she acts as if she's oblivious to where we are. I tell her how I found her purse, and the cricket jars, one in the window on the farm and the other under her sink. I tell her about the deed from the courthouse, and the one among the charred remains of the fire she set. "Creel Hollow Farm," I add.

Not a word comes out of her mouth. She stares at the landscape passing us by, the town behind us by then, fields like a checkered quilt of squares, an occasional fence separating the green from yellow, brown from gold. She begins to tremble. Not an all-out shaking of her body—more like a silent tremor, from the inside out.

I tell her that she owes me the truth.

She continues to stare straight ahead. I allow her to remain in that silence, allow her to work out whatever needs working out, hoping she's aligning the facts in her mind.

As we drive down the dirt road, she shifts in her seat and her eyes scan the surroundings as if she's on the lookout for something.

When we arrive at the farm, she is calm except for the persistent tremor of her hands. She seems to be able to keep her body under control, yet her hands escape her.

My mother gets out of the car and makes straight for the porch, pulls out a fan from her purse. It is ornately carved with a black tassel dangling at the end of it. I wonder where she buys this stuff. She wears a dress and full makeup; she even painted her nails—sloppily, yet they are painted. She continues to fan herself. The motion of the fan renders her face blurry, like an ill-taken photograph.

"Is there electricity?" she asks as if that's the requirement for her to stay. She's trying to camouflage her trembling but I know her well, at least the anxious parts of her: her hands are what she can't hide, even while fanning herself.

"Yes, there's electricity," I say. "I'll get a couple of window units to cool the place down." After I find a job, that is. I can always clean houses, maybe get a subcontract at a local school. Things need cleaning; there's job security in the messes people make. "The plumber should show up any moment," I add and scan the road.

Having electricity restored was an easy feat, but the water is a problem I haven't figured out yet. I thought it'd be as simple as calling the city and asking them to turn on the water but I was told that there's no record of the Creel Hollow Farm ever having received water from the municipality and that there must be a well on the farm.

We both look up as a white van with blue letters roars up the driveway, unsuccessful in avoiding potholes. A ladder strapped to the top of the van bounces and slides about but stays put.

The plumber touches the rim of his hat as he passes my mother, who has her legs crossed and the fan on her lap. "Ma'am," he says and I'm aware that he's checking out her still slim and tanned legs. She's always been attractive, and she still is, even though she's in her sixties.

He inspects the well by the barn—a casing sticking up about a foot out of the ground—then returns to his truck to retrieve tools and parts. He agrees to mail the bill and I breathe a sigh of relief.

"Here's the thing," I say to my mother after he leaves. I sit next to her on the porch, a dirty jar from underneath the kitchen counter in hand. "He exchanged parts and we have running water but we need to have the quality tested."

She continues to fan herself, staring to her right, where the meadow is in full bloom with a carpet of wildflowers.

"I need to find a clean container for the water sample. Any ideas?"

"Just use a plastic bottle," she says.

"Let's see if there's something in the shed we can use?" I insist.

"I'm not setting foot in that shed. For all I know it'll collapse on top of us. I doubt it's safe to go in there."

"I don't have a water bottle that fits into the casing. All I have are gallon containers, and they are too big." She can't argue with that and she doesn't, just stares off into the distance. "Mom," I say, gently now. "I don't know what the big deal is. Just help me find a clean jar. You know your way around here, don't you?" *Know your way around* might be the right choice of words. Not *You should know what's in that shed*, or *You know all about this farm*, or *Tell the truth already*, but a generic statement, hopefully coaxing her out of her shell.

"You can test water from the faucet. Why that man told you to collect from the well, I have no clue, but he doesn't know what he's talking about." She wipes some invisible specks of dust off her dress but makes no attempt to get up and follow me.

"Just help me look," I say and turn my back to her.

I hear the *snick-snick-snick* of the lighter. Then I smell smoke.

"I'll look by myself then," I say.

"Suit yourself."

The shed is about twenty by twenty feet, covered in a red, rusty color, roofed with shingles. There are two small windows on each side of the door but they don't seem to be the opening kind, as if glass panes were used to skimp on building material and were smacked in between the wood panels making up the walls. The door is warped and there's a heavy-duty drop latch below a door pull. It looks rusted and the warped wood has pulled it into a contorted state of being, no longer horizontal, as if the wood of this damned shed holds power to forge metal. I try to wiggle the latch but it's stuck. I look around for a tool of some sort, even a sturdy branch to get the latch to lift, but the only tree is a meek and knotted sapling with leaves as spiky as thorns.

"Dahlia." I hear my mother's voice from behind me. "Come here. Hurry."

"I need to open this lock, it's completely stuck," I say as I shimmy the lock. I turn around. My mother's face seems out of sorts, her forehead wrinkled, her nose slightly curled upward.

"Something's wrong with your dog. She's collapsed."

I run toward the house and see Tallulah in the dirt, flat on her side. I fall to my knees and pet her head, realizing that her ears are burning up. I check her body for any sings of injury or snakebites, but I can't find any. Her eyes are open, staring straight ahead. I think heatstroke but remember her napping in the shade of the porch earlier and that I refilled her water bowl twice.

"I need to take her to the vet," I say and scoop her up. Her weight makes me stumble but I manage to get her into the backseat.

As I drive off, in the review mirror, I see my mother on the porch, lighting another cigarette, lazily blowing smoke out of the side of her mouth.

IT TAKES MERE SECONDS FOR A MALE TECHNICIAN IN MAGENTA scrubs to take Tallulah from my arms. Another tech appears and she leads me into a room with posters of dog breeds and a small sink. I'm close to tears and we check off Tallulah's medical history.

In one word: unknown. *Yes*, she's been eating and drinking, *no*, there wasn't any strange behavior before the collapse, *yes*, she's been going to the bathroom, *no*, there was no diarrhea.

"Her ears are hot. She might have a fever," I say and wipe the tears off my cheeks.

"How long have you had her?" the tech asks, her eyes big, her voice low and calming.

"I adopted her from the pound a few days ago."

"Did she get into the garbage?"

"Not that I know of."

"Was she out in the heat when she collapsed?"

"Yes, outside. We live on a farm," I say, surprised how easy those words come off my lips.

"Any snakes around?"

"No."

"What did she do right before she collapsed?"

"She napped in the shade."

"Was she walking around right before, acting normal?"

"Yes."

"The doctor will be right with you, okay?"

She leaves the room and I sit on the bench staring at the posters on the wall. Within seconds a short freckled female vet in a white coat and Mary Janes enters the room.

"She's stable right now. We are giving her fluids. I did an exam and felt hardening around her uterus. It could be a tumor. We are about to do an ultrasound, but I need a signature from you."

She folds down a small wall-mounted table and checks off every single item once I nod. Between the exam, the ultrasound, and possible surgery, I'm looking at over one thousand dollars I don't have.

"Usually we sedate and do an X-ray but she's in no shape to go under right now. We'll know more after the ultrasound, okay?"

I have no idea how to pay for this bill and I still don't have running water at the farm, and the one check coming my way is already spent on the plumber.

"You can wait or we can give you a call later?"

"I'll wait," I say. "Do you offer a payment plan?"

"The ladies up front will assist you with that," she says and gathers the paperwork.

Later, as I sift through paperwork and tediously sign and initial page after page, I hear the receptionist call my name. The doctor appears, asking me to step back into the same room I was in earlier. My heart sinks as I watch her face. It's blank.

I see a tablet propped up on the folding table with a picture of an ultrasound. I can clearly recognize a rib cage and hip joints. Toward the back, tucked off to the side, is what seems like a half-moon made up of tiny nuggets.

"This here," the vet says and drags the tip of her finger across the screen, "is Tallulah's pelvis. And this"—she drags the half-moon shape apart and enlarges it—"is the mummified remains of a puppy she never delivered."

I stare at the tablet.

"See, she was pregnant at one point and delivered a litter but one remained in her womb. It is very small and would have been stillborn, judging by the size of it, but she never delivered it. It was small enough not to cause any problems, but her body was unable to absorb it. She developed an infection."

"That's horrible" is all I can think of saying.

"We have to operate as soon as she is stable enough."

"How much," I say, my voice raspy.

"About fifteen hundred." She pauses. "If you want to go through with it. I can't make any promises but I believe that she'll be just fine after and her chances of a complete recovery are promising."

"Yes," I say and feel my hands tense up around the paperwork I am holding. "Go ahead with the operation as soon as possible."

"All right. Give me a number where I can reach you. We have to do some blood work but if everything comes back normal, I expect to do the surgery late today or tomorrow morning. For now we have to get her stabilized and hydrated."

After I leave the vet, I drive toward Aurora City Hall's water department. It has a small window with a sign reading *Pay Water Bill Here.* I explain the condition of the well to the man behind the counter. He tells me collecting the water from the tap is sufficient.

"It's free, right?" I ask, counting the days until I can pick up my last check. Today might be a good day to pay attention to *Help Wanted* signs.

"The city will test private well water for free, yes." The man behind the counter is rotund, his nose red. "There's some paperwork you have to fill out," he adds and disappears. He returns just as suddenly with a cardboard clipboard in his hand. "The city of Aurora tests for nitrates and bacteria. If you want water tested for pesticides or organic chemicals you have to use private laboratories that are certified to do drinking water tests. There's a list I can give you."

He pushes the clipboard toward me.

When I leave City Hall, on my way back to the farm, I drive by the Filling Station. It's a hangout spot for local teens and also the only gas station with a convenience store and an arcade. It's the same gas station where I met Bobby before I took him out to the farm, and today, again, his cruiser is sitting in the parking lot. It's backed in, trunk toward the front door.

As I pull in, I catch a glimpse of the Lark Inn, a motel across the street. The motel was once a run-of-the-mill motel but at some point during the past decade, its condition has become dismal. The concrete parking guards have been crushed into dust and crumpled-up fast-food bags blow across the parking lot. Wobbly external stairs lead to a second floor with an identical row of doors. Nevertheless, the motel is still legendary in town; teenagers used to spend prom night there and party twenty to one room on the weekends. *I was at the Lark last night* was a saying in town inferring unspeakable debauchery. During the summer months, seasonal workers stay there until the grapefruit season ends and the fruits ship to the nearby industrial fruit-processing factory.

I cruise through the motel parking lot and spot a *Help Wanted* sign taped to the door. I enter and a bell chimes. A man sits behind the counter, flipping pages of a newspaper. He seems familiar but I can't place him. We gawk at each other.

"You look familiar," he says. He stares at me without blinking then his face lights up, as if something just occurred to him. "Dahlia Waller, how the hell are ya?" He smiles, yet his voice remains monotone and flat.

I scan his sharp nose and his sandy hair. There's a hint of something in the back of my throat but I can't put my finger on it.

"James Earl Bordeaux," he says. His lips curl up but the rest of his face remains stoic. "Don't tell me you don't remember me."

"James," I say and point at the door. "I see you're hiring."

"Look at you," he says.

"There's a sign in the window? Help wanted?" I smile in a noncommittal and generic way.

The lobby itself hasn't changed since I was here for prom night over fifteen years ago; the same wooden counter, a leaflet display tower in the far corner, a couple of tables with chairs. In one corner of the lobby is a makeshift breakfast bar consisting of a grimy coffeemaker, a box large enough to hold two dozen donuts, a leaning tower of upside-down stacked paper cups, and brown plastic stirrers in disarray. The only new things are a flat screen mounted to the wall behind the counter and a large welcome mat by the door. The floor formerly of industrial carpet is now tiled with dreary grout. The air reeks of potpourri. The place is sad, to say the least.

"I need someone reliable," he says. He tells me two of the house-keepers had to take some time off, "some personal problems, you know how that goes," and now all he has left is Ariana, and how "it's like pulling teeth explaining something to her. Lots of attitude," he says. "You've done this before, right?"

"Done what?"

He has a blank look on his face. Blunted, short of something. Then it hits me: James Earl Bordeaux. Ninth through twelfth grade. Stoic. Creepy. Son of the owner, worked here all the time. After school, all summer long. His formerly ashy hair has thinned and turned color to a sandy hue.

"Have you done housekeeping before? Hotel work in general?"

I look around; the place hardly qualifies as a hotel. Someone came up with the word *motel* for a reason; minimal accommodations, the very least of customer service. Far removed from my previous job. "I worked at the Barrington Hotel."

"Yeah? Wow, that's quite the place. What brings you to my superior lodgings then?"

"Like I said, looking for work."

"Tell me why you quit."

"I needed some time off. Medical problems."

Bordeaux nods ever so slightly. "Medical problems? Like I said, I need someone reliable. Are you better now?"

"I am," I say. "I just needed some time off."

"The Barrington, huh? That's a gem of an establishment. You'll feel, what's the right word, a bit overqualified here at the lovely Lark Inn."

"Cleaning rooms and changing sheets and towels is the same wherever you go."

"You haven't changed a bit, Dahlia Waller. It's still Waller, isn't it?"

"Last time I checked," I joke and realize the joke might be on me.

"So, you have a place to stay? We can talk about a room if you need one."

"I'm living with my mother. For now," I say and check my watch. Tallulah collapsing in the dirt driveway of the farm quickly replaces the image of my mother smoking on the porch. I just need a job, that's why I'm here.

"You've caught up with all your friends from high school yet?"

"Not really. Don't care to do any catching up."

"So it's just you and your mom then? No boyfriend?"

He's as creepy as he ever was. "Me, my mother, and my dog," I say.

"You have reliable transportation?"

"I do," I say and point at my car sitting outside. "How much do you pay an hour?"

"Ten an hour. With overtime you can make five hundred a week easily."

"Do you need references?"

"You said you had medical problems. Is that what they're going to tell me when I call?"

"Just about," I say and look out the window. The rooms start at 101 through 120 on the bottom floor, 201 through 220 on top. I shouldn't have any problems keeping the numbers straight. "What shifts do I work?"

"Eight in the morning to eight at night. You can take a lunch hour but as long as you remain on the premises and respond to requests if there're any, I'm not going to fret over paying you through lunch. That's what Ariana does. Works out well."

He explains that he makes coffee at five and gets donuts at eight. There's a room in the unattached building where he lives. He starts the laundry but we're responsible for drying and folding. "Ariana does the eleven to midnight shift, sometimes longer. I hope you're flexible."

I look out the window and see the unattached building with three more rooms. "What's in there?" I ask. "More rooms?"

"One of them is mine. One for storage. But like I said, if you need a place to stay, I can arrange that. I won't charge much for it."

"That won't be necessary. When do I start?" I ask, hoping he won't change his mind.

Bordeaux enters the room behind the counter and emerges with a clipboard and paperwork. "You can start tomorrow. I'd appreciate it. One more thing. Do you want to get paid in cash?"

Cash only. I know what that means: off the books. No paperwork. I fill out the form—name, address, phone number, previous employer.

"What's the matter?" he asks.

"Nothing. Is this all you need?"

"That's all," he says and reaches for the clipboard.

"I guess I'll see you tomorrow?" I slide the clipboard over the counter and smile.

"Eight in the morning. I'll show you around then. Wear black pants and a gray shirt. No one really wears uniforms around here."

Bordeaux goes on about laundry and linen and comforters and I continuously nod but I move closer to the door and look out the window. Bobby is still sitting in his cruiser. From time to time I see him lift up a white cup to his lips. If I didn't know any better I'd say he's watching me. The phone rings and I gesture toward the door, get in my car, and leave the Lark Inn parking lot.

I realize that every single time I've seen Bobby, he was parked at the Filling Station. The day he saw me when I came into town, when he waved at me and I ignored him. We met there before we went out to the farm, and there were other times I passed the Filling Station and he was parked there. Every single time, as if he's watching something. Or somebody.

I make a left and an immediate right and park on the west side of the Filling Station, where the pumps are. I enter the building and I walk through the aisles, pretending to look at Twinkies and cans of Chef Boyardee. I eventually grab a six-pack of water, and on my way to the register, I see smoke drifting from the cruiser's driver's door. I pay and leave through the front door, the one facing the Lark Inn. I walk slowly, and Bobby, with a set of binoculars in his lap, writes notes in tiny squares of what looks like the printout of a spreadsheet.

"Covert operation?" I ask and laugh when Bobby jerks.

"What the hell, Dahlia," he says and tucks the papers inside a file and the file underneath a black canvas bag on the passenger's seat.

"What are you doing here? You sure like this place," I insist, jokingly, but Bobby isn't smiling.

"Catching up on paperwork," he says and turns down the chatter of the police radio. "What are you doing here?"

"Just applied for a job."

"At the gas station?"

"No, the Lark Inn. Remember, I'm in the hospitality business."

He's silent for a long time. His hand jerks as the cigarette's lit tip reaches his fingers. He throws it out and gets out of the car and steps on it. "So you thought the Lark was a good choice?"

"I have to work somewhere, right?"

Bobby stretches as if he's been sitting for quite a while, his muscles stiff and tight. I haven't really thought about him being a cop and I wonder how that came about. His father, Ramón de la Vega, was the first Mexican sheriff in Aurora twenty years ago, but Bobby always vowed to never become a cop. He loved sports and I imagined him as a high school coach, baseball or football.

I tell him about the well, the shed door that won't open, Tallulah being at the vet having surgery. Bobby seems distracted, not really listening, looking over his shoulder one minute, across the street the next, as if he's determined not to miss anything. Then, like a slow-falling hammer, a thought comes to me; he *is* watching the Lark Inn.

"Anything I should know?" I ask.

"About what?"

"The Lark Inn. Working there. It's not like I have a choice—between the plumber and the vet, I need to make some money."

"Did he tell you?"

I look at him, puzzled.

"He? Did he tell me what?"

"Did Bourdeaux tell you Jane Doe stayed at the Lark?" Bobby's voice trails off. There is something in his eyes, they are too brown, too glossy.

My Jane stayed at the Lark. I'm attempting to process his comment.

"No, he didn't." There's the Barrington, the Lark, and a Holiday Inn Express about twenty miles from here. I recall the news, the fact she had stayed at a hotel in town. I had never really thought about it. I'm not sure what to do with that. Not only do I not know what to do with it, but I can't make sense of it. "How would they know she stayed there? Do they know her name?"

"Bordeaux said a woman fitting her description stayed for one night and that the computer was down and he checked her in manually, never updated the system. Claims paperwork got lost. She stayed one night and left the next day. Paid in cash. 'I don't remember her name, if that was her.' Those were his words."

"Are they sure it was her?"

"Witnesses are still being interviewed. It's a motel, and people pass through. It's not ideal. They are still investigating but they are pretty sure it was her. But you can't tell anyone. It's an open investigation."

"Is there more?"

"More what?"

"Bobby, I'm not stupid. There are facts they don't release to the public. Like where she stayed. Is there more?"

"I can't say much else, but she wore this." Bobby reaches into his wallet and pulls out a copy of a photograph. A charm bracelet. A simple chain-link with a lobster clasp. There's a ship's wheel, a compass, a globe, a suitcase and a camera, an airplane and a passport, and a sombrero. Random and cheesy sterling baubles, a dime a dozen. Far from an engraved bracelet with a name and a date that would help identify her. How has no one missed this girl? How did she disappear unnoticed?

"I won't tell anyone," I say to reassure him and wonder why he would carry the copy in his wallet.

"Not a soul. Promise?"

"Are there others?"

"What others?"

"Missing women."

He stares at me. The police radio gurgles, then a dispatcher comes on. A mutter, then a squawking, lots of gibberish, nothing but a fuzzy radio voice. "I have to go," he says and turns the key.

"I guess I'll see you tomorrow," I say and grab my water off the hood of the cruiser.

I watch Bobby take off, and just when I lift my hand to wave at him, he rolls up the window, tires spitting gravel.

Twenty-one

MEMPHIS

MEMPHIS sucks smoke deep into her lungs, trapping it. She craves the nicotine and continues to hold in the smoke as Dahlia reaches the end of the driveway. There are many memories she tries not to hold on to yet she can't help when they arrive and wills them to depart just as quickly.

The dog makes it harder and harder for her to ignore certain things she'd rather forget. Memphis likes the dog even though it's difficult to look at her with her engorged nipples drooping toward the ground, and Memphis wonders how many litters she's given birth to.

How unfair life is, she thinks; everything rises and falls with the womb you emerge from. If Tallulah had had a proper home, she would've been spayed and well fed and sleeping on a couch at night, but she is nothing but a stray with a worn-out body, covered in hairless spots from ticks and bites and sharp fences. Memphis imagines other dogs nipping at her when she tried to get away from them or avoiding sticks swung by callous hands while searching for a safe place to rest. Memphis shudders and her heart aches for the dog. She has always had a soft spot for animals, more so than for humans.

After the dust on the driveway settles, Memphis walks toward the shed. She tells herself that she can do this. She's thankful for the meds, grateful for the escape the little orange bottles allow, appreciative for the log-like sleep at night, twelve hours at a time.

The windows of the shed are nailed shut but partially visible, the panes are cloudy and distorted but it's all the same to her, and there's no need to look through them anyhow. She can name every single item in that shed. The door is still temperamental but she remembers it well and knows just how to coax it open. So are the rules with old and stubborn things; one must know just where and how to push and secrets come rambling out like dice from a cup.

Memphis enters the shed and in a flash she stands in the midst of a vast darkness. There are remnants of sulfur in the air. It's been decades, yet the pungent vapor fills her nostrils, turns her stomach. She looks down at her hands and then her feet, but she can't see a thing. Her eyes can't penetrate the darkness no matter which way she turns; it is brooding and rotating around her and the hairs on the back of her neck stand up. She can almost hear muffled voices bouncing off the walls. There's a ripple of mocking laughter, becoming louder, and it presses in on her.

And so she waits until the ghosts of the past join her and complete the memory of the first time Quinn set foot in the shed.

"What are you working on and what's that paint on your fingers? I washed your clothes and they are splattered with that white stuff. They're ruined. Are you painting something?" Quinn had said.

"I'll be more careful," Nolan had said as he gave his hands a good scrub with the dish brush.

"And?"

"And what?"

"What are you working on?" Quinn had insisted.

"Just something to pass the time."

Quinn watched Nolan dry his hands, one finger at a time. His jeans looked as if someone had taken a paintbrush and with a swift flick of the wrist splattered paint all over them.

"Nolan, what are you doing out there every day in that shed?"

"I told you, something to pass the time." Nolan's voice was hard and sharp, as if she had asked him to divulge some sort of secret.

Quinn turned and shut off the stove.

"Breakfast is ready," she said and went upstairs.

Later, when she heard voices from the TV coming from the living room, she went out the back door, toward the shed. She was going to get to the bottom of this.

MEMPHIS HEARS THE REVVING OF AN ENGINE AND JERKS BACK into reality. She makes her way out of the shed, slamming the distorted door shut behind her. Back on the porch, in the warped kitchen window she sees the trancelike haunted expression on her face.

Maybe it's time, she thinks; *time to tell Quinn's story.* She has nothing left to lose, really. What's done in the dark must come into the light.

Twenty-two

DAHLIA

MY mother and I have been living on the farm for a few days now. After hours of cleaning and moving boxes, she sits ramrod straight in the only chair we found on the back porch that has successfully braved the elements. Its wrought iron back resembles the fanned tail of a peacock and looks almost like some ornate Victorian lawn furnishing. More likely it's just a cheap import. Everything else on the back porch is in shambles: Tons of shattered clay pots lie spattered about as if someone took a bat to them. The screens look like birds have clawed at them, leaving holes the size of fists. Every surface is caked in bird excrement, and abandoned nests are tucked in the rafters—just another part of this house making my skin crawl.

I sit on the front steps with my back propped up against the railing. When I move, it moves as well. Not only does my mother act differently since we've arrived, but her face has undergone a peculiar transformation. Before she had this slightly upturned mouth and somewhat flared nostrils; both now have relaxed. Her forehead, though wrinkled, is no longer tense. I have yet to probe the fact that she owns this farm and the almost fifty acres around it but I decide to let that rest for now and give her time to settle in.

Once the sun has gone down and the mosquitoes descend upon us, we go inside. The floor plan is simple; four rooms on the first floor, kitchen to the right with an attached dining room and a large walk-in pantry, on the left an office and a living room. The top floor has three bedrooms and a bathroom. Two of the bedrooms have old wrought iron headboards and beds and the very last room on the left in the back is a storage room. It is filled with boxes and stacks of books that have collapsed onto the floor.

The day I returned from the vet, we began making the place habitable. We pulled the dusty and mold-covered linens off the beds and replaced them with fresh sheets. The mattresses were in surprisingly good condition. I offer my mother the master bedroom, and she seems to want to protest, but then she thinks otherwise and I claim the bedroom across the hall.

Moving boxes and opening windows, allowing the dust to be disturbed one last time before we wipe, sweep, and mop it all up, reminds me of all the places I lived with my mother. Over the years I have revisited some of them in my mind, although I don't recall them as true memories, but merely as a part of my brain that I allowed to remain unclaimed until I found Jane.

During that first seizure in Jane's hospital room I felt the presence of something *substantial*. It has also occurred to me that maybe I just happened to be with Jane in the hospital at that moment and still I am not sure what it all means exactly. The subsequent seizures felt as if I was transcending this world and I was tuning in to some earlier space in time. There were waves of energy, and something was being communicated to me. I've been ignoring Dr. Wagner, haven't seen a neurologist yet, but I take the meds religiously, and I feel comfortable waiting it out, allowing it to run its course.

Some memories float on the surface: the idling trucks, the stench of troves of cattle by the side of the highway when we lived above a gas station on Highway 281. My mother worked nights and we stayed in a small room above a garage, a small one-man operation with a man in greasy overalls. His last name was Herring and he had a head of gray hair, thick and straight, like bristles of a broom. I told him that a herring was a silvery fish with a single dorsal fin and a protruding lower jaw. And that's exactly how he looked. He wasn't amused and told me to get out of his garage.

The Herring era ended abruptly. One night my mother woke me and told me to pack up and that "we need to get out of here." We hardly owned anything in the room we slept in and within an hour we rushed across the parking lot to our car with a few bags in our hands. As we drove off, I looked back and there was an irate woman getting out of a station wagon, running to the garage door, pounding the metal enclosure.

We drove through the night and when the sun came up, a *Welcome to New Mexico* sign greeted me. *Land of Enchantment.* We ended up on a street with motels, liquor stores, Chinese restaurants, and an occasional used car dealer lot with colorful pennants and balloons swaying in the wind. My mother pulled into the parking lot of the very last building on the street, the Moment Motel. There was a simple black-and-white *Help Wanted* sign in the door. She pulled up to the front door and checked herself in the mirror.

"Wait here," she said and applied lipstick.

"Are we going to stay here?" I asked, my legs propped up against the passenger's seat.

"We'll see," she said and locked the car door.

As I watched her enter the motel, her likeness in the window one of beauty and confidence even after a night of driving though the darkness, only the old Buick stuffed with our possessions belied the picture of her success. I took in the cracked parking lot, the chipped paint, the humming soda machine, and the sound of a vacuum cleaner drifting toward me from afar. My mother emerged what seemed like thirty minutes or so later, with a key in her hand.

If Wichita Falls was Herring's domain, New Mexico was Bruno Nettle's time to shine. He was the owner of the Moment Motel and hired my mother on the spot. In exchange for her work and a paycheck he allowed us to live in the very last room at the end of the T-shaped complex. I even remember the number: 210. The 0 was slightly crooked and the room smelled of lavender. Not the real thing, but the artificial scent of lavender flowers in a waft of alcohol. The Moment Motel was where we stayed for a long time. We got there when I was about six and didn't leave until I was eight. It was the longest time we stayed anywhere.

I don't recall the reason why we left but it was in the middle of the night, my mother's preferred time to get away. Always at night, always just packing what we could fit in the backseat and trunk of whatever shabby car she owned at the time. I remember my mother yelling at me in the car but I don't remember what I had done. I shift the responsibility to her—I was eight, what could I have possibly done?—and there's this explicit conviction that she is to blame. There's an accumulation of moments, definitions from my encyclopedia, adjectives defining me, nouns describing my world. Even with all I now remember, I've grown to hate the blanks I'm unable to fill in, the riddles I can't seem to solve. Being denied that knowledge magnifies the crimes she has committed against me.

Sometimes I stand next to her, in the barn, or at a random spot on the property, and she looks at me as if I'm supposed to read her mind. *Don't you see what I see?* her eyes seem to say. *How come you're so blind?*, and I know she's getting at something, but I'm not sure what.

Looking at her now, in her sixties, on this farm, me no longer a child, I see her for what she is: I believe that my mother is the biggest perpetrator of them all and it's going to take a lot to convince me otherwise.

There's no more time to waste. One day I confront her head-on.

"You used to call me Pet. What was that all about?"

Twenty-three

MEMPHIS

MEMPHIS watches Dahlia wipe the counters, continuously rubbing the same spot, going over it again and again, as if there's some sticky residue refusing to be removed. Then she moves on to the floor using the same approach. Memphis often wonders how much Dahlia remembers about their lives, leaving everything behind, clothes and toys, the only constant the old used cars and a book she used to carry around. *I know her so well,* Memphis thinks. Know her better than she knows herself, even though Dahlia is very cautious with exposing her emotions, giving nothing much or nothing at all away, as if she's playing cards and not permitting anyone to see her hand.

They had left Texas behind, then New Mexico. Nevada was a mere ghost, and then they ended up in California. But life was complicated for a single woman toting a little pretty girl behind her. Men want what they want and they take it too, no doubt about that.

They went to Wichita Falls first—Memphis remembers the tiny room above the gas station—where all Memphis tried to do was keep them fed and a roof over their heads, but things became difficult; she couldn't enroll Dahlia in school without a birth certificate and had to buy old school books at thrift stores, but Dahlia turned out smarter than most kids her age.

There was Elvin Herring, a man she thought might be the answer.

His name did him justice; sweaty hands like a dead cold fish and even now Memphis shudders at the thought of ever having allowed him to touch her. First he pretended he wanted to help because *no woman should be all alone* but then the tables turned and all he wanted was to touch her body and use her. Memphis never knew Elvin had a wife, never knew he had three children, one of them slow, unable to feed himself or go to the bathroom. There were times he'd go home and shower and come back to the gas station—it was busy during the day but still off the beaten path and hardly any cars came through at night—and he'd bring food and wine and he'd put the sign up for folks to ring for service and they'd eat and drink cheap wine out of cloudy and chipped glasses.

Memphis wasn't opposed to being with Herring, he was kind and generous on payday, but his wife showed up in the middle of the night with his son, a boy with eyes wandering aimlessly about, and *that* was too much for her. She'd seen Herring's oldest boy in a wheelchair once in the garage and assumed he was merely watching him for someone. Elvin had rolled him into the back room at some point, and the boy sat there, his hands flailing, his foot stomping, drool dripping off his chin. Memphis doesn't want to think of Herring and the boy and his matronly mother and the other children, and she absolved herself of guilt; she didn't know he was married and even if she had known, she did what she had to do.

It's hard for Memphis to know where to start, where to begin, so Dahlia can understand.

Dahlia found the deed to the farm and began to ask questions, and maybe that's the way to go, not to offer any stories, just tell the truth, but Dahlia asks all the wrong questions, about trailers and hotels, schools and coming back to Aurora—that seems to be at the forefront of it all, *Why did we come back here?*—but Dahlia doesn't know it was all done by then. Anything between leaving Aurora and returning was just the product of what came before. What happened before was what pushed on Memphis' heart, deepening the crack.

One day they walked the property and ended up in the barn, where

Dahlia commented on the well and the plumber, money they didn't have, and other things unimportant.

Look around you, Memphis wanted to say, *see this barn? Forget the well, forget the deed, forget all of this, just smell this barn. Doesn't the smell hit you in your gut? When you lugged open this damn door with its worn-out hinges that creak like the moaning of old tired women, don't you smell the straw? The stuffy musk of animal fur and old, dried-out dung and droppings, and the sharp scent of oily metal and iron machinery? Allow your eyes to get used to the darkness of this barn, allow your sight to compensate for the lack of light, then take in the wooden stalls. Do you hear the barn moan, do you see the insidious process of rot? Look below, Dahlia, look below, and don't judge its surface. See the ghosts, Dahlia, do you see them? They are right there.*

Why did you call me Pet?

In the grand scheme of things Pet means nothing but it's what Dahlia focuses on. She should ask questions that are more important. Memphis tells herself to cut Dahlia some slack. There are all these paths but there's no map.

There was the storm. That's when it all began and that's where Memphis is going to start. With the storm.

It's as good a place to start as any.

Twenty-four

DAHLIA

Y OU used to call me Pet. What was that all about?"

My mother makes a halfhearted attempt at smiling by pulling her lips up but it comes across as distorted and slanted, like she just came from the dentist and half of her face is still paralyzed.

"Forget the name," she finally says and folds her hands in her lap after she angrily swipes at some gnats swirling around her. "Forget your name and my name and forget the deed."

"What is it you're not telling me?"

My mother has an aura of defiance about her, I can feel it coming through her pores. I give up on the counters and stab the mop in the bucket of sudsy water. I feel anger rise inside of me. I move the tattered old rug and begin to clean the foyer floor with wide irritated swipes. From her chair at the kitchen table she watches me.

"After I finish here, we are going to walk the property," I say. I watch her closely—there's the trembling of her hands, the rapid blinking with her eyes, but other than that she has her emotions under control.

"There's not much to it," she says, and I detect a sharpness in her voice.

"According to the deed, it's forty-eight acres of land. That's quite a bit of property."

"Never concerned myself with that," she says and refolds the laundry I brought home from the Lark, where I wash all our clothes. Her movements are severe and angry.

"Why have you never told me about this place?" I ask and look sternly at her, making it known that I will be relentless in hearing the story of how she came to own a farm with almost fifty acres that she's never mentioned to me.

We go back and forth—my asking and her not answering by now a delicate dance we perform, yet she refuses to even get up off her chair.

"I have so many questions and I get it, that was your life and all, but I feel I'm part of a story you're not telling and I . . ." I pause and take a deep breath in. "I kind of have the right to know."

"You have questions?" My mother eventually says, tinged in sarcasm. "Let me tell you a story."

I see this moment almost like my last chance, an opportunity that will never return. I must weigh my options, must make a wise decision, or she'll never get this close again.

"A story?"

"Before I begin, I have a question for you," she says. Her eyes scamper, something only apparent if you know her. "Have you ever been in the eye of a storm?"

LAS VEGAS, NEVADA, 1991

The Gateway Motel is our new home. It's a horseshoe-shaped building that has managed to retain its presence between a pawn shop and a block of apartments. Three floors, each one stacked on top of one another like toy blocks, each one with a view of the courtyard. The backside of the hotel is windowless and hides the Dumpsters and an employee parking lot made of dirt.

When I wake, dust swirls in the white morning light. A donut shop is a short walk away and the air smells of powdered sugar and sweet pastries.

It takes me less than fifteen minutes to put my few belongings in the wobbly dresser. The drawers stick and only slide open after I wiggle the worn knobs just right and pull at them simultaneously. This move was hasty yet again, and some of my things have been left behind. Some of them I've had as long as I can remember. I'm ten and I don't want to cry like a baby. Mom gets mad when I complain.

The bathroom is grimy, the sink is chipped, and the Formica is peeling off the vanity.

"What does Gateway mean?" I ask to distract myself.

"It's just a name."

"Like Camelot? The trailer park where we lived before?"

My mother doesn't answer as she swirls the mouthwash from the left to the right side of her mouth.

"Why did you pick this hotel?" I ask her.

I've been wondering why ever since we arrived a couple of days ago, after a long drive from Arizona in another middle-of-the-night operation I didn't understand. Every time I ask her why we always leave, she tells me it's about paperwork. Out of all the hotels and motels I have seen as we drove down Las Vegas Boulevard, the Gateway Motel was by far the most run-down. And it is just about at the farthest end of the city it seems like.

"It's out of the way," my mother said, "and they were hiring."

I'm old enough to know that out of the way *is code for* I don't have to look over my shoulder *and* they were hiring *means* no one asks questions.

It's a live-in position, my mother says, and explains that we live in one of the rooms and she works the front desk and supervises the maids. "And they are flexible," she adds.

Flexible as in she'll get paid off the books. Everything we do is off the books. Free clinics, Sunday meals in church basements, trips to food kitchens. Those are good off the books. Bad off the books is the fact that I still haven't been to school. When I ask her about it, she tends to slow down her speech as if I can't comprehend words at normal speed.

"Paperwork," she says. "We don't have any of what they're asking for. They're making it near impossible if you don't have the right paperwork."

I wonder how other mothers have the right paperwork. Where do they get what they need and how come we don't? We've been to offices and she tried to get the paperwork straightened out but it never works. At those offices where it takes hours sitting around and waiting and mere seconds to be turned away once you go into rooms with numbers. Below the numbers are little knobby dots and I close my eyes and run my fingers over them, attempting to train myself to discern between the arrangements of the dots and their meanings, but I can hardly feel a difference. Every time a door opens I jerk and look around as if I'm doing something wrong.

"What's that mean," I ask, "not having the right paperwork?"

"Be a good girl, don't ask so many questions." A stern look, raised eyebrows.

I've been difficult lately, according to my mother; I ask too many questions and she's run out of answers a long time ago and something has got to give. While she curls her hair, I sit on the edge of the tub and I inspect my fingernails, which, unlike my mother's, never turn out perfect with my frayed cuticles and uneven nails, and she never has the time to show me how to do it properly.

I'm leaning backward and pretend to fall into the tub, which causes my mother to gasp and then yelp as the curling iron touches the nape of her neck. She's in her Marilyn phase, short hair dyed platinum blond, red lipstick, and thick eyeliner. It might be a Vegas thing. I'm not sure about that.

"You never got me that book you promised me."

My voice is strict, almost as if I'm the parent scolding her for ignoring her chores. I've been turning the tables on her lately, and that's when she began to call me difficult. I like being difficult—it's my new thing.

"What book?" she asks.

"The one with all the answers."

She looks at me, puzzled, then her face relaxes. "Will you stop bothering me if I get you that book?"

"Sure will."

Later, using the free local call feature, she makes a few phone calls asking if they have what she calls The Columbia. *I watch her, intrigued and speechless. She looks beautiful with her blond hair and red lips, completely different from the long brown hair and bangs. It was short before, but never blond. "Would you believe it," she says after about ten calls. "That pawn shop right down the street has one."*

I've lived around pawn shops before and they seem to be nothing more but dusty stores with an odd array of products, like Goodwill. They all disappear between liquor shops and motels and diners with steamy windows and alleys leading to brick walls. But much more expensive. Why a book with all the answers would be tucked away in a pawn shop is beyond me but it seems as if soon is going to be now and so I don't ask any more questions.

"Let me see," she says and checks her watch. She tips her head to the left and rubs lotion into her hands, then she runs her hands through her hair. It's her trademark, Xia Xiang, a beige bottle with a red flower. "I still have time."

As I wait for her to return from the pawn shop, my hands pull the plastic curtain taut as I peek through the gap—something I'm not supposed to do but do all the time—I see her walk up the courtyard with a bag that seems heavy, making her shoulder droop as she walks.

The first word I'm going to look up is paperwork.

Twenty-five

MEMPHIS

MEMPHIS watches Dahlia mop the foyer floor, dragging the mop back and forth. She's been going over the same stain again and again but it seems to only deepen. Memphis is mesmerized by the storm Dahlia makes every time she pulls the cotton fibers out of the bucket, her movement creating a twister on the surface of the water. Dahlia hasn't said anything in a while—she's stewing, Memphis can tell.

"Have you ever been in a storm, one of those that almost rip the roof off a house?" Memphis asks again and Dahlia looks up.

"I've seen storms, of course I have."

"Did they have a name?"

"What do you mean? A name?" Dahlia gives up on the stain in the foyer, pulling the bucket into the kitchen.

"The big storms have names. Back before you were born, all storms were named after women. Did you know that?"

Dahlia dumps the dirty water down the drain and joins her mother at the kitchen table.

"Now they have male and female names. Women can cause a lot of trouble, did you know that?"

Memphis watches Dahlia look at her hands, reddish and scaly as if she'd dipped them in some sort of chemical; the hands of a woman who cleans for a living. "I assume so."

"That stain over there"—Memphis points at the foyer—"do you know what that is?"

"I have no idea. I assume someone spilled something. Maybe the shellac stain soaked in; I'm not sure."

"It's not a spill. Not a wood stain either."

"I guess it's there for the long haul, then, because it's not going anywhere."

"He had just put in the new floor. Cherry. He had sanded it and cleaned it to get rid of all the dust. Then he mopped it to raise the grain and he was supposed to apply the stain with an old rag the next morning. But he never got around to that." Memphis sits in silence, reaches for her mug. She wraps her fingers around it, then realizes it has long cooled.

She feels Dahlia stare at her, can tell she doesn't know what to make of this. Doesn't know who *he* is, can't comprehend how Memphis just went from storms named after women and stains to *he*.

"She had such an odd name," Memphis continues. "I never understood who gave her such a strange name. I'd never heard it before, nor have I heard that name since." She pauses, then adds, "Tain Fish."

"The name of the storm?"

"Not the storm. The woman."

"What woman?" Dahlia's eyes widen. Memphis can tell she's worried that this is the moment her mother will go to the other side and remain there.

"The woman who came during the storm, back when they still named the storms after women. If you ask me, that was only right. Women have a lot of power."

"I don't understand."

Memphis chuckles, then gets up. With a clink she puts her mug in the sink.

"Stop bothering with the stain, okay? It won't come out. It's deep in the grain, it can't be removed short of refinishing the floor. She bled all over it before he stained it."

Dahlia sits paralyzed. "What?" is all she can muster.

"There was a storm. A woman by the name of Tain Fish came to this house, and she bled all over the floors. That's the story of the stain. It can't be wiped away. You might as well not even try."

THE NIGHT OF THE STORM, IT WAS A HURRICANE—MEMPHIS NO longer recalls the name—that hit the Gulf Coast, not once, but twice; first it made landfall in the early morning, then it swerved back out into the Gulf, just to turn around and unleash a second wave of rain all the way to Northeast Texas.

That night, Quinn stood by the kitchen window, filling a glass with water from the tap. She had awakened earlier and been unable to go back to sleep with the rain hammering the roof and the constant creaking in the very bones of the house, and the wind tearing at the structure as if some impetuous wind spirit was determined to destroy the world altogether. All the while Nolan snored upstairs, the scent of chemicals lingering deep in his skin.

As her stomach cramped with a dull ache, a harsh fork of lightning severed the sky. In its wake she saw movement beyond the trees, low to the ground—a coyote maybe, or a fox? Then it dawned on her that it didn't move fast enough to be an animal, didn't make any attempt to seek shelter below the juniper trees to the left, didn't try to find a gap between the wooden slats of the barn. There were no gleaming eyes, no sudden scurry, just a white bundle the size of a large dog. It might be Seymour's dog, Ghost, Quinn thought, large and white and shaggy, herding Seymour's few pitiful goats caked in mud after a bout of rain. Maybe Ghost got frightened by the storm and ran off; maybe he was hurt by a branch striking him as he darted for shelter?

Quinn opened the front door, hit the porch light switch, and watched the night through the screen door. A spray of rain hit her face as the screen flapped so hard she thought it might rip. *Rain* wasn't the appropriate word; it was more a torrent of what hours ago had begun as high winds and a steady drizzle and had turned into the most powerful storm she had ever witnessed. The wind didn't howl, it screamed; the rain didn't just fall, but was driven, hard, mercilessly, lashing the land, determined to punish it for some unknown indiscretion. The trees didn't sway in the gale force winds, they creaked, bent, and moaned as their fine limbs were ripped away. Parts of the sweet pea trellises tumbled and splintered across the meadow; apple trees were uprooted, leaning, battered beyond their ability to recover.

Another flash of lightning; the bundle hadn't moved. Quinn stepped outside and without a further thought ran toward it, her nightgown sticking to her skin in less than a second, her body leaning into the wind, hoping it wasn't going to pick her up and toss her about like the metal bucket that landed right beside her with a thud.

When she reached the rounded and plump shape—the silly words *dinosaur egg* came to mind—Quinn froze. Everything that moved stood still, everything that roared became silent; the wind and rain, as if they were a blender on the highest setting, calmed suddenly, as if she and the giant egg were caught in a composed pocket of a world otherwise in uproar. Another bolt of lightning and she found herself staring at a body with a rather large abdomen, swollen and engorged past normal size. Quinn thought of many things, all of them competing to be acknowledged: stories of caskets and bodies floating to the surface, a corpse floating in water, facedown and bloated.

The body turned and moved, a face appeared, cheeks, forehead, lips, mouth, and eyes—a young face, a woman, barely a woman, more a girl. The face deflated like a balloon, folding in on itself. And Quinn made for the house, up the porch steps, screaming Nolan's name, over and over. *Nolan. Nolan. Nolan. Help me. Hurry. Help. Nolan. Nolan. Nolan.*

Nolan appeared, pants unbuckled and carelessly tucked into his boots, shirtless. He hesitated on the porch, eyes squinting against the rain, his body swaying in the wind. With only a fraction of a second's hesitation, he ran over to the woman on the ground, careful not to tread on her with his heavy boots. He picked her up, gently, one hand under her fragile neck, the crook of his other arm under her knees. Nolan limped to the house and onto the porch as her ragdoll-like limbs swung about. Her ponytail was ragged; loose hair fell over features so peaceful Quinn feared it was too late.

She's dead, Quinn thought. The earth stood still once more, negated gravity, halted. Quinn's thoughts tumbled about like the leaves and branches around her: aimlessly, ending up who knows where, unable to still themselves. The swollen belly twisted and wriggled and she could have sworn that there was a visible outline of a foot beneath the skin stretched tight as a drum underneath the white dress.

Cut her open, Quinn wanted to scream, *cut her open so we can save the baby.* For this was *her* baby. Aella said so, *she said so. Her baby. Hers!*

A wind gust rose, merciless, with a force so strong that Quinn forgot to breathe, pushing her body against the door frame as if the wind was making an attempt to get her out of harm's way while Nolan, with the girl in his arms, tumbled down the porch, the wind having other plans for them. The last image Quinn would later remember was the girl's black hair sticking shamelessly to Nolan's naked chest. It made her uneasy but then Quinn stepped forward and helped Nolan carry her over the threshold.

QUINN HAD SEEN A CAT GIVING BIRTH. A BLACK WATER BALLOON had emerged from the tabby, and then it had busted and five kittens were born minutes apart, some emerging with their heads, two with their legs, one even rear first. Each kitten was wrapped in a jelly-like membrane filled with clear fluid. The tabby forcefully licked the kittens, shredding the sac, allowing them to take their first breath, then chewed off the umbilical cords and began nursing them one by one until the next one emerged. The tabby had purred through the entire birth.

This was nothing like that. The girl clawed at Quinn, pulling at her nightgown, twisting it in her fists as if she was attempting to rip it off of her. As Nolan paced back and forth, as the windows rattled and lightning illuminated the sky, the girl's screams echoed through the house.

Nolan had dropped her in the foyer, on top of the woven oval rug, too spooked to carry her in the kitchen when her screams began to slash at him. Anxiously he tore the phone off the cradle on the wall as if he expected service to be restored and it struck Quinn how silly that notion was, how absurd Nolan was, pacing back and forth, incapable of making sound decisions.

At some point, Quinn didn't exactly remember when, Nolan got in the truck and left to get help, just to return minutes later. "I can't get to the road, it's covered in branches and fallen trees."

Nolan stood motionless and the girl screamed with her whole body—eyes wide, mouth rigid and open, her chalky face gaunt, fists clenched with bleached knuckles, body taut and stiff. Her chest heaved. The girl was coiled up on the rug, writhing and screaming, when she suddenly crumpled into herself and went quiet.

Quinn's mind raced. If the mother died, so would the baby, and nothing in this world was going to keep her from holding her baby. *Her* baby. All that money, all she had done was now coming to fruition. She felt her sanity leave her as if a deranged thief had made off with it and she heard her own voice, yet the words seemed like they'd come from someone else.

"Get me a knife from the kitchen." Nolan didn't move, stood pale and motionless as if he had turned into a statue of salt. "Get me a knife," she repeated, this time slowly, gentle almost, emphasizing every syllable. *Get. Me. A. Knife.*

Quinn pushed the girl's gown upward and there it was. This *thing.* Tiny. Newborn was too much a concept for it was barely the size of a loaf of bread and covered in something thick and white. It wasn't moving at all.

It had all been in vain. There was nothing left to beg for, nothing left to offer, nothing to receive in return. She had done what Aella required, she had held up her end of the bargain, had paid her a king's ransom and all she got was *this*? A *thing* with bulgy eyes and an elongated head, as if there was an immense pressure within this tiny body covered in transparent skin.

There was no cord to be cut. The entire afterbirth lay on the wool rug, a bloody tree with a white umbilical trunk that had served its purpose and was no longer needed, an offering to the gods who had clearly turned a deaf ear to Quinn's pleading.

Nolan handed Quinn a towel he must have grabbed from the kitchen table where the rest of the clean laundry sat in neat stacks. As Quinn wrapped the baby in the white bath towel, allowing the face to show, Nolan picked up the girl and carried her upstairs to one of the spare bedrooms. Quinn followed him and Nolan appeared with a bowl of water and Quinn began to wipe the girl's thighs with a rag until the water turned a dark crimson. It needed changing three times before the girl's body was clean.

After Nolan left the room, Quinn sat by the bed. The girl's heaving and shaking had ceased. Her eyes were puffy and red. Quinn handed her the baby, speaking in a slow and measured voice. "Do you want to hold him?"

The girl held the baby in her arms, and she began to awkwardly rock the bundle as if it were alive. At some point Quinn went downstairs and came upon Nolan passed out on the couch. There was an empty bottle of malt liquor on the coffee table.

Back upstairs, she found the girl sleeping, deep and motionless, no movement behind her closed eyelids. Quinn changed into a dry and clean nightgown, one that buttoned up the front, and she took the bundle from the sleeping girls' arms and went to her own room, where she sat on her bed, gently placing the newborn against her breast—aware of her grotesque behavior but unable to refrain from it—pushing her nipple between the baby's cold purple lips.

Quinn's mind flickered with images of the engorged belly, the blood—there had been so much blood—the girl's screams still echoed in her ears, the lifeless miniature hands, the cold lips on her nipple, and once all that noise and those images drained, sadness was all that was left. Such cruelty, such mockery, to leave her here with the lifeless body of a baby that would never be. Lives wasted, hers, the girl's, the baby's. Quinn looked down at it—a boy it was—and longed to join him. What was the point in continuing to draw breath? Nothing had been achieved, everything was lost.

Later, she would bring the baby back and leave it with the sleeping girl. Outside, the thunder and lightning had all but ceased and all that was left was a steady downpour of rain, only occasionally interrupted by a grumbling in the distance.

THE NEXT MORNING THE SUNNY SKY BELIED THE PREVIOUS NIGHT'S havoc and the entire world seemed to be covered in leaves and branches and other debris, as if it had rained green confetti and rubble from above. Quinn entered the shed and Nolan flinched when she said his name. The air smelled of alcohol and rich wet soil.

"I need your help," Quinn said.

Nolan turned around and looked at her with bloodshot eyes. "Is the girl alive?"

"Yes."

"What do we do? I don't know what to do. Do we call the police?"

"We don't need the police. And the phone's still not working," Quinn said but wasn't sure since she hadn't tried.

"Is the girl talking? Is she awake?"

"She's sleeping."

"I can try to tie the trees to the truck and pull them off the road and take her to the hospital."

"What for, Nolan?" Quinn asked and gently touched his arm. "She's okay. She had a baby, is all. She doesn't need a doctor."

Nolan jerked away from Quinn. "We need to call a priest for that baby. This is not what you do with a dead body. It needs to be blessed and buried properly, prayers need to be said. And we need to take the mother to a hospital."

Mother. That girl was no more a mother than Quinn was. "Can I have this?" Quinn pointed at a wooden box of Ball fruit jars. It was about the size of a large shoebox.

A sound escaped from Nolan's throat, half breath, half gasp. "I'm not digging a hole. The least you could do is ask her what she wants to do with the body. It's *her* baby."

"She is in no shape to dig a hole. And if you won't help, I'll do it myself," Quinn said and grabbed the box. *This was* my *baby,* she wanted to add but then thought otherwise. Nolan didn't need to know of the pact she had made, he wouldn't understand.

Out of all the spots that were appropriate—Quinn had pondered many of them; the center of the meadow was impractical; behind the barn there was a constant standing of water and swarms of mosquitoes; in the flower bed behind the house she'd have to live with the memory of it every single day—she decided on the one underneath the cypress in front of the fence, right by the meadow.

Quinn tiptoed into the girl's room. She was asleep. She pulled the bundle from underneath her arm, glad she didn't have to explain anything. She left the room without a sound and underneath the tree she folded the part of the towel that she had used to cover the baby's face into a makeshift pillow and placed the tiny body into the box. It fit perfectly, as if it was made for it.

She forced herself to get on with it before the girl woke up. She began digging with a shovel but after numerous attempts, Quinn gave up. She had barely excavated a hole one foot deep. The soil was saturated and heavy, and even if it had been dry, the shovel was unable to penetrate the rocky and compact ground. In the barn she found a wheelbarrow full of dry and dusty soil. It wasn't perfect but it would do.

After she placed the wooden box in the shallow hole, she then tilted the wheelbarrow and dumped the dirt high on top of it. Though it was morning, the world around her seemed to be made of shadows, and every breath felt hollow in the chest. She spread the dirt with her bare hands, then packed it down. She imagined how the ground would settle in no time, and there'd be nothing left to remind her but a faint rise of soil.

LATER THAT NIGHT, QUINN AWOKE TO THE HOWLING OF COYOTES in the distance. The air was thick and heavy around her. The wailing seemed theatrical and over-the-top as if they felt some sort of way about what had occurred on the farm. She thought nothing of it and flipped over and settled as far away from Nolan as possible.

SHE ALLOWED THE GIRL TO SLEEP FOR TWO NIGHTS AND THREE days. She never so much as stirred, never asked for food, and never even opened her eyes.

Nolan helped her so they could pull the bloody sheets out from under the girl and replace them with freshly washed linens. After the third day was about to turn into night, Quinn brought her a bowl of soup.

"You need to eat," Quinn said and gently rubbed her shoulder. The girl was on her back, her head turned only slightly sideways. Quinn studied her face; petite with large eyes underneath bushy eyebrows. She seemed foreign in some fashion—yet her skin was white and pale—and something about her was exotic. Was it the shape of her face, the full lips, the black hair? "Please eat," Quinn insisted, wondering if it was okay to stroke her cheek. By then she was worried about her and thought maybe they'd have to take her to a hospital after all.

Nolan had all but cleaned up the road; there was only one large fallen tree trunk he hadn't been able to move, even after he had tied it to the truck. The trunk was still attached to the roots and refused to budge, as if something was dead set on holding them all captive.

"Please, just open your eyes," Quinn begged, hoping the scent of the chicken broth would reach her.

Raspy and unintelligible words suddenly spilled from the girl's lips.

"Say that again," Quinn said and on a whim she grabbed the girl's hand, not bigger than that of a twelve-year-old.

The girl cleared her throat and Quinn handed her the glass of water from the bedside table. She drank the water with greedy gulps, just to break into a coughing fit. After it was over she looked around the room as if she expected to see a crib in the corner.

Quinn's heart sank. "I buried him," she said, then pointed toward the window, where, beyond the house, the porch, and the driveway, the mighty cypress stood with a wooden box underneath barely two feet of dirt. The girl, without any emotion on her face, followed the tip of her finger but didn't say anything. And Quinn sat next to her on the bed, gently lifted a spoon of chicken broth to her pale lips. The girl pinched them shut but then relaxed, and her lips parted. Quinn fed her spoon after spoon, as if nourishing her that way would somehow infuse Quinn's strength into her. She talked to her, softly at first as to not scare her, then raised the volume, told her of the storm, the trees that traversed the road like sutures on an open wound.

Later that night, Quinn woke, and when she entered the girl's room, she saw her standing by the window, holding her still-plump belly. The moon was bright and Quinn took her by the hand and led her down the stairs and out the front door, off the porch and toward the cypress. The ground was still soaked and the rain had carved miniature canyons in the dirt. They stood silently underneath the cypress, holding hands, the girl childlike with her hand quivering. Quinn felt the bitterness in her heart soften, melting away.

Quinn told the girl her name and Nolan's name.

"Tain," the girl said, "my name is Tain Fish."

"You can stay as long as you want, Tain," Quinn said.

Tain seemed to want to say something else but didn't and Quinn wondered what that could have been.

Twenty-six

DAHLIA

BUSINESS at the Lark Inn is slow during the week. There are husbands with other men's wives, an occasional truck driver who got off I-45 looking to spend his mandatory break in a bed instead of his semi, and others who stay for a couple of hours and leave used condoms in the plastic garbage cans underneath the sink. After the rooms are clean, I sit with Bordeaux in the office, we drink coffee, and he explains the Frontdesk Anywhere software program.

"In case I'm not coming in, I need you to know how to work this. If it ever goes down, and trust me, those IT people take days to show, you can use the program offline and assign a room. It actually happens frequently, but not to worry. There are procedures. You just give out handwritten receipts instead of printouts," he says and points at a drawer. "There's a stack in there. Later on you go in and update the system, is all."

Jane Doe stayed here before she ended up in the woods. I wonder if she had coffee and donuts. I want to ask him which room she stayed in, I want to find her missing receipt. But I'm not supposed to know any of this and so I don't ask.

I pull the receipts from the drawer and study them. Room number, dates of stay, and charge per night, pretty straightforward. It's my first double shift and my mind drifts and I yawn even though I've had four cups of coffee.

"These hours are getting to you?" Bordeaux folds the local paper and drops it on the counter.

"I just need more coffee, is all," I say and fill a paper cup from the pump pot on the table by the window.

"You know, you can take a quick nap as long as the sheets and towels are washed and all the rooms are ready. Take room 101, it's closest."

Take a nap. 101. I turn. There's something in the way he looks at me but before I can judge the comment, he blows powdered sugar off the keyboard.

I have the shakes from too much caffeine and not eating. My head pounds and I dump the coffee in the garbage and look outside. The bottom part of the window is covered in handprints from unruly children, jelly smears and some sort of smudged wall art. I rest my hands against the cool pane and my mind drifts to my mother's story about the bloodstain. I gaze outside, imagine the kitchen window at the farm, and when I squint my eyes just right, I can almost see Quinn and Tain standing by the cypress, mourning the stillbirth.

I jerk when Bordeaux slams a drawer shut behind me. He picks up the local paper again. I turn back and above the smudges on the windowpane, the Filling Station comes into focus. Bobby, as always, parked. Waiting.

"Cops don't seem to have much to do around here," I say as I try to remember how to look up a room status on the computer. I'm completely blank.

"Officer de la Vega, you mean?" Bordeaux says over the paper.

"I just see a patrol car parked over at the gas station all the time. I don't know whose it is," I lie.

Bordeaux lowers the newspaper. "Bobby?" Then he refolds the paper into a square. "I forgot you two were an item way back when."

"We've known each other since we were kids," I say. "But we've never been an item. Maybe it's just where he goes and eats."

"Officer de la Vega always parks over there. If one day he doesn't show up, I'll know there's something seriously wrong."

"Is he watching someone? Some cute cashier at the gas station?" The thought stings a bit.

"He's chasing ghosts," Bordeaux says, then points toward the glass door. "Looks like we're about to get busy."

Before I can ask him what kinds of ghosts Bobby is chasing, six people step out of a van; three more follow.

"They sell magazines, always pass through here." Bordeaux wiggles the mouse and the computer comes to life. Nine people pile into the lobby. All but one crowd around the coffeemaker and the donut box from this morning. "Only two per room, guys, you know the drill," Bordeaux calls out. "Discount for group occupancy. Grab a donut and let me see some IDs." Bordeaux grabs the first five keys off the rack, 102 through 106, and slams them on the counter.

Bobby is chasing ghosts. I wonder what Bordeaux meant by that.

"Dahlia, take this to lost and found," Bordeaux says after everyone is checked in. He drops a book on the counter, some sort of cheap paperback horror novel judging by the blood drops and gaudy font on the cover.

I make my way down the walkway and across the street the silhouette of a man comes into view. Seconds later I realize it's Bobby as he exits the cruiser, slamming the car door as if he wants the world to know he's there.

The suite where Bordeaux keeps the lost and found items is dank and dusty and I don't enter the room. From the threshold, I toss the book in the general direction of the bins. I hear a thud and it plops on the floor. I don't bother to go in and pick it up, just pull the door shut and lock it.

WHEN MY SHIFT IS OVER, I LEAVE THE LARK INN AND PULL UP NEXT to the cruiser. The driver's seat is vacant. I enter the gas station and Bobby stands in front of the cooled beverage dispenser with one hand on the handle, scanning the drinks. I sneak up on him and tap him on the shoulder. He turns and smiles. For a second I want to tell him about the ghosts Bordeaux spoke about, but then I think otherwise. It can wait.

"I need a favor," I say.

He pulls two Arizona iced teas from the shelf. "You're turning out to be quite the needy girl, let me tell you," he jokes and hands me one can. "What do you need?" He pays for the iced tea and we sit in the cruiser.

"You are always here. Any reason?" I ask.

"We've had this discussion before," he says and pushes the tab until it pops. "It's a small town and I have to park somewhere. How's the job going?"

"It's only been a few days but it's okay." We make small talk about my mother and the farm and whomever we used to hang out with in high school. He tells me of people whose names seem familiar, but most I can't place, and we laugh at each other's jokes. It feels like old times.

"So what's the favor you need?"

"It might seem like a strange question."

"Shoot."

"How long does DNA last? Like bloodstains?"

"Depends if someone cleans it or not. If it's well preserved, years, if the conditions are ideal," he says and crunches the empty can between his hands. "Why do you ask?"

I hesitate to mention the woman who gave birth at the farm; it seems like it's too tall a tale to tell. "Just something at the farm. It looks like blood and I can't clean it up if I don't know what it is. You know, once you put the wrong chemical on it, it stays forever."

"So what do you need from me?"

"Can I test for blood? Is there a solution I can use so I know what it is before I make the stain worse?" I'm lying. All I want to know is if it's really blood, I don't care about cleaning it, that old woolen rug hides it well.

"Sure, there are ways to test for blood. Crime scene uses chemicals for that. I don't know anything about cleaning it up but I can check into it. There are companies we use to clean up crime scenes—you know, biohazards and things like that."

"Bordeaux said something today."

"Yeah, what's that?"

"He said you're always here because you are chasing ghosts."

"Chasing ghosts?"

"Those were his words."

"What if I told you it would be better if you found yourself another job?"

"I'd take that into consideration but there're not too many jobs around here." I pause and reach for the door. "What did he mean by that? Does it have something to do with Jane Doe?"

"That's just talk. Pay him no mind. I'll come out later to the farm to see if you need anything."

If the first few months since I've been back we acted like strangers, we seem to have found what we lost so many years ago.

But then, a town like this doesn't lose anything. Not even ghosts.

BAKERSFIELD, CALIFORNIA, 1993, COUNTY FAIR

The line is long and it's hot. The muggy heat presses down on me and coats my neck in sweat. By all accounts the weather is perfect for a fair; the clouds look like cotton candy and there's no rain in the forecast for days to come. The line moves forward ever so slowly, and we are serenaded by faint music drifting from beyond the fence, occasionally interrupted by a happy scream piercing the air.

I take it all in: the structures of the roller coaster and the Ferris wheel towering high above, the troves of people strolling past Roll-a-Ball Derby, Balloon Bust, Grab A Bag, and Break a Bottle. There are also a Wiggle Worm, a Merry-Go-Round, a Rio Grande Train, a Dizzy Dragon, and a Jumping Bean Bounce. Children balance wobbly cones, ice cream running down their small fingers.

Mingling with the animal feces from the Live Pony Ride are the scents of hot dogs, nachos, and deep-fried-anything. The aroma of popcorn wafts by and I behold the food choices behind the glass of the trailer: Cotton Candy, Popcorn, Caramel & Candy Apples, Funnel Cakes, Sno-Cones, *and* Soft Drinks.

I glance over at my mother, who stands off to the side. She has changed from the Vegas Marilyn look-alike to a somewhat bohemian woman with sandy-brown curls in sundresses. And she has a boyfriend; his name is Henry Cobb. He's slightly pudgy around the waist, and his hands look as if he gets regular manicures. It is Saturday, and his shop, Cobb Auto Repair, is closed. "I own and run the shop," he told me. "I don't know the first thing about cars."

He doesn't have children of his own, neither at the present nor wanted, and he seems rather dull.

Henry Cobb stands behind me in line, pretending to flip through his wallet. He bumps into me, making my purse over my shoulder slide down to the crook of my arm.

"Sorry," Cobb says, pretending to apologize in a small and shaky voice, almost like a cartoon animal.

He isn't sorry at all. Not only is he not sorry, but he's become weird in a creepy way. I can barely stand him but I make nice for the sake of my mother, who seems to like him a great deal.

Mom and I live in a trailer surrounded by native grasses but in the summer there are mostly bare patches of cracked dirt. An upturned Little Tikes car lies discarded by the wooden front steps leading into our trailer. They sway every time we step foot on them, like a moving floor in a carnival fun house.

By this time my mother has managed to buy a new car and she works at the Wild West Casino off Highway 58. The casino is open twenty-four hours a day and she works as many shifts as she can, so she isn't around much. She hides wads of dollar bills, tips I assume, in various places in the trailer; an empty cookie jar here, a lidded bowl there, in the freezer, even. She doesn't hide the money from me—she actually makes me count and keep track of it, sometimes even uses the moment to teach me to solve math problems—and one day I ask her why she doesn't just put the money in the bank. I'm really embarrassed about the fact she's making me count out the individual one- and five-dollar bills at the market and I'd prefer to write checks or swipe a credit card like everybody else.

"Open a bank account," I say.

"It's not that easy," she says.

"Why not?"

Before she can say anything, I know the answer: paperwork. This conversation took place months before Cobb entered the picture, and she told me that sometimes we have to leave quickly and there'd be no time for accounts and banks and when you have cash you've got what you've got and you take it with you when you leave.

At the fairgrounds, the line collectively takes another step forward and I manage to get behind Cobb because I prefer to keep an eye on him. Cobb preaches about the fallen and I have no idea what he's talking about until I come to understand that the fallen are children, usually girls, who end up in dire straits. That's what Cobb calls it. He doesn't talk like that around my mother. When she's around, he's enamored with her and hardly pays me any mind.

"Girls need a father," Cobb says, "or they get arrested for fighting over some no-good hick boy in a parking lot at a bar surrounded by cacti in large Mexican pottery with cigarette buds sticking out of the dry soil."

He gets flowery like that with his language and for a while it was funny. Mom just rolls her eyes behind his back and changes the subject but now it's no longer funny. At least not to me. He says much weirder things when I'm alone with him; most of them I don't understand. He's particular about how I sit and how I cross my legs. He offered to give me clothes that are too small for his niece to wear. I've never met the niece but the clothes turned out to be underwear. I never told Mom about it, I just try not to be alone with him.

While we wait in line, I stare at people passing by and imagine their lives. I fill in the blanks, connect the dots, because people usually don't tell the truth. One must read between the lines if one wants to get to the truth. Stories present themselves willingly and just about everywhere, as I watch through the window of some motel room, or walk-up above a gas station, or one of the trailers we've lived in. But stories are just stories, they are just make-believe, and I wonder how and where I'm going to get the paperwork to do anything real. Like go to school.

Everything has gotten more complicated and now there are so many unspoken rules that I wouldn't know where to start if I had to explain them. My mother lies a lot but it's not the kind of lies that get you in trouble, it's more little things, like where you are from and where do you live and where have you worked before. She keeps track of dates and names and I've seen pages of her neat and skinny handwriting going beyond the gray sidelines, as if she feels a need to keep track of a life she wouldn't otherwise remember.

I look down at the dollar bills in my hand Cobb gave me. I can feel him staring at me. He always stares at me when my mother isn't watching, stares at my skinny arms, my hairless armpits. He also stares at my legs, and given the fact that they are covered in healed scratches that are a shade lighter than my skin, and mosquito scabs, it's just weird. He has a habit of wiping his mouth with old-fashioned cotton handkerchiefs that have his initials embroidered, HC, in ornate fancy letters; he folds them in half and wipes the corners of his mouth repeatedly.

I wear a white tank top made from stretchy and tight material with a built-in bra even though I don't need to wear a bra just yet. It's a Salvation Army find. My shoulders and arms are covered in bug bites, some healed, and others scabbed over. There is a smear of blood on the strap of my white cami.

Somehow I don't pay attention and Cobb ends up behind me again. He stares at my neck, making me uncomfortable. I turn my back toward him but I can feel his eyes hovering where the shorts frayed an inch below the fold of my butt. I wonder what would happen if all those people around me—parents, kids, grandparents, teenagers, the carnies themselves—were able to hear his thoughts, if they were made public with a megaphone, exposing him. I don't know how to tell my mother—don't know how to tell her that she should never leave me alone with him. It's creepy as it is with my mother just a short distance away from us.

For the first time ever I want to pack up and leave in the middle of the night just to get away from him. I don't like him but I'd never tell my mother because she seems happy when he's around. I'm afraid. But I don't tell my mother that either. I fear she'll trust him completely and he'll come by while my mother is at work and no one will think it odd because he comes around a lot, even with my mother gone. But the day will come. That I know. That's why I'm afraid. And it's just a matter of time.

I have no idea why I know this to be true. Sometimes I go days and I don't even so much as think about Cobb and then suddenly, like a public service announcement on TV, a buzzer sounds and he shows up with bags of my favorite cookies and snacks and books, reminding me that he feels some sort of way about me. He told me when we were alone that once I reach puberty, I must scrub and wash and sponge and rinse, to get rid of the foul stench of my body.

The line moves forward and he's now closer than ever.

"Your mother is so beautiful," he says and smiles at me. We take another step forward; we are next in line. "I might ask her to marry me and then I'd be your daddy."

Suddenly the music slows, switching into a lower key, sad and nostalgic, as if it is being played on some old and rusty instrument. Then it stops for a second, switching back to a childish and cheerful melody. "I don't think she's looking for a husband," I say.

"I'm going fishing tomorrow. Would you like to come?"

"I want to get on the Dizzy Dragon ride," I say and add, "and I don't like fishing."

"I think you'd enjoy it . . ." Cobb furrows his brow. "Your mother might let you go with me if you ask?"

"I don't like fishing, I already told you that," I say with a light sharpness in my voice.

I jerk when I feel Cobb's hand on my neck, nudging me forward. He has never touched me before. I want to jerk away but I don't want to make a scene. Mom told me not to make scenes.

His hand lingers and I can feel every single finger hot on my skin as if his flesh is glowing. I bend down to adjust a sandal strap that doesn't need adjusting and then I turn and see my mother sitting on a bench, waiting for us. Watching. Our eyes meet, her face remains stoic, and I wonder why she doesn't wave at me. Cobb and I take the last step forward and we stand by the counter where he orders three of everything.

"She doesn't like fishing she told me, so that's that. Just as well," Cobb says after we join my mother at a wooden bench. "Let's go check out the Dizzy Dragon after we eat."

Mom watches me like a hawk. When Cobb slides on the bench next to me, she pulls my food over the uneven picnic table. "Sit next to me," she says and points at the bench beside her. "I don't see you nearly enough."

There's a word for what he is and I looked it up. Pervert; a person whose behavior deviates from what is acceptable, especially in sexual behavior.

We eat silently and after the Dizzy Dragon and a shooting game during which Cobb can't hit the target even once, he drives us home.

"*Go inside and turn on the TV. I'll be right in,*" *my mother says and I climb out of the backseat and my plan is, instead of watching TV, to stand by the window, watching them. As I fiddle with the door keys, they drop and fall through the uneven wooden slats of the rudimentary steps and land with a* cling *in the dirt. I jump off and climb under the stairs. I see a couple of coins and reach for them. Through the steps I watch Cobb getting out of the car and I'm expecting him to open the car door for my mother as he always does but my mother exits the car before he has barely reached her side. They stand and talk. My mother's back is straight, like a rod. Cobb's face turns crimson and his eyes pop. He's spitting out words as his neck strains. I can't hear what he's saying but the words are spat out with the ferocity and rapidity of machine-gun fire.*

My mother leans closer into him, her face ashen but unwavering. They stand in the open passenger's door and as he's trying to push Mom back in the car, she spits in his face. Cobb stands with his eyes closed, reaching for a handkerchief in his pocket, holding on to the car. My mother steps behind him and shuts the door with a bang. There's a scream that turns into a whimper as I watch Cobb opening the car door. His hand is hanging lifeless off his wrist, dripping blood around his fingertips.

Without any emotion on her face, my mother walks away from Cobb as if strolling through a park on a sunny day. I sit beneath the wooden steps, surrounded by discarded coins and candy wrappers, and wonder how far she'd go to protect me. I feel elated suddenly, as if the worst I imagined had just been erased to never become true. Because my mother keeps me safe.

I wonder if she would've been mad if I had told her about Cobb. It was probably best not to make a big deal about it. She knows best.

I love you, I'll always be a good daughter.

I promise.

Twenty-seven

MEMPHIS

MEMPHIS knows Dahlia is exhausted from work and worried about the dog but she must go on with Quinn's story. She doesn't want to add any more hurt to Dahlia's already delicate state—but so many other painful things must be brought to light.

"She needs surgery," Dahlia blurted out the moment she entered the kitchen that first night they'd spent at the farm. The dog was nowhere to be seen and Memphis could tell there was bad news.

"What's wrong?"

"She had puppies and one wasn't born and mummified inside her. I have never heard anything like it. She needs surgery."

Her heart broke for Dahlia then, the way she held back the tears, so courageous, not wanting to show her anguish.

Even now, as Memphis watches Dahlia spoon soup out of a pot she had left on the stove, there's a fragility about her that Memphis hadn't been aware of. Maybe the toll their life had taken weighs much heavier on her than Memphis ever suspected. To Memphis it's a sad way to eat supper, holding the pot by its handle, tipping it slightly to get to every last bit. She suddenly feels tears well up in the back of her throat but she isn't worried, she won't cry, she's learned to swallow it all down, allow the acid in her stomach to dissolve it.

Memphis watches Dahlia scrape the sides of the pot with the

spoon. She wishes she had allowed Dahlia to have a dog as a child, but that would have made everything more difficult. Dahlia had begged for a dog more than once but Memphis didn't have the heart; what if they had to leave it behind, or couldn't find a place to live, or the dog got sick and they didn't have money for a vet? So many reasons she had had not to give her what little she asked for. She should have allowed Dahlia to pick a dog from the pound, a small one that was calm and didn't bark a lot, and Dahlia would have had some company instead of spending her days home alone.

As the spoon scrapes the bottom of the pot, Memphis can clearly see the damage that's been done. But she never, *never*, let anything happen to Dahlia, not on her watch. When she was a child, some man had looked at her wrong and they had packed up and left. Where it wasn't safe, they wouldn't stay. And it was never safe. She always anticipated a knock on the door, and they'd take her away and then what would happen to Dahlia? It was a constant worry, that infinite fear of getting caught. But nothing mattered then, she made those sacrifices willingly, and she too had been surprised by the ferocity that girl had brought out in her, that love for her. She should have made more allowances; a dog would not have been the end of the world. She can't shake the feeling that keeping secrets took a much larger toll than she'd expected. "I hope she'll be okay. I like her."

Dahlia looks at her, puzzled.

"The dog. Tallulah," Memphis repeats. "I hope she gets well."

"I hope so too."

"When is she coming home?"

"I'm just waiting for the vet to call so I can pick her up. She's on the mend. Don't worry."

"Do you need money?"

Dahlia looks up, surprised. Memphis sees the stunned look on Dahlia's face; for Memphis to offer money is an odd concept, and Dahlia probably wonders how much social security Memphis can possibly squeeze out of those jobs she got paid under the table for. "No, I don't. But thanks."

"Where are you working?" That dog business is getting to her and Memphis isn't sure if she forgot or if Dahlia never told her.

"The Lark Inn. I'm working double shifts."

"How much is the vet going to cost?"

"A couple thousand."

"I want to pay for it."

"You have that kind of money?"

Memphis can tell Dahlia regrets the comment by the way she pinches her lips shut, but she can't take it back. "Don't worry about that. Let me know if you need money for the vet bill? That's all I'm saying."

Dahlia spoons the last of the soup from the pot. She does the dishes and they share the paper, but Memphis just flips the pages, has to read paragraphs twice and still is clueless. Finally, she gives up. "The story I told you about the woman and the baby?" It sounds like a question, a continuation implied somehow, and Memphis hopes Dahlia won't get up and tinker around the house but stay put so she can bring the story to an end.

"What about the woman and the baby?" Dahlia asks.

Stay with me, Memphis wants to say, *there's a reason I'm telling you this, you'll see, it'll be worth your while.* She watches Dahlia emerge from behind the paper, *here she goes again with this tale of a woman giving birth in the foyer* her facial expression seems to say.

It's difficult to find the beginning every time, a spot from where to start, a point in time that links the story of Tain Fish and Nolan Creel and Quinn together.

Memphis gets up and hugs Dahlia, wraps her arms around her. Dahlia remains stiff. They have hugged before, but never like this, never with Memphis holding on so tight, and it feels right to her. Dahlia relaxes; Memphis feels her body sag and her muscles become loose.

"There's more," Memphis says and brushes Dahlia's black hair out of her face.

Memphis catches a scent of laundry and cleaning supplies coming off Dahlia, like a whiff of nostalgia.

When Dahlia props her legs up on the chair and lights one of

Memphis' cigarettes as if they are friends chatting about people they used to know, Memphis speaks as loud and clear as she can muster.

"Nothing good came after the stillbirth," Memphis says. "Nothing. At least not for a while."

TAIN WAS ALOOF; SHE BROODED AND STARED INTO SPACE. WHEN she did eat, she wolfed down her food as if she were a feral animal, drew strange designs with sticks in the dirt as she sat on the back stoop. Reserved as she was, there was a tightness about her. Quinn studied Tain's body and couldn't make light of her; how she wasn't slumped at all, her body too tense for that; how she seemed not relaxed enough to be present. Tain smiled a lot—a slight pulling upward of her lips as if there was something she was looking forward to—and it wasn't a role she played either, for Quinn made it a point to observe her from afar and she was always the same old smiling and absent Tain. Distant, wound up, in anticipation.

In a bucket in the only upstairs bathroom Tain left her bloody pads, and almost two months after the stillbirth, she was still bleeding. Quinn emptied the bucket daily, and when the bleeding stopped, she made it a point to buy her pretty underwear and matching bras and though Tain wore them, the bra straps remained tangled, her appearance always slightly disheveled.

Through all this, Nolan watched Quinn suspiciously. He spent his days in the shed and if he came inside, he ignored Tain as if she wasn't even there. He wouldn't address her, wouldn't say her name, and eventually he became intolerant of her presence.

"How long is she going to stay?" Nolan asked. "She can't be here forever, she must have family somewhere. It just doesn't seem right," he'd say, gazing out the window, at the tree and the small grave underneath that held the tiny human the size of a baby doll. The dirt still hadn't smoothed out and the small mound within the otherwise flat landscape seemed to unsettle him, a constant reminder of things gone awry.

Quinn knew what this was all about. Nolan was protective of what he considered to be his; his shed, his house—Tain wasn't allowed in their bedroom at all—even down to the smallest things, like his mug. A silly mug, chipped and speckled, blue, cracked by age, and when he saw Tain drink out of it, he stormed off, slamming the door behind him.

"As soon as she feels better and comes around, we'll help her find her family," Quinn said. "She is not in the condition to leave right now."

"What if she is a minor and having her here is against the law? It can get us into a lot of trouble."

"We're not breaking any laws allowing her to stay," Quinn said. "What do you want me to do? Put up flyers in town? That'll cause a stir for sure."

"How old do you think she is?"

"Around twenty, I think," Quinn lied. She knew Tain's back molars were only partially erupted, which could be a sign that she was much younger, but Quinn didn't know enough about teeth to be sure.

"She must go, Quinn. This isn't right."

Quinn was taken aback by Nolan's opposition, his constant griping about Tain and her presence. She didn't cause any problems and did a lot of chores around the house and the farm. It wasn't *right*? If anything it wasn't fair to her, Quinn. Was it right that she had no baby to show for all the money she had paid to Aella? Was it right that her gut cramped and twisted, making her wince every time she picked up a gallon of milk? Was it right that every time her stomach became full and bloated and her breasts stung like needles, she, yet again, was shedding precious skin meant to sustain life? Was it fair that she withered in pain for days on end and just when she felt better and had regained some strength, there came the spasms again as if her insides were a coil twisting themselves into a tight spiral? "What do you want her to do? What if she has no place to go? Do you want me to send her out into the streets? To do what?"

"Quinn, I'm not saying put her out tomorrow, but we should have a plan. I'll ask around."

When he saw Quinn's face, he held up his hands in a defensive gesture. "No, I'm not telling anyone about her, I'm just asking where someone like her would go."

"Someone like her?"

"Homeless, I meant to say. A plan is all I'm asking for. A deadline, a date, anything. She can't stay here forever."

"I won't put her out if she has nowhere to go. Know that."

"What do you want me to do with this floor?" Nolan dropped his breakfast dishes into the sink with a clank. "I can still see the blood-stain. You want me to replace it? Stain over it?"

Nolan was far removed from the man who had carried Tain into the house and gently lowered her onto the ground and tucked his jacket underneath her head. He was no longer the mindful husband who used to hang up fresh wallpaper, plant flowers—he was now a man engrossed with blood that had soaked into the unfinished wooden floor in the foyer. He was preoccupied with making it all disappear as if it had never happened; the birth, the blood, Tain.

"No one cares about the floor, Nolan. No one pays attention to it but you. Don't concern yourself with it, obviously you have more important things to do. I'll take care of it. Just go and . . ." Go and do whatever, Quinn no longer cared. She had this moment of clarity, looking at Nolan and his stained pants and flabby body gone soft over the years, no longer working and hammering, just tinkering around in that shed, and she was done with him. If he walked out right now she wouldn't mind. For all she cared, she might as well walk out with Tain and both of them could start a life somewhere else. *It's an option,* Quinn thought, *I might just leave with her, pack our few belongings in Nolan's truck and take off in the middle of the night.* By the time he stumbled out of bed and limped to the window to see what was going on, they'd be on the road, turning east toward a bigger city, or south, farther into the country, where fewer and fewer houses and farms dotted the landscape. "Go and do what you do," Quinn managed to say with a much softer voice. "I'll take care of the floor."

After Nolan stormed out the back, after she heard the screeching of the shed door, she flung open drawers, rummaging through odds and ends until she found a hammer. When she gripped the smooth wooden handle tight in her right hand, the heavy head resting in her left, she ran her fingertips over the sharp claw, then over the blunt face. She dug deeper into the drawer, collecting the longest nails she could find, and she dragged a rug from the living room into the foyer and positioned it so the bloodstain no longer showed. She held a nail by its length and with one swift movement she lifted the hammer above her shoulder and lowered it on top of the nail head.

She recalled her father but she could no longer remember the scent of his suits or his aftershave. Sigrid too had all but disappeared to wherever the memories of the dead go, but the sound of the hammer making contact with the nails conjured up Benito and his uncle nailing down the rose trellises, and then a vision of the stillbirth was all that remained. Quinn blinked away the briny tears, yet the vision of the lifeless little body remained.

Bam. Bam. Bam.

Quinn continued to hammer, repeating the downward motion without making contact with any nails. She didn't stop hammering until Tain stilled her hand and pulled her into an embrace. Quinn had always been self-conscious when she cried but Tain holding her seemed to allow her to give way to the enormity of her grief. She sobbed, her breathing ragged, gasping. All these years with Nolan she had felt as if she could scream in all four directions and no one would hear her. Tain's body felt gaunt in her arms but her embrace was strong and determined. Tain held on to Quinn and wouldn't let go and even as Quinn struggled to break free, reaching for the hammer, Tain held on.

Together, they sank to their knees and they sat motionless, unaware of the time passing. No thoughts came to Quinn except that her fate was sealed.

NOLAN REMAINED UNMOVED IN HIS RESOLVE TO GET RID OF TAIN.
He became increasingly impatient as Tain clumsily knocked over

coffee cups, spilling the dark steaming liquid over the tablecloth Quinn had just smoothed over the kitchen table, and he'd shake his head as she stumbled walking up the front porch, knocking over a water bucket. The more Nolan watched Tain, the more she attracted disaster wherever she went. Quinn, realizing Tain's clumsiness, took to being around her as much as possible, reminding her, *Steps, watch out*, and *Don't knock over the mug. Careful now.*

After weeks of Nolan's callous behavior Quinn had an epiphany: Nolan's impatience came from the fact that Quinn and Tain had become close. He hated how they giggled and laughed, and he'd shake his head as if he didn't condone their relationship. When Quinn fixed up the upstairs bedroom for Tain, Nolan watched them as they moved a wicker table from the porch to the room to use as a nightstand. Quinn rummaged through the quilts in the linen closet, most of them littered with moth holes and yellowed at the edges, but there was one that seemed in much better shape, a tufted quilt with a large pink wreath stitched in the center. They laundered the linen, gave the floors a scrub, and flattened the quilt over the four-poster bed. All this Nolan observed suspiciously.

Quinn wanted Nolan to see that Tain was pulling her weight, gave her endless chores to complete to keep her busy, and checked on her intermittently. She made her take out the garbage and do the laundry, the ironing and the mopping of the floors, and while it seemed harsh, it kept Tain from brooding and staring off into nothingness. Quinn felt as if she had to protect Tain from herself, and eventually she completed all chores without supervision while Quinn took to her bed, allowing blood to soak pad after pad, which she stuffed in the bucket in the bathroom. Tain emptied the bucket for her and every morning when Quinn awoke, she felt grateful that for once she didn't have to pretend to be strong.

Winter arrived and Nolan came down with the flu, shaking the house with his coughing fits and spitting phlegm and vomiting for days on end. When Quinn couldn't get any sleep next to him, Tain offered Quinn her room.

"No, I couldn't ask you to sleep on the couch."

Tain laughed, exposing her teeth, and Quinn realized that Tain seemed to be more cheerful lately. "You can sleep with me until Nolan gets better. The bed's big enough."

And so they started sleeping back to back, sharing a large quilt and breathing the same air at night and Quinn couldn't help but think that this was as close as she'd ever be to having a sister.

Sometimes, during certain moments, when they squeezed the pits from the sour cherries to make jam, when they folded sheets and pulled them taut and their movements were coordinated and well thought out, Quinn wondered if Tain was the child Aella had assured her would appear in her life. Quinn wanted a baby, still wanted one, but she wondered if she'd be able to settle for Tain, this fawnlike creature slipping in and out of her very own world, as if she had somewhere else to be as she stared out a window or at a picture on the wall without really seeing it.

She might have to settle, Quinn thought, not in a condescending way, but factually, with clarity, and maybe caring for someone who needed her was what the world was willing to give her—not a newborn nestling into her arms—vulnerability came in many forms and maybe this was it and there was no use in waiting around for something that was never going to happen.

Twenty-eight

DAHLIA

THE vet calls and there are complications. Tallulah has been running a fever for the past four days. "It's not uncommon after surgery, not for the first twenty-four or forty-eight hours. But now she seems to be fighting off another infection. We are giving her antibiotics. It'll be a waiting game but I'm optimistic. She's been sleeping most of the time and that's what we want. You are welcome to see her but if you can hold off on visiting her, that might be best. We don't want her to get excited. Our techs take excellent care of her and spend time with her when she's awake."

"Whatever is best for her," I say and fight back the tears. I don't want my mother to see me cry. She's offered to pay for the vet but for as long as I can remember, she has been opposed to dogs. I don't want to show any emotional weakness, knowing how harshly she has judged me in the past, never extended empathy toward me during such moments.

It's not until Bobby stops by and I join him on the porch that I begin to cry. He pulls me closer, folding his arms around me. His embrace is warm and protective as he wraps himself around my body. His arms offer more comfort than my mother will ever be capable of.

Later, Bobby and I sit on the porch, lazily draped across old lawn chairs that squeak every time we move. He has forgotten to buy beer and the only drinks in the fridge are a couple of bottles of sangria, the cheap stuff you buy at gas stations. We have a few glasses of the wine, and after we get used to the sweetness, we sit and talk, the sangria making my knees weak and my stomach tingle.

The sun is about to go down, the light is just right, the colors seem to get stripped from the world and everything turns into shades of gray and out of those grim hues the land and the farm with its buildings float like boats in still water. The crickets start chirping and soon twilight will fall, the sharp shadows will fade into the background, and only the faintest light will come from the moon above.

We remember funny stories from high school—I actually get up at some point and mock the dancing skills of a girl who now works at the Family Dollar, the way she used to bounce her upper body, sidestepping wide and awkward—and we spray my mother's home-made bug repellent all over us, a spray bottle filled with a cloudy liquid and engorged lemon rinds. By the time the sediments collect on the bottom, I shake it up again. I refuse to allow anything to settle tonight. I feel a need for the world around me to remain in motion.

As Bobby relays some sadder stories—the coach who fell off a ladder and remains paralyzed, the pretty cheerleader who now sits in her trailer in a mobile home park we used to refer to as *the worst place to live in Aurora*, with three kids and no husband. How most of the people never made it out of town and never made it in it either, still selling farm equipment or stocking feed store shelves with their tired bodies twice the size they used to be, struggling to make child support payments—the sun sinks lower and lower in the sky. We no longer care to keep the mosquitoes at bay and go inside. Bobby has never seen the interior of the farmhouse but for the stolen glance into the foyer the day we broke down the door. We get fresh glasses from the cupboard and another bottle of sangria from the fridge. The last remnant of the day has drained away and, as if the conjuring of our past has given way to a road we've always refused to travel on, we both know we are taking *us* into consideration.

"This place is something else," Bobby says as he follows me across the foyer into the living room.

The couch in the middle of the room is a chintzy saggy affair that has seen better days. Its velvet-like fabric and large floral pattern is past the point of distress and there are numerous tears and holes. The sun has bleached the once-bright colors, the browns have bled into the pinks, and the fabric puckers around the corners of the cushions. When we sit, we fall in with a thump.

At some point, I don't remember when, after the second bottle of the sangria's sweetness has taken over my body, I feel the strong urge to start my life over, right here, right now, have it going forward from this moment on, everything else, the past and everything with it, fading into the background.

We hold hands. It has an initial tinge of awkwardness, and then we kiss. He tastes of citrus with a hint of apple, and at first the kiss has less appeal than that of a complete stranger, but then it turns into something else. Bobby is known yet unexplored; he's not a dangerous alley but an undiscovered room in my very own house. There's some reluctance in the back of my head, even through the alcohol daze—the fact that we won't be able to take this back, that our friendship will change to some sort of relationship that we can't be sure of, but all the while I know my resistance began to dissolve quite some ago.

I crumble the moment he puts his lips on my neck, and when his hands touch my body, something else does the bidding for us. His hand runs through my hair, as the kisses become harder and more urgent. Another hand slides around my waist and pulls me close to his lemon-scented body. Maybe the room itself does the commanding for us—after all, time has stood still here, and we too are going back to some point in time when we came of age, but simultaneously we are being born right here and right now.

And then I *want*—I just want more of him, more of life and happiness and being in the moment and I want to see him fall apart and at the same time I want to come undone myself. I feel his breath on my neck, then the burning brush of his lips as they make contact with my skin. Our clothes come off slowly, and then his naked body is on top of mine. The sensation of having him inside me, the emotions on his face, in his eyes, the way our bodies seem to hum and vibrate, an overlay of something I can't put my finger on, this descending into each other, is never-ending. Without breaking eye contact, he begins to move slowly, maddeningly almost, and I slide my hands down his back, feeling him beneath my touch. My head is spinning and we are moving, moving, and we still don't look away. We are no longer in this farmhouse, we are not on an old dusty couch with my mother sleeping upstairs, we are who we used to be and who we are going to be, all at the same time.

Later, as my eyes drift to the glass of sangria on the table, I tell him of all those stories my mother has been telling me. He listens as he holds my hand, and I feel like I have my whole life to tell him stories about bloody floors and sheds and chirping crickets. As I relay them, they seem to be nothing but a figment of my mother's imagination, nothing more than the strange outbursts of her slow descent into madness.

After Bobby leaves, I make my way up the stairs and down the hall to my room. I turn the knob slowly and step inside. I switch on the light and my room comes to life: a four-poster bed, a cross-stitch quilt with a pink wreath, a round table as a nightstand. Eerily similar to my mother's story of a woman and a girl who may or may not have lived here before us. I haven't changed the room at all, haven't so much as moved a table, and the only personal things are some cardboard boxes lined up neatly by the wall across the bed. One box is ripped open, with four flaps hanging lifeless.

My eyes are heavy. I lie down and as I switch off the lamp, right before I drift off to sleep, out of the corner of my eye I see the composite of the missing woman tacked to the wall. I jerk from my lulled state. I have yet to open any of the boxes; I haven't taken out the papers, haven't assembled the missing wall, hadn't thought about it in days. Did I, in a moment of stupor, tack up the missing wall like I had in my mother's house? I don't remember doing any of this. I switch on the light on the nightstand but the room remains stubbornly shadowy.

The past materializes and cloaks the present in a layer of dust, as if it is stronger than anything happening in the present. My mother's stories of people who have lived here, stillborn babies, husbands who disappear into sheds, seem all too real.

In the distance, I hear the creaking and moaning of a door slamming shut. Or open, I can't be sure. But this I know: this farm, this house, they have a life of their own.

Twenty-nine

MEMPHIS

WHEN Memphis enters the living room, she knows that Bobby and Dahlia were together on the couch the night before. She heard them talking on the porch at some point, stirring up the past, and one thing must have led to another, that's what disturbing the past does. It's like kicking up the dust that coats everything in this house, putting a distorted layer on a life left untouched for decades.

She remembers the scent in Sigrid's bedroom lingering after Cadillac Man left. She recalls the initial pleasant hint of tobacco and vanilla mutating into a raunchy scent of sweat and bodily fluids. The blanket and Benito in the woods, those scents were different, they smelled sweet and honeyed, fragrant with tenderness. The hunters in the woods had reeked of bruised pine and deer urine, salty and stingy like skin abrasions, intermixed with blood and semen and spoors of pain, raw and aching.

Bobby might cloud Dahlia's mind for a bit, Memphis worries about that, but she doesn't dwell on it. Last night, as she heard their voices and laughter drift up to her bedroom window, she had entered Dahlia's room and opened all the boxes that were neatly arranged against the wall. She finally found the one with the pictures and articles about the missing people Dahlia has been so obsessed with lately. Memphis isn't sure what's happened to the girl Dahlia found in the woods, but the composite, that's the one Dahlia should keep in mind.

And Memphis puts up the wall as she sees fit; the composite in the very middle, and all the other articles around her, as if she's the one on whom everything hinges. She is proud of herself; the story is coming together but Dahlia is suspicious and Memphis knows she has to be careful and spoon-feed her small tidbits at a time, like sipping water after being stranded in the desert as to not overwhelm the body.

Dahlia won't survive if she turns fragile now. And that job, at that motel, scrubbing sinks and changing filthy sheets, polishing faucets and distributing miniature soaps. Memphis knows this all too well, has spent all her life working menial jobs, but the last thing Memphis wants is for Dahlia to be at the mercy of that boss giving her double shifts in that horrid place, at the mercy of men in general.

Memphis doesn't know what to make of Bobby either.

From Texas to New Mexico, across the state border to Nevada and farther west to California, she had always kept Dahlia safe. Yes, they had to pack up and leave often, mostly in the middle of the night, cloak-and-dagger operations that required every dollar Memphis had so painstakingly put away in months of working double shifts herself. Men were the problem, had always been the problem, and when Dahlia turned twelve she could no longer protect her. She became headstrong and independent, just wouldn't stop asking questions, rebelling against their lives, and eventually she'd blow their cover altogether.

Memphis returned to Aurora without knowing if anyone was looking for her or had become suspicious, if someone had found the graves. All the while, all these years, she had shuddered at the thought of a flash flood coming through, exposing the bodies, washing up bones, making them float to the surface.

Henry Cobb, the man who owned a mechanic shop, had started off as if he was a catch but then she'd seen him look at Pet, just a bit crooked in the beginning, but there were moments when Pet's face told a story that Memphis tried to ignore. Inevitably, she had to face it: he made Pet uncomfortable, his hand placed ever so slightly on her shoulder or the back of her neck was an intrusion, but more than that it was a plan in the making. Memphis loved Pet fiercely, she had loved her from the moment she was born, pink and healthy and perfect. Such a happy child, curious, always having to get to the bottom of everything. That never changed. As Dahlia she was just the same, always searching for the truth. Like the other day, when they cleaned out the closets, they had found the quilt Tain had used so many years ago. Out of all the blankets and quilts, this one was the only one not eaten up by moths and bugs, and it had remained in an almost pristine condition. When Memphis tugged at the quilt, a white boucle jacket with a green embroidered rabbit and a zipper that no longer worked fell from its folds. Stuck within the quilt, it hadn't yellowed, and it smelled of the cedar lining Nolan had put in the closets. Memphis hid the jacket among other linen and blankets, but then Dahlia discovered it, handed it to her, probing, digging, asking questions.

"Whose was this?" Dahlia asked, and Memphis took Dahlia's hand in hers.

"Remember the woman I told you about?"

Dahlia seemed like a deer caught in the headlights, not understanding how encountering the past can make you unravel—Dahlia doesn't have enough of a past yet—and make you let go of secrets, as if loosening the laces of a corset. "I thought the woman's baby was stillborn?"

Now might be the time to tell Dahlia what women were capable of, she thought, but only for a second. One spoon at a time, one at a time.

The woman. Memphis wonders if Dahlia ever questions why every single conversation begins with *the woman.* Memphis feels compelled to tell particular parts of the story. She doesn't know why. *In due time,* Memphis thinks. *In due time all shall be revealed.*

And Memphis grabbed the baby jacket and continued with the story. There was still so much to be told, and it was getting harder every day.

But what's done in the dark must come into the light, that's the way of ancient and secret things. Into the light.

"SHE'S A FERAL CAT," NOLAN USED TO SAY WHEN TAIN WASN'T around. "She'll never trust us, never trust anyone. You can feed her, pet her, she'll always be wild. You must know that." Nolan gently squeezed Quinn's shoulder but she shrugged his hand off.

"She's a child, barely grown. Don't talk about her like that. She needs a family."

"I agree with you, for once. She needs a family. But we are *not* her family. Someone is probably looking for her."

"We would have heard by now if someone was."

"Remember the cat that used to come to the back door, wanting to be fed?" Nolan asked, not caring if Tain could hear him in the next room. "The food made her stick around, but then she got spooked when you tried to pet her and we never saw her again. That girl is going to leave one way or another—it's just a matter of time. Let it be on your accord, otherwise it's a heartbreak waiting to happen."

It's my heart to break, Quinn wanted to say, but knew she was on thin ice and so remained silent.

"Do what you want, but her days are numbered. She has to go."

"She's become so independent. She does all the chores and gives me time to rest." Quinn realized that the statement sounded selfish. "I like spending time with her. She's like the sister I never had."

"After Christmas. That's my last word. Come the New Year, she will leave."

"Put her out in the cold?"

"It's then or now. What is it going to be?"

Quinn wanted to cry, knowing that she could defy Nolan only for so long. He was right in so many ways—what if someone was indeed looking for her?—but Quinn was selfish, wanted to keep Tain around, loved spending time with her. She had a plan, to take a picture of Tain, maybe show it around, see if anyone knew her. She had bought a camera and had begun taking pictures and eventually she asked Tain to be in the picture, pose for her.

"This is the barn," Quinn would say and take a picture. "And this is Tain by the barn. Smile, Tain, smile for the camera," Quinn called out with all the cheer she could muster, but Tain would protest, not wanting to smile for too long, or hold a pose. She'd remain still for a second, but never long enough to take a clear picture. Tain always seemed to remain elusive, as if she didn't want to be observed, wanted to remain fleeting and temporary, a mere passing presence in their lives. Quinn took photos of her anyway, hoping a few would come out clear, and it took her months to get a mere dozen or so pictures and still there were many left on the film roll, and most of them were fuzzy at best.

Tain had long picked up on Nolan's hostility and avoided him at all cost. Quinn didn't blame her. There was this feeling Quinn couldn't shake, a hunch really, that Tain was limited in many ways. She had given her books to read—first she'd picked random ones off the shelves, then she'd selected more childlike stories, with large letters, but not a single one of the books engaged her. Tain did wait for Nolan every morning to read the daily paper he bought at the gas station and after Nolan left, she'd pick up the paper and turn the thin pages, one by one, looking at the pictures, and Quinn couldn't help but think of a child pretending to read.

One day, as they were folding laundry, Quinn watched Tain bite on her lower lip and then saw her eyes turn glossy. First she blinked them away, but it was no good, and she just stood there, staring at the ground, crying, and then turning away as if she was embarrassed.

It pained Quinn that Tain wanted to hide her tears with everything that had happened to her, but there was this limited range of emotions, this obvious simplemindedness that seemed to govern Tain, as if she really was a child and her outbursts were guided more by frustration than actual understanding.

"What's the matter?" Quinn asked and forced a cheerful smile on her face, when all she wanted to do was to break into tears herself. Quinn embraced Tain and held her, allowed the shaking to subside, then wiped the tears off her face. Every time she hugged Tain, she was surprised how tiny she felt in her arms, how bony and fragile, with the tiniest hands she had ever seen on an adult. After Tain stopped crying she told Quinn that she didn't like it that Nolan wanted to get rid of her and that she was afraid.

"You are not going anywhere, child," Quinn said, immediately embarrassed at having called her *child*, hoping Tain didn't feel put down in any way.

"Why does he not like me?"

"He likes you just fine. He's just grumpy, is all."

"Is it because of the baby?"

Quinn froze, her eyes stinging with tears. She didn't know how to word it just right; the baby that died? The stillbirth? The baby Quinn never had, never would have?

"He wants a baby, I know he does," Tain said.

Quinn collected her feelings, swallowed down her tears, and continued to fold sheets. "Well, sometimes we don't get what we want. We have everything else, don't we?" Quinn said and made a sweeping gesture around the room, including the house, the farm, everything. "No need to cry about what we can't change, right?"

Tain spoke in a meek and small voice. "I'll have a baby for you," casually, as if she was offering to hang up Quinn's coat.

"You what?"

Tain just stared at her, cocking her head is if to say, *You heard me.* "I'll have a baby for you?" Tain eventually repeated.

"Stop that nonsense right this minute," Quinn said.

Tain shrugged, her eyes red but void of any expression, as if she was unable to choose a fitting emotion for what had just occurred. Quinn doubted the girl even knew what she was saying. And they continued folding sheets, moving backward as they pulled the seams, stepping toward each other, matching the corners, Quinn grabbing edges as Tain smoothed the fabric, stacking them on top of the kitchen table, in the most perfect and organized pile.

CHRISTMAS AND NEW YEAR'S CAME AND WENT AND NOLAN WAS unrelenting in wanting Tain gone. Quinn figured it was the strain of another mouth to feed, a stranger roaming around in the house, forcing him to keep up the facade of having something to do.

Nolan frequently disappeared all day long, tinkering in his shed, and Quinn felt like pinching her nose shut when he returned for supper at night. The pungent odor seemed to seep out of his pores, but Quinn managed a cheerful smile even though her stomach turned. She wanted Nolan to allow Tain to stay, and if that's what it took, so be it. But Nolan remained cold and eventually ignored Quinn as he did Tain. Day in and day out he strolled around the farm, inspecting nooks and crevices, or he disappeared into the shed for hours on end. She'd seen him with a magnifying glass, had seen him inspect the house and the porch, and Quinn thought he was checking for bugs.

"Are there termites?" Quinn asked. She knew termites fed on wood and over years were capable of compromising the strength and safety of any wooden structure, leaving it unlivable. She suggested calling the exterminator, but Nolan never acknowledged any of her questions and so she just let it go.

She could no longer stand for Nolan to touch her. Quinn was willing to bide her time, cook his meals, wash his clothes, be his wife for all intents and purposes, but she couldn't bear his hands on her body. When he reached for her, she turned away from him, not a word was being said, but he understood. Weeks went by without them talking, and soon Quinn and Nolan lay awake at night, pretending to be asleep. Quinn was capable of taking his cold demeanor, but what he did in that shed, she felt she couldn't live with. Now that she had heard the stories from Aella, she knew the Creel men weren't made to be farmers and had their very own peculiar hobbies and that eventually the farm was going to fall into complete disrepair. Secrets they had, Aella had said, dark vices, even. And Quinn became increasingly suspicious of Nolan and his doings out on the farm, especially in the shed.

Years ago Nolan had built the structure, not bigger than a bathroom, as a playhouse for children. He had painted the wooden planks in a soft yellow and even put shingles on the roof. After the years passed and Quinn never got pregnant, he had eventually allowed the chickens to settle in and used it as a paddock for the animals. Last time Quinn remembered setting foot in it, the ground was covered in chicken poop, feathers, and pieces of eggshell. Maybe it was time to find out just what Nolan was doing with his time, and even though it had been years since Quinn had been out to the shed, she had to know.

The shed was warped and she wondered how only four years—she did the math twice in her head—was all it took to distort the rafters and turn the walls and door crooked. She opened the door, fiddled with the temperamental lock, tugged and pushed, and leaned against it until the door swung backward. There was utter darkness. Not a single ray of sunlight fell through the cracks; it seemed as if this was a world that didn't allow for any light to penetrate. The smell of some sort of chemical was strong and suffocating, making her temples pound.

The windows had been removed—she just realized that now, standing there—and Nolan had nailed the openings shut. Once her eyes got used to the dark, she observed old sash windows leaning against the walls like paintings in a gallery. Some of the panels had been removed and now functioned as glass panes for numerous shadow boxes. The table was covered in glass squares and pieces of wood, hammers and nails and glue. Quinn expected saws and scythes and axes with honed blades, tools propped up against walls and the smell of grease and gasoline. There was a scent of ether and chloroform hanging in the air and she immediately covered her nose.

The bench underneath the window was covered in jars, some open, some closed, with a white residue on the bottom and black flecks of something Quinn couldn't make any sense of. There were numerous metal and rubber rings, as if Nolan was canning clandestine objects, but there was none of the electricity or hot plates or wood stoves needed for canning.

Quinn stepped closer, still covering her nose with the hem of her shirt. On the floor, underneath an old table, were storage cases, some wooden boards, unopened boxes of Mason jars, a basket full of vials, and plastic containers filled with powders. One of the boxes—it reminded Quinn of a box of Biz, used for presoaking laundry—said *Plaster of Paris* in bright orange letters. On the wall above the table hung three shadow boxes, crooked and rudimentary creations of weathered wooden boards and window panes. A net leaned in the corner.

Quinn stepped farther into the shed. When her eyes zoomed in on the contents of the shadow boxes, she jerked backward. She wanted her breathing to slow, but it didn't—her breaths came out in gasps, her heart hammering inside her chest like a rabbit thumping its hindquarters. The shed began to spin and she squatted on the floor, and her thoughts tumbled about in her head as if she was free-falling from the sky. Then they accelerated.

She remembered being pinned to the ground, one cheek chafing on the branches and sticks and rocks. Bony Fingers' hand on her neck, his fingers so long they reached across to her other cheek, forcing her mouth to remain open, swallowing pine needles and bark flakes. And as she lay immobilized, Bony Fingers on top of her, a cricket came her way, like a worm wiggling its way to freedom, fighting acorn caps and chestnuts on its way to the top, the cricket crossed the threshold, entering her gaping soundless mouth. Her mind exploded, the antennae tickling the roof of her mouth, its body moving toward her throat, and then her mind collapsed. It had nowhere else to go but turn to madness and like a house of cards, she had tumbled and became someone else, this other person, a ghost of herself. But that day, standing in the shed, looking at what Nolan had been doing, all those hours not tending to the farm and to her, she saw what he was all about.

Quinn had an epiphany, a sudden awareness that a mistake had been made. That instead of turning into a ghostly shadow of herself she should have become a warrior. A fighter with shield and war paint and headdress and a prayer on her lips. But instead she had turned into a ghost and ghosts are powerless except for their ability to haunt the living. Like the trees that had whispered to her that the wind cannot break her if only she bends, she had tried to remain fluid and become someone else, or *something* else, but here she was, in this shed, surrounded by crickets, some stiff pinned inside frames, some trapped inside a jar. Crickets.

Out of all the insects and bugs—colorful butterflies and dragonflies with lacy wings as clear as glass—Nolan chose to collect crickets. And soon they'll all be in frames, behind old warped window panes, all over her house. In every room.

Ever since that day in the woods when those men had tortured her body and humiliated her, Quinn had been unable to even look at crickets. She would avert her eyes when she saw one. The sound of their chirping was something she could barely handle, but the thought of the long antennae and their spike-like tails touching her skin took her to a dark place altogether.

And here Nolan was, his hands nothing but an extension of the crickets' antennae, soiling her body even more. Stirring up all that didn't need rousing because it covered every surface of her and everything around her every day of her life, but Nolan had to stir it up some more, kicking it up like the dust on the cracked road leading to the farm, blinding her, suffocating her, making breathing impossible. She might as well be in that jar, like a cricket, trapped.

Damn him. Damn Nolan and his lofty ways, not knowing how to run a farm or hold a woman the way she ought to be held, unable to lift a tool or hammer a nail, or stain a floor. And once, just this once, Quinn found the strength to blame Nolan for not being pregnant—she no longer saw any reason as to why she was the guilty party here, and if he were the man he ought to be, she'd be pregnant by now. The doctor had told her as much, had told her that a pregnancy would do her good, keep her from bleeding for nine months, allow her body to recover. No one had said it was impossible—difficult, yes, extremely difficult the doctor had said—but never impossible. And she knew it was a matter of time until the bank foreclosed on the farm, nothing but expenses and not ever a profit from anything, but a shed full of crickets and chemicals, and other claptrap and nonsense that did nothing but deplete the little bit of money they did have.

And then Quinn devised a plan, a plan of becoming that warrior she should have been so many years ago. She had to become stronger and gather resolve and then she'd put an end to all this nonsense, these crickets and Nolan acting like he was in charge of everybody. No need to make life complicated. Maybe Tain was all the child she was ever going to have and so be it, and she wasn't going to allow Nolan to send her away. Tain would stay and they'd all live on the farm and if Nolan wanted to leave—so be it.

And Quinn wanted to test her resolve, test her newfound strength. She wasn't going to leap forward, but take baby steps. She thought of the creek on the property behind the house, toward the woods, not *in* the woods, but close enough. She hadn't dipped her feet in a creek in years and she wondered if it was like Nolan had described it, so clear you could see the smoothness of the rocks underneath. She longed to cup her hands, not to submerge them quite yet, that would take it too far, but trap the water in her hands and dump it back into the creek on her own accord. That she could manage. She'd think about it one more day, one more night to gather more courage, and then she'd go out to the creek.

As Quinn stood in the shed, her eyes zoomed in on a wooden crate full of Mason jars. She grabbed one and scanned the ground around her until she found a few dead crickets with their legs poking up toward the sky. With a leaf she found nearby, she scooped the dead carcasses into the jar and closed it tight.

At the house, she put the jar in the kitchen window and she cut up peaches and pitted the cherries and waited for Tain.

Hours passed, but Tain didn't show, and Quinn began to worry.

What if it was too late? What if Nolan had driven her into town, or a nearby train station, or the bus depot in Palestine? Quinn went outside and circled the barn, then went to the back of the house but Tain was nowhere to be found. Minutes later she found Tain in the kitchen, dipping her fingers into the bowl of pitted cherries, fishing out a handful and stuffing them into her mouth. When Quinn asked her where she had been, Tain, she just shrugged, licking the juices off her fingers.

Just when she was about to question her further, she saw Nolan's truck coming up the dirt road. He stopped, climbed out with a large package in his hand. Something was off about him, different; his lips were relaxed, as if he was happy for once. There was a hint of joy in his smile, his cheeks not quite so stiff, but when she called out his name, he froze, turned his back toward her, slipping the package in the bed of the truck, underneath some odds and ends covered up by a large burlap cloth.

Almost as if he had tucked it away in shame.

Thirty

DAHLIA

BOBBY helps move furniture, he fixes stuck drawers, nails down some loose floorboards, and before we know it, it's a nightly thing: we have a couple of drinks, then we go to my room.

We don't even turn on the lights, just stumble toward the bed while my mother putters around the house.

That night, my head rests on Bobby's chest as we lie in the darkness. Our bodies entwine like copper wiring and shimmer with a layer of sweat. Across from us, I catch the shadowy contours of the wall of the missing. I untangle myself from his body and I go downstairs to get some ice and come across a bottle of Johnnie Walker in the freezer compartment.

"Look what I found," I say and pull the door shut behind me, handing him the bottle.

"Remember this?" Bobby asks and grabs the bottle of whiskey after I climb back in the bed. He pulls the golden bottle closure deliberately, circling around exactly three times, starting at the lip, ending at the collar. We both start laughing, remembering a scene from a James Bond movie we'd seen many years ago. He pours two fingers into each glass and I stare at the rich gold color and the amber glints. I inhale notes of soft raisins, toffee, fresh malt, and light cream. I take a sip, feel the whiskey on my tongue, smell a hint of oak and almonds. I'm still processing this Dahlia-Bobby thing, something that I'm not quite used to yet.

Bobby drops some ice into my glass to take the edge off the hard liquor. He empties his glass and pours himself another one. We both haven't eaten and within minutes I go into a buzzy trance, letting the softness flow through me. My body feels pliable and my movements are smooth, and nothing matters but the two of us.

We make love. We are silly. We drink and shower. Bobby talks about his mother dying from cancer, his warm spicy breath in my ear, but we immediately circle around to the funny memories, as if we must have it all and everything at once. He hums a song we used to listen to in high school. My lips creep into a grin and I hum along until he kisses me.

If we'd just met, we'd lie here just the same, questioning each other about our childhoods, parents and siblings, how our parents have failed or saved us, all our teenage indiscretions and lovers we've had, which ones we could have done without and those that got away, but we know so much about each other already. There's something about the two of us that feels right as we kiss and our mouths alternate between laughing and kissing and suddenly I'm overcome with a feeling I'd rather die than let go of him, rather wither away than lose him.

Later, I listen to his breathing, hear it stutter, followed by a sigh, then it goes back to its permanent restful rhythm. The way we are in this world has a pleasant rhythm, a familiar tone, a harmony. It feels comforting. And just when I think I know myself, I realize that there's so much more that's possible, so much more that I haven't even touched on, like the song he hummed that I hadn't thought of in years, the way he opened the bottle in Bond fashion, a memory that would not have returned to me if it hadn't been for him. The past somehow remembers us, it flows and moves us forward, like a sweet cantata, melody and synchronization, waxing and waning—something that tells me there's more. So much more.

I close my eyes and eventually doze off. When I awake, the sun comes at me all at once, not a gradual trickle of rays, but as if some-one has switched on the lights, violent and harsh.

Someone has opened the curtains. Bobby stands naked in the middle of the room, staring at the wall of the missing. He is motionless, as if paralyzed.

I get up, stand next to him. We both behold the wall—the composite in the center, my Jane fanned out around her like wispy stems of a dandelion.

"Bobby," I say softly, wondering for a second if he's sleepwalking. I see him shaking his head as if to say *not now.* "What's wrong?" I ask.

"How does this even happen?" He lifts his hand, taking a sip straight from the bottle. "No one looking for her. No one coming forward."

"The police are investigating." I feel a glimpse of satisfaction; I am not the only one asking questions, not the only one bothered by this dead end that is the identity of my Jane.

"They are just playing a waiting game, counting on her waking up. If I had it my way . . ." He doesn't finish the sentence and takes another swig from the bottle. "They've never cared."

"I don't understand."

"There were other women, Dahlia. Over the years. As far back as when my dad was sheriff." He raises his hand when I open my mouth. "No, wait. Not what you think. Not like Jane Doe, nothing like that. There were no investigations, nothing concrete. Some were illegals; one girl disappeared after she aged out of the foster system. They were women no one cared about, they disappeared and *poof*"—he makes a gesture with his hand—"never to be seen again. No bodies. No missing persons reports. But there was talk. My dad told me when I became a cop, when he still knew left from right. He was adamant about it, made me promise him. Keep an eye on him, he said."

"Keep an eye on him?"

"Bordeaux's father. As we got older, Bordeaux took over for him more and more at the hotel. He spent his last years in a wheelchair. I think he had MS. He died five years ago."

I reach for Bobby's hand and he allows me to hold on to it. I recall Bordeaux's father. We gave him a lot of hell, brought alcohol to the hotel, partied, and left a mess behind. Bordeaux Sr. was clean-shaven, a small man, quiet. Long thin fingers. There were tremors, even back then, and that was twenty years ago.

"He died, and I thought, *So be it. Let it go. Nothing to prove here, nothing to investigate. I kept my promise; it's over.* But then there was the girl in the woods." He turns and looks at me. "And you had to be the one to find her. Out of all people you come back and find a body in the woods."

"But Bordeaux Sr. is long dead. Does it have anything to do with the Lark? Is that why you watch it?"

"I have been watching it ever since you found the girl in the woods. Bordeaux has always been off, always on edge, since we were kids. And then you started working there."

My feet tingle and I imagine termites under the slats scooting about. I feel the pockmarked floor beneath my feet, pitted as if it is about to turn into dust. I stand in silence, the only sound the creaking of the wooden floor beneath me. I don't want to think what I'm thinking.

"Like father, like son," Bobby says.

Part Three

There can be no covenants
Between men and lions.
—ACHILLES

Part Three

Thirty-one

DAHLIA AND QUINN

approach the shed, but I don't enter. I stand motionless by the door and shine the beam of my flashlight inside.

I take one more step forward. Now I smell the air. It hasn't moved in years; it festers like a stagnant overgrown pond. The only movement I can make out is the dust I have dislodged by standing on the threshold. The beam powers through the darkness: the amount of Mason jars in crates is staggering, and there are additional boxes stacked in the corner. Aside from an unruly shaft of light that bursts through a crack in the boarded-up window and the beam of my flashlight, the shed remains in complete darkness.

Something tells me not to enter. It's not so much that I'm afraid but I feel as if I have no right to be here just yet. I remember my mother's face back when we arrived at the farm and she spotted the shed—*Don't go in there* it seemed to say—but now her demeanor takes the shape of something entirely different. Her story has rules of its own, a decorum I must abide by. I can't forge ahead but must wait for her to tell the rest of the story.

I shut the door and turn off the flashlight.

Later, I ask my mother about the cricket jar in the window—the same jar she kept under her sink at her house. As she lights a cigarette, she says, "It's a killing jar." She blows smoke from her nostrils and mouth simultaneously. "You put a chemical in it and bugs and they die."

"But why would you keep crickets in those?" I am perplexed, not understanding what this all means.

"Quinn collected them," she says.

I can't help but think that she's being jangled by invisible strings from above, some awkward puppeteer unable to stay on point.

A long pause turns into a breathless torrent. "Quinn had to prove something. She had to prove it, to herself. There was no other—"

"Prove something?" I ask. "Like what?"

She doesn't answer at first, but then she straightens her back and scoots forward in her chair.

"She wanted to prove that she could be strong. See, some men are cruel beyond what your mind can conceive. One must be resilient."

HER TIME IN THE SHED MADE QUINN REALIZE THAT SHE HAD TO become tough, had to harden as to not lose her mind altogether. *There's nothing to fear,* she kept telling herself as she stared straight ahead. The meadow seemed peaceful from afar—nothing but a shallow basin surrounded by the tallest of pine trees, where the grass grew long and lush in the rich soil—and she gauged the distance after she passed the fence; she came up with about a half mile or so. Behind that, there were the woods and the creek—she had seen the land survey on parchment paper; *legend,* they called it—and she was prepared and determined to forge ahead on her own accord.

As she crossed the meadow, the grass made her legs itch, and she breathed a sigh of relief when she recognized a walking trail at its edge. She watched her steps along the furrowed path with its dips and holes dug by chipmunks. The grass rustled gently in the breeze as Quinn made her way across toward the narrow brook, which she expected to be merely a gentle trickle this time of year. But one never knew, there might have been rain up north and it might have carried rainwater with it. When she reached the brook, she found a slow but steady stream of water. It was choked with weeds but there were spots where dozens of forget-me-nots grew at the edge.

She stood in the woods, trees towering around her, the scent of rich soil choking the air right out of her lungs. She waited for nausea or a pounding heart to overtake her body but none of that happened. The peaceful trickling of the brook was nothing like the creek in the woods of Beaumont where a hunter had stood in her path, not allowing her to pass.

Quinn took off her sandals and sat by the edge, dipping her feet into the water. She had come here to become a warrior. She would not suffer for one more day. For the first time she was going to willingly conjure up the men, their voices, their smells, their hands on her body. She knew if it became unbearable, all she had to imagine was the baby she'd held at the beach in Galveston and everything would be wiped away like condensation off a mirror.

She steadied herself, rocked to the left, and the images appeared immediately:

Bony Fingers had crudely washed blood and evil rudiments off her, then dragged her out of the water onto the spongy forest floor. "Your turn," he had called out to the others.

The men had screamed and shouted, tossing more bottles. The pain was all-encompassing, yet with every man it multiplied; every time she thought it was over, it got worse. Then all went quiet and Quinn stepped beside herself, managed to summon an otherworldly body, one that couldn't be touched, an apparition of herself, standing by, watching, a ghost who'd report back to her at a later point in time, if ever she so desired.

Her body, the one that was shaking and cold, was thrown onto its stomach.

The ghost she'd created wept for her. With a gaping mouth and soundless screams it warped into a shadow, stood a distance away, beholding her, regarding her as if she was a dead branch on the forest floor, disconnected from everything that was lush and green and alive.

When Ponytail and Beard held her down, when the pain and the burning became unbearable, that's when the ghost refused to partake any longer. It stopped weeping for her. Ghost was no longer under her control, just turned away, hid behind a tree, unwilling to watch them tugging on her and pinching her breasts. But before ghost averted its eyes and turned, ghost told her to be strong. Then ghost took off and disappeared into the woods, left her, split in body and mind. As if she had left her body, stepped outside for a gallon of milk, and then returned to someone else entirely, another woman was created that day, but not by name; no, that came years later.

The men's savagery went on and on and on. Pain licked up inside of her, past her back and down her legs, and it burned so deep she imagined being tied to a stake like a witch, flames licking at her thighs. Quinn lay on the forest floor, staring up at the long and narrow tree trunks with their parallel lines. They seemed to converge, almost leaning inward, and she rolled up into a ball. The woods around her were quiet, not as much as a squirrel dashing up a nearby tree. Quinn imagined God had hit some sort of switch, making the wind die to keep the leaves from rustling.

The pain was deep within her, almost as if she were smoldering from the inside out. In the far distance, she thought she heard the men laughing but she knew they were long gone. She remembered a story about a river separating the world of the living from the world of the dead. She didn't care for Greek mythology, for all their gods and heroes, their origins and trials and tribulations, and their significance remained elusive to her, but she remembered the River Styx, the boundary between this world and the Underworld, and how her mind had cracked and left her on the other side of that river.

A hooting call sounded in the close distance. Deep and soft hoots with a stuttering rhythm: hoo-h'HOO-hoo-hoo. *An owl perched in a tree right above her, watching her with soulful brown eyes. It startled and flew noiselessly through the dense canopy. Quinn wasn't sure if she was imagining this, because mere seconds later, the brown-and-white owl snoozed on a tree limb to the right.*

Quinn got up, stumbled toward the stream, blood and fluids running down her legs, converging into a pink tributary by the time it reached her feet. She wanted to crawl beneath the waters and take the pain with her, her body bloody raw and discarded. They had left her behind after they were done with her, the message clear enough: she was worth less than a deer's carcass.

Standing by the edge of the raging stream, a torrent fed by lashing rains miles up north, Quinn aimed for a rock—her foot slipped, almost skidded off, but she willed it to remain—then for a boulder. Her eyes gauged the depth of the creek, and she continued on atop the stones and rocks and boulders, making her way downstream. When she thought she'd reached the deepest spot the creek had to offer, she stepped off the rocks and into the rushing waters.

She immersed herself into the hastening torrent, didn't leave a single inch of her body above the surface. Like Achilles, she yearned to be invulnerable from here on out. Yet the Texas stream was no River Styx and she was no warrior.

She emerged from the waters, her clothes clinging to her body. Yet there was no armor, no protection for future battles. Like Achilles, she would remain vulnerable.

QUINN REMINDED HERSELF THAT THIS WAS JUST A MEMORY, SOMEthing that had happened many years ago. She anchored herself in reality and clung to the sound of the creek and the rustling of the leaves above her; the scent of dark soil; the feeling of moss beneath her hands, plush and velvety.

The time had come and nothing and no one was to hold her hostage any longer. Not a pregnancy, not Nolan, not this property, not this town. Suddenly she recognized how so many things lately had lost their power over her; how she had collected more crickets in the jar—even though she still didn't quite dare pick them up with her bare hand but merely scooped them into the jar—and how it sat on the windowsill in the kitchen as a constant reminder that she could overcome.

She wished Tain was with her but she again had disappeared and it became clearer with each passing day that Tain was simpleminded. If she had been wild in the beginning, unable to clean herself and change her soiled clothes after she ate, lately she seemed to retreat into a world of her own. She hummed strange melodies and collected branches, tied them into bushels and stacked them in the corner of her room. Poor Tain, offering to have a child for Quinn. She clearly didn't understand what it meant to give birth and then give away that child. How had Tain even come up with such a notion?

Quinn pulled her feet from the creek and allowed them to dry before she slipped on her sandals. She made her way back across the meadow, and as she got closer to the farm, she scanned her surroundings. She still didn't see any sign of Tain. The shed sat silent and nothing about it gave away the fact that someone could spend days on end there, tinkering with bugs and chemicals. Even ten or so feet away, she could smell the chemicals, stronger with every step she took.

The shed door was propped open with a large rock and she approached the door slowly as not to startle Nolan. The first thing she saw when she stepped into the shed was an open box atop the table, a wad of tissue paper gently moving in the breeze. The box was from a department store in town.

Quinn heard a noise from behind the shed, the way wooden slabs rub together or as if a stack of firewood was about to tumble, right before the chopped logs collapse. There was also a chiming sound as if fork tines reverberated rhythmically. Maybe a wind chime somewhere, Quinn thought, but the next farm was a mile or so away and she couldn't imagine any sound traveling all the way to Creel Hollow Farm.

Quinn followed the sound and stepped behind the shed.

The first thing she'd later remember was the dress. Blue, sky blue, almost turquois. The shade was utterly out of place with its surroundings. The fabric was silky and glossy, almost like a nightgown. Quinn's next thought was how the bright blue looked beautiful against Tain's olive skin. Then her brain kicked in, able to interpret the scene in front of her; Tain on top of the stack of firewood, a black tarp underneath her. Nolan, his pants undone, gathering around his feet. Tain's spiderlike legs around his waist. Nolan's belt buckle rhythmically clinging against the stacked wood, his hand over Tain's mouth. Quinn knew what was in front of her yet the first thing she felt compelled to do was shout, *Don't ruin your pretty dress.*

Leaves scudded over the ground, hurriedly taking flight up into the air as if the scene created some sort of energy. Tree branches overhead swayed like ghostly arms, daring Quinn to step closer. Quinn's body shook and her brain caught up and she let out a scream.

Nolan turned, his face red, his eyes wide, pulling up his pants, confused, unable to buckle his belt, hands unable to follow his commands. He took off, holding on to his belt. He stumbled once but caught himself.

For a split second Tain lay exposed, her legs spread ballerina-like, and she slid off the tarp and stood bare just before she pulled down the dress. Quinn caught a glimpse of her wiry body, her thin limbs, her sharp collarbone, her tiny breasts, but there was something else. And it rendered everything else nonexistent.

Quinn and Tain stood and stared at each other. Tain jerked forward suddenly, throwing her spindly arms around Quinn's neck, screaming and crying and carrying on. Quinn smelled the sin on her, the wickedness of her body, her pores fecund with the scent of transgression. Yet there was something about Tain, this gangly girl and her desperation, her inability to get out a coherent sentence when she got worked up. Those desperate little cries escaping her mouth and arms that didn't want to let go of Quinn, despite how desperately she attempted to loosen her grip. Tain held on, maintained the embrace, and every time Quinn managed to undo one arm, the other one held on even tighter, and eventually she just gave up and stood there with Tain wrapped around her, allowing her to sob and spasm and cling to her.

Around them, the wind carried the fragrance of the woodland, the essence of betrayal, and something that would change everything.

Tain's stomach. There was a roundness to it, a gentle outward slope that hadn't been there before. Tain was with child.

Thirty-two

AELLA

Q. was different. Aella could tell, by the feverish look in her eyes, the way she stared at the tree line leading into the forest, the way she never held her gaze for any longer than necessary. She knew Q. pretended to want a reading because the cards told otherwise. Eventually she caved.

"I WANT A CHILD," Q. SAID, MATTER-OF-FACTLY, AS IF IT WAS THE most normal thing in the world.

Aella thought she had heard it all, had helped many women conceive, but never had she met a woman asking for a life as if such things just materialized, like morning dew on grass. Q. couldn't conceive, but she wanted a child, and the only way to get one was to take it from another woman. Aella cautioned her against it, but she wouldn't listen. And then she mentioned her husband was a Creel.

Aella knew about the Creels: all the men were off somehow, lived in the clouds, and the women they picked weren't any better. The Creels used to own hundreds of acres, half of the county to be exact, but year after year—taking up painting and gambling, and one even growing orchids—they sold off parcels, and eventually Q.'s husband, the last Creel, ended up with barely fifty acres, a mere watering hole compared to what the family used to own.

Aella was all but indifferent after she made Q. aware of what was at stake.

"I will tell you what I need. No shortcuts, no excuses. I won't know if you lie, but they will," Aella told her. Just who *they* were she never clarified but Q. knew because she was well acquainted with *them* since she'd come undone.

To Aella, Q. looked like a woman who had seen beyond, had seen spirits, and maybe even conjured them to join her. It was in her eyes, her movements, her demeanor; but she had a man who took care of her, a house, a property, and Aella couldn't help thinking what she'd become if she was left to her own devices. How far she'd go to get what she wanted.

They had a talk. Scorned lovers and unfaithful husbands don't require that kind of talk, but Q. wanted a baby and so Aella made it clear.

"Asking for a life demands a price be paid. A child is born. It sounds so easy—the head emerging, pushing its way outward to join the world—but there are powers involved and those powers remain on this earth. A void is left behind, one void for the woman who gives the baby—and I'm using *give* here loosely—and another void, a void much more costly if ignored: that space the baby occupied before, in the other world, before it was born. That space comes forth with the baby, and it enters life, enters *this* world. The void on the other side remains, and it *demands* to be filled."

Q. just nodded.

"Imagine," Aella told Q., "imagine you build a house. Let's say you use local stones, let's say sandstones. There's a literal hole in the ground where you excavated the stones. And you also took stones from the unseen world so they can be seen in this world. We are not talking about a house here. You are not asking for a house—you demand a life. A *life*."

Q. stared at her, and she wasn't sure if she had understood her.

"The holes you leave behind by taking something, they must be filled. Do you understand?"

Q. just nodded again.

"Gratitude demands you fill those holes. You must repay for what you've gained."

"Repay with what?" Q. asked.

"You must repay the seen world with what was given to you. And you must repay the unseen world too."

"Just tell me what to do. I don't understand all that repaying stuff," Q. said, getting impatient.

"You were born in debt, and your death is the ultimate repayment. But in the meantime you must show gratitude until that day comes."

"I think I understand but if you just tell me what you want me to do."

"The powers will not just sit back and be patient. So think it through carefully. Being given a child is adding to your debt. You mustn't forget that. And maybe they'll ask more of you than you're willing to give."

"I won't forget. I won't."

"This is what I need from you, then," Aella said and whispered in her ear.

Q. nodded. She was well versed in deceit and barely flinched. Q. was generous too. Whatever people gave Aella to keep a lover or get rid of an enemy, she added two zeroes and multiplied it by three.

Shortly thereafter they parted ways. There were the demons in Q.'s life—Aella could almost see them as she watched her walk to her truck that day. They were in close pursuit, some so close that they were tightening around her neck. Aella thought Q. must surely feel that they were squeezing the air out of her. There was this conviction about her, as if Q. was convinced a child would persuade fate to let go of her or get tired of suffocating her altogether. Love was what Q. was looking for, a love so strong that it would heal her.

Aella shook her head as Q. took off down the road. If there was one thing she should have told her, it was that love was powerful, but fate was unstoppable.

Thirty-three

DAHLIA

I watch my mother pull clothes from the closet. She haphazardly throws them onto the bed, where they end up in a chaotic heap.

"Are you okay?" I ask as she rips down the last few pieces of clothing from the rod.

"I'm looking for something," she says.

I watch her take a yellow dress off a hanger, gently straightening the folds of the skirt. She shakes it to get off the dust. As if she found what she had been looking for, her body seems to fold in on itself, her shoulders droop, her movements become slow. Before my eyes, she retreats into her very own world, and it scares me to see her this way.

Lately, she's been seemingly fine—no more setting houses on fire, running off, or doubling up on meds—but she has replaced her anxiety with something entirely different. In those moments of metamorphosis, she becomes someone I don't know. This has been happening a lot lately; we talk and suddenly she's far gone, as if she just decided to be somewhere else. It is a visible transformation. Her face changes as if it has been taken apart, just to later emerge from that state, all put back together again. She is in deep thought, almost disappearing, but then she straightens her back and shakes it off.

"I miss her," my mother says, and I don't know who she's talking about.

"Who?" I ask.

She's far away, her eyes are off into the distance, her hands running over the fabric of the now-dingy dress with visible moth holes.

"I love you, Mom. Are you okay?"

She snaps out of it. "I'm fine," she says and puts the dress back on the wooden rod, a lonely example of something she's trying to hold on to while all the rest is in a pile on the bed. I feel as if I'm an intruder and so I let her be.

Back in my room, as I put on my shoes, I stare at the missing wall again. The tacks don't look familiar and it's not exactly as I would have put it up. At that moment I know, *know* with certainty, that I didn't put this wall up, and I know that my mother is the one who did. I can tell by the way the pages are haphazardly arranged—I would have organized them by date—that she put them up for me to see. To behold. To contemplate. But I don't know why. I can't make out what she's trying to tell me. Maybe it's nothing at all, just a random firing of her already detached brain.

The world around me starts to blur like an out-of-focus photograph. My mind is foggy and I'm terror-stricken and excited all at once. The wall swirls and the papers merge as my head tilts toward the floor, and every muscle in my body knots up as the realization floods in: I am seeing something important.

I stare at the photograph of Jane's bracelet, remember her chipped nails, and the ship's wheel charm comes into focus. I'm falling, tilting toward something beneath me that doesn't seem to have a bottom to it—a well, maybe, because I smell dank and standing water—but the expected contact with the ground doesn't come and instead I continue to fall, only the world around me is utterly dark.

A melody plays, accompanied by an image of myself walking through a meadow bursting with flowers. The feeling is joyful, like skipping off to school, but just when I speed up, someone grabs my hand. I turn and there is Jane. She holds on to my hand with a tight grasp. I attempt to twist my hand loose but I can't and I look down and I see a bracelet around her wrist. Clinking charms playing a gentle cantata. What a majestic vision.

But there's more.

Someone is following us. I hold on to Jane's hand and together we run. I'm afraid there's a black dog with bared fangs after us and I try not to be afraid. This fear weighs heavy on me but I know what to do: I talk myself full of courage like I used to when I was alone as a child in some unfamiliar hotel room.

Jane's hand slips out of mine. Someone grabs me by the arm and I jerk to a stop.

Bordeaux has caught up with me.

I fall into the feeling—no, I *fly* into it—and I'm afraid I'll soar through a world filled with spinning silver baubles for all of eternity.

MY MOTHER CALLED AN AMBULANCE AND THEY TOOK ME TO THE hospital. I don't remember any of it. Not the ambulance, not Bobby, not my mother at the hospital, not any doctors or nurses.

What Dr. Wagner does tell me in his office is that I had a big one, the granddaddy of them all; a grand mal seizure. And a second one in the ambulance on the way to the hospital. "It was touch and go, Dahlia, touch and go," he says.

My body is sore but other than that I feel okay. Initially I don't get his comment, but then it sinks in. These kind of seizures can kill.

"Your medication levels are in the therapeutic region, and now we have to assume that medication is either not going to help or your kind of seizures don't respond to it at all. I fear you'll have to make a decision."

"A decision?"

"Surgery. We are going to have to remove your olfactory bulb."

"Brain surgery?"

"Yes."

"It seems radical."

"The next seizure could kill you, Dahlia, let me be very clear about this. The seizures cause the scents and visions, and this one could have been your last one. We have to eliminate the root of the problem."

I want to tell him about my Jane and how everything is coming together and that I'm going to need just a little while longer to sort this all out.

"It does sound radical, I agree," Dr. Wagner says. "I understand you'll need some time to think this through. We'll talk in a couple of days, okay? You'll need to check in a few days early to have a physical, some blood work, some more tests, in order to get you ready for surgery. But you shouldn't hold off much longer."

"What if . . ." I hesitate and struggle to find the right words. *What if I refuse? What if I don't consent?*

"Dahlia, over the course of days you went from partial seizures that went undetected to two grand mal seizures, both within minutes of each other. There's really no room for anything but surgery."

"What will be different after you remove the olfactory bulb?"

"Your sense of smell will be gone. Food will be bland. There might be disruption of pheromones."

I think of the fragrance of the wildflowers in the meadow behind the farm. Spoiled food, smoke, old sheets, spilled alcohol—the kind of smells that hit me when I enter a room at the Lark. The scent of coffee in the lobby, the donuts, the vanilla and lavender room spray. The way the farm smells of wood and Tallulah's scent after she's had a bath. Bobby's skin, sangria, and whiskey. The way an orange smells when you peel it, how it just bursts and comes at you all at once. My mother's cigarettes, the smell of her hair dye, the scent of her lotion reminding me of ripe plums.

I have just days to decide about the surgery, but I have too much on my mind. I get lost in all the *ifs* and *buts* and then I remind myself that I can't stop now. I can't allow for anything to interfere with this *thing* that is going on with me: my mother and her stories, the bracelet in the photograph and the vision I had of Bordeaux. The last thing I need is to halt my life and have brain surgery. There's so much riding on me and my ability to keep this all together. In addition to my mother, there's Tallulah, who is finally coming home today.

I leave Dr. Wagner's office, and at the vet's I cry when I see Tallulah come through the door. She looks good; her eyes are lively and her whole body moves as her tail makes circular motions. She licks my hands and my face. I gently rub her shaved belly. The vet appears and gives me instructions for her care—*Keep her from scratching the incision on her belly . . . the sutures dissolve on their own . . . no need to bring her back . . . call if anything comes up . . . we'll call in a couple of days to see how she's doing*—and we leave. I lift her onto the seat, and the entire drive out to the farm her paws are firmly planted on the middle console.

I imagine having to take her back to the shelter, knowing my mother's ability to care for her in my absence is nonexistent. Right then I know that my surgery isn't going to happen.

Later that night, Tallulah is curled up on the couch next to me, in and out of sleep; she wakes frequently. Every time she opens her eyes, I rub her ears, making sure she knows she's home and here to stay.

My mother sits with me, and she begins her ritual. She starts innocently enough, little vignettes of someone else's life, some outrageous, some less so, all about the woman my mother calls Quinn. There are two kinds of storytellers—the ones who tell good stories and the ones who tell great lies—and I just don't know which kind she belongs to. Judging by her past, she belongs to the latter.

Then my mother's story takes a strange turn. I call it strange because it starts to bleed into the present in ways I would have never thought possible.

Thirty-four

MEMPHIS

MEMPHIS keeps telling herself that she must be fair in her judgment of Dahlia. After all, she knows nothing of sacrifices, nothing about the things Memphis had to give up. Over and over she had to leave everything behind on those moves—most of it inconsequential and menial, yet it meant everything to her—and she hopes Dahlia will come to understand. When she's done telling the story, Dahlia *must* understand.

She watches Dahlia as she listens, her head cocked to the side, hanging on her every word. Memphis tries not to give anything away, spoon-feeds it to her—she's been increasingly fragile lately, those seizures and visions she's been having—and the story of Quinn sometimes feels so far removed from reality and Memphis has to remind herself that she is doing more than just dredging up buried memories. She tells Dahlia a story that was entrusted to her. She has been holding on to it for many years, and now it is her obligation to release it from her memory.

Dahlia was in the shed the day before the seizure that put her in the hospital. Memphis had watched her when she came upon the open door and how she had shone the flashlight into the darkened shed and then just turned around and let it be. Memphis had unlatched the door, had left it gaping as if it was an invitation to enter, but Dahlia didn't see what Memphis sees every time she passes by the warped wooden shack.

Be patient, Memphis tells herself; *in due time*. She repeats it three times, like an incantation she wants to conjure into reality.

She watches Dahlia on the couch, rubbing the dog behind her ears.

Animals have always had a special place in Dahlia's heart. Memphis is still pained that she never allowed her to have a dog all those years on the road, wouldn't even allow her to befriend the stray cats in the motel parking lots, would remove the bowls of food and saucers filled with milk, didn't want her to get attached and then have to leave. It was like setting her up for heartbreak.

Memphis jerks herself out of the past, reminds herself to be on point.

"There was this man who lived around here, long time ago. He had a big white dog. Called her Ghost. It was a fitting name."

Dahlia continues to rub Tallulah's ears, and the dog scoots even closer to her.

"Let me tell you about Ghost," Memphis says. "She had the most beautiful coat you can imagine."

QUINN WAS MADDENED. WITH A DEEP AND POWERFUL ANGER inside her she grew silent around Nolan, became unresponsive toward him as if he wasn't even there. She felt hate for him in such a way that it wasn't even comparable to the indiscretion of having taken advantage of Tain. This was not Tain's doing. It was all Nolan.

Rape. Yes, *rape* it was—after all, Tain was simpleminded, hardly able to keep herself clean. She was naïve and so much more child than adult, dependent on Quinn for so many things. Repetitive chores she did well, but one could never expect Tain to make an independent decision. She'd walk right by an open window through which the rains were splashing on the freshly polished floor unless you had sent her to close it. Only snapped the beans when reminded, never because it was time to prepare dinner.

But the baby—there was the baby. Quinn had stopped hoping altogether. The night of the stillbirth she was devastated but she knew why it had happened. Aella had been clear—*Follow my instructions,* she had said, *don't deviate*, and later Aella had asked Quinn if she had done everything the way she had asked her to.

Quinn answered yes. But that was a lie. She couldn't do what Aella had asked her to do, just couldn't. The instructions had been clear: she had to go find a bitch and before she gave birth, she had to hang her—literally hang her, strangling her to death from a tree, cut open her belly, and take the first living puppy and bring it to Aella.

Those were the instructions, but Quinn knew she wasn't made for such a task. But she needed a puppy and so Quinn had walked down to Seymour's place, the old retired teacher, knowing that his Great Pyrenees was about to give birth. She had been visiting him, asking him how he knew the birth was imminent, and Seymour had told her what to look for—Ghost had been sneaking into the barn, making a nest from straw and old blankets—and that night she went out to Seymour's place. She snuck into the barn and made her way to the straw arrangement where Ghost was going to give birth any day.

But it was too late. Ghost had already pushed the puppies out and they were feeding off her engorged teats as she lay on her side, exhausted, barely looking up. There was one pup, smaller than the others, and it had been pushed off to the side. It was cold and Quinn knew it was dead, stillborn, and what difference did it make it anyway if she passed the dead puppy for the one the instructions required. Quinn had known all along that she'd never be able to go through with such a gory thing, would never be able to cut a puppy from its mother. Quinn didn't put many things past herself—she reckoned she could, given the right circumstances, strike out. If she was completely honest with herself, she knew she could kill in a moment of desperation, but committing such an atrocious crime against an innocent animal—Quinn didn't have that in her.

By the light of a single flashlight beam, she picked up the still bundle and cradled it. She lifted it to her mouth and blew her warm breath on the pink nose as if she was going to be able to resurrect it by breathing her very own life into it. Ghost lifted her head and after she glanced at the suckling pups, she put her head back down and closed her eyes.

Quinn wrapped the dead pup in a piece of fabric she found in the barn and made her way to Aella's trailer in the woods. She knocked on the door and Aella opened it and let her in. The trailer smelled of smoke and herbs, sweet and spicy. She handed Aella the bundle and she took it, unfolded the fabric, and smiled. It wasn't a smile of perversion or one that took solace in the stiff little body, its bare belly and pink pads, just sheer approval of the fact that Quinn had done as she was told.

"What do I do now? Just wait?" Quinn asked.

"You stay and watch," Aella said and stepped toward the stove.

Quinn's stomach dropped but she sat at the kitchen table, a shabby and crooked affair covered in herbs and other plants growing in pots.

She watched Aella do things she didn't understand: there was a joyous fire and herbs were burning, filling the trailer with smoke. At some point Aella put the pup down and went outside. Quinn, through the window, watched Aella dig in the yard, under the oak, just to return and empty the contents of a glass bottle into the pot that was on the stove, turning up the heat. After a while steam developed, more steam than Quinn had ever seen come from a pot of boiling water. In no time, the windows were blind with condensation and there seemed to be a presence in the room. It wasn't visible by any ordinary means, but Quinn felt they were not alone.

Aella addressed the presence—Quinn didn't understand any of the words—and then she fanned the steam coming from the pot toward Quinn.

"Step closer," Aella said and moved aside.

Quinn did as she was told, making sure not to look inside the pot, but she needn't have worried, the steam and smoke coming off the stove were too thick for her to make out anything. Quinn took in a deep breath. The steam mixture was oddly comforting, and seemed to clear her mind. The smoke became thicker then, taking her breath away. Quinn coughed and had to sit down until the spell was over.

"It's inside you now," Aella said. "It's done."

Later, Quinn went to bed but was unable to sleep. She must have walked ten miles or more that night, but exhaustion wouldn't come.

YES, THE PUP HAD BEEN STILLBORN AND QUINN HAD NOT ONLY lied to Aella but had lied to the spirits, had taken them for fools. Maybe that's why Tain's first baby never lived—what other reason could there be?—but in the end, there was going to be a child.

Tain was pregnant by Nolan, and she'd have a baby after all. Judging by her belly, the baby would be due sometime in the spring. And Quinn filled in the blanks, imagined all three of them living on the farm with the baby, a sort of commune like the woman whose name Quinn no longer remembered had told her about at that Galveston beach.

But quickly it became apparent that wasn't going to happen. Quinn smiled at Tain every day, didn't so much as scowl at her, but Nolan, him she hated for what he had done. And that hate didn't ebb—it multiplied. He wasn't just scum, but lower than that: Nolan and Tain had been carrying on behind her back. Quinn didn't blame Tain at all, she loved Tain fiercely, but Nolan was another story altogether.

"She's just a child, Nolan." Quinn tried to remain calm yet she couldn't, had to watch him every Sunday in church, so pious with the hymnal in his hand, yet his mind full of filth. "What are you thinking? She is pregnant. I don't even know who you are anymore."

They'd go on for hours, yelling at each other. Quinn began to plead, tried to make Nolan understand, and sometimes, for a fleeting moment, she thought she had gotten through to him, but then he'd just defend himself all over again.

"I've been telling you for months to make her leave. You wouldn't listen. Now you're blaming me?"

"Your judgment is what I blame. How can you take advantage of her? She's not even all there. You know that." Quinn watched his face closely. Maybe it was the light playing shadowy tricks, but she swore she saw something like regret in his eyes. "Tell me why."

"Why what?"

Was he so cruel that he was going to make her spell it out? "Why are you carrying on with her?"

"You are the dumbest woman I have ever met, Quinn Creel. By far. Don't you see that it's your fault?"

Quinn closed her eyes. "My fault? Are you mad? Are you completely mad?" Putting the blame on her when all she had ever done was be a good wife. She stood in silence, her hands quivering. Shiny objects on the table, on the walls of the shed, they called her name, tempting her to shut him up. The hammer on the table. The saw hanging on the wall. The long silver nails in a neat pile.

"Don't you see what you've done? You allowed her to stay, even though I begged you to make her leave. Then you become her friend. You spend all day with her, you even sleep together. And she loves you, Quinn. She loves you with the few thoughts she can keep in her mind at one time. She wants to please you like a dog pleases its master. She'd do anything for you."

"Just what are you saying?"

"She did this for you. She's watched you cry, cared for you when you bled and you couldn't get up. Wiped your tears. And still you go on and on, talking about babies. You never let it be. I was content, had come to terms with it, but you kept carrying on and on. You poisoned her mind. All she did was give you what you've always wanted."

"You don't know what you're talking about. Tain has no idea what's going on."

"She used me. She might be simpleminded, but she can get anything she wants. Learned it somewhere, I assume. She used me to give you a child," Nolan said. "I didn't use her. Yes, I made a mistake, I'll be the first one to admit it. But don't underestimate her. She knew what she was doing. And it was all because of you."

It was all because of you, Nolan had said.

Her hate remained, yet something else snuck into her head. An inner voice, unfriendly and cruel whispered to her, *Everything has gone wrong and it's all because of you.* The world seemed to close in on her and the air around her became hard to breathe. Her thoughts scattered like some electrical short circuit in her head, too many for anything to make sense.

Eventually Quinn's hatred toward Nolan became rational, void of her emotions, almost as if she had come to some sort of agreement within herself: quite simply, Nolan needed to be punished.

THE ONLY BIRTH ANNOUNCEMENT WAS A SLIGHT DROP IN TEM-perature and the descent of absolute silence upon the farm. As if the weight of what was being set in motion was apparent to Tain, she was afraid to push, had forgotten how to breathe through the contractions, and all she knew to do was scream, her voice high-pitched and tearing at Quinn's patience.

"Is it out yet?" Tain kept asking as if she was blind, sitting off to the side, waiting for the news, while all the while she was the one doing the pushing and the birthing. Quinn understood then how simple Tain truly was, how meek, just short of being completely backward.

In a moment of clarity, Quinn saw the future, *their* future: Tain would remain at the farm with them, she'd conceive baby after baby with Nolan, and maybe even other men in town, like a stray dog in heat. And people would talk, would look at them in church, and even if they quit going to Mass, there'd be trips to the market and city hall, the bank, and doctors, and they'd all stare, gossiping about them living together. Nolan would continue to pin insects and sire babies with the dimwit living in a back room while the wife watched on.

Is it out yet? Is it out yet? Is it out yet? It went on for hours and Quinn said *almost* a dozen times, nodding as if to convince herself. "Almost. Push harder!"

Quinn felt a tremor of pleasure, for she was closer to whatever was going to come of this. Between the stillbirth and Nolan carrying on with Tain, she'd be happy enough if this baby finally got there healthy, she'd settle for that. But if she could have it her way, she'd keep Tain and the baby on the farm, just as long as Nolan left. She'd cried too many tears, had taken just enough abuse and humiliation to want him gone. Yes, this baby belonged to the both of them, her and Tain.

It wasn't until the darkest part of the night that the baby crowned. Quinn instinctively slipped the umbilical cord over the baby's face, hoping she wasn't tightening it by mistake. It slipped out of Tain's pelvis with its umbilical cord coiled and blue. It was a girl. The baby didn't cry, didn't even let out an angry shriek.

Quinn felt her chest tightening. *Not again,* she wanted to scream, *not another one. Fear* was too mild a word for what she felt and she wiped the elfin body vigorously yet gently. The baby began to gripe, timid at first, but then her voice became stronger and she broke out into an all-out wail. After Quinn wiped the baby down and tied a diaper around her, she handed the bundle off to Tain, but she pushed her away.

Tain had become less and less lucid as the labor had gone on, and after it was all over, she stared off into the distance. Quinn remembered the lack of emotion after the first birth, the absence of tears and involvement, as if she had watched a cow give birth and was utterly bored by it.

"You have to feed her. I don't have formula," Quinn said and Tain reluctantly complied, pressing the newborn against her chest. Tain watched in amazement as the baby latched on to her nipple, but then it slipped out of the baby's mouth and she started crying and all Tain did was look around helplessly.

Quinn drove to a neighboring town to buy diapers and rash ointment, and she stocked up on baby formula, anticipating Tain would soon refuse to feed her. Every day from then on out, Quinn had to remind Tain to feed the baby, bathe and change her.

After a week went by, Quinn reminded Tain to come up with a name.

"Have you thought of one yet?" Quinn rocked the baby as Tain twirled her wet hair around her index finger. She had only taken a shower because Quinn had asked her to. She wasn't sure what Tain knew about conception but she hoped she knew the basics, knew that the whole Nolan business had to stop.

"I don't know," Tain replied, "you pick one." Then Tain looked around the room. "Where will she sleep?"

"We'll go and buy a crib. We can put it by the window; there'll be a breeze and she can hear the birds. We'll get a mobile that plays a melody. And a changing table maybe."

Quinn worried about Nolan and buying anything new, knowing he'd gripe about how much money it was going to cost. She had been avoiding him so far, had not spoken to him about much but the bare necessities, but maybe now was the time to have a talk.

"I'll talk to Nolan, see if he can help me with the furniture." Quinn looked down at the baby, her eyes gently twitching, her lips pursing in her sleep. She was beautiful with her perfect skin and black hair, so much like Tain, nothing of Nolan's washed-out complexion and sandy hair. "Get some rest, and if you need anything, I'll be downstairs."

Tain nodded and closed her eyes. She was exhausted, and Quinn couldn't blame her. She tucked the baby by Tain's side, close to her chest.

"She'll hear your heartbeat that way," Quinn said and turned around but Tain was already asleep, the baby molded against her.

Quinn saw Nolan's truck parked in the driveway and she went out the back door and made her way to the shed. She called out his name but there was no answer. Lifting the large metal latch partially with one hand, she pushed the door with both hands, leaned her shoulder into it for added pressure, and then the latch lifted, full of resistance at first, but then the door gave way.

Nolan sat on a stool in front of an old table functioning as a workbench. He smiled as he turned, but then his face froze as if he had expected Tain instead of her.

Quinn felt a tinge of anger ripen once more inside of her. Between the chemicals hanging in the air and the floor covered in a white layer, she felt nothing but disgust for him. He had brought her here, punished her with indifference when she didn't get pregnant. He'd been trying to get rid of Tain ever since she'd shown up, wanted to leave her to some dubious fate and wipe his hands clean. He fathered her child—but in Quinn's mind, just one question remained: how to get rid of Nolan, how to have money and a place to live for her and Tain and the baby, how to convince him to leave. Maybe she should reiterate that fact that he had sinned, that his guilt ought to motivate him to go and let them be?

Quinn opened her mouth, had lined up her case, but Nolan stopped her by raising his hand.

"Quinn, we've known for a while now that this was going to happen. It's been going on for too long, and it's against everything I believe in," Nolan said. "All these lies, day in day out. And now there is the baby," his voice nasal, annoying.

Nolan went on about sin and redemption and what God required him to do and how he could never, *never*, go against the word of God and that a man must care for his and forsake all others, and how sometimes things happen on their own accord and *all of us*, he said, *deserve to be happy*. And that, with a heavy heart, he had made up his mind, and nothing more was to be said about it. "Not another word, Quinn. I have to make this right. Sometimes we make the wrong choices but God demands we can make those wrong choices right."

Quinn ignored the dozen or so frames with gory insects pinned behind glass leaning against the table, and then she realized the frames had braided wire sticking up from the back, ready to be hung on a wall. Quinn scanned the shed, realizing there wasn't any room on the walls of the shed—they were covered in tools hanging off nails, dirty aprons, and rickety utensils, and then Nolan's voice went up in volume as if he wanted to make sure she was hearing and understanding him, as if he wasn't going to repeat it because his word was law.

"I need you to give me a divorce. I want to marry Tain and raise my daughter. I hope you understand."

He went on. Quinn comprehended nothing at first, but then it sank in: he wanted to take from her the only thing that she cared about.

God. Child. Obligation. Every time he opened his mouth, Quinn got angrier. *I hope you understand.* All these years of reproach and criticism, his looks of disapproval, and all those years he'd spent in this shed, devoting himself to what Quinn was most afraid of, what she despised. She could handle the nightmares, could handle feeling imaginary hands on her body, could push that away, but those crickets, those damn crickets ready to be hung in her house, on her walls, that was too much.

Quinn imagined one of those frames on the wall in her bedroom, Tain sleeping in her bed, carrying on with her husband. Not a stitch of hate toward Tain—her simplemindedness had been proven—but for Nolan to be this callous? All these years of her swallowing her retorts and just living this isolated life on this rotten farm, how she had smiled through it and carried on with chores that were Nolan's obligation. And now he made it all go to shit.

"Here," Nolan yelled, and pulled some papers from his jacket pocket. "Here, I've put the farm in your name. It's all yours. I don't want it anymore. I don't want any of this, you can have it all. I just want a divorce and the baby."

All those years of her trying to convince him to sell and buy a house in the suburbs, all the brochures she had brought home, all those times she had shown him floor plans, and he had just ignored her. And Tain came around, and he was ready to give it all up, give up the farm and everything on it, if he could just have a divorce.

All her rage spilled over, fast and destructive. It consumed all of her—everything that she had so delicately hidden over the years, how she had never resorted to violence before, not once, not even as a child, *never*—and as she scanned the table her eyes fell on a hammer claw, shiny and new, its wedge large and blunt. And before she knew it, the smooth handle was in her hands, its grip powerful, as if her reach was now extended and therefore the damage not so much of her doing, but that of the hammer that had chosen to intervene on her behalf.

Quinn was strong, had been the one splitting wood all these years while Nolan was in the shed or the barn toying with unimportant things. Quinn raised the hammer, switched the blunt neck to the back, wanted the claws split like a forked serpent's tongue to make contact. She raised her right arm and aimed at Nolan's head where his hairline had receded, where the claws could penetrate his skull and soft tissue, digging into his brain, destroying his evil ways and his wicked and immoral thoughts, with just one hit.

Her arm was sturdy and so was her shoulder and she paused just long enough so he saw the look in her eyes.

Nolan screamed. Mouth gaped open, about to raise his speckled hands to ward her off. Too little too late.

Quinn's left hand joined her right, her fingers interlacing around the wooden handle. In a perfect half circle she brought the hammer from behind her head down on his skull.

There was a sound, a crack, then a spatter of warm liquid on her face—she closed her eyes—and then she heard glass shatter, thought he'd be upset at her for breaking his jars and glass frames, but then she realized it was over. She was surprised how little effort it took to drive the claws into his head.

Quinn thought of this moment later, the moment she became the warrior, more like a progression toward fate than a choice she made.

He had it coming. Nolan had meant to wind her up, had been vengeful and mean, and this was what he deserved. One minute he was speaking of God and faith, and the next he was a bleeding mess on the floor. He had it coming.

Quinn was taken aback by how little what she had done bothered her.

Thirty-five

DAHLIA

MY body is tired and my mind won't let me rest. My life seems to be spent in anticipation of something big happening, something I can't put my finger on. As I lie in bed and stare at the ceiling, the stagnant air of the room leaves me with an epiphany: it was a mistake to come back to Aurora. No one has to take my blood or shove me in a high-tech tube to know that the past is a ferocious beast determined to turn me inside out, a juxtaposition of my mental state on one hand and my mother unraveling on the other. Then there's Bobby—I haven't even begun to put us in any kind of order—it just seems as if another part of the past comes rushing at me every day: my mother's stories and the flecks of images that have emerged lately from my childhood form strange inkblot shapes.

And then there's the farm, this house, the drag it produces. It catapults my mind into some sort of limbo, as it does my body: there are the uneven floors that make me lose my balance and the past seems to seep through the window frames and then rise and make the wallpaper peel. All those abandoned artifacts that have somehow served their purpose seem to communicate with me—this very quilt I sleep under every night, with its pink wreath, is in perfect condition, whereas the others are frayed and yellowed after moths have waged a decade-long war. That too lacks explanation. The farmhouse seems to shudder, and even if I open all windows, the light still struggles to creep in and its rooms are always dark and shadowy. Would a new coat of paint and the fragrance of a cake baking in the oven change that? I doubt it.

The shed. I have never actually stepped inside—the first time I attempted to enter, I couldn't open the latch; the second time I found the door gaping open but I just stood there with a flashlight, shining a beam into the darkness. I have never set foot in it and maybe I should just go right now and see for myself.

I throw a hoodie over my pajamas. Outside, the sun is up, yet barely there, struggling behind wispy clouds. The sky changes constantly, juxtaposes itself onto an infinite canvas that colors are tossed upon, first blue, then bright pinks and oranges pile on top of each other, only for low-hanging clouds to fill my world with a gray haze the next. The clouds push against one another in anger and everything is alive, growing at each passing moment, a constant changing opus offering itself to me.

I give the door a shove and it screeches on its hinges. It opens, swings all the way back as if it is inviting me to enter, unhindered, without opposition. A thick carpet of dust clings to every object, and the limited light that seems to have snuck in behind me illuminates the dust particles suspended in the stagnant air. A quick appraisal reveals nothing of importance, nothing that proves or disproves my mother's story, but then what did I expect, the outline of a body?

The interior is in such bad shape, covered with not only dust but leaves and spiderwebs and other debris. Short of dusting and wiping everything down, nothing will be revealed here. There are window frames and glass panes covered in spiderwebs, and Mason jars, most of them in shards on the ground. There is a hammer on the table, but why wouldn't there be? This is a shed, and sheds contain tools, so that's nothing to be suspicious about. Even so, I only stare at the hammer, covered in some sort of white substance that has partially flaked off. Webs and spider eggs cover it, some of them round balls, others squishy and fluffy masses of silk. I don't want to touch it.

I hear a cracking sound and I shift my weight. The floor is soft, almost springy it seems, and I twist the tip of my shoe into the ground.

I bend down, wipe the leaves and debris aside, and underneath the floor is solid. And white. Gypsum. Plaster of Paris.

Outside the sun hides behind the clouds, not allowing for a fleck of light within this shed, not so much as a broken window permitting a spear of it to enter.

I can't shake the feeling that this place is alive and dead at the same time. The only thing thriving is the hot and stagnant air, fecund with what has become apparent: my mother's stories may not be stories after all.

AT THE LARK I TRY TO AVOID MY LIKENESS IN THE MIRRORS OF THE rooms I clean. I am as pale as the plaster I discovered on the floor of the shed and there are so many questions circling in my mind: Why is my mother telling me these stories? Is she trying to distract me with Quinn's life so I don't ask other questions that pertain to my very own past? Or maybe she's just good at telling stories, and I know that's a fact about her that is quite true.

Later, as I stock the cleaning cart, Bordeaux appears from behind, making me jump. A feeling builds in the pit of my stomach. Then my heart starts to beat even harder and faster, my hands move irrationally, pretending to count towels and sheets.

"You don't look well," he says.

"I'm okay," I say and continue to count the towels, hoping he'll just go away. "Stop sneaking up on people."

"You're not going to get sick, fall down, hit your head, and then sue me, are you? I'm worried about you. Do you feel as bad as you look?"

Bordeaux seems concerned, yet there are two people covering three shifts seven days a week—he can't afford to lose me.

"Come to the lobby with me. Sit down and rest. I have to run out in a bit."

Later, we have coffee in the lobby, me in front of the counter, Bordeaux behind it, hammering away on the keyboard.

"You frighten me with those looks on your face sometimes. Like you're about to pass out."

"I'm fine. The medication really helps," I lie and scan my cart to make sure it's fully stocked with cleaning supplies, towels, and sheets. "It's the hard core stuff. Don't worry, I won't fall and crack my skull open."

"Are you sure?"

There's something in the way he looks at me, not just looks at me but takes me in.

"Nothing to worry about," I say.

"If you say so." Bordeaux scans his computer screen. "We have three rooms booked, another five about to be. There's a problem up at an RV site, something about the plumbing, and some campers need to stay here until the problem is resolved." He studies the screen some more. "I'm running out to get some more coffee and donuts, maybe even some orange juice. We'll be full for the next few days so I appreciate your commitment. You don't look well, but you're hanging in there. I appreciate it. I'll be back, I won't be too long."

"No problem," I say. Looking at Bordeaux now, he is nothing but a haggard man looking fifteen years older than he really is. There is a shortness about him, the way he deals with customers, always to the point. I wonder if there are hidden things that allow me to appraise him further, in the drawers and boxes all over this office.

After Bordeaux gets in his car and drives off, I go through the drawers behind the counter. I come up empty: nothing but receipts, magazines, pens and pencils, some loose change. Nothing meaning anything. Besides, I have no idea what I'm looking for.

I hear the doorbell jingle and Ariana appears, dragging the scent of fabric softener and dryer sheets behind her.

"Chica," she says and smiles. "So glad you're back." Ariana is in her forties, pretending to be ten years younger with perfectly drawn Sharpie eyebrows and a lip liner making her lips unnaturally pouty. Ariana works in push-up bras and skinny jeans, and she has five girls whose names all start out with the letter A, but I can't ever remember a single one. She still might try for a boy, she told me the other day, if it wasn't for her husband driving a semi and being gone most of the time. "I hate working with Bordeaux alone. He's a creep. You all better?"

"Yes, I'm all better. Do me a favor?"

"Sure, what you need?"

"Keep an eye on the lobby and text me when Bordeaux gets back?"

"Ay, chica, what are you up to?"

"I need to check on something."

"Go ahead. He'll be gone for a bit, he gets the donuts cheaper at the other side of town. Don't worry."

I leave my cart in front of 101 and walk the entire row of rooms down to 120, then I cross the parking lot toward the suites. I don't know what I'm looking for. I know Bobby wouldn't approve of my snooping at all, and it's just a hunch, an instinct of sorts, but the building seems to be sitting there just waiting to be explored.

I know the suites are as old as the rest of the motel and none of the rooms except the lobby were ever renovated since it was built in the late sixties. James Earl Bordeaux Sr. worked at the Lark all through my high school years and beyond, according to Bobby, until he was wheelchair-bound and his son, James Bordeaux Jr., took over.

As I stand in front of the suites, I know one thing for sure; when playing truth or dare, I'd always picked dare. I pause by the first door and wipe the dirty sign with my fingers. 301. This one must be the storage room.

I unlock the door and step inside, leaving it ajar. I pause long enough for my eyes to adjust to the dimness of the room. The air is thick; even the feeblest breeze seems to be unwilling to cross the threshold. I give the room a quick survey: an array of unused furniture, headboards stacked one in front of the other, mattresses leaning against a wall, MicroFridges, about half a dozen of them, stacked on top of one another. The entire room is covered in a layer of dust. I back out, holding my breath in the process, and I wait until the door closes before I breathe again.

302 doesn't unlock with my universal key and so I move on to 303. It's a somewhat intact room, though there's no bedding or mat-

tress. Where a dresser and a TV on a desk should be, there is nothing more than three cheap metal shelves holding nesting bins, numbers written on them. On the floor lies the paperback I tossed in days ago.

I step closer to the bins. I struggle to connect the numbers, miss the connection between them. I sound them out in my head, one by one, and finally a pattern emerges; the bins are numbered by years, 6972 is 1969 through 1972, 7375 is 1973 through 1975, and so forth. I rummage through the bins and find the usual items: stuffed animals, watches, single earrings, books, shoes, clothes, a couple of flip phones, purses, and duffel bags. Most of the containers are dusty, and there are occasional spiderwebs stretching from one bin to another. There's only one item that catches my eyes: a briefcase, reddish leather, with a three-dial combination lock, its surface not as dusty as the rest of the items. Not only does it seem out of place, but it looks like it's been handled recently.

My cell rings and I see Ariana's number pop up. Something tells me that I have nothing to lose, that I can return it later, and even if I don't, no one will miss it, and so I grab the briefcase and on my way back to push my cart in front of 101, I throw the briefcase on the backseat of my car. With a thud it bounces off and comes to rest on the floor, half hidden underneath the passenger's seat.

The rest of the day goes by quickly. The RV people need directions to Laundromats and grocery stores, and after Ariana leaves, I mop the lobby and wipe down the tables covered with powdered sugar.

As I clean up spilled coffee in the lobby, I have a moment of courage. I don't know how far I can go, how far I *should* go, but the feeling has been building up for a while. I'm not alone—Bobby is across the street, just like always. It's how Quinn must have felt after she collected the crickets in a jar. It's as if life can't be lived in a state of fear. You get accustomed and then you forge ahead.

"James," I say, "do I call you James or Bordeaux?"

"Bordeaux is fine."

"So, I was thinking about something. About the girl in the woods everyone is talking about."

"What about her?"

"I don't know if you know but I was the one who found her. I'm the jogger they talked about on the news." I wait for a reaction but there is none.

"Is that right? That must have been quite exciting, finding her." His voice is flat and his features have become lifeless in the bluish light of the computer screen.

"I didn't tell you about the rest, did I?" I say and watch him closely.

"Tell me what?"

"Since I fell in that creek and I hit my head, I've been having these episodes. I see things, and I hear voices."

"You shouldn't underestimate a concussion. Did you see someone about this? Are you still taking your medication?" he asks as he hammers away at the keyboard.

"It's not a concussion, not a medical problem, Bordeaux, it's more like . . . like"—I look past him as if I'm trying to find the right words—"it's more of a psychic thing. I'm just worried something is going to happen to other girls," I say casually.

He looks up then, startled, but immediately catches himself. "You have quite the imagination."

"You never know. Jane Doe stayed here, right?" I check the time and drop a cup in the wastebasket. I feel like I have nothing to lose. "Did the cops ever question you? About her? I would think they must have."

"Like I said, I don't know much about it," he says. "She stayed for one night and left the next morning."

"I better go. Look at me just chatting along."

He flicks on the *Vacancy* sign. It stutters for a second but then illuminates the lobby in an eerie reddish glow.

I leave the Lark and take off faster than I usually do. When I reach the farm, I turn on the overhead light in the car and sit the briefcase on my lap. The three-digit code is stuck at random numbers and as I wonder about a tool I can use to pry the locks, I swipe the rectangles toward the outside and the locks snap open. I open the lid and I stare at twelve rectangular compartments with jewelry boxes neatly positioned in a gray foam layer. *Prized Possessions* is printed in the corner of each box in ornate gold letters. I dig into the edge of the foam and there are two more levels beneath. Only the top layer has three vacant spots; the other layers contain twelve boxes each. I pull out one box and open it.

Within the box rests a bracelet with charms. The pouch in the leather interior of the briefcase holds an inventory sheet: *36 boxes, Assorted Charm Bracelets, 1 dozen each. For demonstration only.* It lists a *travel theme*, a *fairy-tale theme*, a *Chinese zodiac theme*.

I arrange the boxes on the passenger's seat. The Chinese zodiac has animals: rat, ox, tiger, rabbit, dragon, snake, horse, goat, monkey, rooster, dog, and pig. The travel theme: a ship's wheel, compass, globe, suitcase, Eiffel Tower, airplane, passport, cruise ship, sombrero, *Aloha* written across a lei garland. The fairy-tale theme: shoe, key, clock, handheld mirror, teapot, ring, chair, quill, and frog. Nothing seems to make sense, I get confused, can't count, the charms blend into one another. I run out of room, I drop some on the floor mat of the passenger's side, and I attempt to count again. After the buzzing in my hands ceases, my head begins to hurt, but this is where I'm at: eleven zodiac, eleven travel, and ten fairy-tale bracelets. I tuck my trembling hands under my thighs.

Seared into my brain stem are two images: a printout of the charm bracelet Jane Doe wore—a ship's wheel, a compass, a globe, a suitcase and a camera, an airplane and a passport, and a sombrero. The second image is the sparkle among the leaves and soil and acorns when Jane's hand began to move. A shiny glint, a silver flicker, a shiny bauble among the forest debris.

Trinkets to ward off evil or bring good luck, a memory of a trip, a gift, and charms added over years, some girl's rite of passage. To the killer they are bait, a piece of jewelry given for a purpose. I think of Bobby, what Sheriff de la Vega told him years ago. There were more women. Easy prey, illegals, the women no one looks for. The ones who could be anywhere. And they just might be.

I see the Bordeaux connection, yet I can't prove a thing. I take a deep breath. I need more time, time to sort this all out. Yet every scent, every shadow, every memory disguising itself as a vision, could be my last.

Thirty-six

MEMPHIS

A scream sounded in the distance. Its echo traveled toward the shed, pulling Quinn back into the present. It tore through her like a shard of glass: she knew that scream, had heard it many times before. She dropped the bloody hammer and it landed on the table with a thud, bounced and slid across the surface, knocking over everything in its path; bottles without stoppers tipped over, others broke and then spilled, their contents mingled with one another, odors around her so powerful she was about to faint.

Though Quinn felt dizzy, her hearing remained sharp and clear. The screams continued, one after the other in short rapid screeches. She had recognized Tain's voice with the first scream and Quinn feared for the baby, feared for its very life. She had no time to waste, even as she'd only been able to hit Nolan once. She wanted his death to be grand, as epic as his abhorrent treatment of her had been. Quinn wiped off her face, stumbled across the shed's threshold, and tripped over his fallen body, barely able to hold on to the door. The latch, cold and rusty, seemed to be put in her hand by some higher power, the only thing allowing her to remain on her feet, breaking her fall. Trapped is what she wanted Nolan to be, trapped in the stench and the filth and the smut. If he wasn't dead already from the hammer to his skull, he deserved to be engulfed by his chemicals, his lungs full of poison. Quinn slammed the door shut, heard the latch engage. She prayed the shed would crumble and fall on top of him, a fitting burial for the man he was.

With blurry vision she recognized the path ahead, then focused on the cracked dirt underfoot, and stumbled along as the cries got louder and more intense with every step. Her heart fell and Quinn knew what was to come; she'd run upstairs, enter Tain's bedroom, and there the infant would be, blue and lifeless. Birdbrained Tain had rolled on top of the baby in her sleep, suffocating her like an inconsiderate child would fall asleep on top of a doll. But she wasn't mad at Tain. It was *her* fault, she should *never* have left Tain with the baby, half-witted Tain, Quinn should have known, and *she* was to blame.

Quinn busted through the front door, taking two steps at a time. She felt sluggish, the chemicals making her body feel like dough, expanding and folding in on itself. She felt as if she was in one of those dreams where her legs moved slowly as if she was trapped under water, powerless and drained of all energy. Quinn stopped at the top of the stairs.

Another scream. Shrill, piercing. Dramatic. The screams didn't come from upstairs, but from the kitchen. She turned and stumbled, tripped, managed to hold on to the railing, pulled herself up, back to her feet, and she realized going down the stairs was so much harder than up. The steps seemed to merge and she wasn't sure where one ended and another began.

Tain stood in the kitchen, her nightgown sticking to her breasts, milk leaking down the front of her body, and there she stood, rooted to the ground, screaming.

"What's wrong? Where is the baby?"

Tain continued to scream, one cry after the other, as if she couldn't bear silence altogether. Quinn surveyed the kitchen, didn't see anything amiss and went back upstairs, one step at a time, careful not to fall and injure herself this time. Tain's bedroom was empty; so were the other rooms.

Back downstairs, Quinn embraced Tain and finally the girl quit screaming, allowed herself to be held. "The baby, Tain, where's the baby? What did you do with the baby?" Quinn held Tain by her shoulders, shook her until her head bobbed back and forth. But no word came from her mouth but a croak.

Quinn searched the house. She started upstairs again, one bedroom at a time, peeked into the bathroom, moved the shower curtain, even, kitchen, living room, and back porch. Nothing.

Quinn thought about going down to get the sheriff, telling him about the missing baby, but he'd ask for Nolan, and then they'd find him in the shed and he'd throw her in a cell. Creel was an important name, still held weight in Aurora, still contained the power of what once was. But Quinn didn't care, the baby was all she cared about. She went outside, into the barn, then to the well. She took the cap off and peered inside, wondering what she'd do if she heard a whimper. Or if she saw a body, floating.

And like magic there was a whimper. At first she thought it was a figment of her imagination, just a trick her mind played on her, but there it was, a shriek, gentle at first, quickly spiraling into urgency until it was a full-blown cry. It wasn't coming from the well, it wasn't in the barn or behind it, not from the shed, but it came from upstairs, from the bedrooms, through the open window.

When Quinn reached the top of the stairs she heard the cry clearly coming from the bathroom. A whimper echoed off the tiled walls but there was no baby anywhere. She ripped the shower curtain off the rod and there the baby was—no, there she must be—the whimper came clearly from within towels and dirty laundry Quinn hadn't gotten around to yet. She parted the towels and cotton sheets and saw the baby lying there. Safe and sound, her arms flailing and her tiny face contorted.

Quinn had looked in the tub earlier; the baby must have been asleep. Tain must have forgotten she put her in the tub, maybe went to the bathroom, maybe not, who knew what Tain's reasoning was, but Quinn knew one thing for sure: the baby wasn't safe with Tain. The baby wasn't even safe with Tain and her. As long as Tain was around, things like this would happen. Until one day, she'd leave the baby in a stroller somewhere, she'd give her the wrong medicine or too much or none at all, Tain would turn in her sleep and the baby would roll off the bed, or fall down the stairs, or be left in a hot car or outside in the cold. So many possibilities, any of them bound to happen. And one would be fatal. The baby was safe with Quinn, no one else.

THREE DAYS PASSED, AND QUINN KEPT AN EYE ON THE SHED through the kitchen window. Eventually she would have to go out there and deal with it but she wasn't ready quite yet. She was still mad at Nolan—so many things she hadn't said to him, so much she still wanted him to know. She'd never get that chance now.

After five days had passed, Tain began to ask about Nolan.

"Did he leave?" she kept asking, her eyes wide and glossy.

"I'm not sure. I don't know more than you do. Maybe he had business in town?"

"I heard you argue in the shed."

"Maybe he's still out there. Maybe he spent a few nights in the truck or the barn."

"Are we going to look for him?"

"Should we?" Quinn asked, and a tinge of guilt crept into her heart for being so deceiving. Nolan was, after all, the baby's father. By then Quinn had made up her mind, had come to the conclusion that it must all look like an accident, and surely Tain wasn't going to understand or question the circumstances, yet she still had to keep up the facade.

On the seventh day, Quinn told Tain they were going to look for Nolan. In front of the barn she instructed Tain how to safely hold the baby—she kept forgetting to support the head—and put her in the crook of Tain's elbow, the other arm underneath her body, making sure the blanket never restricted nose or mouth.

"Let's go inside," Quinn said and they entered, calling out Nolan's name into the dark and dank interior. Nothing stirred but for the air swirling with dust. Quinn stood by the ladder leading into the hay-loft, looking up. She narrated and explained things along the way—wanted Tain to later recall some sort of story if it ever came down to it—and she described how there was no way Nolan was in the barn, he had not stood on rungs so brittle only a fool would attempt to climb them, that short of a being a small child the treads would break, or if he had made it up there, the flimsy loft would fail to bear a grown-up's weight. Then they strolled from the barn to the shed as if this was just an afternoon walk, and Tain followed Quinn like a duckling its mother.

"Let me just take a look inside," Quinn said in front of the shed. "All those chemicals are bad for the baby. Just wait outside." The moment she placed her left hand on the lever and pulled with her right hand, she smelled it. Not only were there chemical odors of glue and solvent and alcohol—no, there was something additional lingering in the background, a different kind of scent. Sweet, the way rotten fruits reek. Like overripe pineapple, like the pears in the yard when she was a kid, after they'd fallen off the tree and plopped on the ground under-neath, slowly turning brown and soft and then she'd step on one and the sweet stench would hit her right between her eyes, like an arrow. Only this was deeper. More concentrated. Focused. "Remember, wait here," she repeated, "the smell of the chemicals isn't good for the baby."

Quinn stepped over the threshold and found herself standing over Nolan's body. One more step and she would have touched him. The jars and bottles lay shattered, and fragments of glass, clear and brown and green, were strewn about. The hammer, the one Quinn had bashed him with, was on the table. Its claw head was stuck in a puddle of white. And so was Nolan where he lay on the ground.

Nolan's fingers pointed upward, stiff, deformed and warped as if frozen in the middle of a convulsion, and everything about his body was ugly and forbidding in its putrid decay. Quinn felt a sense of triumph. Just like his crickets and beetles, Nolan had died like the bugs in the jars, in this shed. Avoiding his broken eyes staring into space, Quinn stepped closer and grabbed the papers from the table.

The deed seemed to be the only object in the entire shed that was neither plaster-speckled nor doused in chemicals. Quinn took that as a sign. She wanted to chuckle. She long had chased away thoughts of guilt, and all that was left inside her was the notion of the fates having intervened. And just as she had thought he had it coming, it indeed had come to pass. Nolan, trapped like a bug in his very own killing jar, had gotten what he deserved.

Thirty-seven

DAHLIA

QUINN, Nolan, Tain, Aella, they swirl and take form, they lose their ethereal bodies and become more and more tangible. They visit me at odd hours, at work, on the drive home. At the farm, I hear their footsteps in the foyer. They open drapes, slam the back door, but I am convinced there is more to this.

It was a physical shift when we arrived at the farm, as if the property had had a plan all along to do us both in, claiming me and my mother. But how does one verify the stories of an old eccentric woman who, over the years, has had a track record of being vague and irrational at best? Assuming her stories are real and factual, still decades have passed, the town of Aurora is no longer this tight-knit community in which one knows everybody's business, neighbors like Seymour are no longer around. There is a canning factory that brought an influx of people years ago; there is the apple orchard sprawling over a hundred acres or more a few miles from here bringing visitors and tourism; the Barrington and its conventions and meetings; the farmworkers harvesting Texas grapefruits at a farm south from here, season after season. The prison complex thirty miles west. Ramón de la Vega, Bobby's father, would know, but according to Bobby he's senile, and even if he did remember, it might just stir up unwelcome memories—and Bobby would never allow me to question him, he'd made that clear.

Later that night, I tell Bobby how my mother didn't deny the truth of the deed. I tell him the entire story again, beginning with the storm that started everything. I need to lay it all out for him.

"Hurricane, all the way in Aurora. Imagine that," I say to Bobby.

"There've been hurricanes coming from the coast," he says, "and if they carry storms with them, they can dump large amounts of rain hundreds of miles inland. Did she say what year?"

"Before I was born, late seventies. So this girl, Tain, came to the farm and Quinn found her and she gave birth in the foyer. The baby died and Quinn had an argument with Nolan about allowing her to stay. Nolan is the name on the deed, the one who put the farm in Quinn's name. Nolan, in her story, dies in the end, in the shed. Quinn hit him with a hammer and then left him in the shed with the chemicals."

I catch the impression on Bobby's face—eyes wide, eyebrows raised, head slightly cocked to the side—and I have a small inkling of how I must sound, talking about these characters as if they are family members or people I know. I've even caught myself lately, upon waking up in the mornings, wondering what they're up to—is Nolan in the shed, is Quinn fiddling around in the kitchen, is Tain simplemindedly roaming the farm, picking flowers, visiting the grave of her stillborn child?

"Quinn Creel," Bobby says and allows it to sit on his tongue. "Doesn't sound familiar."

"Creel Hollow Farm, makes sense." Something inside of me jerks, telling me to open my eyes. "I should be able to look that up, right? A storm, dumping rain all the way up in Aurora. A birth on Creel Hollow Farm. There should be records."

"Dahlia." He pauses as if he's thinking hard how to say something he can no longer hold in. "The deed and all those stories your mother is telling you, I don't want you to go overboard."

"Overboard?"

"What I'm trying to say is that I worry about you. Everything you've been telling me about your childhood, it sounds overwhelming. It gets to me, just listening to you. But I want you to know that I understand why you won't quit. Not only with your mother, but Jane Doe. I get it. But I still worry."

"I know you do," I say but I'm not so sure about the first part. Bobby was born here, grew up here. The trees he climbed, the house he grew up in, it's all there. His life is an open book, while mine is a vault with my mother holding the key.

I want to bring up the bracelets, and the photograph of the one on Jane's hand, yet I hesitate to tell Bobby about the briefcase. Maybe now isn't the time. To me he still is the teenager looking out for me, stubborn in his attempts to protect me, to make sure I'm okay.

"I don't know what your mother's stories are all about, and short of hiring a private detective you may never know. What we do know is that this farm was signed over to a Quinn Creel and she put the farm in your mother's name, Memphis Waller. There could be a relation, or maybe she bought it from her, I don't know."

"She never had any kind of money."

"What do you expect to find? Why are we doing this now?" he asks.

"Because I'm tired of all the lies, for one. And because finally there's something tangible that we can look into."

As we walk outside, I stop in the foyer.

"Right here?" he asks and lifts the edge of the rug with his boot tip.

"Right here."

"If it's blood," he says as if he's telling me a spooky story on Halloween, "blood evidence is very hard to get rid of, especially if the surface can't be scrubbed or bleached."

"I mopped but the stain is still there."

"If it soaked into the grain of the wood, nothing will get rid of it. Short of ripping out the floors. Wait here," Bobby says and disappears through the front door. Seconds later, I hear a trunk open and close.

I roll up the dusty rug and push it against the wall. I get down on my knees and examine the spot, which is by all accounts rather large with well-defined edges. It looks different than I remember it; maybe it's the fact that I'm mere inches away from it now. I run my finger across the porous floor and the slats that have warped around the stain. It looks refinished, as if another layer of stain was applied at some point— not a particularly thick coat—and that layer has also worn down.

Bobby appears behind me, in his hand a flashlight and a box that says *Luminol Demonstration Kit*.

"You remember you asked me about a blood detection kit?" He hands me the flashlight and I search for the tiny nail holes that used to hold the rug down.

I remember my mother telling me that Quinn nailed the rug down. I also want to believe that there are a dozen or so holes in an almost perfect circle, the exact shape of the wool rug. But I could be mistaken.

"Step back," Bobby says and I do.

He opens the kit and takes out a small spray bottle, coating the entire floor from the front door to kitchen on the right and the living room on the left. There's nothing, not a trace, no glow, not even one the size of a firefly.

"Don't you have to use a blue light?" I ask and Bobby studies the back of the bottle.

"No blue light required. Says here that the area must be completely dark in order to see chemical reaction," he reads off the box.

Bobby shuts off the foyer light and motions me to turn off the kitchen light. The house goes dark.

I look down and freeze.

On the floor a blue orb floats in front of me, but then I recognize it for what it is: a large oval stain, blue and luminescent, with multiple smaller droplets around it. My mind is searching for shapes and forms and figures and there is a realization that I refuse to accept: one shape looks like one of those newborn kits in which you make an imprint of a little foot. Only this one is much smaller, so small it might as well belong to a baby doll.

"Bobby," I say and I sound like a little girl. The flashlight slips out of my hand and lands with a clatter on floor. With only a second of hesitation, Bobby steps around the oval stain, careful not to tread on it with his heavy boots.

I feel like I'm being shaken, like a tree by an ax, not taken down, not quite, but a few more hits and I will drop to the ground. A light comes on—not the dusty pendant in the foyer, but an overall light bathing the entire hallway in a stark and harsh glow.

Out of the corner of my eye I see a silhouette at the top of the stairs, dressed in a white nightgown, staring down on us like a ghostly onlooker. The silhouette isn't moving, isn't talking, just hovering, and I wonder if all the commotion has caused my mother to wake from her sleep.

It can't be my mother, the silhouette is shorter, younger, with long, dark hair, like mine. Judging by her fuzzy outline, she isn't a person after all, more an apparition of a woman in a white nightshirt, a woman who looks nothing like my mother, but everything like me. She holds something rather bulky in her two outstretched arms. I can't help but ask myself if I'm dying, or if I have already passed, and a specter of myself is ascending the stairs. I can't be dead. My limbs are heavy, I can feel my weight, its momentum taking me to the ground. By then I've tumbled, giving Bobby barely enough time to catch me.

My head is buzzing but I can still form thoughts, even though I know I'm about to black out. Who are these people? How does my mother know these stories and why, for the love of God, *why* does the woman atop the stairs look like the composite that is taped to my wall? I understand with every fiber of my being that this is a hallucination, this is *not* reality. There's no woman on the landing looking down on me, yet she *is* real.

I feel as if someone is holding me, carrying me down the stairs and across the foyer. I am being held like a child. Just as Bobby lifts me off the floor, carrying me into the living room and dropping me on the chintzy couch, arms carry *me* through the foyer and down the front steps. Outside, I'm engulfed by tiny specks of ice. The blizzard. I'm surrounded by it, I'm in its very eye.

The vision, for once, doesn't scatter like the others have done before; it continues on. There's an open car door, and the woman whose face

I cannot see—not the same woman who stood on the stairs—puts the child—me?—in the backseat, on top of a feathery mountain of pillows and blankets. And then the blizzard swallows everything around me and there's nothing left but the humming of a car engine.

DR. WAGNER IS RIGHT, IT TAKES ME LONGER AND LONGER TO RE-cover. My muscles remain stiff, my mind can't quite get back to where it was before the seizure, and the first steps I take are unsteady at best. I push the implications aside—now is not the time to worry about that. I still have to tell Bobby about the briefcase and the bracelets; it might change everything.

I wake to the sound of kitchen drawers slamming and the smell of coffee drifting into my room. I find my mother in the kitchen dressed and showered, fixing eggs and toast. I follow her command as she points to the kitchen table, motioning me to sit. She wears the yellow dress. It's too big, but it's a lovely color on her.

"Sit," she says. She's resolute, rigid, as if I'm a child who needs to be taught manners.

"What's going on?" I ask.

Before me on the table lies my book. My childhood salvation, the book that had answers to everything I didn't dare ask my mother. My *Columbia Encyclopedia*.

"You've had this all along?" I ask. I want to reach for it, but I don't.

"I've kept a lot of things that weren't mine to keep," she says. "After Quinn killed Nolan . . ." She pauses. Then, "There's something else you need to know."

The wheels are turning. I don't know what I'm expecting—a tale of Quinn running and getting caught, maybe confessing, I'm not sure—Quinn is so real to me, all alone in her dark and twisted world, and I wonder if karma does exist in the story I'm about to hear.

"Tell me she's getting away," I say, almost as a joke.

"No one ever gets away," she says. "That's not how things work."

Thirty-eight

MEMPHIS

THE scent of the closet hasn't changed at all; it is sharp and spicy like cedar, yet sweet like the sprigs of lavender I used to put everywhere around the house. There is one thing I'm after: the yellow dress.

I slide it off the hanger and lay it out on the bed. It has moth holes, and the formerly bright yellow fabric has faded. I remember it well—the deep back has a tied bow to make the waist fit the body, and a flared skirt has pleats sewn in.

I slip the dress over my head and it rests on my shoulders. My arms find the holes and I reach behind me and tie the bow as tight as it will go. Nothing about it is right. It hovers around my body like an ill-fitting garment made for someone else. It fit Quinn's body perfectly, it was never meant for me, so what do I expect anyway? I won't look in a mirror—a visual would just disappoint me further.

Today, I am going to tell Dahlia the rest of the story. I can only imagine how it must sound and I won't go as far as to admit that my mind is twisted—I'm not pleased with what I've done, that much I will say—but I had no choice. Backed into a corner, there was only one way out, but I'll allow her to be the judge.

When Dahlia sees the book on the kitchen table, she is taken aback, didn't know I had kept it all along, maybe even thought it was just another figment of her imagination.

I hear my own voice, unfamiliar and remarkably steady.

"After Quinn found Nolan in the shed, she told Tain she'd take care of his body. She made her go back to the house, and later that night she went out and dug a grave by the cypress, next to the grave of Tain's stillborn. She put the baby in a basket and it slept silently on the porch but when it woke and wanted to be fed, she took it to Tain and then continued digging Nolan's grave. By the time the sun came up, her fingers were bloody and blistered, but she kept on. It took her all night but she managed to drag Nolan a few inches at a time, until she reached the hole in the ground."

I can smell the dankness of the dress; the dust and mold and decades of abandonment have taken their toll. The other day I saw her walking past with Bobby and the dog. They all paused, Dahlia and Bobby holding hands, the dog sniffing around. I'm glad the dog isn't a digger. I watched them cross the meadow that used to be covered in buttercups. Over the years wildflowers have taken over and they are plenty now, bursting with colors and diversity, just as it should be. Dahlia will, from now on, throw a glance toward the cypress every single time she passes by.

Dahlia must realize I'm telling her a story of consequences, not a mere figment of my imagination or fictional characters on some stage that I control. There is one more thing left I need her to know, and it is probably the hardest part of it all. I am aware that I will have to break her heart. She is strong, but even the strongest hearts have a breaking point, and I also know that if there's any chance of Dahlia becoming who she was meant to be, this has to be done.

I want to hold her hand as I tell her the rest of the story but I won't be able to bear it when she pulls away from me so I don't touch her at all.

"There's more," I say. "About Tain and Quinn."

Dahlia looks puzzled, doesn't know what to make of this. In her mind, the story seemed to have come to a conclusion. I wonder if it clicked, if she put two and two together.

After all, there are three graves by the tree.

Thirty-nine

AELLA

THE tinkers didn't return to claim the girl as they'd promised. Others passed through but not the ones who had left her behind. Eventually Aella got word that on their way through Louisiana the group had been arrested for fraud. Aella told her of their fate yet the girl seemed oblivious.

"When is the baby due?" Aella asked.

"Another two months, maybe three," the girl said.

Aella realized now that she wasn't nearly as far along as she had thought. Her elfin frame made her stomach poke out more than it would have on a taller and bigger girl. "Is it moving a lot? Have you been to a doctor?"

"It kicks. We had a doctor at our camp. We don't go to doctors in town," she said and absentmindedly shredded sage leaves with her fingers.

They'd be no good for smudging but they were abundant and easy to grow so Aella didn't dwell on it. She also taught her about the herbs in the garden but wasn't sure if Tain retained any information. She listened intently, or so it seemed, and was curious about palm reading, and Aella showed her a rudimentary way of foretelling the future. Three lines, their depth and continuity—folks around here were easy to fool.

The girl's attention span was short and she began roaming the woods, came back with flowers that grew nowhere near the trailer—the next field of bluebonnets was miles from here—and Aella hoped the spell she had performed on the girl's behalf would keep her safe. There was no telling what she could get herself into.

SEPTEMBER CAME AND THE STORMS REMAINED MILD—THE RAIN was heavy but never lasted longer than one day and one night, and in the morning there was sunshine breaking through the clouds. Lightning flashed, yet it was a mere flicker and then it died, and when a bolt of light broke through the darkness, it was for the briefest of moments. Aella kept Tain occupied during those times. She gave her tea steeped with herbs that made her fall asleep and not wake until morning, when the storms had passed by.

One day, Aella felt her skin tingling and her ears were more alert than usual. She knew there was a big one brewing. Most birds had migrated by then—for others it was still too early—but there weren't any bees around, as if those winged creatures knew something the rest of the world wasn't privy to quite yet.

Everything Aella had taught Tain about the weather and its patterns came to fruition then. The girl questioned her obsessively about the coming storm and what was going to happen, went on and on about the roof flying off and cars being tossed around by the winds. Aella tried to calm her but when the storm approached and the wind began to howl and the room remained dark as night even though it was noon, the girl turned into pure adrenaline. When the willow in front of the trailer creaked and its limbs whipped against the windowpanes, she sat on the floor rocking back and forth. Aella led her back to the cot in the corner and by the light of a lightning flash she thought she saw red spots on the floor where Tain had cowered. She gave the girl another dose of laudanum and watched her nod off. Hours later Aella awoke to the front door open, and she rushed to scramble for the knob pounding against the wall. She caught a glimpse of the girl running down the steps, her hair whipping violently about her.

"No! Come back!" Aella screamed but she couldn't even hear her own voice above the battered structure. She stood on the threshold screaming and yelling and then the trailer creaked like the trees around her and the noise rose and Aella looked up to make sure the roof was still there. It was nothing like the storms that usually passed through this part of Texas—Aurora was too far off the coast and any storm was bound to lose its strength so far inland—this was much stronger, fiercer.

After it was over, she kept an eye out for the girl, yet she was nowhere to be seen. Earlier that day, after the clouds cleared and the sun burst through, she had found blood on the floor where Tain had cowered in the corner and she knew that the red she had seen hadn't been a illusion. The girl, worked up by the storm, had gone into labor and Aella had mistaken it for panic. There was no telling what had happened to her and the baby. No one could survive out there in such wrath, especially not a woman in labor.

Two years went by—two years of guilt and blame she put on herself—until she saw the girl again. Aella had almost forgotten about the woman she had called Q. but one day she appeared on her property. Aella recognized the powder blue truck and when the door opened, she thought she was looking at a ghost.

Q. emerged from the truck and then the passenger's door opened. At first the woman following behind her, approaching the trailer, was no more than a chill in the air, a shimmer of mist, diffused, like a poorly taken photograph. It wasn't until the woman came within a few feet of her that she congealed into a form; the girl that had run off during the storm over two years ago, Tain. In her arms she carried a small child with brilliant eyes and light, almost silver skin. Quinn told the girl with the baby to sit in the chair under the willow.

Aella did the math and it didn't add up; the baby in the girl's arms wasn't a day older than five months, if that. It couldn't be that it was Tain's baby. She wasn't going to ask any questions, wasn't going to dwell on it.

"She must go," was the first thing Q. said, out of earshot of Tain, and even though there were tears in her eyes, Aella knew she was serious. "I need you to take her back. You sent her to me and now she must go. I love her but I can't allow her to stay."

Aella took a step backward. For a moment all was silent, then Aella understood. She was adept at recognizing people's intentions by their manners and this had nothing to do with petty jealousy or distrust but sheer fear on the part of Q.

"When the travelers come back through we can send her with them," Aella said and made sure to watch Q.'s face closely. It seemed wise to send her the same way she had come; the girl after all had appeared that way and sending her back wasn't farfetched at all.

"When will they be back? Soon?" Q.'s words were breathless and strained. She had a habit of constantly turning around as if she was checking on the woman with the baby.

"They'll be looking for work soon. I'll contact you when—"

"No, no, no. You don't understand. She can't be around the baby. Not another minute."

Aella felt for Q., always had. Broken she was, now more so than ever. "Bring her back tomorrow," Aella said and added, "Money, bring money. They'll take her all the way to South Carolina but I can't guarantee she won't come back. Know that. Unless . . ." Aella was going to offer a spell—in her mind she assembled the items needed, graveyard dirt, nails—

She was interrupted by Q.

"No more spells, just make sure she leaves."

"She might come back. Are you prepared for that?"

"Let me worry about that," Q. said.

"I have a question." Aella turned and watched Tain with the baby. The way she held her, then scooted her from one side of the hip to the other, leaving the baby's hat crooked on her head, and her pants riding up, exposing her legs. "Does she know she's leaving?"

"I'll tell her tonight," Q. said, turning to leave. On her way to the truck she spoke one more time. "Tomorrow?" Q. asked, fear in her eyes, as if Aella was going to renege on her.

"Yes, tomorrow. You can drop her off. She can wait until they pass through."

Q. DROPPED THE GIRL OFF THE NEXT MORNING. SHE GOT OUT OF the truck and without another word Tain disappeared into the trailer.

"What did you tell her?"

"About what?"

"Where she's going? What did you tell her?"

Q.'s eyes became big and glossy. "She's going back where she came from. With her people, where she belongs."

"Listen. Don't take this lightly." Aella paused, searching for the right words. "I'm not looking forward to a big scene here. If there's any trouble, I'll send her back to your farm. Know that."

"Don't worry," Q. said and before she left, she turned around one more time. "I need to talk to someone. Recently departed." She paused and when Aella remained silent, she added, "You must know how to do this."

"There are ways. Salves. Causing dreams. But they are poisonous—you have to be careful."

"There are ghosts. On the farm," Q. added, unprompted.

"People who used to live there? They crossed over?"

"Yes."

"Spirits, you mean. Not ghosts."

"Whatever. I need to speak to them. I need them to go away."

Aella didn't hesitate and opened a drawer. After rummaging for a while she handed Q. a small container of salve with a foot drawn on the lid. It was one of the strongest salves she made, mixed and prepared to remove the barriers between here and there, this world and the spirit world. Her grandmother used to call them a key to the other realm.

A bit of yarrow to protect you on your flight,
A bit of datura, to give you special sight.
Monkswood, foxglove, belladonna, and henbane for a moonlit night.

Aella had never sold the salve or given it away, just used it herself, and only in small portions and never on cut skin, but something in Q.'s eyes compelled her, and she handed her the metal container. "Here you go," she said. "Apply to the top of your feet. But sparingly. It can kill you if you're not careful."

"Doesn't everything?" Q. said.

Aella never saw her again after that. Q. was a strong woman; strong but damaged. Those are the dangerous ones.

Tain stayed for a better part of the week. When the tinkers passed through, she packed her up and Aella watched as a young girl with a doll in her arms grabbed Tain's hand, smiling at her. Tain seemed confused, looking around. "Where am I going?"

"Didn't someone tell you? Remember you came here with them?" Aella said and pointed at the tinkers as the trunks of the cars thudded shut. Aella could tell that she was overwhelmed and she cursed Q. under her breath, yet this was none of her business. "Don't worry now. Remember before you came here? That's where they are taking you."

"Where I came from?" Tain hesitantly followed the girl with the doll toward a car.

Every step she took was light, making no sound at all. She paused, took another step, stopped again. Tain's face was fearful, but Aella saw her bravery. Then her eyes lit up as if she remembered something. She mumbled a few words but Aella couldn't make them out and she didn't ask.

Tain got into a vehicle and the caravan of tinkers took off. After the vehicles had departed, not so much as a fleeting image of them in the distance, Aella remembered that Tain's footsteps had been soundless. That meant but one of two things: parts of her would always remain here or she'd return.

Aella stood underneath the willow tree and stared up into the sky. It was as blue as an ocean. Infinite in its possibilities.

Forty

DAHLIA

A FTER Tain left, Quinn thought it was all over, you know," my mother says. "She thought they'd live on the farm. Be happy."

I remain silent. It's hard for me to see her this upset and I look at Tallulah's legs twitching in her sleep.

"Do you understand now?" my mother asks.

"What am I to understand?" is all I manage to get out. Suddenly I'm afraid of my own thoughts, the connections I make in the back of my mind.

"This farm. This house. Everything."

Usually my mother remains silent to either punish or prove a point, but this is different. For the first time I see her struggling to get words out.

"The deed, the farm, in Quinn's name." My mother is shaking, the tremor now surging through her entire body. She's fearful; I can hear it in her voice.

"Why is it in your name?"

"Remember the day we came to Aurora? The sheriff and Bobby— you met Bobby that day."

"I remember."

"The sheriff. Ramón de la Vega."

"Mother, I know. What are you trying to say?"

It hits me like a thousand bricks all at once. Yet I wait. I need to hear her say it.

She falls apart. *I'm sorry,* she repeats, *I'm sorry I'm sorry.*

I don't dare ask what she's sorry for. She talks about herself, then switches to *Quinn* and back to *I.*

"I saw their faces in every man I passed on the street," she says. "When I thought I had shaken it off, there it was again, as if it was a rubber band allowing me to go only a certain distance away, just to snap me back in. I had to fight it off, again and again."

There's more rambling, more of the same, and then in a low haunting voice, she says: "The way the breath of a man goes from normal to panting, on top of you, how thick the air becomes, how it covers your body in disgust. How you wake up every morning and you think it was a bad dream but then it sinks in. It's not going away. It's your life and you are forced to live it and there's nothing that can be done. It's forever."

She goes back to the part of the story when Quinn wakes up in the woods, after Benito, her lover, leaves. And on and on she goes, every single detail is laid out elaborately, as if she's gone over it a hundred, maybe even a thousand times, everything she's put in a specific place, everything has been assigned a meaning. The moon watched the men rape Quinn, so every time Quinn looked at the moon, it threw the images back at her. The woods had swallowed Quinn and every time she went back into the woods, the images reappeared.

I want to interrupt her, tell her I know this already, know all about this. Something in her eyes demands my silence. And then she speaks of the hunter again, the scent of deer urine, the way he blocked *my* path, and how they dragged—

"Dragged me like a deer carcass, over rocks and roots and brambles, like I was a dead animal, incapable of feeling anything."

Dragged *me.* I remain silent. And then it gets worse. Three words bring me to my knees. Three words I had feared but somehow convinced myself couldn't be true. How could I have been so blind? I was preoccupied with missing women, with myself, Bobby, and Tallulah. I should have connected the dots sooner.

"I am Quinn," my mother says.

As long as it takes to stir a cup of coffee, to fold a towel or tie a shoe, that's how long it takes for me to grasp what's been in front of me all along: Memphis is Quinn. Nolan was her husband.

The air stagnates, I can't breathe. This isn't *a* story, this is *her* story. *I'm sorry.* Those words have no meaning at all. Until.

"Tain was your mother."

"TAIN, HONEY, WHAT WAS YOUR MOTHER'S NAME?" QUINN DIDN'T know where else to start. Any children of hers would have been named Nolan Jr. or Frances after her late mother.

Tain just averted her eyes.

"What was your father's name?"

"Peter," Tain said.

"Was he a good man?"

"Good enough."

"Well, it's a girl so you can't name her Peter. I don't know the female form of Peter, I don't even know if there is one."

"Petra," Tain said. "I like Petra."

"Petra." Quinn allowed the name to dissolve on her tongue. It seemed strong and indestructible but she didn't like it. It was harsh, didn't have any softness to it.

"If you like it, Petra it is."

"Okay. Petra. Her name is Petra."

SHUT UP, I WANT TO SAY. DON'T SAY ANOTHER WORD. YOU'VE *done enough. Shut up Shut up Shut up Shut up Shut up Shut up Shut up Shut up Shut up Shut up.*

"No," is all I can get out, croaky and hoarse. *This can't be* echoes in my mind. I'm not sure if I'm just thinking it or if I say it out loud. All those spaces, dark and deep, now the light floods in.

I am the baby, I am Tain's baby. The baby Quinn always wanted.

My mother—the woman who I thought was my mother—was violently raped. Those were the sins committed against her. I can't deny that. But she killed Nolan, my father, she took Tain's baby, and then sent Tain away. She sent my mother away.

She killed my father and stole me from my mother.

I feel a surge of hate, strong and sure. It quickly fades to sadness for these confessions, these crimes committed by a dark and haunted woman named Quinn. Quinn is Memphis. Is *her.*

It hurts. Not like accidentally slicing your finger with a knife, no, not a sudden jolt of pain that turns into a burn, but more like a knife in your back that remains. With every breath I take, the knife drives in deeper yet I'm required to live and go on. My mother is a knife lodged in my back and I see her as the lunatic she is: a crazy person who has raised me in hiding. She took me and tried to sustain me with her perverted mind, attempted to make me an accomplice in her twisted games. I'm an experiment.

I look at her, *really* look at her. Consider her. Every single movement of hers, her shaking hands, the tears in her eyes, all of it just a reminder that she is a con. A criminal. A psychopath. I was unkempt, neglected, deprived, dragged about, and suffered because of *her.* She is the root of all evil.

I get up, stumble blaringly into the cabinets. Tallulah wakes from all the noise I'm making, runs up to me. She raises on her hind legs, pawing at me, groping my thigh over and over and over as if to say, *It's okay, I'm here. I'm here.* I ignore her and she retreats to the corner, her tail tucked underneath her.

I run to my car, as fast as I can possibly get away from my mother, putting distance in between us. The cypress stops me in my tracks with its bright feathery appearance, mocking me. All those weeks I've lived here close to graves my mother dug. And behind me, in that farmhouse, is a woman who is no relation to me whatsoever. None. There are more dots I connect: Ramón de la Vega is Benito. Everybody is someone else, except Bobby. He's safe. He's just Bobby.

The woman who raised me is a criminal, and I am her biggest crime. I *am* the epitome of all the crimes she's committed.

I jump in the car and speed off. As I drive, as clear as day, a memory: that afternoon at the diner. Like a jack-in-the-box lid bursting open, the jester pops up.

Dahlia. Memphis. Crimes that shook the world.

Pick a number, she'd said, and on page seven she found the article "Crimes That Shook the World." By picking a number, she made *me* pick those names. The Memphis Three. The Black Dahlia. We are newspaper headlines. The woman who took me from my mother made me pick names from a newspaper. Not just random names from articles, no, names of people who have either committed crimes or were victims of crimes. Guilt and blame tied together forever.

She made me her accomplice. She is to blame for everything. A life spent in squalor and in hiding. My mind upturns and then the blame shifts—she too is a victim; there's an accumulation of moments, definitions of words, a collection of adjectives that define me, decades of patterns and habits. I feel the walls closing in on me, the riddles I can't seem to solve test me, and denying myself revenge magnifies the crimes that she has committed.

The sadness turns back to hate and the hate intensifies. I feel wrath. I long for revenge as if turning her in is going to deliver the ultimate blow for the years of suffering she's put me through.

BOBBY, AS ALWAYS, IS PARKED BY THE GAS STATION. WHEN I PULL up next to the cruiser, he looks up, surprised. I roll down my window.

"Follow me," I say but he doesn't move. "Go. Just go," I say, now with a sharp voice.

Bobby starts the engine.

"To the warehouses," I add.

He turns the key in the ignition, pulls out, and we are on our way.

THE WAREHOUSES STILL SIT ABANDONED AFTER ALL THESE YEARS.
The bottom of the chain-link fence around the perimeter is full of
leaves and debris and paper that has been blown about.

Bobby stops by the gate with a large lock on a heavy chain. The
No Trespassing sign is weathered and hard to read. Locals know not to
go in; even today's high schoolers have probably found other hangouts
around town that don't threaten to collapse on top of you.

"What are we doing here?"

My mind is clouded by my mother's confession and I don't know
where to start but I know if I wait any longer I won't be able to get
it out at all.

"My mother's stories, about the people and the farm, they are all
true." I take in a deep breath. "Not only are they true but they are
about her."

"I don't understand," he says.

I tell him everything, I start off with Quinn's rape, and I end with
Memphis and Dahlia and the day at the diner. The day we met. I tell
him Ramón de la Vega, his dad, is Benito. I don't mention that the
mounds at the farm are graves, not yet, but I tell him about the deed
and that his father helped Memphis start a new life.

"I can't even begin to understand. My father knew your mother. I
don't know what to say. When did you find that out? Just now?" Bobby
is less surprised than I expected—maybe it's not a matter of surprise,
but a puzzle that has been longing to be solved. "I had a hunch they
might know each other but I had no idea."

"She told me and I ran, just took off." I choke back the tears, then
I mumble, hear myself—*She killed my father and she's not my mother*—
and it sounds too outrageous to be true, so shocking, so extreme. The
rape she talked about, the rape she revisited in her stories over and

over, that was her. There's something growing inside of me, a hint of compassion, and I'm not comfortable with that. "I have to tell you something else."

Bobby's eyes have grown dark and I know he's thinking about his dad. He wraps his arms around me and when he lets go, while he's still close to me, I want to hold on, want to remain there with him.

"I just don't know what to say, Dahlia. I'm so sorry."

"There's more." I want to tell him that the mounds, those peculiar rises of earth underneath the cypress tree, are graves. I want to call Memphis a murderer and I want Bobby to tell me to go to the authorities, I want him to urge me to turn her in, but before I do that, I must tell him about the briefcase. The bracelets.

"More?" Bobby asks.

"I went into the storage room at the Lark the other day," I say as I unwrap myself from him. "I took a book to the lost and found bins, but that day I didn't really go inside, it's old and dusty. Anyway." I take a deep breath and then I go on. "I went back, just out of curiosity, I went through the lost and found items. I found a briefcase that someone left behind, probably someone passing through years ago. A briefcase, with salesman samples, something like that. They have different themes but anyway"—I'm trying to sound matter-of-fact but the words come out breathless, without pauses and commas, just a long stream of breathy incoherent ramblings—"it was full of charm bracelets." I pause and watch his face. He's stoic. "Jane wore a charm bracelet, remember?"

Bobby remains silent and stares straight ahead. He shuts off the radio that had been hissing and breaking in and out the entire time.

"Where's the briefcase?"

"I took it and I counted the boxes. I put everything back the very next day. In the same spot."

"And they have your fingerprints all over them?"

I feel myself getting impatient. "So what? I wouldn't know if I hadn't gone through them."

"Dahlia, you realize that you are the one who found Jane in the woods. And you work at the Lark, and your fingerprints—"

"So I'm the suspect now?"

"No, but as far as evidence goes, it might be worthless now. Why didn't you tell me you found the briefcase?"

Nothing is lost. Nothing. I hate the fact that Bobby gives up so quickly, how being straight and narrow is more important to him. I feel something settle inside of me, a seed attempting to take hold in fertile ground. This is Bobby, Bobby who would never lie, never betray me, the boy I knew would never . . . But the biggest things that happened to him—his mother dying of cancer, the promise to his father to keep an eye on Bordeaux—he never spoke about. He's a vault, like my mother. "Why didn't you tell me about Bordeaux back then, about your father's suspicions? We were friends, we were so close."

A voice from afar, Bobby's voice. "I need you to trust me now."

"I trust you," I say and know immediately that's a lie. I'm still processing. We are so good together. But then, it's always good until it goes bad. "Did you know about the charm bracelets at the Lark? And you never told me about that either?"

He remains silent.

The sun is beaming on the roof and even though it's hot in the car, I'm shaking.

"Dahlia, listen to me," Bobby says and grabs my hands and holds them in his. "You must stop this now, this must end today. I'm sorry about your mother, and what you just told me is huge. I can't even imagine how you feel. But Bordeaux is something else altogether. That's police work, evidence. Don't get obsessed with that. You need to take a step back and—"

"You're calling *me* obsessed? What about you?"

"What about me? I thought I was doing the right thing. I became a cop. I watched Bordeaux Sr. until the day he died. I kept an eye on him. For years, Dahlia, *years*. In a span of ten, fifteen years, you get married, have children. There are holidays and vacations and birthdays.

A lot of life happens in fifteen years. Imagine, all those years you were gone, all that time. And you know what I did for fifteen years? I lost my marriage, the life I was trying to build, because I couldn't leave this damn town."

"I'm not judging you." I want to say that I know what he went through but that's just one of those empty expressions. I don't know, just as he doesn't know what my life has been like.

"We make promises, Dahlia. I promised my dad to keep an eye on Bordeaux. To be vigilant. I kept my promise. Not only did I keep my promise but I became a cop because of it. And now look at me, I have less power than anyone else. You barge in and find briefcases and bracelets and I just sit in this car, day in and day out, looking at that damn motel."

Bobby grabs me by my shoulders and squeezes. "Do you not see what this does to people? Your mother, look what happened to her, to both of you. What happens when you're stuck, not really making your own choices even when you think you are. No chance of a normal life, not even a remote chance. We both know something about that. And your mother, she lived it all her life. Hiding, trying not to get caught." He turns around and takes off his holster. "I'm not doing this another day." With the last word, his voice cracks.

"What are you saying?"

"Keep my gun for me, okay? Leave it at the farm, hide it somewhere, but don't leave it in your car. I'll get it later."

He hands me his gun and I take it. I'm not sure why—is he worried of what he might do with it, will he confront Bordeaux and is afraid he might shoot him? Maybe he doesn't want to show up as a cop, maybe there are legal reasons to this and all he wants are answers—and so I grab the gun and toss it on my backseat. By the time I turn around, he's in his cruiser.

"Did you hear what I told you? The briefcase . . ." I call after him.

But then I stop. I have to let him go. I sit in my car and I remain there for what seems like hours. My mind is racing and then I realize Memphis and I are not even remotely at the end of her story, our story.

Earlier that morning, when I left, I passed by the mounds and now, even though much of her story still seems like an impossible maze, one path begins to shine brighter than all the others. Three graves, I just saw them with my own eyes, and I know that my mother, Tain, is the third grave. Memphis hasn't told me that part yet.

I know with every fiber of my being that Memphis is guilty of one more crime. And I will demand she tell me why and how she killed my mother.

AT THE FARM, I SHOVE BOBBY'S GUN IN THE BACK OF THE SMALL cabinet above the fridge. Memphis sits on the back porch, smoking, watching my every move. I sit next to her.

When the silence becomes unbearable, I ask the question. "How did my mother die?" I hold her gaze. "That's her out there, isn't it?" I say and nod toward the mounds.

Memphis doesn't blink. She takes a drag from the cigarette to buy time to think about her answer.

"She couldn't care for you," she says. "You must believe me."

I fight back the tears. I'm torn; I want to take into consideration Tain and her limited mental capacity, her inability to care for me, something that Memphis thought she had to do for her.

"I know this is difficult for you," Memphis says and gets up. "Come with me," she adds, "I want to show you something." She points toward the graves and in the blink of an eye I see the future: yellow police tape, white tents propped up, crime scene investigators with paper coats and booties turning this place upside down. I follow her past the two graves, past the cypress, to the third grave.

"When they came," Memphis says. "I should have never opened the door."

Forty-one

MEMPHIS

AUTUMN forced the end of sunny days upon the woman and the child. All through the summer they'd strolled around the property, picked flowers in the vast meadow, played hide-and-seek between the sheets flapping in the wind, fed the chickens, and shucked corn on the front porch. By the time winter asserted its grip, the sun went down early and all that was left was to go to bed. Even the child felt out of sorts and refused to nap and if she did, she'd only sleep for a few minutes and then she'd jerk awake.

A cold front came and the skies seemed to be darker than any winter the woman had ever experienced. A sudden steep drop in temperature brought dark and angry clouds with a bluish tint. At the same time heavy precipitation had moved across the land, making the approaching front seem even more threatening.

The woman explained to the child that there'd be long periods of harsh loneliness and frost forcing them to stay indoors and they'd huddle up by the fireplace. *We just read books and play games,* the woman explained, and the child smiled. She often wondered if the child recalled Tain and their time together, even though she had probably been too young to remember anything. Tain hadn't cared for her more than a nanny would during infancy, and the child had never asked a single question about her. For a while Quinn had felt guilt for how she had sent Tain away—yet whichever way she twisted and turned it, she didn't look at it as having deserted her. She had done what she had to do to keep the baby safe. She tried to forget about Tain altogether, and there were other concerns.

Frightening things happened every day. She had seen a shadow out by the shed. It was the shadow of a man walking with a limp, hunched over, hurrying and dragging one leg behind, rushing to get to the shed. *Nolan,* she wanted to call out to him, wanted him to stop and talk to her. At first she felt as if there were things left unsaid during all those years of marriage—how he'd taken her for granted, had never made any attempt to make her happy, had never listened to her, had betrayed her, had taken her best friend from her—all those things she didn't get to say while he was alive—but by the time his ghost appeared daily, she had changed her mind. The winter was long and by then she had given in to some sort of guilt, wanted to ask his forgiveness, wanted to know what else she could have done, wanted to maybe just acknowledge him, thinking the dark clouds might evaporate if she did. She had been feeling nothing but dread all winter long, and if it wasn't for the child, her bubbly personality and her joyous laughter—who knows what she would have done?

Quinn had used the salve Aella had given her. She had taken the balm—remembered Aella said it was poisonous and to use it sparingly—but the only reason she didn't just rub it all over her body was the fact that it might kill her and the child would find her and once that image had manifested in her mind she knew she could never leave her. She rubbed a tiny dab over her feet where the veins ran across like angry rivers. All it did was make Quinn wake up in the middle of the night, gasping for air, her brain misfiring with random images. She didn't understand why the pressure on her chest was so real when it was all just a dream, but then she saw Nolan's ghost sitting on the other side of the bed. He had returned, getting ready to pull off his boots and climb in the bed with her. She'd jerk then, not because she was afraid, but for the simple fact that ghosts usually have some sort of business with the living. But every time she addressed him, he vaporized, disappeared in front of her eyes, his likeness dissolved and vanished, turning into tiny droplets like the soap bubbles she made for the child with dish detergent and glycerin. Quinn wasn't afraid of ghosts, not even as a child, had been one herself since that morning in the woods, knew that they didn't mean any harm. Yet things had been left unsaid and regardless how hard she tried, she couldn't stop dwelling on it.

During the day she didn't see Nolan's ghost, not in the house at least. The child was three then, and Quinn felt as if the raw isolation of living on this farm was going to swallow her at any moment. Every day, when dusk came, her sanity seemed to slip through her frozen fingers. The fire in the fireplace barely heated the room, and when she fetched a cup of chamomile tea, she'd allow the girl to warm her hands on the earthenware mug, and by the time she drank the tea it was almost cold.

There was the constant worry. Once a person in town opened this hive of secrets, everybody would demand answers. Maybe things would change come spring, but after the summer, the next fall and winter loomed on the horizon.

Quinn was lonely and the child had become trying, demanding to go out, and play, and the days of baby bliss had long passed. She was headstrong and defiant and even though their lives were dreary, a thought took shape in Quinn's mind, a thought as clear as day: she couldn't see herself spending the rest of her life on this farm, tucked away, just so people wouldn't ask questions.

Her mind no longer could conceive of this life on the farm being all there was going to be.

Regardless of her trying ways, the child was heaven-sent, was her salvation. She seemed to erase all darkness when Quinn watched her learn to walk with knees made of rubber, how she wobbled before falling, laughing and clapping. She was such a happy child, never sullen, and so beautiful. The way she giggled and ran toward her, extending her arms, wanting to be picked up, and held, those moments kept Quinn alive, reminded her that people were inherently good and loving; otherwise the weight of her memories would have crushed her by then, would have swept her away.

THAT DAY THEY PREPARED DINNER. IT WAS FIVE IN THE AFTERNOON and every miniscule task and chore Quinn dragged out as long as possible. She allowed the child to wash potatoes in the deep sink, took her time to peel them, check for tenderness.

Just as they leaned over the pot in the sink and inhaled the steam, there was a knock on the door. It echoed through the house and Quinn switched on the porch light. She moved the curtain and saw two shadows standing motionless.

It wasn't until the taller of the two lifted his hand and rapped on the door again that Quinn realized they weren't ghosts; it was Tain and a man with an unkempt beard and matted hair. Not knowing what to do, Quinn just stood there, but the third knock came and she knew it was a matter of time until they'd demand to enter. Quinn thought of Nolan's shotgun that still rested on the mantel. Quinn had no idea if it was loaded or if it even worked. She sent the girl to her room. Opening the door and thinking that the visit wasn't going to end well happened simultaneously.

Tain was thin and her brown eyes were black pebbles stuck in snow. Her face seemed paler than Quinn remembered, her head too large to be held up by her fragile body.

Not long after Tain and the man entered the house, the man, who went by the name of Delbert, demanded alcohol. "Beer if you have it," he said. A crooked smile exposed a row of rotten teeth.

"I don't have any beer. I don't drink. But I have a bottle of whiskey somewhere in the house," Quinn said, "I'd have to go look for it." His smell, repulsive, filthy, grimy, entered the house the moment he crossed the threshold.

"You do that," Delbert said and went to the living room, plopping himself on the couch, his dirty boots resting on the edge of the table. "You got somethin' to eat too?" he yelled toward the kitchen.

She didn't answer him but heard Tain open the fridge behind her, randomly pulling out whatever she could find that didn't require cooking, stuffing cheese into her mouth.

Quinn wanted to rip it out of her hand but then told herself that Tain knew nothing of the long drive she had to make with the child to a neighboring town to buy groceries. She allowed her to eat, remembering that she had never been able to teach Tain any kind of manners.

"How's it going?" Quinn asked and watched Tain pull off her boots, her socks barely holding together with the heel poking out. There were blisters and raw skin and lots of caked-on dirt on her feet.

"I need money," Tain said without looking at her, bending down and pulling off chunks of dead skin as she winced.

"Let me get you some warm water to soak your feet in," Quinn said and walked to the stove to put on a kettle, the calcium making a swirling sound as it swished around on the bottom. "I have some iodine somewhere. You don't want that to get infected."

"We'll spend the night and then we'll leave. But I need money and—"

"Let's just fix you up," Quinn interrupted her and put the kettle on the stove with an angry clang.

Tain hadn't even asked for the child, hadn't even so much as looked around to see if there were any signs of her. Quinn wondered if she had forgotten about her altogether or if the child just wasn't of any concern to her.

After the water was just right, Quinn squirted some soap into a plastic tub and watched Tain grimace in pain when she immersed her feet into the sudsy water.

"Who's that man?" Quinn asked while she prepared sandwiches.

"He's my boyfriend," Tain said and took a hearty bite out of the sandwich.

Quinn put two more sandwiches on a plate. She stepped into the living room, where Delbert was picking his nose with one hand and flipping through the TV channels with the other. Quinn never watched TV and what little reception she got through an air antenna wasn't worth mentioning.

"You found that whiskey yet?" Delbert asked as if to scold her for her sluggishness and snatched the plate from her hands.

Quinn recoiled when his dirty fingertips touched her hands. He looked filthy and she would have to clean the couch after he left. She would never touch anything this man had sat on.

"Not yet," Quinn said. She jerked when she heard a whine coming from upstairs, hoping it was merely a few words uttered in her sleep. "Let me get that whiskey for you. I'll be right back."

Quinn rushed upstairs with a throbbing heart, fearing they might follow her, scare the child, get her upset, and make her cry. She was so small, not used to people, and became uneasy when people stared at her too long. Tain, with her slow-witted ways, might grab her, pull her from her warm bed and hold her tight, too tight—she had never known the right amount of love to give—and then there'd be tears and crying and wailing. What if they just demanded Quinn pack a suitcase for the baby? She was Tain's child, *biologically* she was, but no one was going to take the child from her. No one.

With wide brown eyes she said, "Mommy," wrapping her scrawny arms around her.

Quinn held her for what seemed a full five minutes before her eyelids closed but then she jerked awake again.

"You there, Mommy?" the child asked, as if she was afraid Quinn wasn't going to be there next time she opened her eyes.

She finally fell asleep and Quinn went into her bedroom to get the bottle of whiskey from the closet along with a pair of socks for Tain. She looked around frantically for a knife or something sharp she could use in case things went wrong and she couldn't get to the shotgun in time. There wasn't anything but a glass carafe that Sigrid had given her but it seemed silly to arm herself with that and suddenly Quinn realized it was Friday and she couldn't go to the bank until Monday morning and there was no way she could give them any money until then. The clerk would ask her to wait another day or two because the amount was too high to be withdrawn in cash—Quinn just knew Tain would be outlandish in her demands and ask for an excessive amount—and Quinn couldn't see herself spending all weekend and even longer with Tain and that awful man and his dirty body on the couch. Tain was no longer Tain, she was just someone she used to know, now she was running around with this criminal—Quinn could just tell by looking at him—and she hadn't asked for the child at all, just demanded food and drink and money.

Silence echoed in her ears and she wondered what they were doing downstairs, didn't know if she could do what it took to rip that shotgun off the wall, point it at them and pull the trigger. Did she have it in her to just bust into the living room and shoot that criminal who rested his muddy shoes on her table and picked his nose on her couch? And Tain, what was she going to do about her? She could never hand the child over to Tain, *knowing full well* she was in danger with her, blood or no blood. And then the void of panic slowly filled with a cold, howling storm of resolve that refused to let up. If they took the child away from her, she'd be completely and utterly alone on this farm, entirely alone in the world.

Downstairs, Quinn found the man asleep on the couch and Tain still soaking her feet. She had rummaged in the large drawer of the kitchen table with the odds and ends that were in the way or things Pet shouldn't get ahold of, like matches, a knife, a mousetrap. Aspirin. There were also things that reminded her of Nolan; some of them had been there for years.

Tain held Nolan's mug in her hand, twisted it about, ran her thumb over it, and inspected it as if it held some sort of revelation. She put the mug down with a thud. "That's Nolan's mug. He never liked anyone else drinking out of it. Nolan would be mad at you."

What a simpleton. Quinn wanted to say something, wanted to scream at her, *How dare you mention Nolan and not waste a single thought on your daughter? Have you no sense at all?* But Tain wouldn't understand, would just cry and get upset and then the ruffian on the couch would get involved and then there'd be this whole commotion, waking up Pet, and then who knows what else would happen. His name alone, Delbert, made Quinn wince. Delbert might hold the baby against his body and touch her, run his hands over her backside, she wouldn't put it past him at all, touching a child inappropriately, it was something Quinn could just tell about him, and she'd always had a hunch for things like that. Certain brow ridges on men, too pronounced, like the faces of the hunters had had *bad* written all over them. Delbert was made from the same cloth, she had seen it in his eyes. He was bad news, no doubt about it. Pet wasn't safe with anyone but her. No one was going to touch her.

"Why did you drink out of his mug?" Tain insisted with such authority that Quinn had to force herself not to raise her voice.

"What is it to you?" Quinn replied, getting impatient. "He doesn't care about the damn mug any longer, does he?"

"I'll tell everybody what you did to him."

There. Just like that. *I'll tell.* "What exactly did I do to him?"

"You killed him. I know so," Tain said and reached for the pair of socks Quinn clutched in her hand. "Help me put those on."

The audacity. The guts of this girl. Quinn had taken her in, nursed her back to health, had bought her an entire wardrobe, given her a place to live, had *loved* her, and all she'd done in return was to carry on with her husband. And Quinn had felt for Tain—the only person she had ever loved, except her father, Benito, and Nolan, and him only for a while—but Tain was the sister Quinn never had, she'd given her everything, had even considered leaving her husband and helping her raise Pet.

But Tain was a moron, just a stupid moron, not understanding even the simplest of things. She wanted money and next time, what would she want then? Pet? The farm? She wouldn't quit in her halfwit kind of way, the crazy inside of her would never stop demanding and, most of all, wouldn't understand that eventually there'll be no money left. Like Pet, who saw a picture of a cake in a magazine and wanted cake, not understanding that there was no cake and cakes had to be baked, but childlike minds wanted what they wanted regardless if it was available or not. That was Tain, always asking for things with her childlike demands, but now she had taken up with that thug on the couch and he wouldn't play. He was tall and his hands were huge and he wouldn't care if he hurt her or Pet.

Quinn handed Tain the socks.

"I found this ointment in the drawer," Tain said.

Quinn stared at it. The magic salve Aella had given her, *a key to other worlds* she had called it. A way of seeing the dearly departed. Nolan's limping ghost. *Only a little bit. Never on broken skin. Poisonous.*

"Should I rub it on my feet? Will it help?" Tain asked.

"Give it a try," Quinn said and watched Tain open the round container and grimace when she got a whiff of the salve.

Not too much, it can kill you. Nightshades are nature's ultimate poison, Aella had told her.

Tain looked down at the metal container, inspecting the foot drawing on the small label. Quinn kneeled on the floor and gently lifted Tain's feet from the water. She patted them dry, careful not to rub too hard. Quinn then applied the ointment, generously, in round strokes, making sure to cover both feet entirely. "Is it burning?" she asked as she helped slip the socks over Tain's feet. She felt some fear but mostly she felt relief, something inside her unwilling to stop. She washed her hands and then helped Tain up and held her by her elbow.

"Where's Delbert?" Tain asked and scanned her surroundings as if she was lost without him.

"On the couch."

"I'll stay with him. Take me to him."

Quinn led her into the living room, where Delbert's head had fallen backward and drool had run down his chin. The bottle of whiskey on the table was half empty. Tain plopped on the couch and Delbert briefly opened his eyes, mumbled something, and went back to his alcohol-induced sleep. Tain scooted next to him, her legs propped up on a pillow at the end of the couch.

"I'll see you tomorrow morning then," Quinn said and waited for her demeanor to change. Quinn suspected the potency of the salve had deteriorated over the years. But more than that Quinn knew it had all been for the birds. Looking at the shotgun on the wall above the fireplace, she knew it was old and rusty, hadn't been cleaned in years. She didn't know where the shells were, if there were any in the house at all, and she knew she wasn't capable of shooting them, but run she could. She had to pack, and before they woke up, she'd be long gone with the child.

Quinn went upstairs and dragged out a suitcase, packed all their clothes—which were few—books and toys and all the money she had stashed away. It was a rather large amount and the rest of the money from her father's inheritance was in an account at the bank, set up to pay the yearly property taxes as to not arouse suspicion, and it would be many years before the money ran out. No one would suspect anything if she never returned to the farm—people might think she'd joined Nolan on some job out of town, some oil fields on the coast. They would be safe for the time being.

While Delbert and Tain slept on the couch, it began to snow. It was a fluke really—snow was rare in Texas, Quinn couldn't even remember the last time she had seen snowflakes—it was just a flurry that melted the moment it hit the ground, but Pet, wrapped in blankets as Quinn carried her to the truck, still drunk with sleep and disoriented, woke up and started to ask questions, confused as to why they were up and about in the middle of the night. When Pet saw the snow, she became excited, burrowed out from underneath the blankets. She wanted to feel the snow—she didn't know what it was, kept asking, *What this, what this, what this*—and Quinn managed to calm her and by the time she put her in the backseat, she had fallen asleep again and hopefully she wouldn't remember anything the next day. She'd figure out the story she'd tell her on the road.

Just when Quinn closed the truck door, she heard a noise, followed by the shattering of glass. She wanted to get in the truck and take off, didn't care about Tain nor the hoodlum, but there was a blanket she needed, and crackers from the pantry to make the trip more pleasant for Pet, a magazine she loved to look at. And so she hurried into the house, but the moment she passed the threshold, she knew something was wrong.

Quinn flipped the switch and the living room was bathed in the harsh overhead light. On the couch lay Tain with her arms flailing. Delbert stood above her, swaying back and forth as if he'd been hit by a tranquilizer gun, about to go down. Tain was audibly gasping for breath, her chest heaving. Quinn watched in horror as Tain began yanking on her clothes as if they were strangling her.

"What's wrong, what's wrong?" Delbert yelled repeatedly, out of breath himself. "Babe, babe, babe, babe," over and over, like a broken record.

Served him right, Quinn thought, to be such a waste of life, dragging a girl like Tain around, talking her into doing things she'd never do if left to her own devices. She watched Delbert drop to his knees, shaking Tain as if she was in the midst of a nightmare and all he had to do was wake her and everything would be okay. Quinn stepped closer and she saw vomit on the carpet and her stomach began to heave in a sickly way and her head spun as if the whole room was one large carousel, slow at first but gaining momentum. Delbert turned and stared at Quinn, his face shiny, covered in sweat, and then she watched him collect items from the table; pipes and foil, lighters and all kinds of objects Quinn didn't recognize.

Delbert pulled on his boots and stumbled past her but then thought otherwise.

"What's wrong with her?" he asked, his voice wobbly.

Quinn wanted to slap him but that meant touching him and she was not going to do any such thing.

"How would I know?" Quinn said and turned her head away to escape his stench, looked past him, toward the couch. Tain's skin was gray and waxy, all life was gone, Quinn could tell. The salve had done its deed. She should have taken off in the truck, shouldn't have set foot onto this godforsaken farm again. She could be miles down the road but now there was this brute and she had to figure out what to do with him. "What did you do to her?"

"I woke up and she was like this. I don't know."

"You must have done something. Look at her." Tain's body seemed relaxed but her eyes were wide open, looking upward and back, and there was some foamy spittle on her lips.

Delbert grabbed Quinn by her coat and twisted it so it went tight around her neck.

"Go. Just go," was all Quinn could think of saying. "Forget you were ever here."

"Give me some money."

"I don't have anything to give."

"I'll tell the police. I saw you packing up the truck. There's something you're not telling me. I ain't stupid."

"Give me a few days, I'll get you some money. But now you leave," Quinn spit at him. Time to get away was all she needed.

Quinn stumbled as he let go of her coat and she worried about him demanding the keys to the truck, that he'd take off not knowing Pet was in the backseat, or he'd throw her out of the car, and so Quinn just screamed, repeatedly and high-pitched, and Delbert ran down the hallway and out the front door.

"I'll be back and you better have the money for me or I'll tell the police."

Quinn watched his dirty and greasy hair barely move as he ran like a man who was out of shape, almost like Nolan used to run, and she imagined the brute's lungs about to burst, but she wasn't worried about him. Without so much as looking at the truck, he took off toward the meadow and the woods beyond. Delbert would return, but they'd be long gone. He'd absorb himself into whatever world he had come from before he had found Tain, and he'd remain there, get killed in a knife fight, or end up in jail, or clubbed to death in some alley somewhere.

Quinn took Pet back upstairs and put her in her bed, but left their belongings in the car. She knew the ground wasn't frozen, knew the earth hadn't had time to become hard and solid and, after all, she was skilled in digging graves.

It took her a few hours and she had to take a break and care for Pet, give her a bath and make her breakfast, but once she went down for her nap, Quinn continued to dig, and when it was all said and done, she had added another mound to the two by the cypress tree. She wondered if people who came across the mounds would catch on, but maybe the ground would settle and in a year's time it might be leveled out and no one would be the wiser.

It struck Quinn, just for a second it struck her deeply how odd and unlikely it was for a woman to have to bury three people on a farm underneath a tree and she thought herself somehow troubled—the expression *leaving death in her wake* came to mind—but then she heard Pet call out and she turned and rushed into the house, not wasting another second on the dead.

The next morning they left. Quinn had thought about it—Delbert was not to be trusted and all she'd do was look over her shoulder, jerk every time there was a knock on her door, and that was no way to live. They'd find a new home, somewhere. She'd take baby steps. One state over first, and before they knew it they'd be living in a nice house, maybe all the way in California.

Later, when Pet awoke, she began to cry for a toy, her lavender bunny. Quinn didn't remember if they'd left it behind or dropped it on the muddy ground at the farm. She pulled over and went through the trunk, every suitcase and every bag—Pet screamed the entire time—just to find it lodged underneath the backseat. And not until Pet had gone back to sleep, clutching the toy to her chest, did Quinn weep. Just for a moment, then she consciously thought about what she had gotten herself into.

She didn't dwell on it, for that would take her to much darker places. How hard could a new life be? Compared to what she had done so far, the future seemed like child's play.

Forty-two

DAHLIA

IN the parking lot of the Aurora Police Department I kill the engine. I have called Bobby a dozen times, but his phone goes to voice mail every single time.

In the still air of the car the town's indifference seeps into my skin, makes me feel like a ghost. Sobering and melancholy all at once, the feeling mocks the past few weeks of my life. Time will continue to pass as it always has and the trees in this parking lot will be on autumnal fire in a couple of months. Once fall comes and the temperatures drop, the trees will know it is time to let go of their leaves and expose themselves for what they are.

This is what is about to happen: I will walk into the APD and expose my mother as a murderer. I'm about to tell the police the exact story Memphis has told me. I haven't forgotten a single detail. I will struggle with the names, Memphis and Tain, and whom I call mother, but it'll sort itself out. It's not about telling on Memphis; it's the fact that there are three bodies buried only a few hundred yards away from where I've been sleeping for the past few weeks.

I tell myself to get out of the car and enter the building, but neither does my hand reach for the door nor do my legs as much as twitch. Behind me on the backseat is my long-lost encyclopedia. Memphis should have given it to me a long time ago. Why did she hold on to it? That's another point of contention for me: her unnecessary lies, her needless secrets, the games she plays.

I roll down the window and stare in the driver's side mirror. Not since Memphis has told me she is not my biological mother have I really studied my face. I used to think I had her sharp nose, just a bit more refined, we are about the same height, have the same slim body type. I am taken aback by the lack of emotion on my face. There is so much inside of me, always has been, but I have learned to contain it. There is rage and frustration, all bundled up into something that I can't name. The mirror shows the woman the world sees, not who I really am. It doesn't express how I remain blunted, how I hardly raise my voice, how I never lose control, never allow my hands to get involved. I'm afraid how far I would go. What I would do.

Her audacity. Is that how Memphis felt about Tain? I think of Tain, the simpleminded girl, and Memphis' claim that she was unfit to raise me. I don't know if I can trust her with Tain's story. I want it to not matter, I want to believe that Memphis did all this for me, but regardless of how I twist and turn it, she is still a murderer.

Is there more to this story? Should I go back, clean out the shed, turn the house upside-down? Roll up my sleeves and just get at it, see what comes of it, all those boxes, the dusty shed, the dark corners of the barn. Will it support her story or tell a different one? There is only one way to find out if she told the truth: to have the bodies dug up, exhumed. That also means putting Memphis in prison for the rest of her life. Whenever I think I know what to do, I wait a couple of minutes and everything arranges itself yet again.

This is what I know for sure: by choosing to remain in hiding, she also chose my isolation, the poverty we lived in. The constant beads of sweat on her brow, the conniving and running. If you chose one thing, by default you chose another. You chose to run, you chose I run with you. Your crimes were mine. I am the biggest crime of them all. I let that sink in for a minute: the woman who has raised me in squalor killed my parents.

I suddenly remember the first time I went to school. It was eighth grade in Aurora's middle school, and I was so lost; I had never been to school, had never even sat still in a classroom, had never been around large crowds of kids. Those hallways between classes, all those kids, the bumping and the noise and the smells, the hurrying to get to class. I was on edge the entire time. Bobby somehow picked up on that. I had no problems comprehending any subject—I had spent my days reading and studying ever since I could remember, was mostly ahead in everything but math—but he gave me the shortcuts that mattered. He never went on and on about explaining things, just laid it down. *Don't give a fuck, is what you do.* There were all the girl friendships that I didn't know how to navigate. *If it's hard being friends with her, don't bother. It isn't worth it.* That's what I need right now, I need Bobby to tell me what it all means.

I reach behind me and pull the encyclopedia from the backseat onto my lap. It is heavy and cumbersome and I can't imagine having dragged it around ever since I was nine years old. The book seems familiar and unfamiliar at the same time, a relic I remember in spirit. The brown cover looks like linen but is made of sturdy cardboard, the words *THE COLUMBIA ENCYCLOPEDIA* embossed in green, and a crown with three crosses sits above them. There are little inverted tabs indicating the letters of the alphabet. I open to a random page. The letters are small and I have to squint to decipher them.

Pages pop open as if someone has left a bookmark for me. Some of the words are underlined, maybe an indication that I had studied them, and there are handwritten comments on many pages. I don't remember why I made those notes or what they mean—page 327, carpet and rugs, thick fabrics, usually woolen—I wrote *can be magic and fly* in jittery letters. I keep flipping; randomly my eyes catch a word here or there. Some seem vaguely familiar, more a memory of a memory than a true recall.

The worst part is that I love her. I always have. She was the only constant between Texas and New Mexico, Vegas and California. Just the two of us. As much as I want to walk into this police station and tell them about what she has done, I also want to protect her. I need to talk to Bobby about this; he'll know what to do. I dial his number and again it goes to voice mail.

There is a commotion behind me; multiple car doors are opening and slamming shut at the same time. Vans with roof masts and satellites pull into the parking lot. People shout, run, and then an entire crew of people with microphones and cameras set up equipment on the steps of the police department. Another white van with multiple satellite dishes on the roof pulls up next to my car.

I roll down the window.

"Hey, what's going on?" I ask the first person who exits the van.

"We are setting up for a news conference," he says, positioning a camera on his shoulder.

"What about?"

"The woman from the woods," he says and takes off running toward the police precinct. He turns. "She's been identified," he adds.

"GOOD AFTERNOON. I'M JESSICA VALDEZ, REPORTING FOR KDPN," a reporter says. "Shortly, the Aurora Police Department will update us on the woman who was found in the woods by a jogger. There's information that she is awake and responsive."

I stand off to the side, behind a couple of rows of people. The energy in the air is palpable and I can't bring myself to even form a coherent thought. All I know is that my Jane is awake.

"We've been told the woman who was found by a jogger a few weeks ago in the local woods has now been identified. That's all the information we've been given. As soon as the press conference convenes, we will interrupt the regularly scheduled programming and go live to hear Chief of Police Walter Goode give us the latest details regarding this case that has puzzled the town of Aurora the past weeks. This is Jessica Valdez, reporting for KDPN from Aurora, Texas."

I feel giddy. This is it, everything is coming to a halt. There'll be no more wondering, no more preoccupation. It's about to be done.

The sliding glass doors open and two uniformed officers, the police chief, Walter Goode, a rotund man with a spikey crown of white hair, and two men in suits emerge. There's no greeting, no introduction; Walter Goode jumps right in.

"We are happy to report that the young woman who was found in the woods by a jogger has regained consciousness. After examination by Metroplex personnel it was determined she had been assaulted and suffered major trauma. There will be a separate news briefing regarding her health status at a later point. Her doctors will elaborate on that sometime today.

"She is awake and responsive and her name is Kayla Hoffman. She is from Hot Springs, Arkansas, and is a sophomore at Trinity Methodist University in Dallas. Her college was not aware that she was not attending classes and therefore she was never reported missing." Chief Goode takes a handkerchief from his pocket and wipes his forehead. He unfolds a piece of paper and lowers the microphone. "Kayla Hoffman passed through Aurora and spent the night at a local motel. She was abducted and a suspect is in custody. This is an ongoing investigation, therefore I will not take any questions at this point."

The reporters break out into a frenzy. *How long had she been . . . Can you spell . . . Which hotel . . . Where is her family . . . Will they make a statement . . . Has she been questioned . . . Did the school release a statement . . .* Questions fly at the chief, who steps to the back and ignores the reporters.

I'm not sure what it is I'm feeling. Relief that she's okay surges through me. After all, I wanted to see this through until the end, in all of its madness. I know who she is now, my Jane now has a name, and there's a suspect.

Taking two steps at a time, I enter the precinct. I walk past the front desk, ignoring the question from the officer, and I rush down the hallway.

On the right, several doors down from the front desk, in a room with glass windows, I see Bobby take off his badge. Bordeaux stands on the other side of the room, his hands behind his back. There are two officers and three detectives in civilian clothes crowding the small room. I stare through the window, trying to take it all in; Bordeaux's face is blotchy and red, his eyes bloodshot. As if I'm watching a silent movie, the characters' lips are moving but I can't hear anything. The last thing I see before the officer steps in front of me is Bordeaux crossing his wrists, as if he's telling them to put cuffs on him. He laughs, throws his head back.

"You are not allowed back here," the female officer says and steps between me and the glass window, reaching for my arm. I walk backward, then I turn and run out the door.

Forty-three

MEMPHIS

FROM the perfect spot on the front porch, I position the chair just right—the angle matters more than the placement itself—and I watch Dahlia through the kitchen window. If you had asked me thirty years ago what kind of life I imagined for her, this isn't it. She moves about deliberately, as if she's considering the world over and over, never trusting even the most dependable things. She tries to act as if everything I have told her doesn't touch her, but I can tell that there's fury inside of her. She holds her cards close to her chest, never to reveal them, never to just abandon herself completely. I have told Dahlia everything, every single detail I have disclosed, yet when I ask myself what has been gained, I come up empty. The truth didn't set her free—it binds her tighter to a life she'd rather forget. There are parts of her that never came to fruition, were cut short by the life we led. I poisoned the blank slate she was with what I have done and now here we are.

During those long morning hours before the sun comes up, when the weak morning light is about to turn harsh, creating moving shadows on the walls, I have come to the conclusion there's only one thing left to do: I have to make this right.

I must allow her to begin again as if all this had never been; as if I didn't kill her father, as if I didn't poison her mother. I did the right thing by keeping her, yet by making the pacts I made, by demanding what isn't given freely, I now have to pay the price. Allowing Dahlia to begin again will give her what is rightly hers; this farm for one, her father's farm. It belongs to her, and so does the money that's left from my inheritance that I claimed with my father's estate. And her life—she needs to have a life, but for as long as I am here she won't be able to move on. She will forever be torn apart by feelings she'll never be able to sort out, never be able to put in proper perspective.

From this perfect spot I have created for myself on the porch I have a clear view of the kitchen. I watch Dahlia hide Bobby's gun in the cubby above the fridge where I used to keep a money can for the leftover change from grocery shopping. After Dahlia leaves, I grab the gun and the sturdy rope I found in the barn and put them in a canvas bag. I leave the farmhouse through the back door without looking back. Aella told me once if you want to leave something behind, *truly* behind, retreat from it and let neither the sound of feet drive you to turn back, nor the baying of a ghost dog, nor the slapping of sheets in the wind.

I have been tired, deep down to my bones. Every day feels like an entire year. I carefully scan the ground in front of me; I cannot stumble or fall. A sprained ankle would derail everything. I gather myself and force my steps to be light and energetic. The yellow dress Nolan gave me so many years ago invigorates me. I think of Benito and my heart is heavy. By the time I returned to Aurora he was Sheriff Ramón de la Vega, married, with a son, and his wife was sick. He was a good man. His uncle and family forced him to leave after the rape, he told me later—his family was afraid he'd get blamed and they made him go to Mexico. Eventually he returned and went to live with relatives in Aurora, where I tracked him down when California became too much.

After years on the road, running from one place to another, I got tired. I called Benito, told him I'd be back in Aurora, and I begged him to help me start a new life. I meant the two of us, me and Pet. His wife was dying from cancer and he loved her but he wasn't the same boy I'd known so many years ago, his loyalties were with his family then. He helped me change our names, and from that day on we were Memphis and Dahlia Waller. It took just one form to get Dahlia enrolled in school, and clearly no one asked questions when the sheriff stands next to you pushing a paper across the counter. No one asked, no one connected us to Creel Hollow Farm. We were just a mother and a daughter looking to settle down in a small town.

From the day Dahlia left, I lived with a steady heartbeat. I was at peace. Then, out of the blue, she returned home. Again I had to be vigilant, had to make sure no one found out about us. Old women blend in, but having her with me was always my weak spot. What were the odds of Dahlia coming across that girl in the woods bringing it all to the forefront once again? It is the price I was told I'd have to pay one day. And then Dahlia starts asking questions, turning stones. She was and is my fate and, at last, exhausted and tired of waiting, fate has brought down a sentence upon me.

Spilled milk it is, nothing else.

When I reach the edge of the woods, my plan begins to derail. The tree line is shadowy and even though I keep telling myself that every evil thing has already happened, that there's no need to be afraid, panic sets in. I have to admit that I may not be able to do what I came here to do. It's not about being out of breath, not about fainting or weakness on my part, but I have underestimated the power of these woods.

When I enter the woods, the air turns cool and I shiver in the sleeveless dress. The dirt and the decomposing leaves make the air thick and I stumble—I have no balance to begin with—but I land on my knees. As if these Aurora woods carry the memory of the woods of Beaumont from all those years ago, I'm back in the forest with the hunters.

Shhhhh. Do what I tell you to do.

Just like that, Beard, Bony Fingers, Pimples, and Ponytail fade in, they stand in a circle around me dropping bugs on my naked bleeding body. I will them to disappear, tell myself this is a different place and a different time, the woods have no memory. That I'm safe and there's no reason to be afraid.

I stand up and forge ahead, trusting that I will find what I'm looking for. There's no map, no directions to follow, nothing but a narrow path covered in knotted roots, but they form steps for me. The silence around me is unnerving and all I can hear is my wheezing breath.

Don't scream. Not a word.

I empty my mind but panic immediately fills the void and every time I step on a twig or kick a stone, I freeze with horror. I fear I've left too late in the day; darkness is descending quickly and without mercy. The black trunks against the dark backdrop take the shapes of the hunters with their guns pulled.

In front of me the path branches off. I take the left one. When I see a massive live oak I know I have found what I'm looking for. My eyes scan the thick, dark trunk in the deepest and darkest part of the forest where shadows are abundant. Its branches are interlocking, almost like a stairway, easy to climb, even for an old woman like me. The dense growth leaves numerous spots to hold on to and to tie the rope to. I press my palm against its rough bark, and breathe in the scent of the forest.

I swing the canvas bag with the gun and the rope over my shoulder and start climbing upward. With every inch I gain courage, increase my resolve. Three points of contact—foot, hand, foot; hand, foot, foot—and before I know it I am far off the ground. I find a perch where I can lean against the tree's trunk, take the rope, allow it to dangle, and start tying my body to the tree. I move quickly as not to lose courage. I start with my feet, wrap the rope around my thighs and the trunk, my waist, then my chest. My left hand is last. I loop the handles of the bag through the rope and tie one last knot, binding the gun to my hand. It rests there.

Those jars in Nolan's shed—the ones full of crickets dying on a bed of plaster, their legs curled up, antennae pointing about aimlessly— it dawned on me some time ago that I have spent my entire life in one of those jars. The ghost I had created was out there pretending to live; the other one, the real me, was in a jar, trapped.

You want this. Beg. Beg for it.

The past is so much more than a memory. There's no escaping it, but this is as close as I'll ever come to being free.

The scent of the forest pales in comparison to the wind that rustles these leaves. To think that my last breath will be carried off by it is nothing short of splendid.

I turn the gun toward my heart and I pull the trigger. I'm aware of one last breath and my ears ring.

There is a scent of death. The forest is heaving with it.

Then all goes black and I welcome the darkness.

Forty-four

DAHLIA

JAMES Earl Bordeaux Jr. confessed. Bobby, after he gave me his gun, went to the Lark and confronted him. At the same time the call came in that Jane Doe was awake. Bobby lied, told Bordeaux she had identified him, took him to the precinct, and during the interrogation Bordeaux confessed.

Kayla Hoffman suffered a horrible fate but she survived. The story eventually came together, piece by piece: She left the university campus, told friends she'd be back in a few days. It was something she'd done before, and so her disappearance never raised any suspicion. Whenever the pressure became too much for her, she holed herself up in some hotel and returned days later with a new lease on life. Lots has been made about the fact that her family was tightlipped after it was all over but it was merely a college student bowing under the pressure of school and grades. Kayla is back home and safe. The last thing her family wants is for her to be in the headlines another day.

That time she was looking to get away, she ended up in Aurora and checked into the Lark. Bordeaux smelled an opportunity, never officially checked her into the database. There are conflicting reports but according to Bobby there is no proof that the system was down that day. The minute details will come out at trial, I'm sure. The short story is that Bordeaux drugged her, took her to the woods, where he raped and beat her. He was in the process of burying her when I came jogging up the dirt road and stepped into the woods. He stood nearby and watched me as I came upon Kayla's body. He watched me scream, watched me run, watched me fall in the creek.

And he considered killing me.

"You were lucky," Bobby says. "If it hadn't been for you freaking out and running off, falling into the creek, if you had seen him standing there, if Kayla had been able to speak, if you had just looked up . . ." Bobby stops right then and watches me closely.

"He was that close?" I ask.

"Just behind a tree nearby."

I remember feeling as if someone was watching me, as if some sort of presence was in those woods when I found Kayla.

What sleight of hand and twist of fate had made me argue with my mother that morning, delaying my run, what made me step into the shade of the woods? I go further with those realizations: what made Memphis cross paths with those hunters, what made Tain show up at Aella's trailer, what brought the storm that made Tain end up at Creel Hollow Farm? What if Memphis hadn't stood in the kitchen window, hadn't spotted her out there in the rain?

"Don't think about this too hard," Bobby says. "It's over."

"What about the other bracelets?" Three more are missing from the briefcase. I want to believe that whoever wore them got away.

"The samples in the briefcase are from the late nineties. They are checking into missing women from as far back as the eighties who have any connection to the Lark and Aurora. They are turning the motel inside out at this very moment."

"So it started with Bordeaux Sr. and continued with his son?"

"Seems that way."

I wonder if I could have been his next victim. It would've been plausible for me to leave town—another argument with my mother, another lost job, easy to make my disappearance believable. Who would have missed me? My mother? Bobby's cruiser across from the Lark might have spared me a horrible fate.

"You know, me and Bordeaux, at some point, we were friends."

Bobby tells me how they skipped school and how Bordeaux changed over the years, especially when he had a few drinks. How he pulled a knife once, and boasted how he could get away with anything.

"Goes to show we don't really know what people are capable of," I say and I can't help but think of the real culprit: the secrets people keep. How they eat them up. What is done in the dark.

But light does get in.

Quinn, Tain, and Nolan are as alive as they were all those years ago, on the farm. There are peculiar occurrences that I can't explain: floating lights—nothing remotely resembling a ghost, nothing that concrete—more a presence that seems to be frozen in place. Sometimes there is the outline of a face, but I could easily be mistaken, and certain round shapes seem like wide-set eyes, yet the presence is lifeless and slack. It is indecisive in its passivity and every time I take a step toward it, it disappears. I long to step into its path or even be entirely surrounded by it and sometimes, somewhere off in the distance, a door slams shut or footsteps echo as if Nolan and Tain are playing games with me. Yet they seem less angry, no longer haunt the night as if they chose to step into the light too.

We all need closure.

I never heard the actual words from Memphis. She never said *I killed your mother.* She didn't go that far. She thought her confession was it; she'd told the truth, *her* truth, and now we'd just all go on with our lives.

I will never forget the last time we spoke.

"What about me? What about Tain? My mother?" I asked her.

She cocked her head, then she looked away. I had called Tain my mother.

"Tain was unable to raise you," she said. "You wouldn't have lived to see your first birthday. I did what I thought was right. Please believe me, Dahlia, please."

"Why is this about you? What about me?"

"What about you, Dahlia?"

I just shook my head, fighting back the tears.

"*How was this hard for you? You were fed, safe, I took care of you. Was that not enough?*"

"*Enough? You can't see what you've done to me?*" I said, shaking my head.

She looked at me intently. I know she was racking her mind. "*Because I took you with me?*"

"*So I wasn't raped, my husband didn't get someone else pregnant, and therefore I must be okay? Is that what you're saying? That I have no right to be upset?*"

"*That's not what I'm saying. It's not the same thing.*" *She leaned forward as if a certain closeness gave her more power over me.* "*I've never met anyone more normal than you. You are strong. Resilient. I've done right by you.*"

"*You think I'm normal, Mother?*" *I spit* Mother *at her like a cherry pit.* "*You think the way I grew up was normal? Living in cars, and trailers, and motels, not going to school? You might as well have locked me in a closet.*"

"*I did this for you. Everything I did was for you.*"

I could tell she believed her own stories, but I knew better. A woman who spent half her life living in hiding, under an assumed name, doesn't just wake up one day and tell the truth. I doubted every word she said. Every single word.

"*Don't kid yourself,*" *I told her.* "*None of what you did was for me. You protected yourself.*" *I got up and looked down on her.* "*I don't know if I can even believe you. Look around you. There are graves that beg to differ.*"

"*Dahlia—*"

"*You killed my parents.*"

"*I did it all for you,*" *she insisted, as if she had committed the murders on my behalf and therefore they were somehow less wrong or punishable.*

This is what I know for sure: After a horrendous rape, and after having constructed a duplicate of herself, Quinn married a man named Nolan Creel who owned a once-sprawling farm in Aurora, Texas. Her infertility was known to her, but dreamer that she was, she hoped for a child. She made a pact with something or someone, with the help of a woman named Aella, a pact that didn't go her way; Tain's baby was stillborn. Tain was, in Quinn's mind, not a child, but a childlike creature, and Quinn loved her, even looked the other way when her own husband got her pregnant. When I was born, Quinn wanted to make compromises, was willing to agree to concessions, but Nolan failed her yet again. Nolan took everything from her and he paid the ultimate price. Confronted with a woman who'd never be able to care for me and a man who spent his life among bugs and beetles and crickets, she chose to kill to get her way.

My feelings for her still teeter back and forth, but dragging me over state lines, making me live in motels and cars, not allowing me to go to school, is another thing altogether.

What hurts the most—I also know this with certainty—what hurts the most is that in the years to come, I'll continue to go back and forth, and maybe I'll be forever torn. Having to get used to this feeling might be the worst of all. The blame I assign shifts, at times remains long enough to feel like hate. My entire life, every single memory, is an accumulation of moments, words I looked up in a heavy encyclopedia. I know now that I was attempting to make sense out of what no child can understand; an attempt to fill in blanks that adults leave for us, resulting in a contorted image of just about everything around me.

My second-to-last memory of Memphis: After she confessed to killing my mother, or to whatever blame she accepted in that regard, I watched her take the porch steps one by one, in an easy motion, her gait that of a younger woman, her litheness making her powerful. She was shaken, I could tell, and I wanted to pull away the mask of Memphis to see the person inside, the woman she was all those years ago, the woman who was carried over the threshold of this house, the woman who held a baby on the Galveston beach. I felt shame because I hated her, but then I knew if I listened to Memphis' words and paid attention to her smile, to her eyes, I might catch a glimpse. I want to believe Quinn was still in there as much as she ever was.

Memphis disappeared the day she concluded her story.

I came home after the reporters had packed up, and she was gone. Just like that. Her clothes remained in the closet, her purse sat on the kitchen table, her belongings were strewn all over the house, yet Memphis had disappeared.

For the first time in my life I opened her purse. She used to guard it with her life, maybe set this all in motion when she lost it that night. She had never let it out of her sight, and I can now imagine the panic that must have overtaken her when she realized it was gone.

There's a wallet, worn down, the top layer peeling off. It's a coin purse and within it are folded dollar bills and some coins. Something is tucked in one of the inside pockets. I unfold it. An old photograph, black-and-white, yellowed with age, its surface cracked. I see two women—they are looking at each other, laughing. I recognize Memphis, her curls blowing in the breeze, leaning against a fence. The other woman is shorter than Memphis, so slim that her frame borders on being gaunt. But her grip seems strong and determined; she sits sideways on the fence and one of her feet is propped up by its heel on the horizontal rail. She has long dark hair, wild and untamed. The photograph is too old to make out her face but I know that I'm looking at Memphis and Tain, more than likely the only photograph of them in existence.

They gaze at each other lovingly, they are familiar to one another, laughing as if there is nothing else in this world but them. Their hands are slightly out of focus as if they're reaching for each other the moment the picture is taken.

All her tracks she covered, destroyed everything bound to expose her, set fire to a house. And out of all the things she thought worth keeping, this was it.

After Bordeaux was arrested, Bobby surrendered his badge. There wasn't any fingerpointing at him, to my knowledge my involvement with the briefcase never came up. Between my finding the bracelets and Kayla waking from her coma, it all fell into place like marbles in a jar.

Initially they looked for Memphis on the farm property, on deserted roads, and in town. Then Sheriff Goode organized a search. Her picture appeared on the local news, and quite a few people from town joined the search party. We started at the farm in rows five feet apart, and with sticks we poked and prodded the earth, through the entire meadow and into the woods. There wasn't a trace of her. Not that day and not the next. A month passed and eventually flyers on local shop doors were the only likenesses that remained of her.

I didn't tell anybody but I knew she was dead.

I knew because that same night I saw the ghost of Memphis Waller.

The old clock in the living room ceased to tick and everything went silent. There was no sound, not a bird sang, not even Tallulah's claws on the hardwood floors could break through the dense stillness that fell over the house. The air became cold, and as my body heat quickly drained, an awareness crept over me that she was no longer among the living. I looked up and on the landing she stood, just for a second or so, beautiful in her yellow dress.

She smiled and then she was gone. And that is my last memory of Memphis Waller.

NOW, WEEKS LATER, AS I DESPERATELY LOOK FOR ANSWERS TO ALL the questions swirling in my mind, Tallulah comes from behind and nudges me. It is hours still before the sun sets, and I take her for her daily walk. She trots along the path by the side of the meadow and makes eye contact every few steps to make sure I'm still close.

Looking at her, I realize her face will soon be completely gray; her paws and her belly have already taken on a slight silver sheen. She deliberately stops often and sniffs, taking her time, inhaling every single scent. She's slowed down ever since she had the surgery, and we don't get far anymore on our walks. Down her belly is a jagged scar where her coat never grew back, where the mummified puppy she carried with her was removed. Life is like that, I guess. Some things just won't stay buried. Spaces dark and deep everywhere.

We make it all the way to the woods. When we cut through the tree line, an earthy smell wafts up from the ground, a fragrance that conjures layers of pine needles and dark, fertile soil. Tallulah sniffs the air, nervously, and I call out to her, but she doesn't pay me any mind.

There's a scent in the air that seems peculiar, in a fruity way. The scent is so mesmerizing that Tallulah changes directions every few feet, sniffing the ground, just to walk in a circle and then find her way back to the original spot.

I watch her for quite some time, then I look up, wondering if people ever do that, look upward in the woods when the ground is covered in treasures like tangled roots, acorns, and pinecones. It's an odd thing to do, yet I feel somehow compelled. The tree before me is tall, and it's knotted and peculiar, its trunk wide, five feet or more, and its branches spread close to the ground.

Something catches my eye. I step closer and touch the short, tapering trunk that so generously supports the picturesquely gnarled branches and limbs that over time have spread horizontally to a great distance from the main trunk. A yellow hue stands out, makes me pause and step closer to the oak. At first it's merely a *this is out of place* feeling, the same way a nature photographer might spot a red cardinal among a flock of sparrows.

High above in the barren crown of the tree, a piece of yellow fabric flutters in the wind.

I see it but then I don't. It seems like a vision of sorts, and I think of all the ghosts this farm seems to house—none of them concerning or evil, just present as if they belong—but this vision of buttery color looks like a body in a yellow dress.

The puzzle pieces begin to drop and Tetris-like they stack themselves into place as if commanded by some higher power. Memphis is up in that tree. Perched on a branch, leaning against the trunk as if the tree's growth was meant to accommodate her perfectly. I stare at the body and nothing about it seems human, or at least not alive. It is merely a decomposing form in a yellow dress. The dress from her stories, the one my father had bought her.

I hear her voice. *When he still loved me.*

A rope is knotted around her waist and neck and I know what she's done. I know that she had no more strength to deny those trees and thicket and underbrush, that the woods had begun to claim her some time ago. Memphis had remained tethered to a death wish her entire life and she'd come to deliver on it once her story had been told.

The bark under my hands is crude and warped, yet strong, almost majestic. This live oak holds my mother's voice but also her reluctant kisses. I press my hands against the trunk and I listen to the whispering leaves above, the wind gently rousing them as if to tell her someone is here, someone has come for you, you will not remain in this thicket of hell.

Epilogue

THERE is so much going on with Bobby and Bordeaux and my mother disappearing that I don't realize it at first.

One day, in the barn, a scent with a certain bite drifts toward me. As I shift the bales of hay, they turn to dust and dry yellow flowers and pollen flare up into my nostrils, covering my body in a fine layer of something that I have no name for. At first I confuse it with a seizure, but then the dust settles and nothing more happens. I wait patiently for my world to shift or fall completely off its axis, fry my brain, or leave me a vegetable, yet nothing happens.

The seizures have completely ceased, much to Dr. Wagner's amazement. *Miraculously* is the word he used. I don't dwell on it too much, yet I remain vigilant. When I feel some sort of way, when I lose my footing, when the air around the farm seems to hum and there's a buzzing sound hovering over the property, I wait for a seizure, yet it never comes to pass. The gift, if it ever was one, has ceased, and for whatever it's worth, it has done its duty: everything that was done in the dark has come into the light.

After Bobby quit his job at the APD, he moved to the farm with me. While he ponders what to do with his future, something decides for him. For us, really.

It was a fall afternoon. Bobby had been working on the barn for weeks, had replaced rotten slats of wood and constructed individual horse stalls. We figured boarding horses wasn't going to make us rich but would provide a steady income. We already had most of the requirements in place—a fenced paddock and a field, mowing equipment, water troughs, trails, and areas to store feed—and we cleared out and prepared the barn, getting ready for the inspector who would grant a business license.

As I sweep the floor, a strange scent comes at me from outside the barn door. It seems to be a musty and unhealthy odor and as I turn, a shadow passes by. It is low to the ground, dragging one of its hind legs. I lean the broom against the stall door and step outside.

There stands an animal—is it a dog?—who has skin like stone. I stand paralyzed wondering if I'm imagining it all. It's a female and judging by her size a rather large breed. She looks nothing like a dog, more like a withered barnacle.

The closer I step, the more the stench comes at me. I step back into the barn and she follows me. As Bobby climbs off the ladder, the dog curls up in one of the stalls by bales of hay. I pull Tallulah's treats from my pocket and we sit beside her, gently attempting to feed her biscuits. She doesn't run nor does she flinch, but it seems more from exhaustion than trust. Considering her condition, I'm convinced she came here to curl up and die.

Bobby pushes the treats closer to her without making eye contact or talking. At first she hesitates, then she scoots toward us and begins to nibble; eventually she eagerly reaches out for more. I go into the house and by the time I return with a bowl of water, Bobby is rubbing her scaly and scabby skin. She then curls up and goes to sleep, her head in Bobby's lap.

The vet offers to put her down free of charge. "She's suffering; it's the right thing to do," he says, but I think of Ghost, the dog in Memphis' story and her stillborn pup. Aella's trailer materializes and Quinn and her desperate attempt at bargaining for a baby. I decline and Bobby and I spend the next weeks coaxing her to accept medicine, applying medicated lotion to help heal the dog's hardened skin and her broken heart.

Weeks later she still cowers when she hears a sudden noise, flinches at the slightest movement, yet she is beginning to look more like herself; her skin has smoothed and her golden coat, however reluctantly, begins to grow back. But most of all, she seems to welcome our gentle care. Eventually she becomes unrecognizable; she turns into a sweet-faced golden dog covered in new fuzz, gazing into our eyes and wagging her tail as she plays with Tallulah. Her sorrowful eyes remain heavy with a past we know nothing about, yet she is well on her way to a better life. We name her Buttercup.

Our animal rescue is born, and in addition to the horses we board, we take in dogs, goats, and chickens.

Every time I look out the kitchen window, when I pass through the yard, I see the three graves underneath the cypress, their mounds reminding me of the farm's legacy. I decide that I will leave the past behind and I will never march into the police station, never so much as utter a word of her story to anyone but Bobby. I had allowed myself to hate her for some time, but then I gave in and let go of the feeling. Before she committed a crime against me, there were crimes committed against her. And though I know one cannot understand someone else's pain, I want to say that hers was much heavier, reached much further beneath her skin.

Fall comes to an end and the days grow gloomy, yet the occasional light streaking through the windows remains both brilliant and filled with shadows.

With time the peculiar happenings on the farm cease; there are no more raps on the door, no more knocking deep within the walls, no longer do faint footsteps sound upstairs. No more glimpses of Tain roaming the property, no more does the ghost of Nolan limp toward the shed. The shivers that used to run through me like an electric current have ended and it seems as if the entire cast of characters have found their resting places among us without disturbing the living.

One day, the farm is changed. It isn't a sudden change—at least we don't experience it that way—but one day we realize the farm no longer feels depressing and the thickness and heaviness has been replaced with the scent of horses and the echoes of barking dogs.

The winter days bring early-morning fog. It sweeps in and wraps itself around the buildings, snakes down the dirt road leading to the main road. It blankets the meadow and infuses the tree line leading into the woods.

And everyone and everything is at peace.

You gave me peace in a lifetime of war.

—ACHILLES

THE Good Daughter

ALEXANDRA BURT

DISCUSSION QUESTIONS

1. Some of Dahlia's childhood memories are crystal clear. Others are obscured by uncertainty. What is your earliest memory? Are most of your childhood memories vivid ones?

2. As a teenager, Dahlia felt held back by Memphis, unable to advance and make the most of her life. Do you think she was right to leave home when she did? How different do you think her life would have been had she stayed? How might Memphis' life have changed if Dahlia had stayed in Aurora?

3. Quinn's life changes dramatically after she meets Aella, a woman with mysterious powers. Do you believe in people with otherworldly abilities like Aella? Have you ever been to a psychic or wished a spell could be cast to aid you in an endeavor?

4. Early on in their marriage, Quinn misleads her husband, Nolan, in an effort to strengthen their relationship. Do you think this was wrong of her, even though she had good intentions, or were her actions justified? Have you ever done or said something that was meant to help a situation but you ended up regretting it?

5. Dahlia has a powerful bond with Tallulah, the dog she rescues.

How do you think this bond helps her to navigate the challenges she faces throughout the novel?

6. Do you think Memphis did what she had to do as she raised Dahlia? Or were her motivations more selfish in nature? How have tough choices changed your life and affected your relationships?

7. Dahlia isn't always sure if she can trust her own perceptions and feelings. Do you think that her difficulties stem from a physical cause or does the weight of the secrets she's trying to unravel affect her? Or is it both?

8. The forest is a powerful catalyst for Quinn, Memphis, and Dahlia. How does it shape their lives? Is there a place that has changed the course of your life or contributed greatly to who you are?

9. Tain and Quinn's relationship takes a turn as the story progresses. What do you think of Tain? How do her motivations change over time? Do you view her as a victim or is she in control of her choices?

10. Quinn transforms multiple times over the course of her life. What do you think is her most significant personal evolution? Have you ever had to change how you handle certain situations or people in your life?

11. Dahlia feels a strong connection to the missing woman she found in the woods and has trouble letting go of her story. Have you ever been captivated by a stranger's plight or has a news story significantly impacted your life?

12. Dahlia and Memphis have a very complicated relationship. How does the power of forgiveness come into play for each of them?

Keep reading for an excerpt
of Alexandra Burt's first novel . . .

REMEMBER MIA

Available in paperback from Berkley!

MISSING: SEVEN-MONTH-OLD INFANT DISAPPEARS FROM CRIB

Brooklyn, NY—The New York City Police Department is asking for the public's help in locating 7-month-old Mia Connor.

The parents and the NYPD are pleading with the public for any assistance in the investigation and are asking Brooklyn residents in the North Dandry neighborhood to come forward if they witnessed any suspicious behavior on the night and early morning of the 30th.

Mia Connor was last seen by her mother, Estelle Paradise, 27, around midnight when she laid her down to sleep. The mother discovered the child was missing when she woke up the next morning. The father was out of town when the infant disappeared.

"It's very frustrating," said Eric Rodriguez, spokesperson for the NYPD, when he appeared briefly at a news conference on Friday. "We're hoping somebody will come forward and give us the information allowing us to locate the child."

Immediately call the TIPS hotline if you have any information about the infant's whereabouts. All calls are strictly confidential.

Mia Connor has brown eyes and blond hair, is 25 inches tall, and weighs 14 pounds. The day of her disappearance she wore white one-piece pajamas with a cupcake print. She has two bottom teeth.

One

M RS. Paradise?"
         A voice sounds out of nowhere. My thoughts are sluggish,
as if I'm running underwater. I try and try but I'm not getting anywhere.

"Not stable. Eighty over sixty. And falling."

Oh God, I'm still alive.

I move my legs, they respond, barely, but they respond. Light
prowls its way into my eyes. I hear dogs barking, high-pitched. They
pant, their tags clatter.

"You've been in a car accident."

My face is hot, my thoughts vague, like dusty boxes in obscure
and dark attic spaces. I know immediately something is amiss.

"Oh my God, look at her head."

A siren sounds, it stutters for a second, then turns into a steady
torment.

I want to tell them . . . I open my mouth, my lips begin to form
the words, but the burning sensation in my head becomes unbearable.
My chest is on fire, and ringing in my left ear numbs the entire side
of my face. *Let me die,* I want to tell them. But the only sound I hear
is of crude hands tearing fragile fabric.

"Step back. Clear."

My body explodes, jerks upward.

This isn't part of the plan.

MY VISION IS BLURRED AND HAZY. I MAKE OUT A WOMAN IN BABY blue scrubs, a nurse, slipping a plastic tube over my head, and immediately two prongs hiss cold air into my nostrils. She pumps a lever and the bed jerks upward, then another lever triggers a motor raising the headboard until my upper body is resting almost vertically.

My world becomes clearer. The nurse's hair is in a ponytail and the pockets of her cardigan sag. I watch her dispose of tubing and wrappers, and the closing of the trash can's metal lid sounds final, evoking a feeling I can't quite place, a vague sense of loss, like a pickpocket making off with my loose change, disappearing into the crowd that is my strange memory.

A male voice sounds out of nowhere.

"I need to place a PICC line."

The overly gentle voice belongs to a man in a white coat. He talks to me as if I'm a child in need of comfort.

"Just relax, you won't feel a thing."

Relax and I won't feel a thing? What a concept. I lift my arms and pain shoots from my shoulder into my neck. I tell myself not to do that again anytime soon.

The white coat rubs the back of my hand. The alcohol wipe leaves an icy trail and jerks me further from my lulled state. I watch the doctor insert a long needle into my vein. A forgotten cotton wipe rests in the folds of the waffle-weave blanket, in its center a bright red bloody mark, like a scarlet letter.

There's a spark of memory, it ignites but then fizzles, like a wet match. I refuse to be pulled away, I follow the crimson, attach myself to the memory that started out like a creak on the stairs, but then the monsters appear.

First I remember the darkness.

Then I remember the blood.

My baby. Oh God, Mia.

THE MEMORY OF THE BLOOD LINGERS. THERE'RE FLASHES OF RED exploding like lightning in the sky; one moment they're illuminating everything around me; the next they are gone, bathing my world in darkness. Then the bloody images fade and vanish, leaving a black jittering line on the screen.

Squeaking rubber soles on linoleum circle me and I feel a pat on my shoulder.

This isn't real. A random vision, just a vision. It doesn't mean anything.

A nurse gently squeezes my shoulder and I open my eyes.

"Mrs. Paradise." The nurse's voice is soft, almost apologetic. "I'm sorry, but I have orders to wake you every couple of hours."

"Blood," I say, and squint my eyes, attempting to force the image to return to me. "I don't understand where all this blood's coming from." Was that my voice? It can't be mine, it sounds nothing like me.

"Blood? What blood?" The nurse looks at my immaculately taped PICC line. "Are you bleeding?"

I turn toward the window. It's dark outside. The entire room appears in the window's reflection, like an imprint, a not-quite-true copy of reality.

"Oh God," I say, and my high-pitched voice sounds like a screeching microphone. "Where's my daughter?"

She just cocks her head and then busies herself straightening the blanket. "Let me get the doctor for you," she says and leaves the room.

Two

VOICES enter my consciousness like a slow drift of clouds, merging with the scent of pancakes, syrup, toast, and coffee, making my stomach churn.

A gentle hand touches my arm, then a voice. "Mrs. Paradise? I'm Dr. Baker."

I judge only his age—he is young—as if my brain does not allow me to appraise him further. Have I met him before? I don't know. Everything about me, my body and my senses, is faulty. When did I become so forgetful, so scatterbrained?

He wears a white coat with his name stitched on the pocket: *Dr. Jeremy Baker.* He retrieves a pen from his coat and shines a light into my eyes. There's an explosion so painful I clench my eyelids shut. I turn my head away from him, reach up, and feel the left side of my head. Now I understand why the world around me is muffled; my entire head is bandaged.

"You're at County Medical. An ambulance brought you to the emergency room about . . ." He pauses and looks at his wristwatch. I wonder why the time matters. Is he counting the hours, does he want to be exact? ". . . three days ago, on the fifth."

Three days. And I don't remember a single minute. *Ask him, go ahead, ask him.* "Where's my daughter?"

"You were in a car accident. You have a head injury and you've been in a medically induced coma."

He didn't answer my question. He talks to me as if I'm a child, incapable of comprehending more elaborate sentences. *Accident? I don't remember any accident.*

"They found you in your car in a ravine. You have a concussion, fractured ribs, and multiple contusions around your lower extremities. You also had a critical head injury when they brought you in. Your brain was swollen, which was the reason for the induced coma."

I don't remember any accident. What about Jack? Yes, Mia's with Jack. She must be.

One more time.

"Was my daughter in the car with me?"

"You were alone," he says.

"She's with Jack? Mia's with my husband?"

"Everything's going to be okay."

The blood was just a vision, it wasn't real. She's with Jack, she's safe. Thank God.

Everything is going to be okay, he said.

"We're not sure of any brain damage at this point, but now that you've regained consciousness we'll be able to perform all the necessary tests to figure out what's going on." He motions to the nurse who has been standing next to him. "You lost a lot of blood and we had to administer fluids to stabilize you. The swelling will go down in a few days, but in the meantime we need to make sure you keep your lungs clear of fluids."

He picks up a contraption and holds it up in front of me. "This is a spirometer. The nurse will give you detailed instructions. Basically you keep the red ball suspended as long as you can. Every two hours, please." His last comment is directed toward the nurse.

The gurgling in my chest is uncomfortable and I try not to cough. The pain in my left side must be the fractured ribs. I wonder how I'll be able to stay awake for two hours or wake up every two hours or use this contraption for two hours, or whatever he just said.

"Before I forget . . ." Dr. Baker looks down at me. He is quiet for a while and I wonder if I missed a question. Then he lowers his voice. "Two detectives were here to talk to you. I won't allow any questioning until we've done a few more tests." He nods to the nurse and walks toward the door, then turns around and offers one more trifle of news. "Your husband will be here soon. In the meantime can we call anyone for you? Family? A friend? Anybody?"

I shake my head *no* and immediately regret it. A mallet pounds against my skull from the inside. My head is a giant swollen bulb and the throbbing in my ear manages to distract me from my aching ribs. My lids have a life of their own. I'm nodding off but I have so many questions. I take a deep breath as if I'm preparing to jump off a diving board. It takes everything I have to sound out the words.

"Where did this accident happen?" Why does he look so puzzled? Am I missing more than I'm aware of?

"I'm sorry, but I can't tell you much about the accident," he says. He sounds subdued, as if he's forcing himself to be composed in order to calm me. "All we know is that your car was found upstate at the bottom of a ravine." Pause. "You have a lot of injuries. Some are from the accident. Can you remember what happened?"

I reflect on his words, really think them over. Accident. Ravine. Nothing. Not a thing. There's a large black hole where my memory used to be.

"I can't remember anything," I say.

His brows furrow. "You mean . . . the accident?"

The accident. He talks about *the* accident as if I remember. I want to tell him to X-ray my head, and that he'll find a dark shadow within my skull where my memory once was.

I'm getting the hang of this. Before I say something, I concentrate, think of the question and repeat it in my head, take a deep breath, then I speak.

"You don't understand. I don't remember *the* accident and I don't remember anything *before* the accident."

"Do you remember wanting to harm yourself?"

"Harm myself?" *I would remember that, wouldn't I? Why am I so forgetful?*

"Either that or you were shot."

Was I shot or did I harm myself? What kind of question is he asking me?

I turn my head as far to the left as possible, catching a glimpse of the outstretched leg of a police officer sitting by the door, out in the hallway. I wonder what that's all about.

Dr. Baker looks over his shoulder and then faces me again. He steps closer and lowers his voice. "You don't remember." He states it matter-of-factly, no longer a question, but a realization.

"I don't know what I don't know," I say. That's kind of funny, when I think about it. I giggle and his brows furrow again. I'm getting frustrated. We're going in circles. It's difficult to stay awake.

Then he tells me about my voice. How it is "monotone" and that I have "a reduction in range and intensity of emotions," and that my reactions are "flat and blunted." I don't understand what he's telling me. Should I smile more, be more cheerful? I want to ask him but then I hear a word that puts it all to rest.

"Amnesia," he says. "We're not sure about the cause yet. Retrograde, maybe posttraumatic. Maybe even trauma-related."

When you hear *amnesia* from a man in a white coat, it's serious. Final. *I forgot* sounds casual—*oh, I'm forgetful.* I have amnesia, I'm not forgetful after all. What's next? Is he going to ask me what year it is? Who the president is? If I remember my birth date?

"*Retrograde* means you don't recall events that happened *just before* the onset of the memory loss. *Posttraumatic* is a cognitive impairment and memory loss can stretch back hours or days, sometimes even longer. Eventually you'll recall the distant past but you may never recover what happened just prior to your accident. Amnesia can't be diagnosed with an X-ray, like a broken bone. We've done an MRI test and a CAT scan. Both tests came back inconclusive. Basically there's no definitive proof of brain damage at this point, but absence of proof is not proof of absence. There could be microscopic damages, and the MRI and the CAT scan are just not sophisticated enough to detect those. Nerve fiber damage doesn't show up on either test."

I remain silent, not sure if I should ask anything else, not sure if I even understood him at all. All I grasp is that he can't tell me anything definitive, so what's the point?

"There's the possibility that you suffer from dissociative amnesia. Trauma would cause you to block out certain information associated with the event. There's no test for that, either. You'd have to see a psychiatrist or a psychologist. But we're getting ahead of ourselves. The neurologist will order some more tests. Like I said, time will tell."

I take a deep breath. He's relaying medical facts to me but I just can't shake the feeling that there's something he is not telling me.

"They found me where again?"

"In a ravine, in Dover, upstate. You were transferred here from Dover Medical Center."

Dover? Dover. Nothing. I'm blank.

"I've never been to Dover."

"That's where they found you—you just don't remember." He slips the pen back in his coat pocket. "You were lucky," he adds. He holds up his index finger and thumb, indicating the extent of the luck I had. "The bullet was this far from doing serious damage. Really lucky. Remember that."

Bullet. I was shot or I harmed myself. *Lucky. That depends on whom you ask,* I think to myself. *Remember that.* How funny. My hand moves up to my ear, almost like a reflex. "You said there's damage to my ear. What happened to it?"

He pauses ever so slightly. "Gone. Completely gone. The area was infected and we had to make a decision." He watches me intently. "It could have been worse. Like I said, you were lucky."

"That's some luck," I say, but when I think about my ear, I don't really care.

"There's reconstructive surgery."

"What's there now? I mean, is there a hole?"

"There's a small opening draining fluids, other than that, there's a flap of skin stretched over the wound."

An opening that drains fluids. I'm oddly untouched by the fact that a flap of skin is stretched over a hole in my head where my ear used to be. I have amnesia. I forgot to lock my car. I lost my umbrella. My ear is gone. It's all the same: insignificant.

"And you call that lucky?"

"You're alive, that's what counts."

There's that buzzing sound again and then his voice goes from loud to muffled, as if someone's turned a volume dial.

"What about my ear?"

He looks at me, perplexed.

"I remember you told me it was gone." *Completely gone* were the words he used. "I mean my hearing, what about my hearing? Everything sounds muffled."

"We did an electrophysiological hearing test while you were unconscious." He grabs my file from the nightstand and opens it. He flips through the pages. "You've lost some audio capacity, but nothing major. We'll order more tests, depending on the next CAT scan. We just have to wait it out."

I look at the police officer's leg outside my door, and I wonder if he's protecting me or if he's protecting someone from me.

"I remembered something." The words come spilling out and take on a life of their own. "I need to know if what I see . . . I . . . I think I remember bits and pieces, but it's not like a memory, it's more like fragments." It's like flipping through a photo album not knowing if it's mine or someone else's life. *Blood. So much blood.*

"You may not be able to remember minute by minute, but you'll be able to generally connect the dots at some point. It's a Humpty Dumpty kind of a situation; maybe you won't be able to put it all back together."

"I'm very tired," I say and feel relieved. All the king's horses and all the king's men. Wild horses. I make a decision. The blood was just an illusion. A figment.

"Let the nurse know if there's anybody you want us to call. Don't forget the spirometer—every two hours . . ."

He points at something behind me. "Behind you is a PCA pump. It delivers small amounts of pain medication. If you need more"—he puts a small box with a red button in my hand—"just push the red button and you'll get one additional dose of morphine. The safety feature only allows for a maximum amount during a certain timed interval. Any questions?"

I have learned my lesson from earlier and barely shake my head.

I watch him leave the room and immediately a nurse enters and I concentrate on her explaining the yellow contraption to me. I'm supposed to breathe into the tubing until a ball moves up, and I have to breathe continuously to try to keep the ball suspended as long as possible.

I have amnesia. My ear is gone. I feel . . . I feel as if I'm not connecting like I should. I should yell and scream, raise bloody hell, but Dr. Baker's explanations of my lack of emotions, "blunted affect" he called it, seems logical. Logic I can handle; it's the emotions that remain elusive.

There's something they're not telling me. Maybe because they don't subject injured people—especially those who've been shot, who lost an ear, who were *that close*—to any additional bad news. That must be it. Maybe the police will tell me, or Jack, once he gets here. They already told me I've been robbed of hours of my life, how much worse can it get?

I hold the spirometer in my right hand. I blow into the tube and allow my mind to go blank while I watch the red ball go up. It lingers for whatever amount of time I manage to keep it suspended. I pinch my eyes shut to will the ball to maintain its suspension. Suddenly bits and pieces of images come into focus as if they are captured on the back of my eyelids. My mind explodes. It disintegrates, breaks into tiny particles.

Mia isn't with Jack. She's gone.

The realization occurs so abruptly and is so powerful that the wires connected to my chest seem to tremble and the machines behind me pick up on it. The beeps speed up like the hooves of a horse, walking, then trotting, then breaking into a full-blown gallop. Mia's disappearance is a fact, yet it is disconnected from whatever consequences it entails—there's a part I can't connect with. An empty crib. Missing clothes, her missing bottles and diapers, everything was gone. I looked for her and couldn't find her. I went to the police and then there's a dark hole.

Like a jigsaw puzzle, I study the pieces, connect them, tear them apart, and start all over again. I remember going to the police precinct but after that it gets blurry—hazy, like a childhood memory. My mind plays a game of "telephone," thoughts relaying messages, then retelling them skewed. Easily misinterpreted, embellished, unreliable.

Every time I watch the spirometer ball move upward, more images form: a bathroom stall, a mop, a stairwell, pigeons, the smell of fresh paint. Then a picture fades in, as if someone has turned up a light dimmer: fragments of celestial bodies; a sun, a moon, and stars. So many stars.

Why was I in Dover? Where is my daughter and why is no one talking about her?

As I lie in the hospital bed, I am aware of time passing, a fleeting glimpse of light outside, day turning into night, and back into day. I long for . . . a tidbit of my childhood, a morsel of memory, of how my mother cared for me when I was sick, in bed with the flu or some childhood disease, like measles or chicken pox. But then I recall having been a robust child, a child who was hardy and resistant to viruses, to strep throats and pink eyes.

I don't know what to tell Jack once he shows up. He will question me. Jack will ask me about the day Mia disappeared. About the morning I found her crib empty. Amnesia is just another shortcoming on a long list of my other countless inadequacies. Shortfall after shortfall.

I must be insane, for the only explanation I can come up with is of my daughter and my ear, together in the same place. And above them, floating suspended like a mobile, the sun, the moon, and the stars. Bright as bright can be, surrounded by darkness. A chaotic universe illuminated by heavenly bodies.

I rest my hands on my lap. My body stills, comes to a halt. I was in an accident. I was shot or tried to harm myself. My ear is gone. There's a hole that's draining fluids.

I don't care about any of that. Mia's gone. I can't even bear the thought of her. I want the pain to stop yet her image remains. I raise my finger to push the red PCA button, longing for the lulled state the medicine provides. I hesitate, then I put the box down. I have to think, start somewhere. The empty crib. The dots. I have to connect the dots.

Photo by author

Alexandra Burt is a freelance translator and the international bestselling author of *Remember Mia*. Born in Europe, she moved to Texas more than twenty years ago. While pursuing literary translations, she decided to tell her own stories. After years of writing classes and gluttonous reading, her short fiction appeared in fiction journals and literary reviews. She lives in Texas with her husband and daughter. Visit her online at alexandraburt.com.